A WOLFE AMONG DRAGONS

A MEDIEVAL ROMANCE

BY KATHRYN LE VEQUE

A SONS OF DE WOLFE NOVEL

Print Edition

Text by Kathryn Le Veque
Cover by Kim Killion

Kathryn Le Veque Novels

Medieval Romance:

The de Russe Legacy:
The White Lord of Wellesbourne
The Dark One: Dark Knight
Beast
Lord of War: Black Angel
The Iron Knight

The de Lohr Dynasty:
While Angels Slept (Lords of East Anglia)
Godspeed (Lords of East Anglia)
Rise of the Defender
Steelheart
Spectre of the Sword
Archangel
Unending Love
Shadowmoor
Silversword

Great Lords of le Bec:
Great Protector
To the Lady Born (House of de Royans)
Lord of Winter (Lords of de Royans)

Lords of Eire:
The Darkland (Master Knights of Connaught)
Black Sword
Echoes of Ancient Dreams (time travel)

De Wolfe Pack Series:
The Wolfe
Serpent
Scorpion (Saxon Lords of Hage – Also related to The Questing)
The Lion of the North
Walls of Babylon
Dark Destroyer
Nighthawk
Warwolfe
ShadowWolfe
DarkWolfe
A Joyous de Wolfe Christmas
A Wolfe Among Dragons

Ancient Kings of Anglecynn:
The Whispering Night
Netherworld

Battle Lords of de Velt:
The Dark Lord
Devil's Dominion

Reign of the House of de Winter:
Lespada
Swords and Shields (also related to The Questing, While Angels Slept)

De Reyne Domination:
Guardian of Darkness
The Fallen One (part of Dragonblade Series)
With Dreams Only of You

House of d'Vant:
Tender is the Knight (House of d'Vant)
The Red Fury (House of d'Vant)

The Dragonblade Series: (Great Marcher Lords of de Lara)
Dragonblade
Island of Glass (House of St. Hever)
The Savage Curtain (Lords of Pembury)
The Fallen One (De Reyne Domination)
Fragments of Grace (House of St. Hever)
Lord of the Shadows
Queen of Lost Stars (House of St. Hever)

Lords of Thunder: The de Shera Brotherhood Trilogy
The Thunder Lord
The Thunder Warrior
The Thunder Knight

The Great Knights of de Moray:

Shield of Kronos
The Gorgon

Highland Warriors of Munro:
The Red Lion
Deep Into Darkness

The House of Ashbourne:
Upon a Midnight Dream

The House of D'Aurilliac:
Valiant Chaos

The House of De Nerra:
The Falls of Erith
Vestiges of Valor
Realm of Angels

The House of De Dere:
Of Love and Legend

St. John and de Gare Clans:
The Warrior Poet

The House of de Garr:
Lord of Light
Realm of Angels

The House of de Bretagne:
The Questing (also related to Swords and Shields)

The House of Summerlin:
The Legend

The Kingdom of Hendocia:
Kingdom by the Sea

Time Travel Romance: (Saxon Lords of Hage)
The Crusader
Kingdom Come

Contemporary Romance:

Kathlyn Trent/Marcus Burton Series:
Valley of the Shadow
The Eden Factor
Canyon of the Sphinx

The American Heroes Series:
The Lucius Robe
Fires of Autumn
Evenshade
Sea of Dreams
Purgatory

Other Contemporary Romance:
Lady of Heaven
Darkling, I Listen
In the Dreaming Hour

Sons of Poseidon:
The Immortal Sea

Pirates of Britannia Series (with Eliza Knight):
Savage of the Sea by Eliza Knight
Leader of Titans by Kathryn Le Veque
The Sea Devil by Eliza Knight
Sea Wolfe by Kathryn Le Veque

Note: All Kathryn's novels are designed to be read as stand-alones, although many have cross-over characters or cross-over family groups. Novels that are grouped together have related characters or family groups.

Series are clearly marked. All series contain the same characters or family groups except the American Heroes Series, which is an anthology with unrelated characters.

There is NO particular chronological order for any of the novels because they can all be read as stand-alones, even the series.

For more information, find it in **A Reader's Guide to the Medieval World of Le Veque**.

TABLE OF CONTENTS

AUTHOR'S NOTE

This is the book that my readers have really been begging me to write.

But how to bring back a dead man?

I admit it; I kill off characters left and right. Hey! It's Medieval times – and everybody dies! In this case, I killed off a character before anyone had ever met him. James de Wolfe was a mention in "Serpent", which was the first sequel I ever wrote to "The Wolfe". In it, I named off all of the de Wolfe offspring and James, other than a stillborn daughter, was the only de Wolfe child to die. It didn't really matter much until I started to write the Sons of de Wolfe sub-series for the de Wolfe Pack and then we got to meet James and see what a great guy he was. He was featured the most in "A Joyous de Wolfe Christmas", where he was marrying his love, Rose Hage.

Well, my readers loved him, and I was repeatedly asked why I'd killed him off. We had Scott, Troy, Patrick, and then no James. So, I set about doing what only I, as the author, can do. I brought James back from the dead.

Lazarus, rise!

Now, understand that much like William, I, too, have a son named James, and it is true that I modeled William's son after my own, never thinking I'd have to write about him, but here I am. That means this book is especially emotional for me because when I see James de Wolfe, I see my own son. The opening scene was done with tears. Way too close to home.

The Welsh culture and country features strongly in this novel, so a few things to note – much like the Scots and the Irish did, the Welsh also has a particular way they did surnames – for example, sons had their father's name as a surname (Angus, the son of Fadden, would be named Angus MacFadden), and with the Welsh, it was male/female specific. For example: Evan, the son of Rhodri, would be Evan ap

Rhodri, while the daughter, Morgan, would be Morgan ferch Rhodri. "Ferch" means daughter or girl, as does "merch". Kind of like the English language has several names for a female, so do the Welsh.

Also, I'm going to give you, dear Reader, a pronunciation key because Welsh names can really be tough. In Welsh, the *dd* is a *th* sound, and the double *ll* sound is even weirder – a sound we don't have in English. The best way I can describe it is if you put your tongue just behind your upper front teeth and blow. Air hisses out from either side of your tongue, but that's how to pronounce the double *ll* sound. So, I've kept some of the spellings phonetic for the English-speaking reader. It's easier if you know the phonetic sound:

Blaidd – Blayth is the phonetic spelling.

Fairynne – FAIR-in (not Fairy-anne!)

Merch/Ferch – daughter in Welsh

Ie – this means "yes" in Welsh, but for the ease of the reader, I have changed the spelling to Aye (which is more familiar).

Teulu – (pronounced ty-loo) literally meaning "family". These were the warlord's bodyguards/personal warriors.

Llandeilo – Pronounced with that odd "hissing tongue" noise for the double *lls* – so it's essentially "hissing noise-an-day-low"

I think the one thing you're going to discover about this story is that it's not simple. It's several different factions, for different reasons, and their stories intertwine. Pay attention to the timelines, because some things happen concurrently, and then some things happen days or weeks later. But rest assured, it all makes sense and, in the end, you will come to realize that a great many people had a stake in James in this very complex and emotional tale. Although it is a stand-alone, it has much more impact if you've read "The Wolfe", especially since the older knights of William de Wolfe and Kieran Hage figure in this book.

Bring tissues and enjoy!

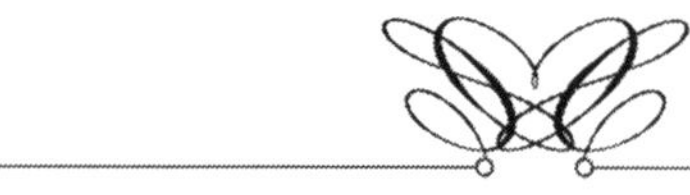

THE NEXT GENERATION WOLFE PACK

William and Jordan Scott de Wolfe

Scott (married to Lady Athena de Norville, issue) Second wife: Avrielle

Troy (married to Lady Helene de Norville, has issue) Second wife: Rhoswyn

Patrick (married to Lady Brighton de Favereux, has issue)

James – Killed in Wales June 1282 (married to Lady Rose Hage, has issue). Second wife (as Blayth the Strong): Asmara ferch Cader

Katheryn (James' twin) Married Sir Alec Hage, has issue

Evelyn (married to Sir Hector de Norville, has issue)

Baby de Wolfe – died same day. Christened Madeleine.

Edward (married to Lady Cassiopeia de Norville, has issue)

Thomas

Penelope (married to Bhrodi de Shera, has issue)

Kieran and Jemma Scott Hage

Mary Alys (adopted) married, with issue

Baby Hage, died same day. Christened Bridget.

Alec (married to Lady Katheryn de Wolfe, has issue)

Christian (died Holy Land 1269 A.D.) no issue

Moira (married to Sir Apollo de Norville, has issue)

Kevin (married to Annavieve de Ferrers, has issue)

Rose (widow of Sir James de Wolfe, has issue). Second husband: Gethin de Lara, grandson of Sean de Lara

Nathaniel

<u>Paris and Caladora Scott de Norville</u>

Hector (married to Lady Evelyn de Wolfe, has issue)

Apollo (married to Lady Moira Hage, has issue)

Helene (married to Sir Troy de Wolfe, has issue)

Athena (married to Sir Scott de Wolfe, has issue)

Adonis

Cassiopeia (married to Sir Edward de Wolfe, has issue)

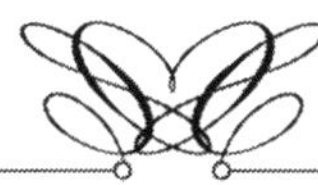

A NIGHT OF DRAGONS

13th c. poem ~ by Fr. Jestin y Dale

In the darkness, 'ere they came,
Children of the night, known by name.
A dragon's call, so high the cost,
A mournful cry, a son was lost.
He died that night, the story told,
But from the ashes, a warrior rose.
A man of iron, of heart and soul,
A man with a past no one could know.
Joy and glee turned night to day,
The Wolfe's son has returned,
With Dragons, they say.

James could match any of his brothers' prowesses in a fight, but he had something more that they didn't – compassion for the enemy, a deep compassion that, at times, had turned him into a brooding and moody man. James felt more deeply than most, was more patient than Job himself, and would much rather negotiate his way out of a fight than quickly draw arms. They were such wonderful qualities and William adored his boy for them. He had a soft spot for James and his wise, gentle ways…

~ A description of James de Wolfe, from "A Joyous de Wolfe Christmas"

PREFACE

St. Jestin's National History Museum
Llandovery, Wales
Present Day

IT WAS THE Children's Hour.

The small museum of St. Jestin's was a tribute to the national history of Wales, but it was mostly a tribute to the spirit and legends based in Welsh folklore. It was a very popular tourist destination because of the Medieval and Dark Ages relics, and it even had some Roman relics that held a good deal of fascination for the folks who came to visit on lazy days, either to get out of the rain or to bring the children for something to do. There was an entire children's area to the museum where Mr. Nolwynn, a local historian known to walk down the streets of Llandovery in historic costumes, would tell stories of heroes or events long ago past.

But he always put the Nolwynn spin on things.

This week, it was stories of Llywelyn the Last and of the near cult-like status the man had earned following his death in 1282 AD. Mr. Nolwynn wore replica tunics worn by Llywelyn and men like him, and he told stories of the battles, bringing weapons modeled after those from the era that he'd made himself. They weren't sharp, and the kids could touch them and get excited about their own history and heroes. Mr. Nolwynn's Children's Hour drew families from all across southern

Wales.

Today, he had an entire class from the local preparatory school on a field trip to the museum. They were well-behaved for the most part, although they were a little noisy at times. The boys wanted to see the weapons and the girls were mostly bored because the relics didn't interest them much. Mr. Nolwynn had walked them through the Medieval section of the museum on their way to the "story veranda", so it was called, but he could see that he was losing about half of his audience. These were young adults, around thirteen years of age, so they were easily distracted and easily bored.

But he had a plan.

The story veranda was full of costumes and fake weapons and models of castles that he'd built himself. He even brought in Lego castles so there was something the younger kids could touch and play with, and he made a tiny dragon flag, the national flag of Wales, to fly on the battlements of the Lego castle. As the group of young people and teachers entered the story veranda, he had them all sit on the floor while he went to a cabinet and opened it up.

Cloaks and costumes were stuffed into the wardrobe and, at the bottom, was a stack of small green and white squares that the kids could stick together with double-sided tape and then cut out a red felt dragon to paste on top of it and make their own dragon flags. But those were for the younger children he often entertained, as the older ones usually didn't go for something so juvenile.

Pushing aside the cutouts, he pulled forth an old woolen cloak that smelled of mothballs. He swung it around his slender shoulders, knocking his glasses sideways as he did so. As he straightened up his glasses, he turned to the fidgety group on the floor.

"This will be an exciting time for you," he told them. "Today is the anniversary of the Battle of Gwendraith Castle. It happened on this day in the year twelve hundred and eighty-seven. It isn't far from us. Have any of you been there?"

The students looked around at each other. One or two raised their hands as the teachers tried to shush those who were giggling. Old Mr. Nolwynn continued.

"There was a very important battle at Gwendraith Castle in the Welsh quest for independence against Edward, who wanted our country for his own." He could see that his words weren't having any impact on the teenagers, so he decided to go for the dramatics. "Did you know that a wolf fought that battle? Have any of you heard of him?"

The students were looking around at each other until one boy, with a round face and shiny dark hair, raised his hand.

"Is that the Dragon Tamer?" he asked.

Mr. Nolwynn nodded vigorously. "Exactly. The man I speak of is a rather obscure Welsh hero and his story is told in a very old tale called 'The Wolf and the Dragon Princess'," he said. "He has been called the Dragon Tamer by some. Other names are the Ghost, the Beast, and I've even heard him called Lazarus."

"Why?" the young man asked.

Mr. Nolwynn fixed on him. "Because local legend said he rose from the dead," he said. "Let me tell you about the story of the wolf who fought amongst the dragons. It's not a well-known legend, but it's one that has appeared in a few historical documents. The man who wrote 'The Wolf and the Dragon Princess' is the Medieval priest this very museum was named after. Jestin y Dale, or Jestin of the Dale as he was called, was a collector of many things. His church is long gone now, although the foundations still survive, but he collected many things from battles local to the *Ystrad Tywi,* the very valley we live in. During Medieval times, there were a great many battles in this area and Father Jestin made a point of collecting what he could from them."

The same boy was holding his hand up, ignoring his friends who were poking at him and snorting.

"Why did he collect the things left over from the battles?" he asked.

Mr. Nolwynn pointed a finger at him. "That is an excellent question," he said. "For safe keeping, perhaps. Or maybe he was just a hoarder."

The kids began to laugh at that, now a little more interested in what he was saying, and Mr. Nolwynn continued.

"In any case," he said, "Jestin collected so many things that the Church, who kept all of it, eventually gave it over to this very town where Jestin's parish was, and it is the town that opened this museum. And Jestin's writings are the only record we have of the wolf who lived among the dragons. There is a famous poem about him, also written by Jestin, called 'A Night of Dragons'. Has anyone heard of it?"

Another boy, with bright red hair, lifted his hand. "I've heard of it. My father has it on the wall of his office."

Mr. Nolwynn nodded eagerly. "It is a very old poem," he said. "It means something different to everyone, I think. National pride or maybe even a metaphor for a second chance at life. Whatever the case, the story behind that famous old poem is the tale you will hear today, some of it told through Jestin's words and some of it told through mine. I'm sure Jestin's account is not complete because it doesn't give us much background on the man, but I would like to believe that the truth of the matter is stranger than fiction."

Some of the kids began to pipe up, asking to hear the poem, and Mr. Nolwynn held up his hands to quiet them. When the room stilled, he fingered the rough woolen cloak he was wearing.

"Heroes aren't just the men you see in the movies or in books," he said. "Heroes come in many shapes and sizes, men of great valor and bravery. Sometimes it's a lifetime of heroic deeds, or sometimes it's just one heroic moment in time, but all heroes have something in common – their moments of bravery make history. Maybe they do it with a sword, or a gun, or by saving a life, or even by wearing a woolen cloak like this one and doing what they believed was right because they believed strongly enough in their destiny – or their patriotism – to make a difference. In any era, all heroes are the same. They do what they have to do, because it is the right thing *to* do."

It was a powerful little speech, one that managed to quiet all of the kids down. Now, Mr. Nolwynn had their full attention as he recited the poem they'd been waiting for:

"In the darkness, 'ere they came,
Children of the night, known by name.
A dragon's call, so high the cost,
A mournful cry, a son was lost.
He died that night, the story told,
But from the ashes, a warrior rose.
A man of iron, of heart and soul,
A man with a past no one could know.
Joy and glee turned night to day,
The Wolfe's son has returned,
With Dragons, they say."

When he was finished, the young people seemed very eager to hear more. And that was how Mr. Nolwynn had planned it.

"Now," he said quietly. "From that poem, we know that the Dragon Tamer was a great warrior, the son of someone named Wolfe. That's not a Welsh name and scholars have speculated that he was English, or even Teutonic, but we may never know. What we do know is that he was part of Rhys ap Maredudd's rebellion in 1287 AD, and that he led a great uprising in the south before disappearing completely. But we can find no documentation of his death, or even his birth, leading some scholars to believe that maybe such a man never even existed. But something tells me that he did, because Jestin said he did. And, as we all know, priests don't lie."

That brought a chuckle from the group. The boy with the red hair was raising his hand again.

"So if this Dragon Tamer had a story, what do you think it is?" he asked. "You must know what his life was like."

Mr. Nolwynn grinned, showing off his brand-new dentures. "I

would imagine a very good adventure for him, for the brief time we assume he existed. I hope Jestin will forgive me for speculating on, but this is the way I believe his story goes. It all starts at the Battle of Llandeilo in the summer of 1282 AD…"

PROLOGUE

Llandeilo, Wales
June, Year of our Lord 1282

"PAPA! YOU MUST let him go! We must retreat!"

Sir Troy de Wolfe was screaming at his father. Coming from a man who did not scream, it was indicative of the horrific situation.

The Welsh had been waiting for them.

It had been such a stupid folly on the part of the English, something William de Wolfe, Troy's father, had warned against. The English had been victorious in a battle that had seen them sack the Welsh stronghold of Carreg Cennen Castle. Edward I's campaign against the Welsh had them in Southern Wales at this point in time, but William had warned the Earl of Gloucester, who was in charge of this particular movement, against proceeding so far into the country without adequate troops. Unfortunately, the arrogant earl wasn't apt to listen to England's greatest warrior, a man who had seen more battles than most.

And that lapse of judgment had led William, his sons, and many other English knights right into an ambush.

They were paying the price.

"Papa!" This shout came from another son, Patrick. The largest de Wolfe son was holding off an attack of rabid Welsh warriors as William sat on the ground with his dying son in his arms. "Papa, we must flee! You must leave James!"

But William was in a world of anguish as he held his child against him. The man had been struck in the head by a morning star, which had knocked him off his steed, while several Welsh rebels had swarmed over him and used his body like a pin cushion. William couldn't even count the number of injuries on his boy; all he knew was that there was blood everywhere and the man was dying. Truth was, he was probably already dead, but William refused to admit it.

He *couldn't* admit it.

Not James!

"I will carry him," he rasped. "I will carry him and he will be healed."

He shifted the body, trying to stand up even as his sons and several soldiers tried to protect England's greatest knight who was, in fact, a very old man. That was the reality of it. William de Wolfe had no business being in battle at his age, but he was healthy enough and there was no reason for him not to except his advanced years.

But at this moment, England's greatest knight was very close to losing his life in an inglorious Welsh ambush.

Scott de Wolfe, Troy's twin and a fine healer in his own right, pushed his way out of the fighting to get to his father and dying brother. Tears stung his eyes as he looked down at James' pale face, seeing the extent of the head wound and knowing that if his brother wasn't already dead, he wasn't long for this world. As a healer, he could be somewhat logical about it but, as a brother to James, he was devastated.

But the problem wasn't James as much as it was William – the man was so grief-stricken that he couldn't even see his way to comprehend what was happening around him. All he could do was clutch James fiercely and weep openly over the man. *My boy… my sweet baby boy*, he said, over and over. But Scott could see what was going on around them. They had been ambushed and they were outmanned. If they did not leave Llandeilo at that moment then none of them were going to survive.

"Papa," he said as calmly as he could, putting his hands on James to try and pull him away from his father. "You must leave him. We cannot risk carrying James with us, as he will slow us down. He would understand. Do you hear me? We must make all due haste away from here."

But William shook his head, violently. "I cannot leave him," he wept. "I will *not* leave my son behind."

Scott could see his brothers, Troy and Patrick, and several other cousins and family members struggling with the Welsh. So far, the ambush had been a massacre of English knights and unless Scott pulled his father out of harm's way, it would claim even more of them. He yelled at his brother, Patrick.

"Atty!" he boomed. "Help me or we all die!"

Atty was the nickname for the biggest de Wolfe brother, Patrick, and Scott had summoned the man for a reason. William had a stable of very strong sons, but Patrick was the largest and the strongest. If he had any chance of separating his father from James, then he was going to need help and Patrick was probably the only one strong enough to do it. Physically, it was going to be a battle.

But Patrick had his own problems. Because he was so big, the Welsh seemed to be determined to take him down, so he was fighting for his life even as Scott called to him. There was no way for him to break away.

Yet, Scott's call did not go unheeded. Two older knights, the oldest and dearest friends that William had, were also in the fray, fighting with their sons, trying desperately not to be killed. In the midst of the chaos, of the fighting and screaming and death, they heard Scott's cry and they managed to disengage from the Welsh enough to stagger over to where William sat with his son in his arms.

It was a shocking sight. Neither Kieran Hage nor Paris de Norville had realized James had been struck down because they'd been fighting off to the south and they'd missed the moment when James had been toppled off his horse and attacked. Paris was a great healing knight, a man who was trusted by everyone under William de Wolfe's command, and he had been known to heal even the hopeless. He rushed up to William, trying to separate the man from his son.

"William," he said breathlessly. "Let me see him. Let me have him!"

William was reluctant to release his son, even to the man he had trusted with his very life for many years. The bond between William and Paris went beyond blood but, at this moment, William couldn't seem to trust anyone with his son's body, not even Paris.

"Uncle Paris!" Scott hissed. "James is gone. We must leave my brother here and flee!"

Paris' fair face was pinched with exertion, with fear, and now with rage at Scott's words. He shoved the man away.

"We will *not* leave James behind!" he barked. "And we do not know that he is dead!"

With that, he yanked James from William and placed the man on the ground. What he saw shook him to the core; James had been hit so hard in the head that his helm was dented. There was blood and bits of blond hair and scalp everywhere, leaking from the helm and onto James' mail. He also had several arrows sticking out of him, and a huge gash on his neck, making him look as if he'd taken a bath in his own blood, literally.

A bloodbath.

As Paris lifted his eyelids, trying to see if the pupils were reacting, he really couldn't tell because it was so dark around them. The Welsh had struck at sunset, just before the English had reached the safe haven of Dinefwr Castle, and the fighting in the dusk had created mass confusion and panic.

"Is he dead?" Scott demanded. "Uncle Paris – *is he dead*?"

Paris looked at the man on the ground. He tried to remove the helm, but it was so dented that it was nearly impossible. He tried to feel for a pulse, but with all of the jostling going on around him and layers of clothing, he couldn't seem to find one. He could only form an opinion based on his years of experience and with tears in his eyes, he nodded.

"I believe he is," he said quietly. "God, William… I am so very sorry."

William was already weeping, but with Paris' confirmation, Scott couldn't fight back the tears. His kind, gentle, and wildly humorous brother was dead. He couldn't even stomach the news but, in the same breath, it didn't change the situation as a whole.

They had to get out of there.

"Then we must leave him," he said, reaching over to pull his father away from his brother's corpse. "We cannot carry him. It will only slow us down and the Welsh would eat us alive. We must get out of here, Papa!"

Paris was weeping, too, and over his shoulder, big and broad Kieran Hage gazed down on his daughter's husband and felt as if he'd just lost his very own son. As Scott and Paris struggled to pull William away, Kieran fell to his knees beside James' body and gathered the man into his arms as William had done. Now, they had another problem on their hands; William was separated from his son, but the father of James' wife had taken his place.

"Your children shall not forget you, I swear it," Kieran whispered, tears popping from his eyes. "They will know how bravely their father met his death, and you shall live in their hearts every day. You shall be well remembered, my sweet James. Godspeed, lad, and know that you are loved."

With that, he struggled to pick James up and carry him, much as William had tried to do. By this time, the English were retreating, including Kieran's own sons, Kevin and Alec. Kevin, who was James' best friend, hadn't seen him fall. So when he saw James in his father's arms, panic and rage set in. He rushed to his father's side, as did Alec and the rest of the de Wolfe brothers, now trying to herd the old men back to the horses that had been scattered in the ambush.

"Oh… *God!*" Kevin erupted when he saw James' body in his father's arms. "God, not James. Please… *not James!*"

It was a cry from the heart, and Kieran couldn't even answer his son. He was devastated, struggling with the body even as Kevin tried to take it from him. But the Welsh were following, and Kevin was needed for the intense fighting that was taking place to cover their retreat. Scott and Troy were urging their father along, while Paris, his sons Apollo and Hector, and Patrick were fighting off the Welsh who very badly wanted to get their hands on the *Saesneg*. They'd already claimed a few English knights and their bloodlust was fed.

They wanted more.

It was utter chaos and somewhere in the retreat, Kieran stumbled and dropped James onto the ground. But the Welsh were right up behind them and he wasn't able to reclaim the body. It was his life or James' corpse, and Kieran's sons were dragging him along so that he couldn't retrieve James. They were all fighting for their lives, all scrambling to leave that dark, green-covered valley without succumbing to the Welsh.

Somehow, the English found their horses and were able to reclaim them. Even after William mounted his steed, he tried to go back for James, but it was to no avail. The Welsh had his son, and they were stripping him of everything of value. When William saw that the Welsh had put James de Wolfe's tunic onto a stick and were waving it high like a victory banner, horror and grief consumed him. But he also knew that there was no chance for him to recover his son's body.

The Welsh were fed by victory, and he had to leave in order to save himself.

On that day, William de Wolfe lost a piece of himself in Wales, never to be recovered again.

PART ONE

RISE OF A LEGEND

CHAPTER ONE

August, Year of our Lord 1287
Carmarthen Castle, Wales

IT WAS A gathering among gatherings, a most important meeting that could, and would, determine quite a bit in a world where the English held parts of Wales, while still other parts were ruled by various warlords.

But this gathering was different.

Carmarthen Castle was awash with Welshmen, rebels from the mountains, from the seaside, and everything in between. All of them were gathered for a most important conference. Patience, they didn't have.

But vengeance… they had enough to fill the ocean.

The castle sat on a rocky outcropping above the River Towy, which meandered through the green and lush land on its way to the sea. Gulls flew this far inland, swooping over the river banks and diving for meals from the scraps left on the river banks by the fishermen.

But in the village itself, tension could be felt because the roads and alleys were full of Welshmen from different tribes and ruling houses, all of them converging on the castle. There were many rivals and allies, even though every Welshman considered every other Welshman a *cymry*, or fellow Welsh. There was a good deal of infighting and hostility among the factions but, in all cases, those hostilities were put aside when it came to the *Saesneg.*

The English.

And that was why they'd gathered at Carmarthen Castle, which had been through some rough times over the past century. For the past ten years, it had belonged to Howell ap Gruffydd, who had taken it from William Marshal the Younger, but Howell hadn't done much to effect repairs the castle so badly needed, mostly because he didn't want a repaired castle to fall back into English hands. The castle had been tossed back and forth between the Welsh and the English over the years but, at the moment, Howell had it. But there was no guarantee that would be the case next year, or even next month.

It was, therefore, symbolic that this meeting take place at Carmarthen. And even as Welshmen flocked to the castle, men were wearing their long, woolen tunics and carrying the weapons that were traditional to Welsh warriors. These were men of mail and shields, *teulu* to great warlords, and always prepared for a fight. They employed effective fighting methods, and they were rabid in their love of their country.

Howell knew this because he was one of them. Standing on the second floor of the gatehouse of Carmarthen, he was watching the Welshmen as they filtered into the castle. His men were keeping watch to ensure no tempers or old hostilities flared. The peace must be kept, especially in light of what was to come. There was renewed rebellion in the air and Howell was at the head of it, but he couldn't do it alone. If he could rouse the men of Southern Wales, then perhaps they could reclaim their country once and for all. As he stood there, envisioning the glory to come, one of his *teulu*, or personal guard, joined him on the wall.

"Almost everyone we have invited has come," he said. "Men are gathering in the hall and await you."

Howell was still looking out over the countryside, over the river that flowed like a murky, muddy ribbon. "But Morys has not arrived yet."

The *teulu* shook his head. "He has not," he said. "Morys ap Macsen has not arrived, nor has the man who fights with him."

Howell drew in a long, thoughtful breath. "Say his name, Hew," he said quietly. "*Blayth yn gryf.* They say that any battle Blayth the Strong is involved in is an assured victory because he can read the minds of the *Saesneg.*"

Hew had heard that, also, but he wasn't so willing to give credence to the rumors. "Is he a witch, then? I am not certain that I want to follow a witch into battle."

Howell smiled faintly. "He is not a witch," he said. "He is something... more."

Hew was uncomfortable with such talk. "*What* more?" he demanded. "Lord, must I remind you that we really know nothing of Blayth the Strong?"

"We know enough."

Hew sighed sharply. "Morys said that he simply appeared in the village one day and no one seems to know where he came from," he said. Then, he lowered his voice. "I have heard rumor that Morys found him half-dead on the field of battle and brought him back to life. Back to life! Mayhap Blayth is a wraith or a phantom that has taken the form of a man. I do not trust such a man."

Howell looked at the man. He was an excellent soldier and a loyal servant, but he was also a worrier. He smiled. "You fret like an old woman," he said. "There is no denying Blayth and his reputation. Many men have fought with him over the past five years and swear by his tactics. Even you have fought with him, Hew, at the skirmish near Pembroke. Do you recall how he outmaneuvered the *Saesneg* knights and was able to destroy the postern gate at Wiston Castle?"

Hew grew frustrated at the talk, mostly because he knew Howell was correct – the man they called Blayth the Strong was as amazing as everyone said he was. Perhaps there was even some jealousy there.

"The man moves like magic," he said, almost sarcastically. "But he fights like a *Saesneg*. Mayhap he *is* a *Saesneg.*"

"You cannot know that for certain."

"How can you say that when no one knows where he has come

from?"

Howell shrugged. "Morys knows," he said, "and I trust the man. He is a strong leader who commands many men, including Blayth. He would not betray us."

Hew knew better than to question Morys ap Macsen's reputation. He was a warlord that lived high in the mountains near Brecfa, about a day's ride from Carmarthen, in a stronghold known as *Mynydd Gwyn* – White Mountain. He was a man of royal blood, descended from the kings of Deheubarth, from the House of Dinefwr, and was considered a great leader in the south. But he was also petty, ambitious, and conniving, and he very much wanted control of the region that had once been Deheubarth, so much so that it had driven a wedge between him and his younger brother, Cader.

Cader was supposed to be in attendance today as well, which would make things interesting when the brothers ap Macsen were in the same room together for the first time in a long while. Cader at least had some restraint, but Morys had none at all, and that was why Hew was so reluctant to trust the mysterious warrior with no past, the man who led the Welsh to victory time and time again. Morys would say anything, about anyone, if it gained him victory.

Hew didn't trust him even if Howell did.

"Then I hope you are right," Hew said after a moment. "I hope Morys' mysterious warrior can do what we all hope he can do."

Howell nodded faintly. "As I said, we have all seen him in battle. It is not as if the man hasn't proven himself." He paused, his attention moving to the horizon. "But I seriously wonder if Cader will make an appearance. Surely he knows his brother will be here today."

Hew cleared his throat softly. "I have been wondering the very same thing," he admitted. "The grandsons of Rhys Gryg are not at peace. In fact, it will make this gathering… interesting."

Howell grinned, a lopsided gesture. "Let us make sure we keep them on opposite sides of the hall," he said. "Morys is fearsome, but Cader is as fast as a cat. I do not want them tearing into each other."

"Nor I."

"This gathering is not about their relationship. We will remind them of that if we need to."

Hew nodded, knowing that it might come to that. In all of the skirmishes over the past few years, never once had Cader allied with his brother, so what Howell was about to propose might leave a bitter taste in the mouths of the ap Macsen brothers.

But it couldn't be helped.

Hew was about to reply but something caught his eye. He leaned forward on the gray stone wall, peering at the road that led up to the gatehouse. Down the road, a party approached, coming closer by the second. Finally, Hew pointed.

"There they are," he said. "I recognize Morys' steed."

Howell saw it, too. "Go," he said. "Keep the man with you. I will watch for Cader. Meanwhile, make sure everyone has gathered in the hall. I will join you as soon as Cader arrives."

"And if he does not arrive?"

"We shall know soon enough."

Hew fled the wall, heading down to inform the *teulu* in the bailey that Morys ap Macsen was approaching. The man was royalty and would be received as such. But even as the Welshmen in the bailey scrambled to greet the incoming warlord, Howell took a moment to watch them approach until they were nearly underneath him. When Morys saw Howell, he raised a hand. Howell lifted one in return.

But he wasn't really looking at the grizzled old warlord who was so hairy and big that he looked like a beast more than man. He was looking at the enormous warrior that rode to his right, the very man they'd been speaking of. *Blayth the Strong*. Howell took a moment to look over the man who was well on his way to earning a legendary reputation; he was a big man, no doubt, with scarred arms and legs, and a massive scar that ran from the left side of neck and disappeared beneath his tunic.

But the most pronounced distinction of Blayth was the left side of his head, which had clearly been damaged in battle at some point. The man had a handsome, symmetrical face and, according to the Welsh women, he was quite alluring in a mysterious, masculine sort of way. His eyes were the color of the sky, his skin fair, and his hair was blond with a hint of red to it. He had a beard, which was neatly trimmed, but he kept the sides of his head shorn, leaving the top longer so that it flopped over his eyes unless he raked it back against his skull. It was that shorn style of hair that made the injury on the left side of his head so much more pronounced; his temple, left cheekbone and nearly the entire left side of his head was badly scarred. His left ear had been mangled and was barely something that even resembled an ear.

But Blayth didn't hide the damage. He proudly displayed it, like a badge of honor. Howell watched the man and the rest of Morys' *teulu* as they passed beneath the gatehouse, his thoughts lingering on the frightening-looking warrior who had already led many a victorious battle. Truthfully, much of the success of the meeting on this day hinged on Morys and his warrior, and Howell prayed that today of all days, the Welsh would once again find a passion for rebellion. He prayed that the *cymry* were once again fueled with the love of their country and for their freedom from the *Saesneg*, because for certain, if they weren't, then all would be lost. He prayed that Blayth the Strong could help fuel that which was dying.

It was time to stir the fires of rebellion yet again.

CHAPTER TWO

"BE CALM, *MERCH*. Your Uncle Morys does not need your anger. The rift is between my brother and me, and you are not part of that."

The great gatehouse of Carmarthen Castle spilled forth a group of men and one woman into its innards. They were from the village of Talley, an area that Cader ap Macsen controlled. It was high in the mountains, one valley over from the valley where Morys lived with his gang of *troseddol*. Criminals, Cader's wife called them. A large collection of men with questionable backgrounds, all of them living off of Morys and obeying his commands.

It was a strange, unholy tribe.

Cader had spoken the quietly-uttered words to the woman riding to his left, a long-legged lass astride an equally long-legged stallion. This was no ordinary woman; she was Cader's eldest daughter, a young woman who was more capable in battle than any young man Cader knew. She was intelligent, well-spoken, and beautiful. But she was also bold, unruly at times, and could fight like a man. Having no sons, Cader had indulged her. Now, he had a lovely daughter of marriageable age who could best any husband in a fight.

And no self-respecting man wanted a wife who could beat the spit out of him.

"By virtue of the fact that I am your daughter, I am, indeed, part of the rift," the woman said in a voice that flowed like warm honey. "You need not try and distance me, Dadau. I will defend you from Morys' deceit and venom at all costs."

"He is Uncle Morys to you."

"*Morys.*"

She didn't consider the man part of the family and, therefore, refused to show him such respect. Cader eyed the woman for a moment before turning his attention to the collection of men near the great hall of Carmarthen. It was a powerful group of important men, and he and his party came to a halt just inside the gatehouse.

"Asmara," Cader said, rather sternly, because if he wasn't stern with her, she would damned well ignore him. "At this gathering, you will not speak. You will not shoot daggers at Morys with your eyes. In fact, you will remain silent as the grave in all matters. Is this in any way unclear?"

Asmara ferch Cader cast her father a long look as she dismounted an excited but weary stallion that was throwing its head around. As she soothed the animal, she avoided giving her father an answer, but Cader was on to her. He dismounted his own steed and made a point of standing next to his daughter as she crooned to her beastly stallion.

"Well?" he demanded quietly. "Do we understand one another?"

Asmara sighed heavily. "Aye."

"Look me in the eye."

Asmara gave him an exaggerated look. "Aye."

Cader fought off a smile at his daughter. Had she been born a man, she would have been a magnificent warrior. As it was, she was still a magnificent warrior, but she was like a young colt – wild, strong, and difficult to tame. The fact that she'd been born a woman didn't seem to matter to her. Sometimes, Cader had a difficult time reining her in.

"See that you do," he said. Then, he pointed off to the stables where the horses were being watered. "Tend to the horses. I will meet you inside the hall."

Asmara took both her horse and her father's horse. Behind her, her father's *teulu* were splitting up the duties, some of them gathering the horses while others went to accompany Cader to the great hall.

Great warlords did not travel without their personal guards, and Cader ap Macsen was a great warlord, a son of royal blood. As Cader slogged off across the muddy bailey, Asmara led the pack of horses heading for the stable area. She hadn't taken five steps, however, when she heard the thunder of hooves charging through the gatehouse behind them and nearly crashing into the rear of Cader's party.

Nervous horses danced and tried to bolt, and Asmara struggled to hold on to her stallion. The horse ended up kicking rancid mud onto her chest and neck, and she groaned with frustration. She was fully prepared to rant at the rider who startled the horses when she happened to see who it was. Her eyes widened.

"Fairynne!" she gasped. "*What* are you doing here? Dadau told you not to come!"

Fairynne ferch Cader, Asmara's younger sister, appeared quite defiant as she struggled to control a horse that was far too much animal for her. It seemed to be a trait both ferch Cader sisters had.

"I will *not* remain behind with the women and children," she declared. "I do not deserve to be treated with such disrespect, so I came. It is my right!"

Asmara shook her head at her sister. While Asmara was long-legged and beauteous, Fairynne was shorter, wiry, and believed she could do anything her sister could do. Truth be told, she was a fierce fighter, a little reckless, and she tended to spook easily. Cader had permitted her to fight in one battle, mostly because she had given him no choice, and because of it, she believed herself to be just as good as the seasoned warriors.

But the truth was that she was a child. At ten years and five, Fairynne was too young and too unruly. She thought she knew everything there was to know and rarely listened. Cader was afraid the girl was going to get herself killed, as was Asmara.

Like now. Fairynne had been told to remain at *Mynydd Gwyn*, but her arrogance and foolishness had her following her father's party all the way to Carmarthen Castle. It was a dangerous journey, especially for a lone woman, and clearly she had tailed them all the way. Frustrated, Asmara marched up on her sister, grabbed the girl's leg, and yanked her right off the horse.

The men within eyeshot laughed uproariously as Fairynne ended up on her arse in the mud. When she came up swinging, Asmara pushed her down by the head.

"Cease," she snapped quietly. "You are making a fool of yourself in front of everyone. Dadau told you not to come, yet you disobeyed him. *Again*. Someday, your disobedience will get you killed, Fairynne."

With mud covering her backside and a slash of mud on her cheek, Fairynne glared at her older sister. "You cannot tell me what to do."

Asmara cocked an eyebrow. "If you want to be a soldier so badly, then you must know that soldiers follow commands. We all follow commands. You will never be a soldier as long as you cannot follow orders, you little fool."

Fairynne's confidence took a hit and, for the first time since her arrival, she appeared uncertain. But only for a brief moment. Then, anger took over and she bolted to her feet, grabbing her horse's reins and pulling the animal over to the stables.

At that point, Asmara gave up on her sister. If the girl wanted to make a fool of herself, then that was her business. Asmara had more important things to tend to, like her father. He would be expecting her. Leaving the horses with her father's men to be tended, she turned for the great hall where the men were gathering. Her long strides took her across the bailey and towards the one-storied, stone building with open oak and iron doors that had seen better days.

The men were gathering with those they knew, allies and family, and she could feel their stares upon her. In this world of men, she was an anomaly. Some of the men knew her, as they had fought with her in the past as part of Cader's contingent. *Rhyfylwr dywsoges,* they whispered. *Dragon Princess.* As a woman of the House of Dinefwr, she was indeed royal. Asmara returned their stares boldly, noticing the *teulu* from great houses, men wearing the traditional red tunics that signified their elevated status, and bearing wooden shields that had been painted white or blue, or both.

In fact, Asmara herself wore a red tunic, one that had been given to her and it was too short for her long body. It rested about mid-thigh, but she had heavy woolen hose and another tunic underneath, a pale linen one, that went past her knees. In any case, she was well-covered. With boots up to her knees, held on with strips of leather, she was also well-protected.

Every inch the Dragon Princess.

It was, therefore, her manner to challenge those who stared at her, and her threatening glare began to turn men away. She was feeling rather powerful until she went to enter the hall and realized that her Uncle Morys was standing just inside the door.

In fact, had she taken another two steps, she would have run right into him. However, not having spotted her father yet, Asmara didn't want to walk right into Morys and a potential confrontation, so she quickly rolled away from the door, clinging to the rocky wall and rounding the corner of the hall. It was a blind move, meant to get away from Morys as quickly as possible before he could see her. But before she realized it, she was stumbling over someone who was crouched against the north side of the hall.

Asmara flipped right over him.

Now, she was the one sitting on her arse in the mud, looking up at a very big man who had been crouched against the wall. It wasn't as if he was doing anything; relieving himself or anything else. He was simply crouched there, perhaps even resting from the long journey to Carmarthen. Asmara's first reaction was one of rage, but the moment she looked into his face, the anger building inside of her was instantly doused. She found herself looking into eyes of the purest blue, with pale lashes and pale, but defined, brows. The man was wearing a sleeveless tunic, and his pale and freckled arms were bulging with beautifully defined muscles.

She'd never seen a male specimen like him.

"What… what are you doing, crouching there like a stump?" she managed to demand, sitting up and wiping her muddied hands on the wall. "You could have killed me."

The man simply looked at her, a glimmer in his blue eyes. "And you could have looked where you were walking."

His voice was deep and quiet, his speech somewhat slow, but she didn't receive the impression he was a dullard. Simply deliberate in what he said. And, in truth, he was entirely correct in what he'd said, so she cast him a frustrated expression as she picked herself out of the mud, trying to wipe herself clean.

"Next time, I suppose I shall have to," she said. "With you around, I will have to watch every corner I turn."

He didn't say anything, but he did watch her as she stood up, his gaze lingering on the long, slender legs in snug hose, the shapely female form beneath the belted tunics, and the face of an angel that was now twisted in disgust as she tried to wipe the mud off her arse. She had dark hair, pulled into a messy braid, and eyes that were a shade of hazel that made them appear golden. None of her alluring attributes escaped his scrutiny; that was clear. He eyed her as if he'd just found something delicious for supper. As she stood up, he suddenly stood up next to her.

Now, he towered over her by well over a head. Considering how tall Asmara was, the fact that the silent warrior was so much taller was a serious testimony to the man's size. As he stood next to her, he also turned to face her fully, and Asmara could see that the entire left side of his head was scarred and damaged. He virtually had no ear. As he shaved the sides of his skull and left the top of his blond hair long, the shorn scalp only emphasized the damage. Most men would have grown hair to cover it, but not this man. In truth, his shorn head didn't distract from what Asmara was realizing was a truly handsome man. In fact, all of that battle damage seemed to make him even more attractive in her eyes.

But he was also rather intimidating and frightening if she thought about it. He abruptly grabbed her by the wrist and began pulling her away from the hall. Startled, not to mention fearful, she dug her heels in to resist him.

"Let me go," she hissed, beating at the hand that held her. "Did you hear me? Release me!"

He ignored her. He dragged her all the way back across the bailey, past groups of men who were watching but did nothing to help Asmara. They simply turned back to their conversations. Asmara didn't want to create a huge scene and start screaming, but she was close. The man had a grip of iron. Still, she figured she could fight off anything he tried to do to her so, at some point, she stopped dragging her feet, purely for her pride. It was embarrassing to let people see her being dragged, so she started to pretend she was going along with it. She simply started walking behind him.

The warrior pulled her into the stable yard where so many horses were being watered and rested. There was a well in the stable yard, which was an unusual feature, and also a very long drinking trough. He took her right over to the trough, picked her up easily, and tossed her in.

Asmara landed with a big splash. Horses scattered as the water flew, and she howled when she realized what he'd done. The water was freezing. Quick as a flash, she leapt out of the trough, infuriated that she was now soaked to the skin.

"Why?" she demanded, enraged. "*Why* did you do that?"

He still had that glimmer to his eye as he looked at her. He pointed to the lower half of her body. "The mud is gone now."

He was right. Asmara realized that the mud was now almost completely washed off and although she was clean again, she was also soaking wet. Enraged, she balled a fist and threw a punch right into the man's jaw.

His head snapped back at the force of the blow, and he took a step back as well, but he didn't stagger. The move simply surprised him. As he put a hand to the spot she'd hit, Asmara shook her fist at him.

"That is for getting me dirty in the first place, you dolt!" she raged. "And you did not have to try and drown me. I am quite capable of cleaning myself!"

The man eyed her as he rubbed his chin. "Forgive, demoiselle," he said. "As you pointed out, I caused you to fall in the mud. It is my responsibility to clean you."

Demoiselle. That wasn't a term Asmara heard frequently. That was a *Saesneg* term for an unmarried miss, a term of respect. This enormous, scarred warrior with the slow, deep speech had her curiosity; she could admit it.

He was unlike anything she'd ever seen before.

"Well," she said, feeling her outrage fade somewhat at his explanation. "You could have at least told me what you were going to do."

All he did was look at her, a slight lift of the very broad shoulders. Then, a smile flickered on his lips, which spurred her outrage. She was about to berate him again when she realized that his smile also spurred her humor in what was truly a ridiculous situation. She'd fallen over him, and gotten dirty, so he threw her in the water. He'd taken responsibility for what he'd seen as a consequence of his actions. As stupid as the situation was, she couldn't really fault a man who took responsibility for his actions. When she saw a flash of his teeth, surprisingly straight and white, she fought off a grin.

God, what was happening to her? When she should be beating the man, she was grinning at him.

Who is the dolt now?

"I shall make sure I look where I step from now on, with you around," she finally said. "My name is Asmara, by the way. You may as well know the name of the woman you tried to drown."

He simply dipped his head as if pleased to make her acquaintance. "You are a queen, demoiselle."

That low, slow speech was intriguing. "Nay," she said. "Not a queen. I am a warrior, as are you."

His gaze lingered on her, the glimmer in his eyes now held a touch of warmth, she thought. "You *should* be a queen," he said quietly.

The way he said it made her heart beat, just a little faster. She opened her mouth to ask him his name, but a shout from the great hall distracted them both. Someone was calling the men into the hall and the big warrior with the scarred head began to move towards the call, quickly, leaving Asmara standing there, dripping all over the ground. She watched him go, thinking that he looked sorely out of place among the Welsh warriors. As if he didn't belong in the least.

Her thoughts lingering on the mysterious warrior, she began to follow the herd of men as they headed towards the hall, hoping she could find a place by the hearth to dry herself out. She also hoped she could find a location where she could keep an eye on the strange warrior and, perhaps, even discover his name.

Why the interest? She had no idea.

But no ordinary man would have the courage to throw Asmara ferch Cader into a watering trough.

Somehow, she sensed the pale warrior was no ordinary man.

CHAPTER THREE

"MY FRIENDS, MY allies, you honor me with your presence," Howell said as he stood on the dilapidated feasting table in Carmarthen's great and rather run-down hall. "We have much to discuss and little time to do it, so please quiet your conversations. Allow me to speak."

The hall was packed with men, all of them turning their attention to Howell, with Hew and a few of his *teulu* standing off to the side. The table couldn't take the weight of more than one man, it seemed, so it was Howell's podium. He smiled at the group, holding up his hands.

"I know that you are men with families and with duties to attend to," he said, "and I will therefore keep our gathering as short as possible, but this is necessary. I beg your patience as I explain."

There was a low hum of men mumbling to one another, shifting around nervously in the hall that was full of smoke from a hearth with a partially-blocked chimney. But it was more than that – they all knew why they had come, men who had suffered over the years from English overlords and English battles. Not one of them was inclined to knuckle under and accept English rule. And now, in this defining moment, perhaps there would be the opportunity yet again for them to show their resistance. All they needed was organization and a strong leader. Over near the edge of the table, a strong voice spoke up.

"Tell us, Howell," Morys said loudly. He wanted all of the men to know that he was in full support of whatever Howell had to propose. "You have my attention. What is so important that you would call such a gathering?"

Howell looked at Morys. "Something of tremendous importance, great lord," he said. "Your cousin, Rhys ap Maredudd, who is also the great-grandson of last king of Deheubarth much as you are, has confided in me his plans to retake the *Ystrad Tywi*. He has asked that I coordinate a similar attack to help him secure his legacy." He returned his attention to the group. "That is why I have summoned you, great men. The time has come for us to reclaim what the *Saesneg* has so wrongly taken from us. We shall reclaim the south and from there, the rest of Wales. But it must start somewhere – it will start with us."

Morys, who had been willing to go along with Howell on anything, wasn't so pleased to realize that his cousin, Rhys, was at the head of the coming revolt. Because of Rhys, and other great-grandsons of Rhys ap Gruffydd, the lands that men like Morys and Cader controlled were greatly reduced. The grandsons and great-grandsons of the last king took precedence, something that Morys and Cader's father and grandfather had fought against. Therefore, Morys was greatly displeased to hear that his cousin was behind this latest push.

Ystrad Tywi was the larger area that used to comprise Deheubarth, an area of great rivers and valleys, both strategic and rich. The English knew this, which is why they'd settled heavily in the area. Loosely translated, it meant the Vale of the Towy River, which was a major river that cut through the land.

It was key.

"A bold proposal," Morys finally said, saying what everyone else was thinking. Then, he shook his head, perhaps in disapproval. "Does Rhys truly think he can take the *Ystrad Tywi* from the English? They've sunk their claws into it and it will not be an easy thing to take it back."

Howell wasn't a fool. He knew that a bold proposal like this would be met with doubt. "We have a plan, Morys," he said. "I know that you and your cousin are not on the best of terms, but Rhys has a plan that he believes will work so long as you and your men are willing to try."

Willing to try. Morys didn't like the sound of that. Trying wasn't succeeding as far as he was concerned. It was a foolish effort. In fact, he didn't like the sound of any of this because the truth was that he thought that he would be leading this revolt, or at least helping to lead it. Instead, he was being asked to *try* something. That didn't sit well with him.

"Did he ask you to relay this plan to me?" he finally asked.

"He did," Howell said. But he looked at the room once more. "He asked me to relay it to all of you. We are *cymry*, after all. This is *our* land. We have suffered the Norman invasion for over two hundred years and, still, they come. Still, they live on our lands and claim them as their own. Many men have fought to reclaim it, and many men have failed. But I believe that this time, it will be different. If we fight hard enough, if we show them how unwilling we are to have them in our country, then surely they will grow tired of losing men. Or are you so willing to return to your villages and let the English dictate terms to us in our own country?"

That was something that every Welshman abhorred, and Howell knew it. He was hitting their pride now. As the collection of men continued to mutter to each other, discussing the possibilities, Howell turned to Cader to see how he was reacting to the situation.

It was typical Cader behavior; he remained calm, impassive. He was standing on the opposite side of the table, his focus on his brother from a distance away. Cader was the reasonable brother, but this was where some strategy came in. Howell knew that if he addressed Cader directly, Morys would be offended since he was the older brother. Moreover, if Cader agreed to listen, then Morys couldn't let the man be more reasonable than he was, so he would agree to listen, too.

Howell was counting on that sibling rivalry.

"Will you at least listen, my lord?" he asked Cader. "Surely you wish to reclaim what belongs to us."

Cader's gaze moved from Morys to Howell. After a moment, he

nodded. "I will listen."

As Howell knew, Morys would not be outdone. "As will I," he said loudly. "Tell us the plan, Howell. What does my cousin wish from us?"

That was what Howell needed – the two ap Macsen brothers willing to listen. That would spur the rest of the group to listen, too. When Howell spoke, it was to all of them.

"Rhys and his men plan to move on Pembroke Castle." A great hiss of disbelief went up and Howell held up his hands, begging for silence. "Listen, if you please. William de Valence, Lord of Pembroke Castle, has left Pembroke. Our spies tell us that the man has been sent to France and that he took nearly half of his army with him. This means that Pembroke is weakened and it is Rhys' intention that we take advantage of that. While Rhys and his men move to encircle Pembroke, he asks that we move on Llandarog, Idole, and Gwendraith castles. If we can claim these, then we can block off the main roads leading from Pembroke to Cardiff and beyond. We can then starve out the garrison and claim Pembroke."

It was a shocking plan, but one that was opportunistic and, in truth, feasible. Morys listened to it with flaring nostrils, not at all happy that his cousin had relegated him to laying siege to smaller castles, but he also saw the brilliance of the plan as a whole.

"It is true that my cousin has an intriguing plan," he said loudly so all would hear him, "but there are other castles near Pembroke that we would have to consider as well, some of them English garrisons. Carew and Narberth castles are English. Then there is the bishop's castle of Llawhaden. If we cut off the roads, there are still plenty of English who will try and break our blockade."

Howell nodded patiently. "That is why I have sent word to the northern warlords," he said. "Morys, we cannot reclaim our country if we fight in splintered groups, and that is what has happened. With the south of Wales subdued, King Edward has gone to the north. He has mostly subdued the north as well. But if we can work together and take back our country piece by piece, then we may have a chance of taking it back as a whole. Are you opposed to trying?"

Morys shook his head. "I am not," he said. "Who comes from the north to support us?"

Howell glanced at the group because he wanted to see their expressions as he spoke the names of some of Wales' most powerful warlords.

"The sons of Dafydd ap Gruffydd fight to the north," he said. "There are several. There is also Bhrodi de Shera, the King of Anglesey. I plan to send word to Bhrodi myself and I am sure he will support us."

That drew a strong reaction from the crown. "De Shera is in league with the English," one man shouted. "His father was English and he married a Saesneg!"

Howell shook his head. "He married her for peace," he said. "That does not mean he sides with the English. He is a Welshman at heart, and a great one. Do any of you doubt de Shera's loyalty to Wales?"

The men backed down after that, for no one doubted Bhrodi de Shera's loyalties. He was a great warlord who had proven his worth time and time again. But he was a man with a Norman name and Welsh blood, making him something more than a Welsh warlord. He had the trust of the Edward, oddly enough, and that made the Welsh somewhat wary of him. A man could only have loyalty to one country, so they believed. But still, no one was ready to denounce the man who held the title of Earl of Coventry as well as being the hereditary King of Anglesey. Better still, his wife was from the great House of de Wolfe, a family of knights who commanded thousands of *Saesneg* warriors.

Bhrodi de Shera was a man to be feared, above all.

"He is loyal," Morys said after a moment. "I would not speak ill of the man, for he has proven himself many times over. But we have something more powerful than even de Shera here in the south, something that will turn the tides for us once and for all."

Howell was curious. "What is it?"

Morys turned to look at the pale warrior standing behind him. His eyes fixed on the man, proudly, as a father would show pride in a son. He walked towards the warrior, pointing to him.

Now, it was Morys' time to show his worth in all of this.

He was a man with a secret.

"Blayth," he said, drawing out the name to ensure everyone heard him. "We have Blayth, the man whose very name means wolf. He knows what the *Saesneg* are thinking, and if anyone can lead this fight, it will be our battle wolf. I would put my trust in no one else; not even de Shera."

Men began grumbling again, some of them agreeing, some of them not. Given that Blayth had earned an almost legendary reputation in a few short years, men weren't ready yet to contradict Morys, but they were uncertain.

Morys knew this, but he had something else in mind, something that would put these men right into the palm of his hand. It was something he'd been working on the day he realized that badly wounded warrior he'd found near Llandeilo was going to live. He'd known even then that the man was something special, and he knew what no one else knew about him – that he was, indeed, a *Saesneg*. But Blayth had no recollection of who he was, or where he'd come from. In fact, his very name stemmed from nearly the only word he'd been able to say as he recovered from his injury those years ago – *wolf*.

That word had become his Welsh name, Blayth, and from that name sprang a warrior of legend, something that Morys had perpetuated. He'd created the stories, and spread many of the rumors, but the one thing he hadn't needed to exaggerate was Blayth's prowess in battle. The man was unbeatable. His men, and the Welsh in general, were badly in need of a hero since the death of the lasts Welsh prince.

Morys intended to give them one.

"I give you the man who will lead us to freedom," Morys finally boomed. "Some of you have fought with him and know the truth of my words, but some of you do not know. You have heard rumor how he came into my service, but I will tell you the truth once and for all. I have been protecting the man's identity because it has been entrusted to me. I swore an oath never to reveal his true family lineage, but since my cousin has decided to once again throw the south into turmoil with his plans for Pembroke, I find that I must reveal the true identity of Blayth, the greatest warrior Wales will ever know. He, and only he, can lead us to victory. And do you know why?"

Morys was, if nothing else, a man who could stir crowds. He had a magnetic presence and a natural air of command that made men take notice of him and as he spoke most passionately, the men were naturally drawn to what he was saying. One of the men shouted the obvious question.

"Why, lord?" the man demanded. "Tell us of Blayth!"

Morys pointed to Blayth. "See his head?" he shouted. "See the damage to his head? The *Saesneg* did that. They tortured the poor lad and tried to burn the Welsh right out of him, but they could not do it. They could not destroy his Welsh heart!"

The men in the room, Cader and Howell included, were looking seriously at Blayth, who was solely focused on Morys. It was as if there was no one else in the room, oblivious to an entire room of men staring at him. Enjoying the fact that he had everyone's attention, Morys continued.

"The *Saesneg* tried to destroy him," he said passionately. "They tried to destroy his heart, because it is a pure Welsh heart. The *Saesneg* knew who he was, but those loyal to *Cymru* smuggled him out of his prison and gave him over to me. These men, these smugglers, were old and beaten, because they were the *teulu* of our greatest warrior. They knew who Blayth was and they entrusted his care to me."

By this time, Howell had made his way over to Morys. He was still standing on the worn and beaten feasting table, but he climbed down in order to be at Morys' level.

"We have all wondered where Blayth came from," he said. "From the looks of him, it makes sense that the English tortured him."

Morys nodded, putting a hand on Howell's shoulder. In truth, Morys was enjoying the performance of a lifetime because, for his own glory, he had to sell this. The man with no sons, and no children at all, had to cement legacy. It all rested with a story he'd spent years building about a wounded warrior who had no memory.

Morys would provide him with that memory.

"The *Saesneg* captured Blayth at a very young age and kept him in their prisons," he said. "It was the loyal *teulu* of Llywelyn ap Gruffydd that freed Blayth from the *Saesneg*. That is because the English knew, as you will now know, that Blayth the Strong is, in truth, Blayth ap Llywelyn. He is the bastard son of the last Prince of Wales, Llywelyn ap Gruffydd."

A collective gasp went up in the group. No one had been expecting that answer, least of all Howell or even Cader. They looked at each other in shock before Howell returned his attention to Morys.

"He… he is *Llywelyn's* son?" he said, incredulous. "But – how? We have not heard of such a child of Llywelyn. He only had a daughter, and she has long been a ward of the *Saesneg*. Now you are saying that the man had a son?"

Morys nodded confidently. "Blayth was sold by his whore of a mother to the *Saesneg*," he said. "The bitch sold her child for gold and the *Saesneg* took him to their great city, to their great Tower, and there he has been his entire life. Men believe he is a *Saesneg* because of it, but that is not true. He was freed and brought to me to protect him, and it is Blayth who shall lead our countrymen to victory against Edward. Who else but a man who has been tortured and wronged to lead the charge against those who tried to destroy him?"

It made perfect sense to the Welsh, who were increasingly excited about what they'd been told. A buzz filled the room as men began to speak of the unknown bastard son of Llywelyn the Last, but the conversation wasn't entirely positive. There were those who were not thrilled by such news.

"Llywelyn was a northern prince," one older man shouted. "His gain was only for the north. Why should we want his bastard for us?"

Morys suspected that might be an issue, but he would not allow old prejudices to mar his glory seeking. "Llywelyn may have been a northern prince, but he fought for all of Wales," he said. "He did what was necessary to secure our country for north *and* south. Now that we have his bastard in our midst, a man who has already proven that he has greatness in his blood, would you truly allow old hatreds to ruin our chance to take back our country from the *Saesneg*? It is a very real possibility, now that we have Blayth among us. Would you deny a Welsh prince his destiny?"

Of course, no one would. Wales was full of history of Welsh princes fighting the English, and sometimes each other. But England was the greater threat and they were all united against it.

Now, they had renewed hope.

It was almost too good to be true, but gradually, men began to realize the opportunity that was presented. Morys ap Macsen was a passionate patriot and the men trusted him. Over the past few years, Blayth's record on the battlefield spoke for itself. He was a fierce warrior, fearless in the face of the enemy, and his reputation had been cemented. Surely such a man could have only sprung from Llywelyn's loins.

And now, he would fulfill his destiny.

At that point, there were no more voices of protest. In truth, it was a thrilling prospect. But standing next to Morys, Howell's reaction was decidedly different. He couldn't decide if he believed Morys or not. He knew the man; he was a teller of tall tales, but he was also a fearsome warrior and deeply dedicated to Wales. As the men of the hall began to take up a cheer for Blayth, Howell grasped Morys by the arm.

"Swear this to me," he muttered. "Swear to me that all you have said is true."

Morys looked him right in the eye. "It is true."

Howell shook his head, still torn. "Then why have we never heard of Llywelyn's bastard? No one has ever spoken of a bastard son."

Morys was completely confident in his answer. "I told you," he said patiently. "His mother was a servant and she sold the lad when he was but an infant. Do you truly think she would then tell everyone that she sold Llywelyn's son to the English?"

Howell glanced at Blayth, standing like a massive sentinel behind Morys. He was pale, scarred, and every inch the seasoned warrior. If one wanted to believe that he was from Llywelyn's loins, then it would be easy to do so. Men seeking hope, something to cling to, would be willing to believe such a thing.

But Howell still wasn't sure.

"But you said that Llywelyn's *teulu* knew of him," he said. "Are you telling me that in all of these years, they never once bargained for his freedom?"

Morys fixed him, pointedly. "Would *you*?" he asked. "The fact that the English did not kill him as an infant was a miracle in and of itself. Do you think if the *teulu* had tried to bargain for him, that Edward might not change his mind?"

That was the truth. Any true Welsh prince wasn't long for this world if the English had anything to say about it. The fact that they evidently kept the man alive, and tortured him, was something beyond horrific, and Howell began to soften, just a little.

"So they knew of him," he finally said. "Then what? Have they been tracking him all this time? The man must be forty years old. He is not a young man."

Morys shook his head. "He is not," he said. "And to answer your question, it is true that Llywelyn's men spent years tracking the child who eventually became a man. Always, they kept their eye on him, even if it meant serving the English king himself. Anything to be close to him. When the time was right, they moved to free him."

The entire situation sounded too wild to believe, and Howell still wasn't convinced. "But why you?" he demanded quietly. "Why should they bring him to you?"

Morys lifted an eyebrow. "Because I can protect him," he said simply. "Think on it, Howell. My father is the fifth son of a prince of Deheubarth. My cousins, like Rhys, are entrenched in fighting each other. All they want to do is kill each other. But Cader and I are not so engaged in politics, or in trying to kill each other, but we still understand the need for discretion and protection. If you want to hide a man like Blayth, then you would choose someone like me. Only I would understand the importance of Blayth, and I have kept him protected accordingly for the past five years. But now… now, he must fulfill his destiny and I must help him. Surely you can understand this."

Some of what he said made sense, but Howell was still torn. It all seemed so outlandish to him but in the same breath, it was a fantastic story that he wanted to believe. He wanted to have faith. The cries of the men in the hall were growing now as the warlords began to understand that a great man was among them and Howell looked around, knowing that if he were to publicly dispute Morys' claim, it would only tear apart the group as a whole. And for what they were about to do, this group needed to be cohesive. If a man they believed to be the bastard son of Llywelyn the Last was the adhesive, then so be it. It was with misgivings that Howell let the subject drop.

But he knew, instinctively, that wasn't going to be the end of it. When he sent his missive to Bhrodi de Shera, he would make sure to mention Llywelyn's bastard. It would either cement the matter, or complicate it.

ASMARA, WHO HAD been standing by the hearth during the entire conversation between Howell and Morys, could hardly believe her ears when she heard her uncle's revelation. She heard the shouting and the buzz of the men but, unfortunately, she couldn't see the warrior that had the entire room rumbling with shock.

Blayth the Strong.

Nearly dry from the heat of the hearth, and coughing on the smoke she couldn't avoid, Asmara finally stepped away from the fire as she tried to get a look at the man known as Blayth, who was evidently, in reality, the bastard of Llywelyn the Last. It was an astonishing disclosure. She tried to push between the men to get a look at him, but the men were standing in tight groups and wouldn't move. They didn't like a woman trying to push them around, anyway, so she ended up skirting the room, making her away along the walls until she caught sight of her father standing near the feasting table.

Then, she was more assertive pushing through the crowds of men, shoving them aside until she reached her father's *teulu*, who moved aside for her easily. Once she came to stand next to her father, she had a clear view of the table and of her Uncle Morys on the opposite side. She tugged on her father's sleeve.

"I heard what Morys said," she said, leaning in to him. "Where is Blayth?"

Cader glanced at her. "Where have you been?" he asked. Then, because she was butted up against him, he couldn't help but notice that she was damp. "What happened to you? Why are you wet?"

Asmara was too ashamed to tell him. "It is nothing to worry over," she said, trying to distract him. "Dadau, Fairynne is here. She followed us even though you told her not to."

As Asmara had hoped, her father's attention veered away from her wet clothing and on to his disobedient daughter. "Where is that foolish chick?" he said in a rare display of emotion. "She will sorely regret having disobeyed me. Where is she?"

Asmara shrugged. "I do not know," she said. "That last I saw, she was heading for the stables."

Cader sighed heavily. "I am going to make it so she'll have to walk home because her arse will be too sore to ride."

Asmara didn't care much about her sister at that point; this was a discussion they had about her frequently, so it was nothing new. Increasingly, she was curious about the warrior known as Blayth, the man whose true identity had been revealed, so she strained to see over near Morys, who was still lauding the lineage of his greatest warrior.

"Morys' voice carries all the way over here," she said, disapproval in her tone. "*Who* is Blayth, Dadau?"

Cader was still lingering on his youngest, and naughtiest, daughter, but he managed to point in Morys' direction. "There," he said. "See the big brute standing behind your uncle? The one with the scarred head?"

Scarred head. A bolt of shock ran through Asmara as her gaze fell on the pale warrior she'd tangled with earlier. Her mouth popped open with astonishment when she realized who her father meant.

"*Him*?" she asked, aghast. "That… that beast of a man?"

"Aye."

"*That* is Blayth?"

"Aye."

Asmara's mouth was still hanging open as she came to understand what her father was telling her. Truly, it took a moment to sink in; the man with the slow, deliberate speech, the one who had looked at her with eyes that seemed to look right into her soul, was none other than the mysterious warrior known as Blayth the Strong.

Good Christ… was it actually true that the man was a bastard of royal blood in disguise? It was all so overwhelming. Shocking, for certain. Now, Asmara didn't know whether to feel privileged or embarrassed that Llywelyn's bastard had thrown her in the trough.

She settled for embarrassed.

"What now?" she asked, averting her gaze from the warrior across the hall. "Do we fight with him, Dadau? Is that what we shall do?"

Cader nodded. "It would seem we are to be part of a resurgence of rebellion," he said. "Morys has stirred the hearts of men with his tale of Llywelyn's bastard. Can you not see that?"

Asmara looked at the men around them, men who were shouting their excitement for what was to come. There was indeed rebellion in the air now that the situation had been explained to them – Howell had proposed the plan and Morys had sealed their fates with his talk of a new hero among them. Indeed, Asmara could see what was coming. She looked at her father.

"Do you believe Morys?" she asked.

Cader was certain that men were listening to her question and even more certain that they were interested in his answer. He could not, and would not, go against his brother, even if he did have misgivings. Sometimes, there were things more important than the truth and, much like Howell, he would not tear this group apart by disputing Morys' claim. He could see that Morys' words were like a tonic to men who had been so beaten down by wars with the English, and oppression, that the mere mention of a new hero to lead them was feeding them all with renewed hope.

He couldn't take that away from them.

After a moment, he turned to his daughter.

"I will not question him," he said. "For now, I want you to find your sister and keep her with you. It is too dangerous for her to wander about with all of these men. Both of you will retreat to the stables and remain with the horses while I speak with Howell and my brother. I must discover what they intend for us to do in this plan to assist Rhys ap Maredudd, so you will wait for me whilst we have our war council. Go, now."

Asmara didn't want to leave, not with battle plans to be discussed, but she decided to respect his wishes by obeying him. It was one thing to dispute her father when no one was watching, and entirely another to do it in front of a room of *cymry*. She would not shame her father so. But before she departed, she spoke quietly.

"Whatever happens, Dadau, I will ride with you," she said. "Swear this to me. If you do not, I will follow you into battle. You will not go without me."

Cader looked at her. He knew she meant every word. "Nay," he said after a moment, reluctance in his tone. "I will not go without you. I have fought many a battle with you and your skill with a bow, so I do not plan to leave you behind. You are valuable to me."

"And Fairynne?"

"She is not so valuable, but do not tell her that. In fact, do not tell her anything about this. I shall tell her myself."

"Aye."

When she turned to leave, he grasped her arm to stop her. "Can you tell me when you plan to stop being a warrior and start being a woman?" he asked. "I should like to have grandsons and that will not happen so long as you can outshoot most men with your bow. Men do not like to be humiliated so."

Asmara grinned at her father, who simply shook his head in resignation. He knew her answer without hearing her answer; it was always the same. *Someday, Dadau, but not today.* Releasing her, Cader's thoughts lingered on his strong, intelligent daughter, realizing that, yet again, they would soon be heading into battle. Only the coming battles, he suspected, would be unlike anything Asmara had experienced in the past. She'd fought in ambushes, and in the siege of Weobley Castle when the English tried to build stone fortifications. She was cool under fire, possessing her father's innate sense of calm, and she was quick-thinking and resourceful. Cader had seen it. But, God, he didn't want to take his beloved daughter into the coming battles against English who wouldn't care if she was a woman. They'd kill her regardless.

But he knew he couldn't make her stay at home with her mother, either.

With some concern for the future, but resigned to what was to come, Cader made his way over to Howell and Morys to discuss the coming plan of attack.

God help them all.

PART TWO

A MAN AND HIS DESTINY

CHAPTER FOUR

Two weeks later
Llandarog Castle, eight miles east of Carmarthen Castle

THE HEAVENS HAD opened up and hell had poured forth.

The summer had been unseasonably wet and, true to form, storm upon storm had rained across the area for the past two weeks. The storms had been cold, too, and the feeling in the air was very much like autumn or even a cold spring.

But it wasn't something that bothered the Welsh. Wales could be wet even in the best of times, so they were used to the discomfort of constant rain and the chill of the wind. The weather did nothing to dampen their spirits or their determination in what needed to be done.

The time to act was upon them.

The plan outlined at Carmarthen Castle was that the three castles in question – Llandarog, Idole, and Gwendraith – would be taken simultaneously. It was decided that the castles needed to be seized all at once to prevent the English from sending reinforcements to one or more of them.

Therefore, the Welsh fighting force in the south, comprised of about four thousand men, was split into three groups. One was led by Morys and Cader, the second by Howell and his men, and the third by another warlord named Kimble whose lands lay to the north near Cilgerran. He carried men from the mountains with him, Welshmen who fought with guerilla tactics rather than in organized groups.

In fact, given that the siege of a castle wasn't something the Welsh normally did because they didn't possess the big siege engines necessary for such grand operations, the smartest tactic for them to take was stealth. That was how they worked best. A head-on siege wouldn't work on any of their targets because all three had serious defensive features, so it was decided that only a few select men would make their way into the castles to open the gates for the rest of the Welshmen to enter and engage in hand-to-hand combat with the English inside.

It was the kind of tactic that Blayth was best at.

Even though it was Morys and Cader in charge of the siege of Llandarog Castle, it was Blayth who would lead the breach of the gatehouse with the enormous portcullis. He had an uncanny knowledge of the English defenses and the night before their assault on Llandarog, Blayth stood outside of Morys' tent, listening to the conversation of the men gathered with Morys. In particular, he could hear two familiar voices, men who had become his friends over the years. Aeddan was one of them, a warrior of thirty years and three, with big brown eyes and a quick temper, and Pryce was the other, a sometimes-foolish younger man who was Aeddan's brother.

Both men were Blayth's shadows. Where he went, they went, and he couldn't remember when they hadn't always been by his side. In fact, their faces were some of the first Blayth could remember after awakening from the weeks of unconsciousness after his terrible injuries.

Morys, and Morys' wife, Auryn, had mostly taken care of him, but when it came time to regain his strength and re-learn even the most basic things, Aeddan and Pryce ap Ninian had helped a great deal. It had been the brothers who had helped him learn to speak again, and the brothers who had helped him strengthen the right side of his body, which the head wound had terribly weakened. They had worked with him, side by side, sympathizing in his frustrations but never allowing him to quit.

Because of them, Blayth had grown bigger, faster, and stronger. He chopped wood, lifted stones and tree branches, rode horses, wrestled men, and any number of extreme activities that saw the weakened, nearly-dead warrior build himself up into something broad and muscular. His body had healed faster than his brain and, in truth, that was something of an ongoing process. He still forgot certain words and, at times, his speech could be slow. But the thought processes behind those damaged traits were still sharp, perhaps sharper than they had ever been. It was simply difficult for him to express himself at times.

Yet, the hard work had paid off. The result had seen them develop a close bond and Blayth considered Aeddan and Pryce his brothers. Since he had no other family, he loved them as if they were his blood, and as he stood on a rise watching the town of Llandarog in the distance, he could hear Aeddan and Pryce as they squabbled with a few other warriors over the game of dice they were playing.

The brothers were fond of gambling and, too many times, they had tried to gamble for every possession from anyone they ever knew. They had a bit of a reputation. When Blayth heard a smacking sound, as if someone had been struck, and then instant silence, he fought off a smile. He knew that Pryce, who could be rather obnoxious, had pushed too far. When he glanced over his shoulder to see Pryce leaving the tent with his hand over his eye, he couldn't hold back the smile then.

Some things never changed.

But some things did. Even as Pryce wandered away, Blayth's attention moved to Cader's encampment towards the north. He could see them through the trees. There were no fires, nothing to alert Llandarog Castle that there were Welsh watching them in the forest, but he could see the outline of the tents nonetheless because the rain was starting to lighten and the moon was quite bright behind the gathering clouds.

Seeing Cader's encampment had him thinking of something he'd tried to push out of his mind for two weeks, ever since Carmarthen Castle and the chance encounter with a woman he hadn't been able to shake. He'd discovered that she was Cader's daughter, the brother that Morys rarely spoke to, but spoke *of* a good deal. Blayth felt as if he knew

Cader simply from Morys' frequent mention of the man, but if Blayth was to believe anything Morys said, then he would believe that Cader was a quiet, meek man who was stubborn and grim.

He wasn't a brother Morys was proud of.

But Blayth had been around Cader during their time at Carmarthen Castle when they were planning their attacks on the three castles, and he came to see Cader as a man who was quiet but intelligent. He had excellent insight into the battles to come and his suggestions were sound. But he'd also been the one to suggest the breach of Llandarog, and even now as Blayth watched the castle in the distance, he didn't like Cader's suggestion for one particular reason.

The man suggested using his daughter.

Blayth sighed heavily at the thought of a woman in battle. It wasn't unheard of, but Blayth personally didn't think women belonged in warfare. Cader had lauded his daughter's skill, and the others who had fought with her seemed to agree, and it was Blayth who was to take an advance party, including Cader's daughter, and scale Llandarog's one exterior tower.

The tower was set in the curtain wall, high on a rise, so Blayth and his men were to scale the hill and then the daughter and Pryce, who was tall and skinny, were to climb the tower as Blayth and the others protected them with their long bows. Once the woman and Pryce slipped into the slender lancet windows on the tower, they were to make it to the curtain wall where they would lower ropes so Blayth and the rest of the party could climb up. Then, they were all to make it to the gatehouse and open the gate for the rest of the army and try not to get killed in the process.

That was the plan for taking Llandarog.

It wasn't a bad plan. In fact, it was an excellent one providing they weren't seen. The moon would be setting towards morning, making the land quite dark, and that was when Blayth was to take his group to the tower. That was when he was to help that leggy, beautiful woman climb that tower.

Nay, he didn't like it at all.

So, he stood there and brooded, thinking of the woman he'd been unable to shake. That wasn't like him, considering he wasn't one to think of women in general. Something told him that, once, there had only been one woman for him, although he really had no memory of her, or of anything else for that matter. He remembered nothing prior to the day he awoke, somewhat lucid, in Morys' sod hut those years ago. He didn't even remember his name; all he could say was one word.

Wolf...

He gave himself that name and he didn't even know why.

The lack of memory didn't bother him like it used to. Morys had told him who he was, and where he'd come from, and he accepted the man's word on the matter. But there were times when he dreamed of men he knew he loved, of women with Scottish accents, and of castles he'd never seen. But on nights like this, with an impending battle, he felt more at home than anywhere else. He knew he'd been born and raised a warrior, and even if he couldn't remember his past, he was certain about his future.

He would lead the fight to free Wales from the English.

"Great Lord?"

A quiet, feminine voice roused him from his thoughts and he turned to see Cader's daughter standing a few feet away. He'd never even heard her approach, but his hearing on his right side wasn't very good because of the head wound, so events like this weren't unusual. He usually had Aeddan or Pryce watching his back for such things but tonight there were no such observers.

Looking at her, Blayth began to feel the same way he did the first time he met her – interested, perhaps even a little giddy. Two weeks of trying to put her out of his mind, and then ignoring her when she was nearby, just went up in a puff of smoke.

He turned in her direction.

"Lady Asmara," he said in his low, deliberate speech. "Your presence honors me."

Wrapped in a dark, oiled cloth against the rain, Asmara's features were pinched red from the cold. She had come from her father's encampment, moving with stealth through the damp foliage, until she reached Morys' encampment. She was wet and weary from what had been two weeks of a rather difficult existence on battle campaign, but her golden eyes were bright.

"My father has sent me," she said. "He wishes for me to speak to you about our coming operation on the morrow."

"What do you wish to know?"

Asmara opened her mouth to say something, but she quickly shut it. She simply looked at him as if scrutinizing him and, after several long moments, she cleared her throat softly.

"I wish to know why you did not tell me who you were when we met at Carmarthen," she said. "I introduced myself. It would have been polite for you to tell me who you were."

Blayth sensed some indignation in her tone. "Does it matter?"

Asmara's eyebrows drew together. "Of course it does," she said. "It would have been the polite thing to do."

"You said that."

"I meant it."

Blayth was coming to sense more than simple indignation. Was it possible she was still angry at him for throwing her in the trough? Truth be told, once he realized who she was, he'd been rather embarrassed that he'd done it. Asmara ferch Cader was royalty, the woman that the men called the Dragon Princess. Aye, he knew all about the Dragon Princess and he knew about her skill.

After he'd discovered her identity, he'd made a few inquiries about the woman and was told a few amazing tales. Wanting to find out more about the woman was certainly not the behavior of a man who'd been trying to shake thoughts of her.

Truth be told, now that he was faced with her, he didn't know what he wanted.

... to forget her?

Or not.

"If my lack of introduction offended you, then I am sorry," he said after a moment. "Our encounter was brief and once you introduced yourself, there was no opportunity for me to give you my name. It was not intentional."

She stared at him a moment, as if debating whether or not to believe him, before finally relenting. Her brow eased, as did her expression.

"I've heard tale of Blayth the Strong," she said. "Since my father and Morys do not speak, and have not fought a battle together in years, I have only heard tale of you. We've never met."

"Nay, we have not."

"I expected to find a man ten feet tall, with arms the size of tree trunks."

His lips twitched with a smile and he lifted one of his arms. Even though it was cold and raining, he wasn't wearing a cloak or warm clothing of any kind. The tunic he wore, of a faded brown color, had the sleeves ripped off it because his enormous arms were bare. With his right arm lifted and flexing, the muscles beneath his pale skin were bulging and defined. He inspected both arms, in fact, before replying.

"They are," he said simply.

Asmara's gaze lingered on him for a moment before breaking down into soft laughter; she couldn't help herself.

"Aye," she agreed. "They are. And you are not a modest man. But, then again, I suppose you have no reason to be."

Blayth lowered his arms. "Modesty is for men who are unsure of their strengths," he said. "I am sure of mine."

It was a curious thing to say. Asmara's interest in the man was a little less guarded because, in truth, he was rather fascinating. But she knew that from the first moment they'd met. She'd spent two weeks thinking about the man and watching him from a distance, but all of that changed tonight.

Cader, in fact, hadn't sent her.

She'd boldly come on her own.

"Of that, I have no doubt," she said after a moment. "And Morys clearly trusts you, for I have heard that you have fought many great battles for him."

"Morys seems to have more battles to fight than most."

Asmara snorted; she couldn't help it. "That is because he has more enemies than most," she said before she could stop herself. Realizing she probably shouldn't have said such a thing to Blayth, who was loyal to Morys, she hastened to change the subject. "The last time my father had regular conversations with Morys was more than five years ago. I think that was before you came into his service."

Blayth nodded vaguely. "So I am told."

"That Morys has not spoken regularly to my father since then?"

"Nay. That I have been in Morys' service for five years."

She cocked her head. "That is a curious thing to say," she said. "You do not know exactly how long you have been in his service?"

Blayth scratched a big shoulder, his gaze moving from Asmara to the castle in the distance, a black silhouette against the cloudy sky. She was asking questions that would lead him to speak on things that were probably better left unsaid. Knowing that Morys and Cader were at odds, he suspected that Cader might have put her up to it. She'd said that her father had sent her, after all, and that was a grossly disappointing thought. He'd rather hoped she wanted to know about him on her own.

"Tell your father that your attempts to discover more information about me have come to failure," he said. "I will see you in a few hours and we may go over the plan to breach Llandarog at that time. I will not speak of it until then."

Asmara stiffened and the glimmer went out of her eyes. "My father did not send me to discover more about you, only the plans for the coming operation."

"I am not stupid, woman. Return to your father."

Her features tensed. "So you think I have been trying to… to *probe* you? What should I want to probe you about?"

"Whatever it is, it is not your business."

He seemed very guarded all of a sudden. As if a curtain of defense was raised, and Asmara was truly at a loss. She wasn't probing him for her father's sake, only for hers, but as she tried to figure out why Blayth seemed so defensive, she recalled the moment in the great hall of Carmarthen Castle and how men questioned Morys' statement of Blayth's identity.

Truth be told, he was a mysterious man, now with a great legend attached to him. Perhaps, he'd learned to be defensive about who he was. Perhaps, it was instinctive for him to protect himself, and understandably so. But his assumption that she was attempting to probe him upset her greatly.

"I told you why I was here," she said, her voice low. "If you do not believe me, that is your misfortune. I do not lie, and I do not seek personal information from you on behalf of my father. That is twice you have insulted me now. There will not be a third time."

With that, she turned on her heel and disappeared into the trees. Blayth kept his gaze on the distant castle until he heard the foliage moving and he knew she was no longer standing there. Only then did he turn to look at her, watching the dark figure move towards the distant encampment.

Oddly enough, he believed her. He didn't know the woman, but something told him that she was being truthful. Perhaps, she really had wanted to know something about him, on her own, and he'd ruined the moment by chasing her off. He wasn't much good with women, anyway, and he certainly was out of practice when it came to wooing one. Not that he wanted to woo Asmara, but she was a long-legged beauty and those long legs had his attention.

As did the rest of her.

Perhaps tomorrow he might apologize to her for insulting her yet again.

It was coming to be a habit with him.

WITH THE MOON down, the darkness before dawn was inky.

A group of ten Welsh were moving in almost complete darkness, heading across a field, a thicket, and a bubbling stream, before reaching the village of Llandarog.

It was a small village, built up around the hill with the castle perched on top of it, rising like a jewel above the green Welsh countryside. It was a prosperous little village, and peaceful for the most part, because the English garrison wasn't an active one.

Even though the road that Llandarog Castle guarded was one of the main roads through the south of Wales, the road to the north, where Carmarthen Castle was located, was more heavily traveled. Therefore, the garrison at Llandarog, which was held by Lord Pembroke, had grown lazy and fat. Without much to do, the soldiers were not on their guard when Blayth, Asmara, and eight Welsh warriors made their way through the village and straight to the hill with the castle on the top.

Unfortunately, with the wet weather, the hill was thick with soggy grass up to their knees, and trees with branches that were heavy with water. For every three steps they took in scaling the hill, they would slide a step or two back. It was slow going to mount the hill, but Asmara and Blayth were leading the charge. Asmara was smart enough to use her dagger to anchor herself into the hill so she could pull herself up, and Blayth was making headway by sheer strength alone. With great effort, they made their way to the base of the enormous tower of Llandarog.

Once they reached the stone, Blayth silently called the men to him, motioning in the darkness. Everyone gathered close to him so his voice would not carry. The last thing they wanted was for any sentries on the walls overhead to hear him. With the group of Welshmen crowded around, Asmara was in the front and she was literally pushed right into Blayth, who had to reach out a big hand to steady her. They were so close that he could feel her hot breath on his cheek and see the glimmer of her eyes in the weak light. As misplaced as it was, it was quite arousing, and he found himself fighting off the allure that the woman's close proximity provoked.

It was a struggle to focus on the plan ahead and not her sweet body next to his.

"We must get to the window overhead," he said, pointing up the tower to a window that was about twelve feet over their heads. It was long and thin, about two feet across, with a lip on the bottom of the sill that stuck out a few inches. "The lady and Pryce will scale the wall with ropes and make their way inside. Once in the tower, they will make their way to the wall next to the tower and lower those ropes for us to climb. Are there any questions?"

Asmara and Pryce were the closest to Blayth. They were already looking up at the great stone tower. "If the weather was not so wet, scaling the wall would be a simple thing," Pryce said. "But the stone is wet, Blayth. I fear we shall lose our footing."

Blayth had already thought of that. He, too, found himself looking up at the tower, realizing their plan to scale it was in great jeopardy, especially since the rain was picking up. He even reached out to touch the stone; it was slick. It would be very difficult to scale. His mind began to work quickly for an alternative plan, knowing he had to think fast if they were going to salvage the situation.

And then, he saw it – there was a vine about eight feet up, a bushy thing that was growing all over the eastern side of the tower. He thought that if maybe they could get to it, then they could use it to climb to the window, because it was growing over the window itself.

It was worth a try.

"There *is* something else we can do," he said. "I am tall enough so that if the lady stands on my shoulders, she can pull herself up to the cluster of vines and use it to climb to the window."

The entire group looked up again, seeing the massive growth of vines over their heads. Wet, perhaps even weak vines. It wasn't much of a back-up plan, but it was all they had. Just as they were about to put the plan into action, they could hear someone else moving up the slope and they turned to see a figure struggling through the slippery grass. Every one of them was armed, so daggers were unsheathed.

Aeddan was part of their group, and he pulled his knife from its sheath. They could all see the figure moving in their direction, but Aeddan didn't wait for the body to come to them – he slid down the slope and grabbed the small figure by the neck. Everyone could hear a decidedly female gasp, quickly stifled by Aeddan as he slapped a hand over the mouth. Somehow, he managed to drag the figure up the slope, shoving it to the ground in front of Blayth. When the muddy head came up, it was Asmara who reacted most strongly.

"Fairynne!" she gasped, trying to keep her voice quiet. Furious, she reached out and grabbed her sister by the arm, practically pulling it out of its socket. "What are you doing here?"

Fairynne was defiant and repentant at the same time. "You may need me," she said. "I came to help!"

"Does Dadau know you are here?"

"Not… exactly."

"What do you mean by that?"

"He told me not to come, but I did not listen. I knew I could help you, Asmara. You must let me!"

Asmara was so enraged at her foolish sister that she started hitting the girl around the head and shoulders, slapping at her, only to be separated by Blayth and Aeddan. While Aeddan pulled Fairynne away, Blayth managed to get hold of Asmara's slapping hands.

"Enough," he growled. "You are going to cause every *Saesneg* soldier in the castle to hear us. Who is this woman to you?"

Asmara was so embarrassed that she could hardly look at the man. "My sister," she said. "My reckless sister. She followed the army when we left our home and my father could not spare a man to return her. She has been with us ever since, like a disease we cannot be rid of."

She'd said that to insult her sister, who was glaring at her, wounded. Blayth eyed the offended woman in the darkness. She was small, and very slender, and from what he could see, not a ravishing beauty like her sister. He shook his head with both disbelief and regret.

"Another ferch Cader female," he muttered. "Can she at least fight like you?"

"Nay."

"I can!"

The sisters answered at the same time. Blayth eyed the pair before shaking his head again, realizing they now had an unwanted woman as part of their group of skilled warriors. Before he could comment further, however, Asmara pushed Fairynne aside, so hard that the woman rolled backwards and crashed into the men behind her.

"Come on," she said to Blayth, hoping to divert the attention away from her disobedient sister. "Stand up and I will climb on you. We must hurry. The sun will be rising soon."

Blayth thought it seemed as if she were giving him orders, but she was right in one respect – they had to make haste. They couldn't continue to stand around and argue about a silly young woman who had followed them. Therefore, he forgot all about the younger ferch Cader sister as he stood up, trying to anchor his big feet into the mud of the slope as he leaned forward against the tower.

As he knew, it was slippery – all of it. The stone, the grass, everything. He was having a difficult time anchoring his feet because of the heavy grass, and he could feel someone butting up against his lower legs, trying to give him some support. Throwing his substantial weight forward even further, he pressed himself against the stone of the tower.

"Go," he hissed to Asmara. "Climb."

She did. Aeddan had put himself against the back of Blayth's legs, trying to bolster the man, so Asmara took the hemp rope that was handed to her and climbed on his back, using him as a stepping stone to climb onto Blayth's back. As she literally scaled his broad back and onto his shoulders, he lifted a hand and pulled her up. With her knees on his shoulders, Asmara clung to the wet, stone tower for support as she made her way to her feet.

Beneath her, Blayth and Aeddan were grunting with effort, trying to keep from slipping in the very wet footing. Asmara knew this, and she didn't want to particularly fall if they lost their footing, so she quickly grabbed on to the vine, which was stronger than it looked. She could feel substantial branches beneath the foliage and was able to grab hold and pull herself up.

Blayth felt her weight lift from him and he looked up in time to see her scaling the wet vines. She managed to climb with ease, quickly making headway up the tangle of vines to the slender lancet window. As he watched with some trepidation, she peered inside the window for several long moments before moving away. Blayth watched with concern as she suddenly backtracked on her climbing, enough so that she was nearly to the bottom of the vine again. Either she was refusing to go through the window, or there was something she wanted him to know.

Her actions were concerning.

"What is it?" he hissed at her.

Asmara was trying not to raise her voice, fearful she would be heard. "The window narrows on the interior," she whispered loudly. "I believe I can squeeze through, but your man cannot."

She was describing an arrow slit – windows that were wider on the exterior and then narrowed on the interior to protect the man firing the arrow at attackers. Sometimes they could become quite narrowed, like a funnel, and Blayth didn't like the thought of Asmara going in alone. He wouldn't have liked the thought of anyone going alone for what needed to be done, but he was particularly concerned for the Dragon Princess. She was trying to do a man's job and it simply wasn't right that she should go alone.

Turning his head, he could see his men crouched behind him, and he saw Pryce in particular. He motioned the man forward, grabbing his arm when he came close.

"Get up there with her," he said. "You will go through that window if I have to get up there and pound you through it."

Pryce nodded. He was slender, but he had big bones. Big knees, big joints, and the like. He wasn't tiny by any means. But he was skinnier than any of the other men, including his brother, so there was little choice. And he knew for a fact that Blayth would climb up and pound on him if he became stuck, which was an embarrassing thought. Blayth started to boost him up so he could grab hold of the vine, but Asmara waved him off.

"He is too large," she hissed. Then, the men heard her sigh heavily. "Give me my sister. She can make it through."

So the little rebel was to be part of this, after all. Blayth frowned as he turned to look at the small woman, several feet away and crouched in a muddy ball. Although he didn't argue with Asmara, the thought of sending two women into a castle full of English was starting to give him hives. He was leery enough with only Asmara breeching the castle, but sending her younger sister in with her was less than ideal.

Still, there was little choice if the window was narrowed on the inside, and he had to trust Asmara in the matter. She knew what she was looking at; he didn't. The Dragon Princess surely knew what she was doing, didn't she? Men had spoken of her prowess in battle and of her skill, so even though Blayth hadn't fought with the woman, and hadn't yet developed a trust for her, he had no choice if this endeavor was going to have a chance of succeeding.

He had to trust the woman.

Therefore, he motioned silently to Fairynne. She'd heard her sister's request, but she hadn't moved, fearful of being pushed down again, until Blayth beckoned. Then, one of the Welshmen grabbed her by the arm and pulled her up, passing her over to Blayth, as someone else put a coil of hemp rope around her neck.

As Fairynne adjusted the rope so she could climb with it, Blayth heaved her up in the direction of her sister's outstretched hand.

"Listen to your sister in all things," he rumbled in her ear as he passed her up. "For if you do not, I shall find you when this is over and blister your arse."

Fairynne's eyes widened with fear as Blayth lifted her up as high as he could. She ended up with her feet on his shoulders, much as Asmara had done, but her sister was there to pull her up onto the vine. Fairynne held on tightly, now climbing the vines and following her sister to the slender window of the tower.

Their entire success now rested on the shoulders of two small women.

"What do we do if they are captured?" Aeddan was standing next to Blayth, his dark eyes watching the sisters climb. "Cader will never forgive Morys if that happens."

Blayth was watching them also. Truthfully, he didn't know what to say about the situation. It had all happened so quickly and they'd had to improvise with the changing of the circumstances, but as he watched Asmara insert her head and then the rest of her body into the window above, he was beginning to wonder if this wasn't a very bad idea.

But they'd come too far to turn back now.

"Cader raised his daughters to fight like men," he said simply. "He only has himself to blame."

Aeddan didn't reply because he knew Blayth didn't mean it as coldly as it sounded. He knew for a fact that Blayth had more feeling than most and, at times, would rather negotiate out of a situation than fight it. But he was also a man who was unafraid to do what was necessary in the end.

There were just over a thousand men waiting for a handful of men to open the portcullis of Llandarog Castle so, in this case, sending two women to make the initial entry was necessary and Aeddan knew the man well enough to know that he was harboring a wicked sense of guilt because of it.

Sending women in to do a man's work.

Now, all they could do was pray.

CHAPTER FIVE

"ASMARA HAS GROWN."

In the darkness of the early morning hours, Cader was watching Llandarog Castle from a distance, knowing that Asmara had gone with Blayth and the others to secure entry to the castle. He had been hesitant to let her go, but he also knew that she was quite capable. Still, it made him nervous that she was out of his sight.

He was unable to help her should she need it.

But his brother's softly-uttered words broke his concentration and he turned to see Morys heading towards him, through the skinny cluster of trees. He hadn't talked to his brother in many years until the summons to Carmarthen Castle, and even though they'd been traveling together, they still hadn't spoken very much. They were so used to ignoring each other that it came naturally. Therefore, Morys' appearance was something of a surprise.

"Aye," Cader said belatedly. "She has seen eighteen years now. She is a woman grown."

Morys nodded as his attention moved to the castle in the distance. "Dragon Princess," he muttered. "That is what they call her now."

Cader snorted softly. "She hates to be called that," he said. "She simply wants to be a warrior, like any other man."

Morys looked pointedly at him. "But she is *not* like any other man," he said. "She is a woman, and a beautiful one. Has she not even been betrothed yet?"

Cader rolled his eyes at the touchy subject. "What man wants a wife who can best him in a fight?" he said. "Nay, Brother, no betrothal yet. No suitor of any kind. Until I can get her to behave like a woman, there is no point."

"Yet you send her into battle."

"Because she is an excellent warrior."

"It is your fault for making her one."

Cader turned to look at his brother; Morys was older than he by fourteen months, so there wasn't much of an age gap between them at all. They'd grown up together, played together, fought together. When their father died, Morys decided that he was head of the family and he'd gone out of his way to make his brother feel insignificant and weak. Morys was married, but he'd never had children, while Cader's marriage had produced two daughters. Their branch of the family was dying out and it killed Morys to realize that. He always had to be the bigger, stronger, and smarter brother, but his one failing had been in his inability to father a child, male or female. Oddly enough, he liked to make Cader feel guilty for only having females.

But Cader wasn't feeling guilty today. He was proud of his daughter.

"Is that what you came to tell me?" he finally asked. "That it is my fault for making Asmara a warrior? I didn't 'make' her a warrior, you know. She chose to be one. There was no way to discourage her."

Morys eyed his brother in the weak light. His younger brother who was kind and compassionate, everything Morys was not. He'd tried for a very long time not to hate him for it, but he couldn't quite seem to manage it. There was so much about Cader that he hated.

And so much he was jealous of.

"So now you have an unmarriageable daughter on your hands," Morys said quietly. "Will she be a spinster, then? Or will she lead your armies?"

Cader wasn't going to let his brother mock him. "We have not spoken to one another in over five years," he said. "If you are going to taunt me about my children, then you can go back to your men. I have no need or desire to tangle with you."

The line in the sand had been drawn already. Morys simply dipped his head. "I was not taunting you," he said. "I was merely asking a question since I have not seen Asmara in so long. What of Fairynne? Has she married?"

Cader shook his head. "She has not."

Morys pondered his brother's unwed daughters but he could see that any further comment about them would not be well met. In truth, he hadn't come to taunt his brother. He really didn't know why he'd come, other than he'd missed the man and didn't want to admit it.

"Well," he sighed, "Asmara has gone with Blayth and we must be moving our men into position so we are ready when they open the portcullis. My scouts say that we can skirt the village over to the east and come in through the trees directly across from the castle. They will not see us until it is too late."

Cader nodded, turning to the men nearest him and issuing a quiet whistle. As the men stood up and began to come to him, he turned to Morys. "I will tell my men to be ready to move," he said. "Are your men ready?"

"They are."

"Then let us depart."

Cader's men came to him and he quietly issued orders. When those men left to rouse the rest of Cader's army, Cader happened to see that Morys was still standing there.

"Is that all?" he asked.

Morys nodded. He started to turn away, but something made him stop. When he spoke, it was without looking at his brother. It was almost as if he couldn't bear to.

"Why did we stop talking to one another, Cader?" he asked softly. "I have forgotten."

Cader looked at him. "You called me weak," he said. "Do you not recall?"

"I am not certain. Mayhap."

"You said you were ashamed of a brother who was so weak."

Morys almost turned to look at him. *I was stupid for saying so.* But he couldn't bring himself to say it, nor could he bring himself to apologize. He remembered exactly what he'd said to his brother, and when he'd said it. He was only hoping that Cader hadn't remembered. Then he would have nothing to apologize for.

But Cader did, indeed, remember. Morys simply nodded his head and began to walk away, but a word from Cader stopped him.

"I will say this to you, Morys," he said quietly. "I am not weak. I have never been weak. I am able to show emotion and feelings that you were never able to, and if you believe that to be weak, that is your misfortune. But I will tell you this; my daughter, Asmara, is anything but weak. She is the strongest woman in Wales and tonight, she will prove that to you. Mark my words. And when you see how strong she is, you will tell me so. Are you listening? I will hear it from your own lips."

Morys still couldn't bring himself to look at him or even agree. Without another word, he continued on, heading into the darkened trees and for his army, which was preparing to move out. Cader watched him go for a few moments, thinking of his haughty, arrogant brother. He didn't exactly hate the man, but it was close.

But tonight, they had to put their feelings aside for a common goal.

To take Llandarog Castle back from the English.

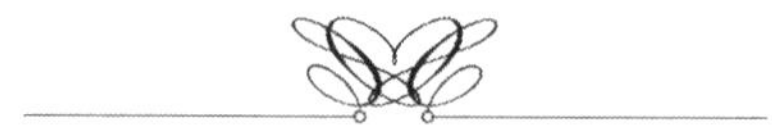

IT SMELLED LIKE a barnyard.

That was Asmara's first thought as she slithered in through the narrowed window of Llandarog's tower and ended up falling to the floor. It was dark, quiet, and smelly. Fortunately, the chamber was also empty and she quickly found her feet, pulling Fairynne through the opening behind her.

But the women huddled near the open window for a few moments as their eyes became acclimated to the near total darkness. The tower itself was small in diameter, so there was only one room per floor. They had no way of knowing just how many floors there were because the base of the tower seemed sunken into the hillside. Since it was an hour or so before dawn, they couldn't hear anyone stirring, but that didn't mean an entire army of English soldiers wasn't sleeping on the floor below them.

They had to get moving.

Asmara pulled her sister close.

"We must find a way to get to the wall on the west side," she whispered. "It is attached to this tower and if there is an opening on to the wall, it will be on the level above us. Follow me and stay close; do not wander and do not make any noise. Do you understand?"

Fairynne nodded, but it was clear from her expression that she was frightened. Perhaps helping her sister had seemed brave enough until they entered the lion's den, but now that she was here, she wasn't so sure. Still, her pride prevented her from doing anything other than pretending she had some measure of bravery. She held tight to the rope that was coiled over one shoulder and down under one arm, just like the rope that Asmara was holding, and when her sister began to move, she followed.

There was a flight of stone stairs built onto one side of the room; a hole in the floor had stairs going down to the floor below while a small flight built into the wall went up to the floor above. Staying close to the wall, the sisters mounted the stairs that led to the floor above, making their way silently until Asmara could just stick her head through the hole in the floor above them, peering into the chamber to see if there anyone was there.

Fortunately, it was empty but for a few shields and metal-tipped staffs against the wall. It also contained a small door that led to the wall walk, just as she'd hoped. As far as Asmara could see, there didn't seem to be anyone on the wall walk, so she came to the top of the stairs, holding out a hand to her sister to indicate caution. Even though there didn't seem to be anyone around, they still needed to proceed carefully. Once they were on the wall walk, they could lower the ropes for Blayth and the others.

Their goal was so close, but yet so far. The wall walk was just a few feet away, but it seemed like it stretched for a mile. Once they left the tower, they would be exposed to the ward below, and Asmara's heart was thumping in her chest. The apprehension was almost more than she could bear, but she had a task to complete and she focused on it. As they neared the doorway that opened out into the wall walk, she came to a sudden halt and backed up against the wall to stay out of sight.

Fairynne looked at her sister curiously as Asmara took the hemp rope and tied a loop at one end of it. The curtain wall had battlements, meaning it had regularly spaced, square openings so defenders could shoot enemies below and then use the battlements for protection from incoming enemy projectiles. It also meant that if they could get the big loop of the rope around one the solid square features in between the openings, they could use that to anchor the rope so the men waiting below could climb up the wall.

Soon enough, Fairynne understood what her sister was doing and she, too, tied a big loop in the end of her rope. The wall itself was perhaps eighteen to twenty feet high, and their ropes weren't quite so long, but long enough that Blayth and his men would be able to get hold of them when lowered.

With both ropes looped at the end, it was finally time to act. Asmara dropped to her hands and knees as she crept onto the wall walk, keeping a low profile until she could see just where the English soldiers were. As soon as she emerged onto the wall walk, she could see the English – there were a few in the darkness, over by the gatehouse, and only three on the vast wall walk, as far as she could see. The men on the wall walk were also over near the two-storied gatehouse, clustered there, as one of them sat on the edge of it, his legs dangling over the side.

Clearly, these were men who were not expecting an attack this night, but something had their attention over by the gatehouse because that was where they all seemed to be gathered. Asmara wondered if they had sighted her father and Morys, who would be moving their army into position in anticipation of the gate opening. If that was the case, then the element of surprise would soon be lost. With that in mind, Asmara knew she had to move quickly while their attention was diverted.

She and her sister may not have another chance.

Heart pounding, palms sweating, Asmara moved to the battlements. Quickly rising to her feet, she looped the rope over the nearest stone square and tossed the rope down the side of the wall. Fairynne was a little slower in getting her rope secured, so Asmara quickly moved to help her, making sure both ropes were over the side so the men could climb up. Peering over the side of the wall, she could see men moving towards the ropes through the darkness.

They were coming.

But so were the English. No sooner had they thrown the ropes over the side than someone saw them. Shouts drifted in their direction and the women turned, startled, to see the men from the gatehouse looking at them. A brief moment of horror in realizing they'd been seen was replaced by determination as Asmara swung into action.

"The staffs and shields," she hissed, pointing to the tower. "Quickly – we must get them. I will fight them off. You must protect the ropes until the men can mount them!"

Fairynne might have been young and foolish at times, but she shared Asmara's sense of determination. She, too, understood that this was critical, so she rushed ahead of her sister into the tower room and began grabbing items. She shoved a shield at her sister and then a staff, and as Asmara ran back onto the battlements to fight off what was sure to be an incoming horde of English, Fairynne also picked up a staff and returned to her post by the ropes. She wanted to be armed in case anyone made it past her sister.

She was prepared to fight to the death.

Asmara, too, was ready for them. She stood her ground several feet down the wall walk, giving her sister and the incoming Welsh plenty of room as she faced off against several English soldiers who were now heading in her direction. Two of them had torches, lighting up the faces of the enemy against the early morning darkness. Although she'd been nervous about facing a moment like this, as the reality of it approached, Asmara found that she wasn't nervous at all. She was angry; angry that the English were here, angry that she had to fight them off. Anger fed her bravery. With the shield in one hand and the staff in the other, she braced herself.

Oddly enough, the English were slow to move. Seeing two women, and really having no idea why they were there, had them moving cautiously, which was to the advantage of the Welshmen on the ropes. Four of them were already climbing, Blayth being one of them, and he was already almost halfway to the top. But the English weren't looking at their walls, at least not yet. They were still trying to figure out why two women were on the wall walk and that distraction would work against them. As several of them moved closer to Asmara, their manner remained almost timid.

And she sensed it. Asmara was, if nothing else, extremely intuitive. She could see that they were quite confused and perhaps even slightly interested. She could only surmise that they didn't see what was going on behind her, and that men weren't climbing the walls at that very moment and that, soon, the castle would be under attack. It was dark enough that they could only see two women on the walls, but if they moved those torches any closer, they would soon see the ropes being used.

Then, it would turn into battle.

Therefore, Asmara took a step towards them, lifting her staff and shield, and smiling hugely. He had a lovely smile, in fact, with straight white teeth and slightly prominent canines. It was a gesture that lit up her entire face, something not missed by the English. Not only was a woman on their wall walk, but a beautiful one at that.

"*Cyfarchion*," Asmara said in Welsh. *Greetings.* "I would wager to say that you did not expect to find two lonely women here tonight."

The Englishman had no idea what to make of it. The man in front, an older man in well-used mail, peered strangely at her.

"Lonely?" he repeated. "What *are* you doing here, lass? How did you get here?"

Asmara turned her smile on him. "What else would I be doing here?" she said. "I am looking for a little… amusement."

The English soldier was greatly confused by her response. He indicated the shield and staff in her hands. "What *kind* of amusement?"

Asmara shrugged lightly, hoping she could keep them talking until someone got to the top of the rope and she could have help fending them all off.

"You fight me," she said. "If I lose, I become your prisoner. But if you lose…"

The soldier folded his arms in front of his chest expectantly. "I will not lose to you," he said. He wagged an irritable finger at her. "Come along, now. *Why* are you here? Tell me the truth. And tell me how you got here."

Asmara lifted her shoulders. "I flew in, like a bird," she said. "If you beat me in a fight, then I shall tell you. But until you do, you will simply have to take my word for it."

The soldier opened his mouth to reply but something behind the woman caught his attention. In fact, he watched in shock as two men vaulted over the top of the battlements. But his shock wasn't so great that he didn't realize what was happening. Suddenly, he let out a bellow.

"*Breach!*"

The game was over. Realizing that Blayth and his men were showing themselves, Asmara did the only thing she could do – she charged the English soldiers standing in front of her, using the shield to literally scoop them backwards. The older soldier tried to grab her, but she kneed the man in the groin so hard that he immediately fell to his knees, blocking the way for the soldiers behind him to charge.

That moment of respite allowed Asmara to bring the shield up and slam them in the face. She caught two of them squarely, with one of them falling straight off the wall walk and into the bailey below. But there were still men to take their place and she fell into a frenzy, striking and stabbing at everything that moved.

The English were unprepared for her onslaught. Because they'd been on watch when she'd come onto the wall, they had nothing more than crossbows with them, no broadswords, and now they had a woman who was fighting furiously, driving them back further, and further still. She was doing a marvelous job of fighting them off, but there were more of them than there were of her.

It was only a matter of time before they turned the tides.

Unfortunately for the English soldiers, there were now men on the wall walk that were not English, men who had climbed the wall on ropes evidently provided by the very woman they found themselves fighting off. The only possible explanation was the Welsh were going to try and take the castle, so the English were scrambling to gather their weapons and preparing to fight off the invaders.

Very quickly, chaos reigned.

But Asmara didn't back away and she didn't run, not even when she saw more English soldiers running for the wall walk. She held her ground, fighting and struggling, kicking and punching, until one of the soldiers managed to rip the staff from her hand. He turned it on her, preparing to strike, when a big body suddenly appeared between Asmara and the English.

Blayth had arrived.

The man had carried his short sword with him up that treacherous rope, and he dispatched two of the English soldiers before the rest began to run, backing away from the enormous Welshman with the deadly strike. When one man tried to challenge him, he punched him in the face, sending him to the ground and, in the same motion, stealing the man's broadsword. Armed with a big weapon now, he moved menacingly towards the rest of the soldiers rushing up to the wall walk as Asmara, Aeddan, and Pryce tucked in behind him.

"We need to get into the room with the pulley that will open the portcullis," Blayth said. "If I had to guess, I would say it is on the upper level of the gatehouse. Aeddan and I will hold off those coming up the ladders if Pryce and the lady can make it into the chamber on the upper level. See how they are already trying to form a blockade on the chamber entry?"

They could all see a group of soldiers with torches bunched up around an opening that led into the second floor of the gatehouse. Oddly enough, if there was a door on the opening, they hadn't shut it. The doorway remained unsealed.

Asmara could see the portal clearly, and she could feel the thrill of battle rushing through her veins, for a variety of reasons. To begin with, she loved the rush of battle and the feel of a weapon in her hand. But it was also her first time fighting with Blayth and she was beginning to see what all the fuss was about. He was absolutely fearless in movement, fluid in motion, and moved with surreal power. She'd never seen anything like it in her life.

As the four of them moved towards the gatehouse, more English soldiers came running at them. Blayth and Aeddan were in the lead, fighting the men back, and as they did so, Asmara managed to pick up a short sword that someone had dropped in the chaos. As Blayth and Aeddan fought off the onslaught, and tried not to get pushed off the wall walk themselves, Asmara dropped to her knees and pushed through the legs of the men who were fighting.

She was in a perfect position to do a lot of damage, and damage she did. Men ended up with cut Achilles' tendons or sword thrusts to the backs of their knees. In fact, Blayth had no idea why men were falling away from him so swiftly until he saw Asmara on her knees amongst the English, slashing viciously with her sword. It was one of the more impressive things he'd ever seen, and he found himself fighting off a smile at the very plucky Dragon Princess.

Now, he understood what men had been saying about her.

She was fearless, indeed.

In fact, he'd seen her fighting off the English the moment he'd arrived on the top of the wall. She'd had a shield and a staff, and she was creating serious problems for several English soldiers who were trying to fight back. For a brief moment, he'd admired the woman and her obvious skill, but then it occurred to him that the lovely, leggy woman who had his interest was in a great deal of danger, and that brought about a side of him he never knew he had. Certainly, he was fearsome in a fight – there was no one more fearsome – but the thought of Asmara in danger did something to him.

It spurred him to another level of fighting fervor.

He'd rushed up behind her, putting himself between her and the English, and that's when men started dropping. Blayth was fighting to claim the castle, but he was also fighting for Asmara. As if the woman needed his help. But the chivalrous man in him was determined to give it.

In the midst of everything, he was trying not to feel like an utter, complete idiot.

The English had cleared up now between his slashing and Asmara's stabbing, so he reached down and pulled her to her feet amidst wounded English on the wall walk.

"Well done," he told her. "I think there are a few men around here who may never walk again, thanks to you."

Pink-cheeked from exertion, Asmara looked at her handiwork of injured men, kicking one soldier when he didn't move out of her way fast enough. He groaned when she kicked him again.

"Do you think so?" she asked seriously.

He nodded, his eyes glimmering at her. "I do," he said. There was a warm moment as they looked at each other, and Blayth felt something shocking bolt through his veins. Fear? Excitement? He didn't know. He couldn't ever remember feeling it before. All he knew was that when he looked at her, he felt a distinct shock, but there was no time to linger on the sensation. He pointed to the two-storied gatehouse. "Now, let us see if we can lift that portcullis. Hurry, now; dawn is upon us and there is no time to waste."

Asmara charged off, swinging her sword and engaging men who were far better protected than she was, but it didn't seem to matter to her. She used those long legs to kick, and she wasn't afraid to aim for a man's groin. She did whatever she had to do in order to disable them. Once she had them off-balance, she lashed out, gravely injuring or even killing. Blayth saw her do it twice as they pushed their way to the gatehouse. Just as they neared the open door, a large soldier emerged.

Unfortunately, Asmara walked right into him and he reached out, clamping a big hand around her neck and giving her a good shake. The sword dropped from her grip as her hands moved instinctively to the big mitt around her neck, squeezing the life from her. She kicked out, twice, and caught the man in the abdomen and thigh, but not hard enough to cause him to dislodge his grip. Just as her vision began to dim, Blayth thrust his sword into the man's belly.

Asmara fell aside as Blayth stabbed the man again and then tossed him over the wall walk. When he should have been heading into the gatehouse to locate the mechanism for the portcullis, he found himself more concerned for Asmara. He pulled her to her feet.

"Are you well?" he asked. "He did not hurt you, did he?"

Asmara was rubbing her neck where the soldier had gripped her. "Nay," she said. "Thanks to you. I think he was trying to kill me."

Blayth's lips flickered with a grin. "What was your first indication?"

Asmara stopped rubbing her neck and looked at him, thinking he was making some kind of nasty remark about her. But she saw the grin, and the mirth in his eyes, and a smile creased her lips.

"I am not entirely sure," she jested in return. "It could have been that big hand on my neck. Or the fact that he was English."

Blayth snorted, a humorous sound. "It was both, demoiselle," he said. "But never fear; I would not let him do it, to you or to your sister.

You were both quite valuable this night."

Asmara's smile vanished as she started looking around, almost in a panic. "My sister," she gasped. "Where is Fairynne?"

Blayth turned around, too, looking for the tiny woman who had helped liberate a castle. The sun was starting to rise and the sky above was turning shades of blue and gray, casting a moderate amount of illumination on the castle. He thought he could see the younger ferch Cader sister over by the tower, still near the ropes that she had helped secure. He pointed.

"Over there," he said. "But I would not worry over her. It seems that both ferch Cader sisters can take care of themselves."

Asmara could see Fairynne also and it eased her mind considerably. "That is not a bad thing," she said. "We have always been able to take care of ourselves."

He cocked his head slightly. "You should not have to. Menfolk should protect you."

"There are no menfolk that can protect me any better than I can do for myself."

His smile was threatening again. "What about English soldiers who try to break your neck?"

She grinned and averted her gaze. "I would have overcome him, eventually."

"And yet, you did not have to," he said. He paused before speaking again. "I would do it again if you needed me to."

There was something chivalrous in the way he said it, something that made Asmara look up and take notice. There was fighting going on all around them but, at the moment, it was as if they were the only two people in the whole world. When their gazes met, the corners of his eyes crinkled in a way that was difficult to describe. There was something… warm there. Something that suggested his concern for her wasn't purely soldier to soldier. It was simply man to woman.

She began to feel faint for an entirely different reason.

God, how the man could make her heart race!

But the warm moment was dashed by the sound of the big portcullis as it began to lurch open. Chains groaned, iron creaked, and men began to yell. When Asmara and Blayth ran to the edge of the battlements to see what the fuss was about, they could see Morys and Cader's men at the gatehouse below. Blayth turned quickly, rushing from the wall as he gestured to the open door of the second-floor of the gatehouse.

"Help them raise the portcullis," he told Asmara. "I will go down below. I have a feeling the English will not take kindly to their new visitors."

With that, he quickly descended the ladder that led to the bailey below, and Asmara charged into the second floor of the gatehouse, helping Aeddan and Pryce and two other men fight off English soldiers who were trying to do them great harm. Once Asmara entered the fight, the English limped away with kicked groins and other unmanly injuries, pain she wasn't afraid to inflict, and the portcullis went up just enough so that Morys and Cader were able to flood in with their hundreds and hundreds of men.

Within an hour, the English of Llandarog Castle were subdued and the banners for Edward I were torn down from the battlements as the fortress was once again claimed by the Welsh. Even in the town of Llandarog, which had been shut tight against the battle, the peasants were starting to emerge, cheering the fact that the great castle was now in the hands of the Welsh. They began bringing food and drink to the castle in droves, and the men of Morys and Cader's armies soon found themselves stuffed with sausages, marrowfat peas, and watered ale.

A feast fit for victors.

When Cader got over his anger at Fairynne's part in securing Llandarog, he realized that he was most proud of his daughters. Blayth had told him that breaching Llandarog would not have been possible if it weren't for the women warriors. He was, in truth, quite pleased with them, and when Asmara wanted to sit and eat and drink with Morys' men, he didn't stop her. She'd earned a place among them. But he sat with his own men, across the bailey, with an exhausted Fairynne sleeping on his lap, and watched his oldest daughter as she listened to Morys' men tell great stories of valor.

But the feasting and stories of valor soon came to a halt when they received word from Howell stating that his siege of Gwendraith Castle had suffered a setback and they'd been unable to breach the castle. His missive asked Cader and Morys to spare what men they could, including Blayth, and send them along to Gwendraith to aid in claiming the castle.

Morys decided that Cader and a few of the men should remain with Llandarog while Morys took his men, and more than half of Cader's, on to Gwendraith. Cader didn't argue with him; he was happy to remain at the castle they'd worked so hard to capture. Before the day was out, Morys and his men rode out for Gwendraith, which was less than ten miles from Llandarog. To the cheers of the peasants of the village, Morys took his men and headed off to another battle.

Much to Asmara's dismay, Cader had intentionally kept her and Fairynne with him. She was furious about it and had argued strongly but, in the end, Cader would not be swayed and Asmara marched off to sulk. What she didn't know was that Cader had his reasons, petty or no – his arrogant, conceited brother who, when told Asmara and Fairynne's roles in the breach of Llandarog, couldn't even congratulate them. Asmara had proven herself worthy, as had Fairynne to a certain extent, but Morys wouldn't acknowledge them. His pride wouldn't let him.

It was pride that was starting to drive an even deeper wedge between him and his brother. And because of it, Cader kept his daughters with him. While Morys and his men went on to confiscate Gwendraith Castle, and remain there, Cader and his daughters, and his men, remained at Llandarog.

Asmara didn't know why her father wouldn't let her go join up with Morys' army, but her father seemed particularly embittered after the siege of Llandarog. He didn't want to talk about Morys at all, even worse than before. All Asmara knew was that it would be some time before she saw Blayth again, and in those weeks of separation, she didn't forget about the man. On the contrary.

She was very much looking forward to the day when she would see him again.

And she *knew* she would see him again.

CHAPTER SIX

Four weeks later, Mid-September
Lioncross Abbey, near Lyonshall, England
The Welsh Marches

LIONCROSS ABBEY CASTLE was named because it was built on the site of an ancient Roman house of worship and incorporated portions of two walls and part of the foundation into the structure of the castle itself. A former owner had christened it "Lioncross" after Richard the Lionheart, a man that the de Lohr family shared a great history with.

In truth, the castle had only belonged to the de Lohrs for less than one hundred years, when it passed into the family through marriage. It sat atop a low ridge overlooking a lake and the dark mountains that marked the Welsh border could be seen in the distance. The land around Lioncross was relatively flat and the Romans, as well as subsequent builders, had seen the advantage of building on the only rise for miles around. With the enormous curtain wall that surrounded the castle, the grounds of which were as vast as some of the largest castles in England, Lioncross Abbey was a force to be reckoned with.

The first Earl of Hereford and Worcester had been none other than Christopher de Lohr, the man known as King Richard's Lion's Claw. He had been with Richard on his crusade to The Holy Land and had made a name for himself there. When he'd returned to England, it had been with a litany of nicknames and titles, not the least of which was

Defender of the Realm. In those turbulent days of Richard and John, when the Plantagenets fought brother against brother, or brother against father, or anyone else they decided to battle, Christopher and his brother, David, had been right in the middle of it, strongly supporting the crown.

The current earl was also named Christopher de Lohr, after his famous grandsire. The son of Curtis de Lohr, eldest son of Christopher and his lady wife, Dustin, Christopher the Second was a man in his fifth decade and had assumed the earldom at his father's death only two years earlier. He had two younger brothers, Arthur and William, and so as not to confuse him with his legendary grandsire, he was known simply as Chris. Chris de Lohr meant the current earl, while Christopher meant the Lion's Claw.

Not that Chris was any less powerful or decorated than his father or grandfather; on the contrary, he'd made a name for himself fighting with King Henry's army and in the battles against Simon de Montfort. He was a proud tribute to the de Lohr name and he'd married well, having four sons and a daughter. Morgen, his eldest son, was also a fine tribute to the de Lohr name, but those who had known Christopher whispered that Morgen was much more like David, his great-uncle, than his grandsire. Morgen de Lohr had that quick temper in him that David de Lohr had been so famous for.

But Chris could not have been prouder of the young man, and of the rest of his brood – Rees, Dru, Kade, and Rhianne. His wife, Kaedia, was Welsh, a lass of a local chieftain he'd long had an alliance with, so his sons were a hybrid of an old English family and an old Welsh tribe, giving them all a particular view of the world. The boys had been raised English, and had fostered in the finest houses, but there was a part of them that was sympathetic to Welsh causes and to the Welsh fight for independence against Edward, which had made things rather difficult for them with Edward's ongoing battles.

That was the reason Chris hadn't consulted with Morgen or Rees when the news came out of Wales, via de Lohr spies in fact, that there was a new rebellion rising in the south. Although Morgen tended to side with the English in all things, as he would be an English earl when his father passed on, Rees had the heart of a rebel. He was passionate for the underdog; in this case, the Welsh. Dru and Kade were mostly English, like Morgen was, but Rees could get them worked up if he truly believed in a cause.

Therefore, when Chris received the men who watched the Welsh Marches for him, it was in secret for the most part. Chris' captain, a powerful knight by the name of Augustus de Shera, had admitted the spies and brought them in through the postern gate, sneaking them in through the kitchens and into Chris' solar.

It was there that Chris was told a great and troubling tale of a new Welsh rebellion, and the conversation with his two spies went on for more than an hour as he made sure to get every piece of information out of them. When he was certain they could tell him no more, he sent them to the kitchens to find something to eat and settled down in his chair as Augustus closed the solar door. Only then did the knight speak.

"I suppose I should not be surprised to hear that there is rebellion in the wind," he said. "But I am concerned to hear of the rise of a bastard of Llywelyn ap Gruffydd."

Chris drew in a long, thoughtful breath. A big man in size and stature, he looked very much like his grandsire with his shaggy blond hair and reddish-blond beard. His leather chair creaked as he sat back in it, gathering his thoughts.

"Gwendraith, Idole, and Llandarog Castles," he said slowly. "I know of these places. They are near Carmarthen Castle. In fact, as I recall, they guard some of the major roads leading to and from Pembroke Castle."

Augustus nodded. Much as Chris had a great family legacy, so did Augustus. His father was Maximus de Shera, one of three brothers known as the Lords of Thunder. Back in the days of Simon de Montfort, the de Shera brothers were legendary, now having bred several legendary sons. Augustus had his father's size and temper, a big man who was deadly with a sword. He'd served Chris for six years, and Chris depended heavily on his strength and insight.

"They were all garrisons of Pembroke Castle before this happened," Augustus said. "They are also very close to Carmarthen Castle, which is held by the Welsh."

"And Dinefwr Castle," Chris said. "Do not forget that one. That also secures a major road into the north of Wales and it also belongs to the Welsh these days."

Augustus scratched his dark head. "If I was to guess about this, I would say that the Welsh are looking to cut off Pembroke from the rest of the Marcher lordships."

"It is certainly possible."

"Divide and conquer, mayhap?"

Chris shrugged. "Your guess is as good as mine, but it looks like that to me, too," he said. "If they manage to starve out Pembroke which, in any case, they cannot do because the garrison can always receive supplies by the sea, but still – they can cut off all land access, and that will make it very difficult for de Valence. It could be a prelude to creating quite a problem for the Marcher lords in the south, including me."

Augustus folded his big arms across his chest. "We have had peace for some time," he said. "I should not like to find ourselves in battle mode again if the Welsh are truly rebelling. And what of this bastard son? Blayth the Strong? I've never even heard that name before."

Chris shook his head. "Nor have I," he said. "But I know who might have – your cousin and mine, Bhrodi."

Augustus knew that name would come up. Bhrodi de Shera was Augustus' close cousin by blood, the eldest son of his father's brother, and just a year older than Augustus himself. Bhrodi was another Welsh-English hybrid, perhaps one of the most powerful lords in both Wales and England because not only had he inherited the Earldom of Coventry from his father, but he'd inherited the Kingdom of Anglesey through his mother's father. He was a prince among the Welsh, and he'd married very well for himself – the youngest daughter of England's greatest knight, William de Wolfe.

Therefore, Bhrodi was many things to many people, including an ally to the House of de Lohr because there were more family relations there in that his father's mother had been a de Lohr. She'd been the youngest daughter of Christopher de Lohr, the Lion's Claw, so the House of de Shera and the House of de Lohr were deeply intertwined. It made Augustus a cousin to Chris also, and the relationship between both families was a cultivated and mutually beneficial one.

"It is possible that Bhrodi knows about the man," Augustus said after a moment. "But if he doesn't, then he certainly should, although you know the northern Welsh princes are somewhat removed from southern Wales. They are the ones who have historically stirred up the trouble."

Chris turned to look at him. "Then it makes sense that this bastard of Llywelyn's should be stirring up trouble," he said. "In any case, our spies seem to believe the Welsh are following this man. Tales of Blayth the Strong are spreading. He's already managed to capture three castles and tie up major roads, and if we are not vigilant, Blayth and his followers may push our way. We must send word to Bhrodi and find out what he knows of this. We may need his help."

Augustus wasn't hugely keen on the idea. "In most of the battles between the Welsh and Edward, Bhrodi has managed to stay clear of them," he said. "He has been involved, at times, but the only reason Edward leaves him alone is because he married a de Wolfe. Even Edward will not violate that treaty and risk alienating William de Wolfe. That would be a very bad thing, indeed."

Chris knew that. "I am not asking Bhrodi to get involved," he said. "At least, not yet. But I would like to know what he knows so we can prepare. If this Blayth intends to invade my lands, I want to know all I can about him."

Augustus couldn't disagree. The idea of trouble in the Marches again was not a pleasant thought. "Very well," he said. "I will prepare a rider if you wish to scribe the message. If the weather remains good and the rider is able to cover several miles a day, he should be able to deliver it in four or five days."

"On your way, then. There is no time to waste."

Augustus was about to go about his business when the solar door rattled. Then, there was a loud and obnoxious knock. Augustus had bolted the panel for privacy because the de Lohr sons seemed to have no respect for their father's personal space, so he cast a long look at Chris and watched the man roll his eyes.

"Open it," he said, flicking his wrist.

Fighting off a smile, Augustus went to the door and unbolted it, pulling the panel open only to find Morgen, Rees, and Dru de Lohr standing outside. The three older brothers were fair and blond, a distinct de Lohr trait, and wasted no time pushing into the room. They frowned at Augustus before turning their displeasure on their father.

"Are you whispering behind locked doors now, Father?" Morgen demanded. "What goes on in here?"

Chris lifted an eyebrow at his nosy son. "That is for me to know," he said. "If I wanted you to be part of it, I would have invited you."

Morgen pointed to Augustus. "So he gets to stay?"

Chris rolled his eyes again. "You act as if the man is not your best friend in the world."

Morgan frowned at Augustus even though his father's statement was true. "Not when he gets to have a private council with you and I do not."

"Stop complaining, Morgen. You and your brothers will sit down and shut your mouths. I will tell you everything, but I do not appreciate your tone."

Morgen was usually the calmer one and he was rather embarrassed to realized he'd come across rather whiny about the whole thing. His brother, Rees, had seen Augustus usher in the two spies and had immediately run to his brothers to tell them what he'd seen. The fact that his father had not invited him to what was evidently a secretive meeting had offended Morgen deeply, and the three brothers had been watching the solar door for the better part of an hour.

However, they knew better than to interrupt their father. They weren't so offended that they were ridiculously bold in what was clearly a private matter. But they watched the two men leave their father's solar and head for the kitchens, and then waited an appropriate amount of time to enter their father's solar, only to discover that the door was locked.

Still, he wasn't so disrespectful to his father that he didn't realize that everything the man said was true – had he wanted him present, he would have sent for him. With an exasperated sigh, Morgen plopped down in one of his father's fine leather chairs.

"Well?" he asked. "Why the secrecy? What is happening?"

"We were discussing a wife for you," Augustus said, taunting the man on a sore subject. Like most young knights, Morgen did not feel he was ready for a wife, something his father poked him about mercilessly. "Were we not discussing such a thing, my lord? That woman from the tavern in the village."

Chris was on to Augustus' game. "Aye. That one. The one with the bulbous breasts and missing teeth."

"Aye, that one."

"Wait!" Morgan practically shouted. "That is *not* funny!"

Augustus was trying very hard not to grin. "Good Christ, Morg," he said. "She owns the place. Think of the money!"

Chris nodded his head seriously. "Forget the money, lad. Think of the whores."

Morgan looked at his father with his mouth hanging open. "I am going to tell Mother you said that."

Chris broke down into gasps of laughter, as did Augustus. "No need," Chris said. "We were not really speaking of a wife for you, although it is something that is increasingly on my mind even if it is not on yours. We were speaking on information we have just received, news on a rising rebellion in Wales. It is possible we may have trouble in the future."

Morgen calmed dramatically. All thoughts of a missing-tooth wife faded at the expression of concern on his father's face. "Is it that bad?"

Chris shrugged. "It could be," he said. "We are sending a missive to your cousin, Bhrodi, to see what the man knows."

"May I take it to him, Father?" Rees asked. "I have a new horse that is very fast. I should like to give him his head and see just how fast and far he can go."

Chris looked to his second eldest. "If you would like to," he said. "If you are confident that your mount will not be exhausted after a day or two."

Rees nodded eagerly. "He will not be," he said, quickly moving for the door. "I shall go and prepare him now."

As Rees rushed out, Chris opened the painted wooden box that contained vellum. His quill and ink were nearby and he pulled them closer as he thought on what he would say to Bhrodi.

"What *of* this rebellion, Father?" Morgen asked. "What have you been told?"

Chris paused, quill in hand, and looked at his son. "There are rumors that a bastard of Llywelyn the Last is rallying the Welsh to his side," he said. "A man named Blayth the Strong. Three castles have already fallen to this rebellion and it is possible there will be more."

Morgen's brow furrowed with concern. "Blayth the Strong," he repeated. "I've not heard of him."

"Nor have I."

"Doesn't the word *blayth* mean wolf in the Welsh tongue?"

"It does, indeed."

"Then there is a new Welsh prince rising?"

Chris' expression darkened as he pondered the rise of a new Welsh prince. "Nay, lad," he muttered. "There is a storm rising and we must be prepared."

Rees departed Lioncross Abbey on his long-legged stallion within the hour, heading for northern Wales.

CHAPTER SEVEN

Gwendraith Castle
Wales

HER FATHER HAD no idea she had come.

Asmara rode astride her frisky stallion, gazing up at Gwendraith Castle as she neared the bottom of the hill that it was perched upon. As far as Cader was concerned, she was still at Llandarog, going about her boring duties and generally being occupied as a commander of men who were now in charge of Llandarog Castle.

But that was far from the case.

Four long weeks and she was ready to scream. Cader and his men were quite happy holding fast to the castle, eating their daily meals, going about their duties, and any number of utterly unexciting and dull tasks. Fairynne had been sent home, back to their mother in their small village of Talley, but Cader had kept Asmara with him. She'd earned the right to stay as far as he was concerned, but remaining at Llandarog was the last thing Asmara wanted to do.

She wanted to go to Gwendraith.

Therefore, on a sunny, autumn afternoon when her father was out with some of his men, hunting in the countryside, Asmara had slipped out of Llandarog and headed northeast towards Gwendraith. The weather was surprisingly calm, as the terrible rains they'd suffered had been gone for over a week, so the roads were passable, and the ride north had been a pleasant one. Asmara had given the horse its head, and it had glided with swift and sure hooves.

Truly, it had been foolish leaving Llandarog, but something was drawing her to Gwendraith. *Someone* was drawing her there. She'd tried to pretend as if he were of no concern to her and that she simply wanted to go where the action was but, increasingly, she knew that wasn't the truth.

She couldn't get Blayth out of her mind.

She'd missed him. What a fool she was! She hardly knew the man but, still, she'd missed him. No man had ever intrigued her like the big, scarred warrior, and she didn't want to remain at Llandarog, dying of boredom, while Blayth was at Gwendraith and living an exciting life. How exciting, she didn't know, but she intended to find out. She wanted to be where he was.

She was most definitely a fool.

The ride to Gwendraith went without incident and she arrived in the late afternoon. Having never been to Gwendraith, she didn't know what to expect, and what she found was a big castle on a hill overlooking a small village and the green, green Welsh landscape below. A small river carved a blue ribbon at the base of it, drifting out into the valley beyond.

A road led up the rocky hill and she passed a few stone huts and herds of puffy sheep being tended by shepherds bearing nasty-looking crossbows. She thought she recognized them, some of the *trossodol* that her mother had referred to, the mercenary-like criminals who followed Morys. She didn't remember seeing some of them in the battle for Llandarog but now, they were at Gwendraith. Undoubtedly, they'd come from Brecfa. But she turned her attention away from them and to the road that led to a big gatehouse, with twin towers on either side. Once she was through the gatehouse, a massive lower bailey opened up that covered nearly the entire hilltop.

The bailey was full of outbuildings and men, and she continued up the road which now led to the keep at the top of the slope. Although the curtain wall and exterior defenses were grand, there wasn't much to protect the inner ward, so it explained how easily the Welsh were able to overtake the castle. There was simply a gate to protect the inner ward, so once the army came over the walls and through the main gatehouse, there wasn't much to stop them from taking the keep.

It was an interesting flaw in an otherwise magnificent castle. Given the vastness of the outer ward, the inner ward was quite small. In fact, it was more of a courtyard in the center of a keep, which was built up around it. A servant, a Welshman with an accent so thick that she could barely understand him, indicated for Asmara to follow him into the keep. Dismounting her horse, she collected her satchel and complied.

Upon entering the foyer, Asmara was surprised to see that she was in a big chamber that was two stories tall. To her left was an enormous, arched door that opened up into what she thought might be the great hall simply for its size, but to the right was another doorway with heavy iron bars attached to it that led into what was evidently the lord's chambers and more. It was a rather low-ceilinged doorway that led into dark passages beyond.

The servant took her into the hall, which had a floor made of stone. That was rare, when most halls on the ground level had dirt floors. Asmara sat down at a very big table, propped up by stones on one side because it was missing a leg, as the servant rushed off to find her something to drink and eat.

She found herself looking around the hall of Gwendraith, impressed with the sheer size of the place. Behind her, several very tall lancet windows emitted some light and ventilation into the room, and above her head was a minstrel's gallery. Most Welsh castles didn't have that feature, which led her to believe that, at some point, the Normans built this hall. The size of it and the details had their mark all over it.

Even though Asmara was weary from her travels, she couldn't seem to sit still. She stood up and wandered over to the hearth, a massive thing that was taller than she was. It had been cleaned of the ashes, ready to burn tonight as the hall filled with Welshmen. She touched the stones around it and noted the iron fire back that, when hot, would project even more heat into the room. As she stood there and fingered the stone, she didn't hear someone enter the hall behind her.

It was Blayth.

In truth, he couldn't believe his eyes. He had been in the outer bailey, preparing to enter the forebuilding that led down to the vault, when he saw her ride in. At first, he thought that he might have been seeing things, but the long-legged woman with the long, dark hair rode past him, at a distance, and he knew there couldn't be two like her in the entire world. Asmara ferch Cader was making an appearance and Blayth dropped what he was doing to follow her trail into the inner ward.

For a man who never gave women much thought, he'd given Asmara a good deal of it. She'd impressed him greatly with her skill the night Llandarog was captured, and as man with a warrior's heart, he was coming to appreciate a woman with the same. He still didn't believe women belonged in battle, but Asmara wasn't just any woman. She was quite different, as he'd seen, and when he'd departed Llandarog last month to come to Gwendraith, he was genuinely sorry to have left her behind. The little minx had grown on him and instead of letting her memory fade during his time at Gwendraith, it had only seemed to grow stronger.

He wasn't hard-pressed to admit that he was glad to see her.

Now, Blayth stood in the massive arched doorway of Gwendraith's hall, watching Asmara over near the hearth and thinking that, quite possibly, she'd grown more beautiful since the last time he saw her. He simply watched her, digesting the way her body moved, her graceful limbs and lovely hands. It seemed so strange to him that such beautiful fingers could kill a man. He watched her drag her hand over the stone of the hearth.

She was as flawless as he'd ever seen.

"Why are you here?" he heard himself ask.

Asmara whirled around to face him, surprise evident on her face.

Shock was more like it. But she covered it quickly, coming away from the hearth and heading in his direction.

"My… my father sent me," she lied. "There is nothing happening at Llandarog these days. The men are growing fat and lazy. He thought that you could use me here at Gwendraith."

That voice, Blayth thought. Like warm honey, pouring into his ears. He felt like a fool to realize that he had actually missed that voice, but the truth was that he didn't care why she'd come. Only that she had.

"The English have not tried to take back Llandarog?" he asked.

She shook her head as she drew closer. "Nay," she said. "What about this place? Have they tried to regain it?"

Blayth lifted a challenging eyebrow. "They would not dare."

There was that dry wit again. He'd used it on her one or twice, and Asmara had thought he might have been mocking her with it. But now she was coming to think that it was purely his personality. It was a very small insight into a mysterious and complex man, so she decided to play along and see where it took her.

"Why?" she asked. "Because *you* are here?"

"Why else?"

She grinned. Before she could reply, however, the servant returned with a tray of food and drink, and Asmara realized how thirsty she was. She headed over to the table, pulling the cloth from the tray and peering at the contents – watered ale, hard white cheese, crusty bread, and small apples. Asmara plopped down on the bench and began to pour herself some ale.

"Will you join me?" she asked Blayth.

His response was to move to the table and sit opposite her as she drained her cup of ale, smacking her lips. He watched her as she poured herself another cup.

"I have not eaten since early this morning, so forgive me for being rude," she said. Then, she looked around the table as if searching for something. "I do not see another cup. If you wish to drink from the pitcher, I do not mind."

His gaze lingered on her a moment before reaching out to take the pitcher. A smile flickered across his lips before he downed nearly the entire contents. Asmara watched him closely, studying everything about the man. She was thrilled to be sitting with him, just the two of them. There was so much she wanted to say, and wanted to know, that she hardly knew where to start.

"If you will recall," she said as she popped a piece of cheese into her mouth, "the first time we were alone together, you tossed me into a water trough. The second time, you accused me of trying to pry information out of you on behalf of my father. I wonder how you will insult me the third time?"

He wiped his lips with the back of his hand. "You said there would be no third time."

"That is true, but here we are. If you are going to offend me, then get on with it."

His lips twitched with a smile again; that smile that always seemed to be right on the surface. "I am afraid of what will happen if I do," he said. "I emerged unscathed the first two times. I fear my luck will not hold out again."

Asmara grinned, flashing that toothy smile. "I will be truthful with you," she said. "The night before we moved on Llandarog, my father did not send me to pry information out of you. I will swear that upon my grandmother's grave."

He believed her. Truth was, he had always believed her. "I was wrong to slander your honor," he admitted. The tone of the conversation was comfortable enough that he did not feel the need to keep his defenses up, his natural guard. He was very anxious to speak with her. "But you must understand that I knew virtually nothing about you up to that point, and Morys has never spoken fondly of Cader."

Her smile faded. "I know," she said. "I can only imagine what he has said about my father. Whatever it was, it is not true. My father is a fine man."

Blayth nodded. "He must be to have raised so fine and strong a daughter," he said, watching her eyes widen in surprise at what was clearly a compliment. "Some men have different ways of commanding men. Morys' way is to shout and, at times, color the truth. Your father's way seems to be far quieter."

"Quiet and trusting," she said, although she was still feeling a bit of a thrill from his compliment. "He tells his men what must be done and he trusts them to do it. That does not make him weak."

"I know."

"I am glad you do. Morys does not think that way."

Blayth knew Morys well enough to know just how the man thought. Sometimes, it was overbearing, in truth, but he didn't say so. He owed Morys much in life and he would not speak ill of him, not even in a private conversation.

"As I said, Morys has an aggressive manner, but it is one that men respond to," he said.

She looked up from her cheese. "Like you?"

"I owe him a good deal."

Asmara nodded faintly, her thoughts moving to Blayth's mysterious background. She couldn't help her curiosity and, somehow, now that it was just the two of them, it didn't seem intrusive. There was no one to listen in on them, and she was genuinely interested.

"It sounds as if he owes you a good deal, too," she said. "Truly, you do not have to speak of it if you do not want to, but I heard Morys at Carmarthen Castle when he spoke of how the English purchased you from your mother and then tortured you for your entire life. I… I simply want to say that I think that is horrible and I am very sorry they did that. No man deserves that kind of treatment, and certainly not you. The hatred and resentment you must feel for the *Saesneg* is beyond my comprehension."

They were wandering into an area that Blayth never spoke of. His past was a strictly taboo subject, except for Aeddan and Pryce and Morys. Those were the only people he ever felt comfortable discussing his limited memory with.

But Asmara… he'd only ever sensed that the woman was brave, truthful, and pure. He'd never thought anything else. Every man who had ever fought alongside her had a very high opinion of her, and the night Llandarog Castle fell, Blayth had the opportunity to see just how brave and skilled she really was. The woman was impressive on so many levels.

But did he trust her enough to speak of his past with her?

He was so used to avoiding the subject that he simply wasn't certain.

"Feelings of hatred and resentment are unproductive," he finally said. "I am not a man to waste effort on things beyond my control."

It was a simple answer, but a truthful one. Asmara received the impression that he didn't want to speak further of it, which was something she'd sensed that night before Llandarog fell.

"That is a sensible attitude," she said. "I am sorry if you do not wish to speak of it. You warned me off the night Llandarog fell and I suppose you had every right if you thought I was trying to pry but, as I said, I honestly was not. I just thought… I thought I should tell you how I felt about what happened to you. You endured a terrible thing."

There was pity there, something he wasn't used to in the least. It made him feel strangely adverse to her pity yet, in the same breath, welcoming it. He'd had absolutely no comfort in his life that he could recall, although sometimes he would dream of a woman with dark hair, a woman that he held some affection for. There was also the older woman with the Scottish accent. But those were only dreams. In reality, Morys' wife, Auryn, was the only women he'd spent any length of time around, and she was limited in her ability to show emotion given that she was married to a man who showed her nothing at all.

The truth was that he was to blame for his aversion to women. What was he? A man with horrible scars, ugly to look at, and certainly not a man that any woman would want as a companion or husband. So, he avoided women, keeping a wall up around him so that nothing and no one could break through that wall and hurt him.

It was safer that way.

But now… now, a beautiful, brave woman was showing him a measure of compassion and he had no idea how to feel about it. All he knew was that it touched something in him, something deep that was kind and soft and wanted to be nurtured. There was something in him that was responding to her compassion, whether or not he was comfortable with it. As Asmara turned back to her bread and cheese, he spoke softly.

"I do not remember very much, to be truthful," he muttered.

She looked up from her food. "You do not remember much of your captivity?"

He sighed, a long and thoughtful sound, as he leaned forward on the table, his arms resting on the tabletop and his hands folded.

"What we are to speak of does not leave this room," he told her.

Asmara sensed his seriousness right away. "Of course not," she said. "I would never repeat something you told me in confidence."

"See that you do not. If I hear that you have told others of this conversation, you will not like my reaction."

Her features stiffened. "So you have managed to offend me a third time," she said. "I told you that I would not speak of it. I meant it. But since you clearly do not trust my word, do not speak of anything you do not wish for me to hear. Let us speak on the weather instead."

She turned back to her food, angrily tearing at the bread and shoving it into her mouth. Blayth watched her, realizing that he had insulted the woman yet again. He couldn't seem to *not* insult her. Watching her frustrated actions, he felt remorse for his behavior.

"I have spent my life, or what I remember of it, protecting myself," he said. "I did not mean to offend you, demoiselle. Mayhap I am accustomed to dealing with unsavory characters all around and that leads me to treat everyone the same way. I… apologize."

A surprising response. At least, Asmara thought so. She cooled somewhat, but not entirely. "If you keep insulting me and then apologizing, at some point, I am no longer going to accept your apologies. Do you understand?"

"I do."

"Good."

Her gaze lingered on him as she returned to her food, but her movements were far less angry. Blayth watched her peel apart her cheese.

"As I said, I do not remember much of anything," he said quietly.

His tone sounded so… *lost*. Confused, even. Asmara pushed her food aside because she realized that she was no longer hungry. Her conversation with Blayth was taking precedence over everything. For the first time since she'd known him, Blayth the Strong sounded vulnerable.

Human.

"You mean of your captivity with the English?" she asked. "I am not surprised. I am sure it was a terrible existence."

He shook his head. "That is not what I mean," he said. "I do not remember anything prior to Morys finding me."

Her brow furrowed with confusion. "*Morys* finding you?"

He nodded. "I awoke five years ago in Morys' sod hut in the Vale of Brecfa, with the sounds of the River Marlais nearby," he said. "Morys told me that I had been saved from the English and he told me who I was. What memories I have, he has given to me."

Asmara was still confused. "But you remember nothing?" she asked. "How does Morys know so much of your past?"

"Because my father's *teulu* told him," he said. "They delivered me to Morys for safekeeping, so I could hide from the English who will capture me once again if they find me."

That was essentially the same story Morys had told everyone that day at Carmarthen Castle but, to Asmara, it was beginning to sound strange. Blayth had no memory of his life before he came to Morys, and it was Morys who told him of his past. But Blayth couldn't remember any of it so he had to trust that what the man was telling him was the truth.

... but was it?

"That is a terrible story," she said. "And... and you remember nothing prior to Morys?"

He lifted his big shoulders, averting his gaze as if that would help him draw on long-buried memories. "Not really," he said, "although sometimes I have dreams. I dream of men that I feel as if I should know. I dream of them frequently, in fact. I can almost call them by name, but not quite. As if their names are right at the forefront of my mind but I cannot quite bring them forth."

Asmara was listening intently. "Surely that is frustrating."

He gave her a wry smile. "It is," he said. Then, his eyes took on that faraway look again. "In my dreams, I can see their faces. I know they are English because I can see the armor they are wearing. Not all of the time, but sometimes. Morys has told me that those men were my captors. Those are the bastards who did this to me."

He had his hand up on the left side of his head, touching the area that was so damaged and scarred. Asmara was deeply surprised to see the emotion in him, the vulnerability of a man who had such a fearless reputation.

"It is possible," she said. "Surely you would not forget men who harmed you so terribly."

Blayth dropped his hand from his head as it brushed over the ear that was no longer there. "That is the strange part," he said. "I see these men and I do not feel as if I hate them. It is hard to describe, but when I dream of them, I feel... love. The love that one would feel for a family, I suppose. I do not think these men were the ones who tortured me, as Morys has said. I feel as if they are something else."

"*What* else?"

He sighed heavily. "I do not know. I wish I did."

Asmara couldn't help but feel a good deal of pity for the man. "Your story is a tragic one," she said, "but you have come through it. You are a man that everyone admires, and you have a great destiny to fulfill. Mayhap through you, Wales will finally know a measure of freedom, as your father had once hoped for."

He lifted his eyebrows, as if not at all convinced of that. "Either that, or I will end up dead like my father," he said. "Morys says that the English will kill me if they capture me. That is why he has kept me away from them, even in battle. In fact, we have the English garrison commander of Gwendraith in the vault at this very moment that he has not let me go near. Morys has interrogated the man for more information on English plans in the south of Wales but, so far, the man has not told him anything he did not already know."

Asmara found that most interesting. "Does Morys plan to kill him?"

Blayth shook his head. "Nay," he said. "I told him not to kill the captive. I think we can use the man to our advantage."

"How?"

A glimmer came to his eye. "Because even if the man refuses to tell us anything more of the *Saesneg* plans in this area, we can send him back to England with a message of our own. A message to the Marcher lords that a new force is rising in Wales. I will succeed where so many other Welsh lords have failed."

Asmara shrugged. "How?" she said. "Please do not take offense to this, but it seems as if Morys tries to think for you. You are clearly a strong and intelligent man. Do you really need Morys to tell you what to do?"

That smile was on Blayth's lips again. "Make no mistake," he said. "Morys may be louder than I am, but it is I who give the commands. Morys has taken many of my own ideas and claimed them as his own, and I suppose I do not care. Morys is a man who needs glory and attention. I do not. All that you see, every successful battle, every successful move, is because of me."

Asmara didn't doubt him for a moment. "I believe you," she said. "Speaking of Morys, where is he?"

"He has gone to Carmarthen Castle, taking his *teulu* with him, including Aeddan and Pryce. He went to confer with Howell."

"And you remained here?"

"He left me in command. And I have an English knight to send back to the Marcher lords with a message."

"Does Morys know this? I thought you said he kept you away from the English."

He shrugged. "He is not here, so whatever I do is of my own decision," he said. "In fact, I was heading to the vault when I saw you arrive. Mayhap you would like to attend me as I speak to the man? Nothing will insult the *Saesneg* more than to realize the Welsh Dragon Princess has the power over his life or his death."

The thought was a pleasing one. "I have never met an English knight before."

Blayth stood up from the table. "Nor I," he said. "At least, not that I recall."

Because he was standing, Asmara stood up as well. "I would like to see this *Saesneg*," she said. "I am curious about him, I admit. English knights are difficult to come by. At least, captive ones are."

Blayth's smile broke through. "You can look, but you cannot touch. No beating the man to death."

She feigned shock. "Me? Why would you say such a thing?"

His grin broadened. "Something tells me that you have a rabid hatred for the English," he said. "And we need this one alive if our message is to make it back to England."

They were walking to the hall entry now, with Asmara walking beside Blayth for the first time. Normally, she'd been behind him or far away from him but, this time, she walked alongside him. It felt right and natural to her.

She liked it.

"I will not move against the man unless he tries to capture you," she said. "It is wise of you to bring me as your bodyguard."

He looked at her, amused. "Demoiselle, I am quite happy to have you as my *teulu*," he said. "I will be the envy of every man."

Something about the way he looked at her made Asmara feel hot all over. If he continued to look at her like that, she would swear fealty to him as his *teulu* and never look back.

It was a rather wonderful feeling, after all.

THE VAULTS, OR dungeons, of Gwendraith were rather strange. Since the castle sat atop a rocky hill, much of the rock was incorporated into the structure of the castle, and that included the vaults, which were actually old storage pits that had been converted for use as cells.

At some point, great iron bars were used to cap the pits, held in with mortar and stone. These pits were in the lower level of the keep but they were accessed in the outer ward by a narrow doorway in the base of one of the keep's corner towers. A long, cramped passageway led to the former storage vaults, now a prison.

An iron grate covered the access doorway, too, and it was kept bolted. When Blayth and Asmara approached, the Welsh guard from the inside unbolted the grate, pulling it open on sticky hinges. Before Blayth and Asmara headed back into the dark passage, the guard at the gate handed them a torch to light their way.

The passage was narrow and low-ceilinged, as black as pitch if they hadn't been carrying the torch. The ceiling was black and greasy from the numerous torches that had been used to light it. But the passage was also mercifully short, and they emerged into the former storage area with the big pits sunk into the rock. It was already lit by a torch, but it was hardly enough light to see by, as the space was fairly vast. As Blayth put the torch in an iron sconce, Asmara drifted over to one of the pits.

They were dark and smelled heavily of urine. There were six in total; she could see two men stuffed into one, and then one man in another, but the other four remained empty. They couldn't have been more than four feet deep, meaning the prisoners couldn't stand up in them. They remained stuffed into them like corks in a bottle. As she looked at them, she couldn't help feel that the conditions were rather barbaric. It surely must have been a hellish existence for a man to be rammed into one of these small pits.

Even if the prisoners were English.

Over to her right, Blayth had finished securing the torch and he headed to the pit with the single man in it. Throwing the bolt in the top of the grate that covered the pit, he opened the grate, braced his big legs, and reached down to pull the man out.

There was a good deal of grunting and groaning from the prisoner as his stiff body was moved around. Blayth dragged him across the stony dirt floor until he came to a wall. Then, he propped the man up against it as Asmara came up behind him and unsheathed her sword. When Blayth caught a flash of her blade, he looked at her curiously.

"I told you that you could not kill him," he pointed out.

Her gaze was on the prisoner, but she tore it away long enough to address him. "This is not to kill him," she said. "This is to protect you should he try to move against you."

Blayth couldn't help the grin. "I see you take your position as my *teulu* seriously."

Asmara merely shrugged, her gaze returning to the prisoner. She was quite serious about her stance and Blayth couldn't help but be flattered. To have the Dragon Princess as his defender made him feel rather important, but it was more than that. Her intention to protect him made him feel as if her feelings on the matter were personal. She *wanted* to protect him, almost as if he meant something to her.

Was such a thing even possible?

It was difficult not to ponder that very thought as he turned his focus to his prisoner.

The man was in terrible shape. Having been kept in a ball for nearly a month had done awful things to his body. He tried to stretch out his legs, grunting with pain as he did so, and it was apparent that he was a fairly tall man. Asmara stayed out of his range as he twisted and grunted, trying to straighten himself out.

"Tell me your name," Blayth said in a low, threatening tone.

The man was rubbing the back of his neck. "I respectfully refuse," he said. "I will not have you ransom my family. I am sure you understand."

He was speaking the language of the English. Most Welsh in the south spoke that language, as it was important to understand the language of their overlords, so both Asmara and Blayth understood him.

"I do understand," Blayth said in the knight's language. "But I do not intend to ransom you. It is my intention to release you but before I do, I want to know your name. I do not address, nor do I show mercy, to men I do not know."

The man sighed heavily, still rubbing his neck, now trying to straighten out his head and neck. "My lord, I mean no disrespect, but until you release me from this hell, I cannot believe your intentions," he said. "I have been lied to since the day I was captured and if my lack of belief in your word is slandering your honor, I do apologize. But you can surely see things from my perspective."

Blayth did. He took a few steps in Asmara's direction, coming very close to her, before lowering his voice.

"Have the guard at the door send for food and drink," he said. "Let us show the man some decent treatment because it is an important message I wish to send with him. Mayhap if I show him some kindness, he will do as I ask."

Asmara nodded, handing over her sword to him. "If he tries anything, kill him."

She turned on her heel, rushing for the entrance to the vault, leaving Blayth standing there with a smile on his face. She certainly was a no-nonsense lady, unafraid to put a sword between a man's ribs. He went over to the torch he'd stuck in the wall, removing it from the brace and bringing it closer so he could look at his prisoner. There was a sconce in the wall over the man's head, so he pushed the torch into it, securing it.

"I am looking at things from your perspective, but you must look at them from mine," he said to the captive. "You are my prisoner. I can do anything I wish with you or to you, as is my privilege. A captor is not honor-bound to tell a captive the truth, but if you give me your name, I shall give you mine. That shall establish trust, and I say to you that I lie to no man, especially a man with whom I have trust. Would you agree with that statement?"

The prisoner stopped rubbing his neck and moved to his shoulders, trying to rub the kinks out. "I would," he said. "Give me your name first and I shall consider giving you mine."

Blayth didn't hesitate. "I am called Blayth."

The man slowed the hand rubbing at his shoulders. "Blayth," he repeated, drawing out the word. "That means wolf in your language."

"It does."

"Then my name is Corbett."

"Do you have a surname, Corbett?"

"Do you?"

"I am a bastard. It would do no good to give you my surname."

It sounded like an honest answer, so Corbett continued. "My surname is Payton-Forrester," he said. "My full name is Sir Corbett Payton-Forrester. Now, I will hold you to that promise of not ransoming me to my family."

"You have my word," Blayth said. "Will you tell me what you were doing at Gwendraith?"

"I am the garrison commander for the Earl of Pembroke, William de Valence," he said. "You *do* know that this is a Pembroke property?"

He was speaking rather easily for a man who hadn't told Morys anything for an entire month, but Blayth was pleased that he'd been able to coerce the man's trust, something Morys would have believed beneath him. He folded his big arms across his chest.

"It is not a Pembroke property anymore," he said. "Now it belongs to the Welsh. A castle in Wales should belong to the Welsh, don't you think?"

Corbett snorted ironically. "In theory, I suppose," he said. "But, much like you, I serve a higher power. I go where I am told to go and fight whoever I am told to fight. My presence at Gwendraith was not a personal insult to the Welsh. I am here because I was ordered to be here."

Blayth's gaze lingered on the man; he was tall, and he'd been better fed in his life because he looked rather pale and weak. He had hair to his shoulders, some dirty shade of blond, and very large hands. Blayth could see that as the man continued to rub the knots out of his damaged body. As he stood there, Asmara came rushing back into the storage area and he turned to her, noting her serious expression. As she came close, he held out the sword to her, giving it back.

"Did he try anything?" she asked.

Blayth's lips creased with a faint smile. "I do not think he is in any condition to," he said. "We have simply been having a conversation. This is Sir Corbett Payton-Forrester, the garrison commander of Gwendraith Castle for the Earl of Pembroke. Sir Corbett, this is Lady Asmara. Treat her with respect or you shall have to answer to me."

For the first time, Corbett looked up. His neck was straighter now and he was able to hold his head up, looking at the man and woman standing before him. But his gaze was on the woman, a long and shapely lady with the face of an angel. But she was dressed like a soldier. He simply nodded his head.

"My lady," he greeted.

Asmara wasn't sure how to respond. The man was an enemy, but Blayth's tone hadn't suggested anything hostile between them. She looked at Blayth, confused, but his impassive expression told her nothing at all. Her focus returned to the English knight, sitting against the stone wall.

"Sir Corbett Payton-Forrester," she repeated. "You were in command of this castle, then?"

Corbett's eyes were adjusting to the light. He'd spent so much of his time in the darkness that the torchlight was like bright and blinding sunlight. He blinked as the light hurt his eyes.

"Aye, my lady."

"Why?"

"Because Pembroke honored me with the command."

"Why should he honor you? Who *are* you to him?"

Corbett could see a very sharp-minded and very hostile lady behind the questions. "My father is a great knight, much decorated in the service of King Henry," he said evenly. "Because of my father's service, Pembroke accepted my fealty."

Asmara's gaze moved over him, seeing a very dirty and very beaten man. She cocked her head, a thoughtful gesture. "Then you come from a legacy of great English knights," she said. "But you do not look so great to me at the moment."

Corbett grinned, his dry lips cracking. "I am positive that I do not."

"Are you married? Was your wife here at Gwendraith?"

"My wife died a few years ago, my lady. And before you ask, I do have children, but they were not here with me. They live in the north of England, with my parents."

An English knight with a dead wife. Asmara thought on that a moment, fighting off the pangs of both curiosity and pity. As she'd told Blayth, she'd never seen an English knight before and it was a rare and interesting event.

But she was quickly coming to see something else – that Payton-Forrester wasn't the omnipotent, fire-breathing *Saesneg* knight she'd heard tale of. He was human, not *super*-human, and she saw nothing in the man that suggested he was any better than the Welsh warriors she had ever known, Blayth included. He seemed rather… ordinary. After a moment, she simply shook her head.

"This is the English knight we are all afraid of?" she asked, almost rhetorically. "I see nothing terrifying about you."

Corbett's gaze was fixed on her. "Mayhap not," he said. "But you have yet to see me in battle, my lady. In spite of the fact that I was captured, it took a very long time for the Welsh to do it. I held them off until I could hold out no more."

Asmara looked at Blayth to confirm the boast. He caught her expression. "I will admit, he was fierce until the end," Blayth said. "He held us off and then was captured when he tried to escape down the castle walls on a rope. It was only by luck that he was captured."

Blayth was honest in his assessment and it was clear that there was some respect for the man, from one warrior to another. That made the situation not so tense, which was a brilliant move on Blayth's part. He wanted Corbett to feel more comfortable so their communications would go more smoothly. An irate or rebellious prisoner wouldn't be of any use.

His tactics worked. Corbett appreciated the compliment, especially from his enemy. That was the greatest compliment anyone could pay him.

"Thank you, my lord," he said. "I did my best. I more than likely would have gotten away with it had the rope not unraveled and dropped me on my back."

"And yet, you are here," Blayth said. "I know that you have been interrogated repeatedly by my lord, but that has come to an end. You are my prisoner now and we are to have a discussion."

Corbett was happy to hear that the interrogations by that loud-mouthed Welshman had ended, as uncomfortable and painful as it had been at times, but he was wary of the suggested "discussion". He was concerned that if he didn't tell this enormous Welshman what he wanted to hear, then there might be repercussions. He couldn't even really see the man because of his sensitivity to light, so he couldn't see his expression to see if there was anything to read into it. He went back to rubbing his neck, his eyes closed.

"Very well, Blayth," he said. "What do you wish to discuss? But you must know that if you are going to ask me about English future plans for Wales, I will not tell you. In truth, I do not know anything. I am simply a knight; I am not in Pembroke's inner circle and I do not know what he is planning."

Blayth moved closer to the man, crouching down a few feet away. "I was not going to ask you that," he said. "But I *am* going to tell you something."

"What is it?"

"I told you that I am going to release you. But when I do, you are going to take a message back to the English on my behalf."

Corbett sighed faintly, wondering just what kind of message he would be charged with. "I see," he said. "Then I am to be your messenger?"

"You are."

"What would you have me deliver?"

Blayth didn't say anything for a moment; he didn't want to speak to a man who wasn't looking at him. The longer he remained silent, the more perplexed Corbett became until he finally opened his eyes and looked up, squinting against the torchlight with bloodshot eyes. Their eyes met, and Corbett blinked rapidly, several times, because his eyes were paining him so.

"Well?" he asked. "Will you tell me?"

Blayth nodded. "I will," he said. "But I will not speak of something so important to a man who will not look me in the eye. What you are to tell your English overlords is simple – you will tell them that a new rebellion is rising in the south of Wales, led by the bastard son of Llywelyn the Last. Surprised? I can see by your expression that you are. This new prince has led the Welsh to capture three smaller castles in the past few weeks – Gwendraith, Idole, and Llandarog. Soon, we will be moving on more castles kept by the English, and we will not fail. I want you to tell the English who control the south of Wales now. Soon enough, we shall capture Pembroke and all of the large castles as well. Then, we shall move north, where we shall purge the English from our country. Do you understand what I am telling you so far?"

In truth, Blayth wasn't sure if Corbett understood at all because, suddenly, he wasn't blinking his eyes so much. He was staring at him with his crusty, red eyes, and his pale face seemed even paler. His mouth was hanging open now, too, and he was clearly shocked at the mention of a bastard son of Llywelyn the Last. At least, that's what

Blayth thought until Corbett uttered one word.

"*James*?" he hissed.

Blayth had no idea what he meant. "Nay, the bastard son's name is not James," he said. "Do you understand what it is I have told you? Acknowledge that you do."

But Corbett wasn't listening; he was quite obviously astonished by something, so much so that his hand flew to his mouth as he stared at Blayth.

"James," he breathed again. "My God… is it *you*? My God… I hardly recognized you!"

Blayth was increasingly baffled by the man's reaction to what he'd been told. It was as if Corbett didn't understand him at all. It didn't occur to him that the man thought he was someone else, someone he recognized, but the way Corbett was looking at him was making him feel awkward and confused.

"I do not know what you are saying," he said. "Who is James?"

"*You* are!" Corbett gasped. "James… do you not recognize me?"

"My name is Blayth. I told you that."

Tears were filling Corbett's eyes, his hand still over his mouth. "Aye… it means wolf," he whispered. When his hand came away from his mouth, he was smiling. "It means *de Wolfe*! James, it is me – Corbett! You know me! Surely – *you know me*! My God, man, we were told you were dead!"

De Wolfe. Blayth had no idea why, but hearing that name hit him in the chest, like a physical blow. He could hardly breathe. *De Wolfe, de Wolfe… have I heard that name before*? Blayth didn't know, but something about it sounded… familiar. Oddly familiar. In fact, it made him feel quite unsettled and he stood up, off-balance by the course of the conversation.

"I know not what you mean," he said. "My name is Blayth. Whoever you think I am, you are mistaken. Now, will you take my message to your English overlords or will I lock you back in your hole again? If I do, I promise you that you will not make it out of this place alive."

Corbett was weeping, overcome by the sight of a man he thought was dead. A man he knew. Or, at least, he *thought* he knew. James de Wolfe was standing in front of him, looking as if he'd been chewed up and spit out by some great, terrible force, and he had to admit that it didn't look like the James he remembered. He was bigger, battered, and his head – so scarred. But… he knew that face. He knew those eyes, sky blue in color and a sort of cat's eye shape.

Aye, he knew them well because he'd fostered with the man for seven years. They'd been squires together, and their families were close friends and allies, but swearing fealty to Pembroke had separated them those years ago. He hadn't seen James de Wolfe in years before the man had been killed in Wales, and Corbett had been devastated when he'd heard of it.

But now… dear God, now the dead was rising.

James de Wolfe in the flesh.

But he was a man who evidently had no memory of who, or what, he was. Above Corbett's shock, he could see that the man who called himself Blayth, *wolf*, either had no idea who Corbett was referring to – or, better still – perhaps he couldn't acknowledge it. It was possible that the news of James de Wolfe's death was a cover and James was, perhaps, invested in the rebellion in Wales, perhaps even an agent of Edward in an attempt to control the Welsh. The House of de Wolfe was heavily invested in Edward's wars, so it was possible that James was deeper than anyone realized.

Corbett glanced at the woman introduced to him as Lady Asmara. She was standing behind Blayth, in the shadows, but he could still see her outline. He couldn't see her expression, but he suspected he might have gotten James into trouble by recognizing him. What if he destroyed the man's cover? The speculation was enough to make Corbett's head spin but, above it all, he knew he had to get out of there. A great deal was happening in Wales, beyond a man's comprehension, and the English needed to know. Blayth had been right about that – the English needed to be aware of the latest turn of events.

A Welsh prince was rising – and James was trying to get the message out.

God's Bones, he'd been such a fool! Thinking that, perhaps, he was now part of whatever spy game James was playing, Corbett became quite obedient and compliant.

"Forgive me," he said after a moment. "You… you looked like someone I once knew. But clearly, I am mistaken. Forgive me. I… I understand your message. I will take it to the English, I swear it."

Blayth was relieved at the man's compliance, even though it seemed quite rapid and rather strange. Still… he couldn't shake the odd sense of discomfort at the name de Wolfe. It was ringing around in his head like a bell even as he tried to ignore it.

"Excellent," he said. "Take the message straight to the Marcher lords. They will want to know."

Corbett nodded quickly; perhaps too quickly. "I will, my lord," he said. "Is… is there any preference to whom I deliver the message?"

Blayth's eyebrows lifted. "Pembroke is not in residence, so you cannot take it there," he said, noting a flicker of surprise on Corbett's face. "Aye, we know he is not at Pembroke Castle. It would do no good to take it to Chepstow or any of the other castles between here and the Marches. You must take it to someone who has great importance along the Marches. De Clare, mayhap. Or even de Lohr."

De Lohr! The Earl of Hereford and Worcester was allied with the House of de Wolfe. Surely he would know if James was an agent for Edward. And perhaps in suggesting de Lohr, James was *telling* him where to go.

"I will go to de Lohr," he said. "When would you have me leave, my lord?"

"You will be given food. You may leave on the morrow."

Corbett eyed the hole in the ground that had been his home for the past month. "You will not put me back into my cell, will you?"

Blayth shook his head. "I will not."

Corbett was greatly relieved to hear that. "Then mayhap you will allow me to leave tonight," he said. "My eyes are greatly affected by the light and it might be better for me to travel when it is dark."

Blayth didn't see any issues with that. Besides… he wanted to get the man out of Gwendraith before Morys returned, and he wasn't entirely sure when that would be. He knew Morys would be displeased that he'd let the garrison commander go because he was certain that Morys was looking at interrogating the man as a sport. But Blayth thought it was more important to send his message to the Marcher lords. He simply didn't want Morys returning and delaying those plans, so the sooner Payton-Forrester took his leave, the better.

"Very well," he said. "You will remain here for now. Food is being brought to you and I will have a horse brought around. But as soon as the sun sets, you will ride from here and head straight to de Lohr's seat. Is that clear?"

"It is, my lord."

"Fail me, and I shall find you and I shall kill you."

"I will not fail you, my lord."

Blayth's gaze lingered on the man for a few seconds longer, as if to drive home his threat, but he soon turned away. Asmara was still standing behind him, where she'd been the entire time, and he took her politely by the elbow to turn her for the vault entry.

Without a second thought to Corbett Payton-Forrester, the pair headed out of the dismally dark vault, leaving the prisoner to ponder what he'd seen, and what he'd been told, and feeling a desperation as he'd never felt before to leave Gwendraith for the sweet green fields of home.

England.

When the sun finally set later that day, and a dark and cool night settled, Corbett was given an excitable young stallion to ride, and ride he did, heading at breakneck speed for Lioncross Abbey Castle.

CHAPTER EIGHT

THE WELSH FILLED up the feasting hall of Gwendraith that night as if they'd been feasting there all their lives.

It was a loud, festive gathering. A massive fire burned in the hearth as men ate and drank and laughed. The feasting table with the broken leg was crowded with men, and there were no other tables in the hall, so men sat on the floor, eating the mutton that had been roasted over an enormous fire in the kitchen yard. Great hunks of roasted meat were being passed around by servants, and men stuffed themselves on the cooked carcass.

After seeing Corbett off into the moonlit night, Blayth and Asmara had returned to the hall, lured as the other men were by the smell of food. When they'd entered the hall, however, it was already packed with bodies, and Blayth had bodily removed two men from the end of the table so that he and Asmara could sit. He'd then proceeded to steal the food that other men were eating to give over to Asmara, who was both touched and embarrassed by his chivalry.

She'd never known anyone to be chivalrous towards her before and she was quite used to fighting her own battles or grabbing her own food, but Blayth was quite happy to do it for her. She watched him as he confiscated food and utensils, and in a very short amount of time, she was sitting with a full trencher in front of her that included meat, bread, and boiled beans, and someone else's knife. She didn't know who it belonged to, but Blayth had given it to her, so she used it to stab at her food, which was quite good and salty. After he finished stealing her a meal, he stole one of his own and delved into it.

He didn't say much at all, really. Small talk and comments as he stole food but, after that, he shoved food in his mouth as if he were starving and the conversation died. But even as they ate, surrounded by a room full of eating, noisy men, Asmara couldn't seem to tear her attention away from Blayth.

James, the *Saesneg* knight had called him. He swore he knew him, and he was evidently quite convinced of it because he'd been very emotional about it. *James, it's me! We were told you were dead!* Those had been the astonished words out of the man's mouth, but it had been obvious that Blayth had no idea who the man was, or what he was talking about. Still, Corbett had been convinced that he was someone named James. But that recognition had abruptly, and oddly, ended and the knight had seemed most apologetic about it. Fearful, even.

But what could he be afraid of?

It was a brief instance of mistaken identity that Asmara should have easily forgotten, but she couldn't quite seem to shake it. So much of Blayth's past was a mystery. From what Blayth had told her, he didn't remember anything prior to waking up in Morys' hut. It was Morys who had told him who he was and had given him his past, and his legacy, but everyone knew that Morys could color the truth to suit him. Even Blayth had said so.

So… what if Blayth's past was something Morys had also colored?

"You are quiet," Blayth said, interrupting her thoughts. "And you are staring at me. What are you thinking?"

Asmara hadn't even realized he'd glanced at her. She'd been too caught up in her reflections. Grinning with embarrassment, she looked to her food.

"I am thinking of the *Saesneg* knight," she said. "I… I was simply wondering if he will do what you told him to do."

Mouth full, Blayth shrugged. "There is no knowing for certain, at least not for a while," he said. "He seemed as if he was agreeable, so I can only hope he values his word."

Asmara tried to eat but she couldn't seem to. There was far too much on her mind.

"He seemed to know you," she said.

It was the statement she'd been hesitant to make but, in the same breath, they couldn't avoid the obvious. They had both been present when the knight seemed to recognize him. But Blayth shrugged, apparently unfazed by the event.

"Too much time in the vault drove the man mad," he said. "He was seeing things in the darkness that were not there."

Asmara wasn't so certain even if Blayth sounded positive about it. She was about to say something when a chorus of cries arose from men near the hall entry, and she turned to see Morys entering the hall.

He emerged into the crowded room to a hero's welcome, lifting his hands to his men and absorbing the adulation, when he caught sight of Blayth and Asmara at the end of the table. Asmara swore the man's expression darkened when he saw her, but his focus was mostly on Blayth, his shining star.

Morys had eyes only for him.

"Ah," Morys said. "Here I find you. Is the food good tonight?"

Blayth glanced up. "Good enough," he said. "How was your conference with Howell?"

Morys pushed the man seated next to Blayth down the table, opening up a spot, which he gladly took. "Something we shall discuss on the morrow, in private," he said. Then, he turned his attention to Asmara. "What are you doing here?"

It wasn't a polite greeting and Asmara could feel herself tensing up.

"My father sent me," she said steadily. "There is nothing happening at Llandarog. The castle is secure, and the men grow fat and lazy. My father thought you could use me at Gwendraith if the situation was not so settled."

Morys cocked his eyebrow. "*You*?" he said. "We do not need you.

You can go back to my brother and tell him to keep his children away from Gwendraith."

It was a nasty thing to say and it was a struggle for Asmara not to rise to it. If she rose to it, they would fight, and he would surely order her away. That would be a problem because she had no intention of returning to her father. Instead, she chose to ignore him, turning back to her food. But as she took a bite, Blayth spoke.

"She may remain," he said. "She has wisdom and she is strong. She is a fine addition to our ranks."

Morys looked at him in surprise before snorting rudely, grabbing at a cup of ale a servant brought for him. "So, the Dragon Princess has you under her spell, has she?" he said. "Very well. I will not contest you, but she will be your responsibility. I want nothing to do with her or her weakling father."

Bashing her was one thing, but insulting her father was another. Asmara's head shot up, a nasty comment on her lips, but Blayth caught her attention and shook his head faintly to discourage her from replying. There was something in his eyes that conveyed reassurance and trust – that he would not let such a thing to go unanswered. More of that chivalry that he'd been intent on showing her as of late. Confused and upset, Asmara returned to her food, but it was clear that she was upset.

Blayth knew this and, in truth, he was not particularly thrilled with Morys' obvious attempts to offend Asmara. She didn't deserve what the man was so callously dishing out. Keeping his focus on his meal, he spoke to Morys.

"I found Cader to be a sensible and thoughtful warrior in my dealings with him," he said. "I would watch who I insult, even if it is your brother. He is still our ally and I am not in the habit of insulting men I would trust with my life."

Morys wasn't sure he liked Blayth's attitude. This was the man he'd nursed back from the brink of death, the man who was leading this great new rebellion, and nothing could interfere with that. Blayth always agreed with him, in all things, and they understood one another.

At least, Morys thought they did. This was the first time that Morys could recall that Blayth even remotely came close to chastising him, of all subjects, over his brother.

And then, it occurred to him.

Asmara was sitting across the table, head down as she ate her food, but it began to occur to Morys why Blayth was defending Cader. Asmara was here, and he suspected that Blayth might have an interest in the woman. She'd come to Gwendraith, uninvited, and latched on to him. He'd never heard of the Dragon Princess having feminine wiles, but she wasn't an un-handsome woman. Some might even call her beautiful. Therefore, it was more than possible that she'd learned to use that beauty to her advantage. It made Morys wonder what had gone on at Gwendraith since he was away. Given how he felt about his brother, it was difficult not to feel animosity towards Asmara.

My father sent me.

Was it possible that Cader had sent Asmara to lure Blayth away? In Morys' paranoid mind, all things were probable.

"He is my brother and I shall say what I please," Morys said as a servant put a trencher of roast mutton and beans in front of him. "Furthermore, I will not discuss him with you. I want to know what has been going on at Gwendraith since I have been away."

Blayth drained his cup of ale before replying. "Nothing but what you see."

Morys wasn't sure if he believed Blayth; given that Asmara was there, certainly, there had been some activity. But he didn't press him, at least not at the moment. With Asmara there, Morys was coming to think that Blayth was, indeed, under her spell.

"I have much to discuss with you from my conference with Howell," he said. "There is much to say."

Blayth simply nodded, holding his cup up as a servant filled it. "More plans, I will assume?"

"We will discuss that tomorrow."

Morys effectively cut him off, which was unusual. Morys was usually more than happy to run off at the mouth about plans and schemes and dreams of glory. Blayth suspected his silence was because Asmara was there, something that didn't sit well with Blayth. He trusted the woman, and she had proven herself to him. The siege of Llandarog had seen his respect for her irrevocably cemented, and it was beginning to bother him that Morys saw fit to treat the woman as if she were dirt beneath his feet.

Nay, he didn't like that in the least.

More than that, he was making it clear that he didn't respect Blayth's opinion on either Asmara or Cader. That, more than anything, saw his ire rise.

It was time to assert himself.

"There is something else we must discuss that cannot wait until tomorrow," he said to Morys. "We must discuss the captive English knight."

Morys was chewing loudly on his meat. "What about him?"

"I sent him back to Lioncross Abbey with a message."

Morys stopped chewing, his eyes opening wide with shock. "You… you *what*?" he swallowed the bite in his mouth, nearly choking. "You released him?"

Blayth turned to him, looking him fully in the face in a direct challenge for the man to contest his decision.

"I did," he said flatly. "You left me in command, and command I did. The man has served his purpose. Your continued interrogation of him was futile, Morys. He wasn't going to tell you anything. Therefore, I used him for a better purpose – sending a message back to the English Marcher lords that a rebellion is rising in the south, a rebellion the likes of which the English have never seen before, and it will be led by a bastard son of Llywelyn the Last. Do you think capturing these castles is going to frighten the English? Of course not. But telling them *why* we have captured them – and that they will not be the last castles taken by the Welsh – will put the fear of God into them. I cannot imagine they want to face another Welsh prince, and certainly not one that will unite all Welshmen against them. There is nothing so fearsome as the spark to the fuel of rebellion."

Morys looked at him as if debating how to react to the news. Truthfully, he was shocked that Blayth had done such a thing. He'd told the man to stay clear of the prisoner and Blayth had never disobeyed him, so this news was astonishing, indeed. It was the second time that night that Blayth had shocked him by going against him, but in Morys' opinion, this infraction was much more serious.

But there was a reason he'd told Blayth to stay clear of the English.

The reason he feared most of all.

It wasn't just the English prisoner he wanted Blayth to stay clear of. It was *all* English. On that June day five years ago when he'd participated in the ambush that had seen several English knights killed, Morys had been there when the English had retreated, leaving their dead and dying behind. He'd been there when his men had swarmed over a dying English knight bearing the black and dark green of de Wolfe, the distinctive tunic worn by the house that was headed by one of the greatest knights England had ever seen.

William de Wolfe.

Morys had been fighting the English for a very long time. He knew the colors of the great Marcher lords and beyond – the blue and yellow of de Lohr, the blue and red of de Clare, and so forth. He knew their allies, like de Wolfe, but rather than kill the dying as his men were doing, Morys had protected the downed de Wolfe knight. He'd let his men take the tunic and wave it around like a flag, but he hadn't let his men kill the man who was already dead.

Or so Morys thought.

The knight was a very strong man. His head had been badly damaged, but he was still breathing and still living. Much as Morys had done with the garrison commander of Gwendraith, he had the idea to save the knight's life if only to keep the man captive and interrogate him. That had been the ultimate goal when he'd taken him back to

Brecfa, to his sod house where Aeddan and Pryce and his wife, Auryn, had helped him tend the man. For the first three months, they had no idea if the man would even live, but he did. He opened his eyes and Morys was thrilled that he'd have a captive to interrogate.

But his excitement was dashed when the man had no memory of anything.

His mind was like a clean slate.

Morys had been forced to change his plans.

As he tried to figure out what to do with the English knight, now working with Aeddan and Pryce as they helped rehabilitate him, he came upon the idea of a new Welsh prince rising from the ashes. Who better to lead the rebellion against the English *than* an English knight who had once tried to subdue the Welsh? He thought it had been a rather brilliant plan, and he'd fed it to Blayth, and to Aeddan and Pryce and his other men, until they were all convinced that Blayth was who Morys said he was.

The only potential hole in the plan had been Aeddan and Pryce, who had been at Llandeilo, although they hadn't been involved with Blayth until well after the battle when Morys brought the man back to Brecfa. Even then, Morys had been vague about who Blayth was, mostly because he didn't want it to get out that he was trying to save an English knight. He could have been viewed as a traitor, in fact, and that was a real fear.

Therefore, Aeddan and Pryce knew Blayth had come from Llandeilo, but they didn't know much more than that. It had been Morys who had convinced them of Blayth's true identity with a rather madcap story about Llywelyn's loyal *teulu* being at Llandeilo at the same time. Aeddan and Pryce believed him because they had no reason not to.

But Morys was always fearful his elaborate story would unravel.

The more he entangled himself in it, the deeper the story became.

And that was why Morys kept Blayth away from any contact with the English, fearful that it might trigger memories in him that were long buried or, worse still, someone might recognize him. Morys had no idea of Blayth's true identity other than the fact that he was wearing a de Wolfe tunic, so clearly, he was from the House of de Wolfe, but that was all Morys knew.

That torn, bloodied de Wolfe tunic was still at Brecfa, buried in a trunk and hidden away from the world.

Now, what Morys feared had evidently happened. Blayth had contact with an English knight. Astonished as he was that Blayth had undermined his authority, that really wasn't his primary concern. What he was most concerned with was if that contact had stirred something in Blayth. With that in mind, he swallowed whatever outrage he might be feeling.

There were things he had to discover.

"I see," he said after several long moments. "Did you speak to the man, then?"

"I did," Blayth replied.

"And what did you tell him, exactly?"

"Just what I told you – I sent him with a message for the Marcher lords."

Morys eyed him. "And he agreed?"

Blayth nodded. "He did," he said. "He gave his name as Corbett Payton-Forrester, the garrison commander of Gwendraith. He serves William de Valence and, I would imagine, that means he is a man of honor. He said he would deliver the message and I believe him. But he also said something odd."

"What is that?"

"He mistook me for someone he used to know."

"James de Wolfe," Asmara spoke up. She had been listening to the conversation and spoke up before she really thought that perhaps she shouldn't. "He seemed quite sure that Blayth was someone named James de Wolfe."

Morys looked at her, such surprise on his face that it was difficult to conceal. "How – how would you know any of this?" he demanded.

"She was there," Blayth said. He couldn't help but notice that Morys was suddenly quite upset; the man's entire countenance had changed and his body was coiled as if ready to burst. "I took her with me as a witness in case the knight said anything of note. But he did not; the only thing he really said was that he believed I was someone he once knew."

Morys' heart was beating heavily against his chest as he realized his fear, that godawful fear he'd been living with for the past five years, may have very well happened. What were the odds of such a thing? Dear God, he'd tried so hard to keep Blayth away from the English for this very reason.

He could hardly believe what he was hearing.

"You should not have permitted her to be there," he snapped, rising to his feet. He was so unsteady that he had a nearly panicked urge to leave. "Did you tell him who you were?"

He was nearly barking at Blayth, who cooled dramatically. He didn't like being barked at. "Of course I did," he said. "It was dark. The man could hardly see. Clearly, he was mistaken. It is nothing to become irate over."

It was a succinct answer and over his panic and anger, Morys realized something – that Blayth was *still* Blayth. He still believed he was the bastard son of Llywelyn in spite of the English knight evidently recognizing him. Now, Morys had a name to put with Blayth's mysterious past.

James de Wolfe.

And it meant nothing to Blayth.

Morys wasn't quite sure how to feel now. Was it possible that this would be an event to be quickly forgotten? Certainly, it would be remembered if Morys continued to have a tantrum over it, so he labored to calm himself. He had to push aside his shock if there was any hope of salvaging the situation. Therefore, he forced a smile, putting a hand on Blayth's broad shoulder.

"Forgive me," he said. "It has been a long day and a long journey. I am simply weary, and news such as this has upset my exhausted mind. I will retire, and I shall see you come the morrow."

With that, he abruptly left the table, wandering out among the happy, drinking men, presenting a far more subdued figure than when he had entered the hall.

If Morys had hoped to ease the situation and not make it such a major event, then he had failed. Asmara was watching him leave, wondering why the man had become so upset over the English knight mistaking Blayth for someone he once knew. It seemed very odd that Morys should become so upset over such a thing.

... unless it wasn't a mistake at all and Morys knew it.

Asmara glanced at Blayth, who had returned to the last of his food. If Morys was displaying bizarre behavior, Blayth didn't seem to care about it. But he wasn't seeing what Asmara was seeing – a man who had clearly been unbalanced by the English knight who had addressed Blayth as someone else. The truth was that before Blayth was the man sitting with her, he *was* someone else.

The mystery behind the mysterious man deepened.

PART THREE

TIMES OF CHANGE

CHAPTER NINE

Lioncross Abbey Castle
Early October

"YOUR FATHER WILL be very glad to hear of your release," Chris said. "Praise God that the Welsh released you."

Corbett was wolfing down a bowl of warmed-over stew and cramming hunks of bread into his mouth. He was absolutely starving, exhausted from his ride from Gwendraith. It had taken him a little over two days to reach Lioncross, and he'd forced himself to ride through the day as well as the night, regardless of his discomfort. As long as the horse held up, he could make it.

And he did.

He almost wept when he saw the enormous, squat towers of Lioncross' curtain wall come into view. It had been mid-morning on the third day since leaving Gwendraith, and as he'd passed through the iconic gatehouse of the castle, with its massive lion-head corbel over the entry, the tears he'd been trying so hard to hold back finally made it to the surface. He told the sentry who he was, where he had come from, and why he was there, and it seemed to throw the entire castle into a frenzy.

De Lohr's knight, Augustus de Shera, was a friend of Corbett's. His family was allied with the House of de Shera and it was Augustus who had run out to meet him, and then nearly carried him into the hall.

Even now, Augustus sat next to him with an expression of great concern on his face, watching him eat.

Chris was a little more subtle, but not much. He sat across from Corbett, trying to make it seem as if all was right and well in the world again with Corbett's release. But that was far from the truth.

"The Welsh overtook Gwendraith in three days," Corbett said, mouth full as he tried to speak and eat at the same time. "They had over a thousand men, at the very least, and they rained arrows on us so much that some of their men were able to build ladders and mount the walls. While we were protecting ourselves from the hail of arrows, the Welsh were aggressively trying to get into the castle."

Chris thought of the news his spies had brought to him not long ago, and how he'd sent his own son north to Bhrodi with the news of a rising Welsh rebellion.

"I have heard of this new rebellion," he said. "I have men in Wales that watch the countryside for just this very thing. I was told over a week ago about Llandarog, Gwendraith, and Idole Castles and how the Welsh had taken them. We speculated that the Welsh were trying to starve out Pembroke by cutting off the roads east, but we do not know for sure. Do you?"

Corbett shook his head, shoving more bread into his mouth. "Nay," he said. "I have been kept in a tiny cell for the past month, in the dark. I have not been told anything, nor do I know anything, but I have come to you with a message."

Chris' brow furrowed with interest. "Me?" he said. "Someone is sending me a message?"

Corbett shook his head and swallowed his bite. He took several big gulps of wine before continuing. "Not you in particular, my lord," he said. "The English Marcher lords. My message is for all of you. That was the only reason I was released – to bring you this message."

Chris was growing increasingly interested. "What is this message?"

Corbett stopped shoveling food into his mouth for the moment and his expression grew serious. "I am to tell you that a new rebellion is rising, led by a bastard son of Llywelyn the Last."

Chris sat forward, his arms resting on the feasting table. "I have heard this already," he said. "My men have told me that because they heard it from their Welsh contacts. They said someone named Blayth the Strong is leading the rebellion."

Corbett seemed to appear inordinately pale. "That is true," he said. "I met the man they call Blayth. He is the one who told me to deliver this message."

Chris' eyebrows lifted. "You *met* him?" he repeated. "Did he tell you anything else?"

Corbett suddenly lost his appetite. He wiped his hand over his face in a nervous, weary gesture, and both Chris and Augustus could see that his hands were shaking. He'd been steady enough until the subject of Blayth the Strong arose, and on the entire ride to Lioncross he had been eager to tell de Lohr what he had seen, but now… now, the whole thing seemed mad. He was coming to wonder whether or not he'd imagined it all.

The dead had returned.

"It is not *what* he told me, my lord," he said hoarsely. "It is what I saw. I am coming to wonder if I was momentarily insane because, in truth, I saw a ghost. A ghost from the past."

Chris wasn't following him, nor was Augustus, but they could see how upset he was. Augustus put a brotherly hand on the man's back.

"What ghost?" he asked. "What did you see?"

At first, Corbett couldn't even bring himself to say it. He knew that once he did, there would be no stemming the flood. The dam would have broken and men would either call him mad or they would praise him. He would be a lightning rod for controversy and speculation. Aye, he knew all of this, but he also knew he had to speak. He took a deep breath.

"You must understand that I have spent almost a month in total darkness," he said quietly. "Any light at all is torture to my eyes and, even now, the light hurts them. I do not know if I will ever see clearly again. I was pulled from my cell by a beast of a man, very big and blond and scarred. So terribly scarred. The first thing I noticed about him was that the entire left side of his head is battered and scarred. His ear is missing. As he spoke to me, my eyes adjusted to the light and I saw his face. The man identified himself as Blayth the Strong."

Chris still didn't understand his meaning. "But why did you say you saw a ghost?"

Corbett sighed heavily and closed his eyes. "Because I believe that Blayth the Strong is James de Wolfe," he nearly whispered. "I will swear upon my oath that James de Wolfe has returned from the dead."

Chris stared at him a moment as the news sank in. Then, it hit him; his eyes widened and a hand flew to his mouth in disbelief. As he sat back and nearly reeled off the bench, Augustus was the one to grab Corbett's arm as if the man had snakes coming out of his mouth.

"De Wolfe?" he gasped. "*James* de Wolfe? But… but that is not possible. He was killed five years ago at Llandeilo!"

Corbett nodded, peeling Augustus' fingers from his arm because they hurt. "I know," he said. "God help me, I know. We were told that James died there. But I swear to you upon my grandmother's grave that James de Wolfe is calling himself Blayth the Strong, and it is he who is leading this rebellion."

Chris was standing up now. He didn't even know how he ended up on his feet, only that he had. His hand was still over his mouth as he struggled with the news he'd just been told. It was outrageous in so many ways, something no sane man would believe. Finally, he shook his head.

"That is not possible," he muttered. "It is just *not* possible."

"Why?" Corbett nearly demanded. "Were you at Llandeilo? Did you see his corpse?"

Chris began wiping at his mouth as if to wipe away the shock, his mind going back five years to that terrible and turbulent time.

"Nay," he said. "I was with Roger Mortimer to the north of Llandeilo. Originally, I had been with de Wolfe and Gloucester, but

Mortimer demanded more men and Edward told me to ride with him, so I did. Had I been with de Wolfe and Gloucester, the outcome of Llandeilo might have been different, but it was not. When I heard… when I heard of James' death, I was devastated for William. I have been told it is something he has never recovered from."

"Yet he married his youngest daughter to Bhrodi," Augustus pointed out. "I heard that he did it because he did not want to lose another son in Wales, so he did it specifically for the alliance it would bring him. He did it for peace."

Chris was looking at Augustus at this point, both of them overwhelmed by the possibility that James de Wolfe might not have died in Wales. "My God," Chris finally breathed. "I know he had to leave James' body behind. William was crushed because of it."

Augustus lifted his eyebrows. "Then if he had no body to bury, it is possible that James did not die at all."

"But William swore he was dead when he left him," Chris said. "I spoke to him and to Paris de Norville shortly thereafter. In their retreat, they had to leave James behind. But they both swore he was dead."

Corbett could see the shock between the two men as they tried to rationalize what they'd been told. There was urgency in their tones, and disbelief coupled with the pain of a lost knight, who might not be so lost after all.

The realization was staggering.

"I have a theory," Corbett said, trying to stop the building perplexity. "You know that the House of de Wolfe is intertwined with the crown. I do not know how deep it goes, but we know that Edward greatly admires and respects William. I, too, have been wondering in earnest why we were told James was dead, yet I clearly saw him in Wales, claiming the identity of another man. It occurred to me that mayhap he is there for a reason – a *royal* reason."

Chris and Augustus looked at him in confusion. "Explain," Chris said.

Corbett had been harboring this crazy idea since he first realized he was looking at James de Wolfe and he could only hope it made some sense to Chris and Augustus.

"It was the man who called himself Blayth who released me from the vault after a month of confinement and torture," he said evenly. "He seemed very insistent that I ride to one of the major Marcher lords to deliver his missive – that this new rebellion was rising, and that the bastard of Llywelyn was behind it. It was the way he said it that made me think… it made me think that, mayhap, James had assumed the identity of this Blayth."

Chris was greatly puzzled. "*Assumed* this identity? Why?"

"So that Edward could have a man inside the rebellion," Corbett replied. "Edward could have a man lead the Welsh to defeat. What better way to destroy the Welsh than from the inside?"

It was frightening to realize that it all made sense. Suddenly, Chris caught on to exactly what he was saying.

"An agent for Edward?" he breathed.

Corbett nodded. "That was my thought, my lord."

Chris pondered that possibility. "But… but I saw William after James' death. The man was genuinely distraught. I have never seen a father more grief-stricken."

"It is possible Lord William does not know of his son's mission," Corbett insisted. "It is possible no one does *but* Edward and James. Mayhap, it was James' directive to fake his death and become someone else. In any case, I know that I saw James de Wolfe. He is alive, and he is leading a rebellion."

Chris could hardly believe it. He looked at Augustus, seeing the same astonishment reflecting in the man's eyes. It was all so overwhelming he didn't know what to think or where to start with any of it.

"Either way, the implications are staggering," Chris finally said. "If James is leading this rebellion and plans to destroy it from within, we cannot interfere. But if he is not an agent for Edward and he is, indeed, leading the rebellion as Blayth the Strong, calling himself the bastard of Llywelyn… I simply cannot comprehend why he would do it. None of it makes any sense."

The mood between the three men plummeted. It was a dark and confusing time, with no one really knowing where to turn. They couldn't contact Edward about it, especially if James was an agent, and they couldn't risk reaching out to James in any fashion.

"What will you do, my lord?" Augustus asked quietly. "Surely you cannot keep this news from Lord William."

Chris eyed his knight for a moment before turning away, shaking his head. "Nay," he muttered. "He must know. If my son had been found living years after I believed him to be dead, I would certainly want to know. I cannot withhold such information. But I am not sure how to tell him, either, especially since no one else but Corbett has seen him. Although I do not doubt the man's word, a second opinion is needed, don't you think?"

Augustus nodded. "I knew James," he said. "Would you have me go into Wales to see for myself?"

Chris cast him an odd look. "Surely you jest," he said. "You? An English knight? They would kill you on sight."

Augustus didn't subscribe to the fact that he would be killed on sight, for he could defend himself, but he didn't argue. "Then what will you do?"

Chris scratched his head in a thoughtful gesture. "There is someone who can get closer to him than we can," he said. "Bhrodi de Shera."

Augustus frowned. "But Bhrodi married James' sister well after James was killed. He has never seen the man."

Chris looked at him. "Nay, he has not," he said. "But his wife has. Let her confirm that her brother is indeed alive and then we will send word to William. For certain, the man will want to know."

It made sense. Augustus was ready to carry out any orders to that effect. "Rees should have already reached Bhrodi right now with the first message you sent," he said. "Shall we send a second one?"

Chris nodded. "Indeed," he said. "I will scribe one before the day is out. Prepare our fastest messenger for the journey. I am going to invite

Bhrodi and his wife to Lioncross so that we may discuss this issue in person, for certainly, they will want to know about it. And Bhrodi's counsel on the matter will be welcome, for I doubt his wife can be rational about it. We will determine once and for all if James de Wolfe is alive or not."

"And if he is?" Augustus asked.

Chris exhaled slowly, with feeling. "If he is," he said, "then William must know. But, as I said, we cannot interfere in anything James is doing if he is an agent for Edward. A faked death, five years of infiltrating the Welsh… we could ruin everything if we try to contact the man."

"True," Augustus said. "But what if he is *not* an agent for Edward? What if he has simply gone mad and is now calling himself Blayth the Strong, bastard of Llywelyn?"

Chris shook his head. "If that is the case, God help us all," he said. "Because not only will he lead a rebellion, he will bring down everything the House of de Wolfe has stood for. He will ruin his father's legacy."

Augustus digested that statement. Then, he said what they were all thinking. "If he is not an agent for Edward, then surely William will not let him destroy his legacy and the legacy of his entire family," he said. "Surely… surely the man will do something to prevent that."

Chris looked at him. "He will not," he said. "But *I* will. My grandfather's best friend in the world was Edward de Wolfe, William's father. Did you know that? Edward de Wolfe and my grandfather were very close, all their lives. Even though we are not related by blood to the House of de Wolfe, they are still family, and family protects family. If James has lost his mind and is actively trying to destroy his father's legacy, then I shall do what needs to be done. I will make sure James does not accomplish his goal. William lost his son once before; he will have to stomach losing him again and this time, for good."

It was an ominous threat, but an understandable one. The Houses of de Lohr and de Wolfe were that intertwined, and very protective of each other. Even when it came to sons ruining fathers. Augustus knew that Chris meant every word of it.

Blayth would have to die.

Before the day was out, another rider was heading north into Wales, to Rhydilian Castle, the seat of Bhrodi de Shera.

CHAPTER TEN

Gwendraith Castle

IT WAS VERY late.

The full moon was in its zenith in the sky, a great silver ball shining over the land, bathing the landscape in a ghostly glow. Inside Gwendraith's hall, Blayth was sitting by the hearth, gazing into the snapping flames as Morys, Aeddan, and Pryce also stood around the hearth, speaking of mundane things at this point.

But it wasn't always thus.

Since his return from Carmarthen Castle, Morys had kept Blayth at his side. That had been two days ago, and Blayth was sick of the sight of the man. It had been two days of plans, of speculation, and of glorious goals for Morys and his men in the new Welsh order once the English had been purged.

Blayth was used to Morys and his dreams of grandeur, and talk like this normally didn't bother him. He, too, wanted to see a free Wales, and Morys' enthusiasm for his country was patriotic and proud. Normally, he was content to sit and listen to Morys spout off and lend his advice on such matters.

But this time, it was different.

This time, Blayth got the distinct impression that Morys kept him close for one very good reason – he didn't want him finding company with Asmara. Morys had made a point of speaking ill of both Cader and

Asmara, as if trying to poison Blayth's opinion of the pair, but Blayth could see through the man's attempts. He'd seen it the night he'd returned from Carmarthen and how disrespectful he'd been to Asmara.

Now, Morys was only succeeding in making him angry.

Two days later, Blayth had been fed his fill of the man. He was no longer tolerant of his foolish opinions, or schemes, because his thoughts were elsewhere. They'd been elsewhere for two solid days, lingering on the golden-eyed woman he seemed to be increasingly obsessed with. He didn't want to hear Morys anymore.

He wanted away from the man.

"Did you hear me?" Morys cut into his thoughts. "Blayth, do you *hear* me?"

Broken from his mental wanderings, Blayth lifted the nearly empty cup of cheap ale to his lips. "What about?" he said. "All I have done is hear you for two days. What more do I need to hear?"

Unusually belligerent words from a man who was normally quite docile. Morys wasn't stupid; he knew that Blayth was irritated at him and he knew why. But Morys needed to ensure that he had Blayth's loyalty and attention, because he knew for a fact that his niece was a far more attractive prospect than he was.

Not knowing Asmara's motives, or if Cader really had put her up to it, Morys had to assert his position in Blayth's life and in the chain of command. He was Blayth's leader, his mentor, and the man who had brought him back from the brink of death. It had been an uphill battle keeping the man close to him, but the past two days had been insurance against the woman creating so much of a distraction that she would fill Blayth's attention for good. Morys had to purge the woman from his thoughts, whatever the cost.

In the end, Blayth would understand it was for his own good.

"We are to return to Carmarthen Castle in several days," Morys said patiently. "Howell is calling his armies to him once again. I have explained this to you; now that we hold Idole, Llandarog, and Gwendraith, Howell plans to move on larger castles now. He will expect us to lead the charge."

Blayth had heard all of this, numerous times. "And then what?" he asked. "Where is Rhys ap Maredudd in all of this? He has put out the call for support, yet we do not fight with the man."

"He is to the north, as I have told you. He has taken Cilgerran Castle, among others."

Blayth turned to look at him. "He takes castles that are of no real importance, whilst we put a stranglehold on Pembroke and the south," he said. "Have you not looked at it this way? *We* are the ones taking the greater risk, Morys, not Rhys."

Morys' dark eyes flashed. "That is because we *are* the greater glory," he hissed. "The son of Llywelyn the Last is leading this rebellion and all men will rise to follow you. It is only right that we take the greater risk."

Blayth eyed him. "I am not leading anything," he said. "You and Howell are planning this rebellion."

"Blayth," Aeddan said quietly. "I would not fight with just anyone. I will only fight with you. All of the men feel the same way."

Blayth looked at him. "These are not my plans, Aeddan," he pointed out. "Just like you, I am accountable to Morys. In battle, I make the decisions, but this rebellion as a whole… I have not planned this."

It was the truth, the rather convoluted chain of command when it came to Morys and Blayth. In battle, Blayth was formidable, but he was only in the battle to begin with because Morys wanted him there. Men were naturally drawn to Blayth and his flawless capabilities in battle and Morys knew this, which is why he needed to keep the man close.

Without Blayth, the men would lose confidence.

It was more important than ever to keep him close.

"You are the spark to the kindling, Blayth," Morys said. He needed to encourage the man, not fight with him. "I have told you this before. You are the light to whom all men look. You bear the blood of the Welsh princes, men who have died for this country. You give all men hope as the last of that line."

Blayth's gaze lingered on him before he turned back to the fire.

"You speak of men I do not know, of a family I have no memory of," he said. "I may as well be a stranger."

"But you are not. You are Blayth ap Llywelyn and you bear a proud heritage."

Blayth wasn't looking at him; his mind was going back to the vaults of Gwendraith when the English knight had called him James. Even as he heard Morys speak of his lineage and, subsequently, his destiny, it just didn't seem right. He'd always accepted what Morys had told him and he'd never contested it, but even so, it never felt *right*. There had always been a sense of loss with him, of wondering about his past life. After hearing the English knight call him by another name, Blayth wasn't certain of who he was any longer. Initially, the knight's words hadn't bothered him, but they were beginning to.

They were beginning to get under his skin.

"Are you so certain?" he finally asked. "In all the time I have known you, Morys, not one man has come forth to confirm what you have told me. Look at me; I am not a young man. I do not know how many years I have seen, but I am older than Aeddan, and he has seen thirty years and three. In all that time before I came to you, not one man has seen me and is able to confirm the identity you have given me."

Morys struggled not to rise to Blayth's mood. He suspected this skewed outlook might be coming from Asmara, who had undoubtedly asked questions of Blayth's true identity. But it could also be coming from the English knight who had called him by a name – *James de Wolfe*.

It had been that event that Morys had been so fearful of and, in truth, he'd hoped that Blayth had forgotten about it. He'd spent two days trying to hammer home Blayth's destiny and the future of their rebellion in the hopes that it would drive whatever doubt Blayth was experiencing right out of his head.

But it hadn't.

This is what he had feared – a man he'd given a mythical identity who was now starting to question that.

"It *is* your identity," Morys said, not at all kindly. "You were brought to me, nearly dead, by your father's *teulu*, old men who vanished back into the north to draw the English away from where they'd left you. They retreated north so the English would look for you there, and not here in the south with me. They fled to save your life. Do you want me to find those men? Do you want me to tell them to come back to you because you do not believe you are your father's son? Tell me now and I shall send for them, Blayth."

"Then send for them."

He said it without hesitation and Morys looked at him as if he'd been struck. That wasn't the answer he'd been expecting and, given that there were no men to send for, he was very close to losing credibility. He was almost panicked at the thought. He couldn't lose Blayth, not when he'd worked so hard to build the man's reputation and build glory for himself in the process. Damn the man… now, he was going to ruin it all, everything he'd worked for.

That brought out the anger in him.

"It is a sad day when the man whose life I saved doubts my word," he growled. "Did you doubt my word when I was making it so you could breathe? So you could eat? Who washed your dirty body and cleaned away your filth? You trusted me then. But now, you would doubt me?"

It was the same thing Morys said every time he feared that Blayth was doubting anything he said, that reflexive action that always brought an apology from Blayth and assuagement to Morys. But this time, Blayth was looking at him without remorse, but more with an expression of a man who was curious and intent. That wasn't the man Morys wanted to see.

"I do not doubt you," Blayth finally said. "But I would like to speak to the men who brought me to you. Mayhap they can give me more background on the past I cannot remember. Morys, I remember nothing. You know this. And two days ago, a man was quite convinced I was someone he knew from the past."

Morys' temper was growing. "He was a fool! He mistook you for someone and you are a fool if you believe him!"

Blayth wouldn't let Morys belittle him. He stood up, at least a head taller than Morys, a great and imposing presence. "I am not a fool," he muttered, "and you will not call me one ever again. Do you understand me?"

Morys was so angry that his lips were white. He turned away, refusing to answer. "You will not tell me what to do."

"If you call me a fool again, I will walk from this place and never turn back."

Morys glared at him. "And go where?"

"That is for me to know."

Morys could see that his anger and threats weren't working, and he wasn't entirely sure Blayth wouldn't walk away from him. *It's her!* He thought angrily. Ever since Asmara appeared, Blayth hadn't been entirely predictable. Therefore, he took a deep breath and tried to calm himself. It wouldn't do any good for them to continue arguing, so he switched tactics.

"If you want me to send word to the men who brought you to me, then so be it," he said, throwing up his hands in a surrendering gesture. "It will take time, however. I do not know where they have gone or if they are even still alive. They were very old men, you know."

"But you will send word."

"I will."

If Blayth didn't believe him, he didn't let on. He had what he wanted, although he had to admit that he wasn't entirely sure Morys would follow through. Still, he would keep an eye on the man. Morys didn't want to lose his faith, so it would be a touchy situation for them both.

And the consequences could be dire if faith was broken.

Meanwhile, Blayth reclaimed his seat by the fire, eyeing Aeddan and Pryce, who were sitting quietly by the hearth. The brothers usually remained quiet in matters between Blayth and Morys, but it was clear they were siding with Blayth in this matter. They had a liege who always had to be in control, and who was known to manipulate men. Still, he was a prince of Deheubarth, and that tie alone garnered him some respect.

But sometimes, it was difficult.

"Someone recognized you, Blayth?"

The question came from Aeddan. He'd not heard of the event on the day it happened, as he simply hadn't spent any time with Blayth when he'd returned with Morys from Carmarthen. It was also true that other than Morys, Blayth hadn't told anyone, so it wasn't common knowledge. But it was clear that Aeddan and Pryce, seated beside his brother, were curious. Before Morys could stop him, Blayth answered.

"The garrison commander I released the day you and the others returned from Carmarthen," he said. "The man called me James – de Wolfe, I believe. When I told him my name was Blayth, he pointed out that the name means wolf in our language. But he swore he knew me, at least at first."

Aeddan was very interested. "De Wolfe," he muttered. "I know the name. I have heard it. They are allied with the great Marcher lords, I believe. De Lohr and de Lara. They are a great family from the north of England."

"It was rambling words from a sick man," Morys said, trying to keep the speculation down. He didn't want the ap Ninian brothers asking a lot of questions, not when he was trying to downplay the entire incident. "The man had been in the vault for a month, in darkness, so he mistook Blayth for someone he thought he knew."

Aeddan simply nodded, not voicing what he was thinking. He knew how protective Morys was over Blayth and to bring about the subject of the man's past would only upset Morys further. It was best to let the subject drop, as they often did in the times when it came up. Morys didn't like to be questioned. But something occurred to Aeddan, something he couldn't get out of his head.

He had been at Llandeilo, and had been there when Morys brought the battered, nearly-dead body of Blayth home with the tale of him having been delivered by Llywelyn's *teulu* to Llandeilo, coincidentally, exactly when the battle was taking place. It hadn't made a lot of sense to Aeddan at the time but, in hearing that an English knight had mistaken Blayth for someone he knew, someone named James de Wolfe, Aeddan was coming to think that something seemed quite strange about the entire situation. He wasn't sure he ever believed Morys about how he came into possession of the gravely wounded man, but now, a thought was occurring to him, something he couldn't get out of his head.

The de Wolfe army had been at Llandeilo.

He wondered if Blayth knew that.

It was an odd situation, indeed.

CHAPTER ELEVEN

THE SKY AT sunrise was truly something to behold. It was a pink sky, with great ribbons of golden clouds streaked across it and a sun that was just peeking out from the eastern horizon. The vibrant green landscape of Wales was coming alive beneath the warm glow, awakening to the dawn of a new day.

Asmara was in the stables of Gwendraith, seeing to her horse. It seemed to have developed an abscess on its hoof. She noticed that the horse was favoring his right front leg yesterday and when she'd come in this morning, the abscess was evident. Bent over the animal, with an iron lamp casting a soft golden light on the floor of the stables, she was working on cleaning out the hoof itself before going in search of the items she would need to cleanse the abscess.

In fact, Asmara had been spending a good deal of time with her horse. Her presence with the animal had been constant over the past two days, ever since Morys returned from Carmarthen Castle. He'd kept Blayth with him, sequestered as they discussed more plans for the building rebellion, and Asmara has been left on her own. Not that she minded, because it was better than returning to Llandarog. As long as she was near Blayth, she was content.

But being away from him had given her time to think. In truth, all she'd done was think about Blayth and what she was coming to feel for him. They hadn't spent a lot of time together before Morys returned and ruined everything, but she felt as if they'd gotten to know one another fairly well in that time. He'd spoken of his past, or what he could tell her, and of the memories Morys had given him.

But in hearing of Morys' part in Blayth's life, Asmara was even more suspicious of her uncle than she had been before. When Blayth told her that Morys had "given" him his memories, that had set off a warning bell in her mind. Then, when the *Saesneg* knight had called Blayth by another name, that had only confirmed what Asmara was already suspecting.

Then, Morys' very strange behavior the night he returned from Carmarthen was questionable at best. It was a litany of clues, all adding up to something, telling Asmara that Morys knew far more about Blayth than what he'd told the man.

It also told her that Blayth wasn't who Morys said he was.

But she would not speak of her suspicions, not to anyone, and especially not to Blayth. He didn't remember anything, but he seemed comfortable in the memories Morys had given him. More than that, those involved in the rebellion were looking to Blayth as if he were their new savior and she would never take that hope away from her people.

It was an odd position she found herself in.

So, she spent time with her horse, stewing over Morys and his lies and wondering if, in the long run, they would end up hurting Blayth. If that happened, then Asmara was prepared to defend the man from any backlash to Morys' lies. She would not let him be hurt, and least of all by Morys. If her greedy, self-serving uncle was on a path to destruction, then she would not let him take Blayth down with him.

That was what her father had said to Morys once, back when they were still speaking to one another. Morys had grand dreams of purging the English from Wales, as did Cader, but Morys was far more reckless about it. Cader preferred to be sly and calculated in his movements against the English, while Morys preferred to be loud and rash. Morys had always called Cader weak because he didn't approve of Morys' bold manner, but Morys had called Cader weak one too many times and

Cader swore at him and told him he would not be pulled down by his brother's path to destruction. That had been the beginning of the estrangement between them.

Asmara hadn't spent much time around Morys before the separation. But in the moments she had spent with him as of late, she developed a healthy hatred for the man. She didn't like anything about him and his manipulative ways, and she didn't like the way he controlled Blayth.

Blayth was a good, loyal warrior and Morys took advantage of that.

Then came the silly daydreams of what it would be like if Blayth was free of Morys, and if that gentle chivalry he'd shown her meant something more than simply manners. What if it was something he wanted to show her? What if he didn't look at her as another warrior, but as a woman fully grown? Her father was always asking about future grandchildren and her answer was always the same – *Someday, Dadau, but not today.*

What if that someday had finally come?

A noise shook her from those foolish dreams and she turned to see Aeddan and his brother, Pryce, entering the stable. Asmara had seen them since their return from Carmarthen with Morys, but she hadn't really spoken to them. They had duties that kept them very busy. When the brothers entered, Aeddan's dark eyes fixed on her and he smiled politely.

"My lady," he said. "You are up early."

Asmara turned back to her horse. "I thought my horse was coming up lame yesterday," she said. "I came to check him."

Aeddan had a cloak and a few other items in his hands. He set them down and came over to Asmara as she bent over her animal.

"How is he?" he asked.

Asmara held up the hoof, showing him the beginnings of the abscess. "Poison has somehow gotten into his hoof," she said. "I must make a solution of salt water to help drain it."

Aeddan was peering at the wound. "Indeed," he said. "You should soak it several times a day with the salt. It should heal. It does not look too terribly bad."

Asmara had a tool to clean out the hoof and she picked at the area carefully. "I hope not," she said. "He has a propensity for hoof wounds."

Aeddan's gaze lingered on the hoof for a few moments before he looked up at the animal in general. He gave the beast an appreciative slap on the withers.

"He is a fine horse," he said. "How old is he?"

"He has seen three years this summer. I raised him from birth."

Aeddan passed a practiced eye over the long legs of the horse. "I would wager that he can run like the wind."

"And he does not like to be captured, either. When I put him out to pasture, sometimes it takes me an hour to catch him. He thinks it's a game to run from me."

Aeddan smiled, petting the horse on his dark face. "I have a horse that looks a good deal like him," he said. "Morys gave him to me. He once belonged to a *Saesneg* soldier."

The mere mention of Morys brought down Asmara's mood. Blayth had even mentioned that Aeddan and Pryce had been with him from the beginning of his memories so, with that in mind, Asmara's curiosity took hold. There was something in her that wanted to know about Blayth and Morys from Aeddan's perspective. He knew the situation as well as anyone.

"You have been with my uncle a long time, then?" she asked, sounding rather innocent in her attempts to probe him.

Aeddan wasn't on his guard. He answered immediately. "Aye," he said. "Since I was young. My father served him, too, so it was natural that we also serve him."

"Is your father still alive?"

Aeddan shook his head, patting the horse's head. "My father died several years ago," he said. "It was Morys who practically raised my brother and me."

"Then you are close to him?"

"Nay."

The answer came from Pryce, who was standing back in the shadows. He had been listening to the conversation and could no longer remain silent. When Asmara and Aeddan turned to him, he seemed rather uncomfortable with the attention, but it didn't stop him from speaking up.

"He is *not* like a father to us," he said, stepping forward into the light. "He is our overlord and that is all. Morys does not treat anyone like family and God was wise when he did not allow the man to become a father. He would have been a terrible one."

Aeddan was giving his brother a warning look, but Asmara pressed him. "Yet you still serve him," she said. "Why do you serve him if you do not like him?"

Pryce simply shook his head. "We owe him a great deal," he said. "When our father died, he fed us. He did not turn us out. But he expects something for that kindness."

"Morys is a strict taskmaster," Aeddan said, cutting of Pryce because the man was starting to complain. "Pryce does not appreciate a man who has a strong sense of control. But we appreciate that he has provided for us and continues to do so. He is a prince of Deheubarth, after all. It is a privilege to serve him."

Asmara hadn't had much contact with the ap Ninian brothers during the raid on Llandarog, or even afterwards, so this was the first real conversation she'd had with them. She could see that Pryce seemed to be somewhat discontented when it came to Morys and Aeddan tried to be tactful. It was a rather interesting take on Morys, but not a surprising one. She dropped the horse's hoof and tossed the hoof pick aside.

"My father is also a prince, but he treats his people well," she said. "He and Morys have never gotten on."

"We know," Aeddan said. "Morys is hard on people who do not think as he does."

Asmara lifted her eyebrows. "I could see that the night he returned from Carmarthen when Blayth did not agree with what he was saying," she said. "Does he always keep Blayth so close to him?"

Aeddan nodded firmly. "He does," he said. "It has always been that way."

"But why?"

Aeddan shrugged. "I suppose because of who he is. Morys protects him."

"Protects him? Or hides him?" Asmara asked. Then, she noticed the change of expression on Pryce's face; he wasn't very good at hiding what seemed to be disbelief. "You have been with Blayth since Morys brought him back from Llandeilo, haven't you?"

Aeddan looked at her. "Did Blayth tell you that?"

"He said that he recovered because of you."

Aeddan's focus seemed to hang on her for a few moments and Asmara was afraid he was becoming wise to the fact that she was trying to pry information out of him. The man gave the horse one last pet before dropping his hand.

"He is like a brother to me," he finally said. "I would trust Blayth with my life many times over. I would trust Morys with my life, too."

Asmara could sense that he was becoming either defensive or suspicious, so she stopped questioning him. Hopefully, there would be another chance but, for now, he was shutting her down.

"It is good to have friends and allies like that," she said, taking the conversation in another direction. "You are very fortunate. I have my father and my sister, whom I trust, although Fairynne can be rather silly at times."

The corner of Aeddan's mouth twitched. "As my brother can be rather silly, also, I understand."

Pryce made a hissing sound, a somewhat threatening sound, and Asmara knew the conversation was over for the most part. But it had been good while it lasted. She turned around, hunting for a bucket.

"I suppose I should find some salt now to soak the hoof," she said. "You would not happen to know where I can find some, do you?"

"Find what?"

A fourth voice entered the stable and Asmara turned to see Blayth entering just as the sun came over the horizon. The light behind him was bright and beaming, as if the man had a halo. She felt her heart skip a beat at the sight of him.

"Salt," she said. "My horse has a wound on his hoof that needs to be soaked."

She was pointing to her horse, but Blayth was only looking at her. He had arisen early that morning with the specific purpose of finding Asmara before Morys also rose. The man liked to sleep past dawn but Blayth was counting on the fact that Asmara, an industrious woman, didn't. He'd hunted in the hall for her, and all around the keep, before wandering down into the outer bailey only to be told by a soldier that he'd seen the woman heading for the stables.

Now that he'd found her, he intended to soak up every single moment he could with her, but he couldn't do it with Aeddan and Pryce hanging around. In fact, he felt the unfamiliar stab of jealousy to realize the brothers had been alone with her.

"Aeddan," he said. "Go and find salt for the lady. She should not have to hunt for it herself."

Aeddan pointed to his brother. "Pryce can do it," he said. "I am expected out on patrol."

"Then get about your duties, both of you."

As Pryce left the stable and Aeddan headed into one of the stalls to bring forth his horse, Blayth took a few more steps in Asmara's direction.

Now, it was just the two of them, without an audience. Blayth could feel the excitement of her proximity, making his fingers tingle. Simply looking at the woman was beginning to feed his soul in ways he could hardly comprehend.

In her presence, all seemed right with the world again.

"I am sorry to hear about your horse," he said. "Is there anything more I can do?"

Asmara's heart was pounding against her ribs. She'd never in her life been so glad to see anyone and she had no idea how to elegantly handle the situation. When it came to social graces, she had none.

"Nay," she said, thinking her voice sounded rather giddy on a serious matter regarding her horse. "Soaking the hoof should ease the situation."

If he noticed the tremble to her voice, he didn't acknowledge it. "Aye, it should. I hope it works."

"So do I."

An awkward silence followed as Aeddan moved past them, leading his horse out into the stable yard. When he was gone, Blayth turned to Asmara with a glimmer in his eye.

"I thought he would never leave," he said.

"Why?"

"Because the man is not wanted."

She cocked her head. "I do not understand."

He started to chuckle. "I am not doing a very good job of this."

"Of *what*?"

He scratched the scarred side of his head. "Of speaking with you. I wish to speak to you."

"About what?"

He lifted his big shoulders. "*Things*," he said. "Morys has kept me by his side for two days until I am sick of the sight of him. I had hoped you were still at Gwendraith. I was afraid his rudeness might have chased you back to Llandarog."

Asmara shook her head. "He cannot chase me away. Did he tell you that he wanted to?"

"Nay," Blayth said. "But he seems to see his brother when he looks at you. The same animosity is there."

"You noticed, did you?"

Her tone was jesting, but the statement was a true one. He grinned.

"Unfortunately, I did," he said. Then, he sobered, but his gaze upon her was most intense. "I… I was wondering if you might accompany me to Carmarthen, demoiselle. I am displeased with the smithy here at

Gwendraith and I know that there is a superior smithy in Carmarthen that I should like to have repair the blade of my sword. It has been damaged and the smithy here has only made it worse."

It was a surprising offer, one that Asmara had not been prepared for. But the thought of accompanying him into town did not displease her at all. In fact, she was most eager to go with him except for one rather major concern.

"I would be honored to go with you," she said. "But if Morys is going also, then I shall decline."

Blayth shook his head. "He is *not* going with me," he said. "In fact, he does not even know that I plan to go. I swear, I cannot take another day of the man. I must have some time away from him and I should like you to go with me when I do."

Realizing it would just be the two of them, Asmara was thrilled at the thought. "I will go," she said, hoping she didn't sound too eager. But then she remembered her horse and her manner cooled. "But my horse must be tended. I cannot simply leave him."

"I will have the grooms soak his hoof. And you can ride with me."

The self-reliant Dragon Princess had never once ridden with a man. In fact, she'd scorned those who had tried, men who wanted to make her anything other than what she was – fiercely independent and strong. She would look at women as they fawned over men and think poorly of them, and that meant she would ride her own horse.

No man would tell her otherwise.

At least, that was how she used to think, but since the introduction of the damaged warrior with the deliberate, and sometimes slow, speech pattern, that independent woman was coming to think that a little dependency – and a little chivalry – wasn't such a bad thing, after all. He commanded that she should ride with him, and she would not argue. She wanted to do it.

For the first time in her life, she was starting to feel like a woman.

But there was some confusion as well as chagrin with that thought. Asmara had to admit that she was glad Fairynne wasn't around to see such a thing. She'd often chastised her sister for her foolish, romantic notions, but now Asmara was starting to see what the fuss was about.

The right man changed everything.

"I always ride my own horse," she finally said, though there was a twinkle in her eye. "I have never ridden with a man on his horse."

"Why not?" Blayth asked. "Is it against your religion?"

Asmara burst out laughing. "Nay," she said. "I suppose there is no one I would consider riding behind."

"Will you ride with me?"

"I will make an exception with you."

It was, perhaps, the first flirtatious thing she'd ever said to him, and Blayth took it as an open invitation. It did his heart such good to realize that the long-legged beauty was willing to put aside her own standards to agree to ride with him. As simple as it sounded, it was an important milestone.

She wanted to ride with him.

But the excitement in his chest began to wane when he thought back to their conversation on the day she'd arrived, and how he'd been unused to the compassion and understanding he'd shown her. Blayth was a man with demons, and perhaps one of his greatest demons was his own insecurities.

When it came to a woman, it was a demon that was almost stronger than he was. He started to think that perhaps her agreeing to ride with him was just another act of pity. She'd shown him so much understanding and grace. He'd asked her to ride with him and, perhaps, this was just more of her grace.

It wasn't as if he'd given her a choice.

Now, he was starting to feel foolish.

"If you do not want to, you do not have to," he said. "If you are more comfortable riding a horse of your own, then I am sure you can borrow one. I will find it for you myself."

He started to step away but Asmara reached out to stop him. "Wait," she said, grasping his arm. "I told you I would ride with you.

Did you ask me hoping that I would refuse?"

"Nay…"

She cut him off. "Then you do *not* want me to ride with you?"

"It is not that at all, but…"

She cut him off a second time. "That what? You are very close to insulting me for the fourth time. You ask me to ride with you, but now you have changed your mind?"

She could bring words to her lips faster than he could even though his mind worked far more swiftly than hers. His head injury prevented him from finding the correct words sometimes, or speaking with any speed, and this was one of those cases. He could see that she was growing increasingly upset, so he put his hands up and grasped her firmly by the arms to stop her momentum.

"*Stop*," he commanded quietly. "Shut your lips. I have not changed my mind, but you have yet to allow me to explain. You keep interrupting me."

He was holding her very tightly and Asmara could feel the strength in those hands. If nothing else about the man had impressed her, the first touch of his hands upon her did. The power radiating from them was indescribable. It made her heart race so vibrantly that she could scarcely catch her breath.

"Very well," she said. "Explain."

He could see that she was still angry. She wasn't going to make this easy for him, and he knew that anything other than the truth wouldn't be well-met, so he swallowed his pride. His relationship with the woman was deepening, or at least he hoped so, and he decided that it was right that he should confess what he'd been thinking. If she didn't understand, then perhaps all of that pity and compassion he'd felt from her was insincere. But if she did understand – and he prayed she did – then perhaps all of this was real.

He very much wanted it to be real.

"It occurred to me that I did not give you a choice," he said. "It occurred to me that I have forced you into agreeing to ride with me.

There is no reason why you should want to do so."

Asmara was confused. Her brow furrowed as she peered at him. "Why would I not want to ride with you?"

He dropped his hands and averted his gaze. "Let us be honest," he said. "I… I am not the most attractive man. My body is damaged. I do not blame you if that repulses you, so I did not mean to force you to do something that would mean… we will be close together by virtue of riding on the same horse, and… you do not need to be faced with the scars that cover me."

He trailed off, putting his left hand up to cover the side of his head that was so badly damaged. He was covering it from her view. As he did so, it began to occur to Asmara what he meant and the pity, the sorrow, she felt for the man knew no limits.

"Is *that* what you think?" she said. "That I think you are repulsive somehow?"

He shrugged. "I would understand, demoiselle. You are such a beautiful woman and such perfection deserves perfection. I am far from it."

Asmara's heart just about broke. She'd always thought she was a hard woman, hardened to the feelings and emotions of others. She kept her composure through almost any situation, but not this one. It occurred to her that he was so very ashamed of the way he looked, at least when it came to a woman. But the truth was that she found it rugged and exciting.

She always had.

The stable was being filled with the warmth of the early morning sun as she took a few steps in his direction. When she was close enough, she reached out and put her hand over his as it covered the left side of his head. Curling her fingers around his, she pulled his hand away. When he looked up, wary of her intentions, all he saw was a gentle smile on her face.

"All I see is a man who has seen much in life," she said softly. "I see a handsome man I would be delighted to ride with. You are strong and fearless as a warrior, but beneath that façade, you are kind and humorous. I also sense a gentleness in you that I cannot explain, but it is there. I can see it, just below the surface. I agreed to ride with you because I wanted to, not because you forced me to. No one can force me into anything I do not wish to do. Or haven't you figured that out yet?"

Blayth could hardly breathe through the pounding in his chest. "I have," he said. "But… are you certain?"

"Very certain."

Asmara's touch was so very gentle, and warm, and it was like nothing he'd ever experienced before. That this beautiful, accomplished woman was saying such things to him was beyond his wildest dreams. He'd never been very good with words, but always much better with actions. The only action he could think of was to take her in his arms and kiss her.

He did.

Enormous, freckled arms pulled her against him as his mouth slanted over hers. Initially, Asmara stiffened with shock and Blayth fully expected a fist to come flying into his jaw, but she didn't hit him. She put her hands up, on his chest as if to push him away, but he simply pulled her closer and suckled her lips with a glorious hunger. It was enough of a hunger that Asmara felt it, too, and soon enough, he could feel her body relax. Slowly, but surely, she began responding to him.

In little time, she was limp and boneless against him.

It was like heaven.

Blayth couldn't remember ever having a woman in his arms like this, so his actions weren't from practice. They were instinctive. It was instinctive that his tongue snaked into her mouth, licking at her, and then feeling the woman tremble in his arms as his kisses became more forceful.

In truth, he was overwhelming her. The scent of her in his nostrils fed the primal beast within, the one that was greatly aroused by a woman. It was the most basic male in him, the one that wanted to mate with her in the worst way, and he put his big hands on her back, between her shoulder blades, and pulled her straight into his seeking mouth. He wasn't feasting on her lips any longer, but on her neck and shoulders, and on the delicate flesh on the swell of her full bosom. The more he tasted, the more he wanted and through it all, Asmara had yet to utter a sound.

She was letting him do whatever he wanted to do.

Blayth was blinded by his lust for her, the soft warmth of her body, and he was thinking about pulling her into the shadows and exploring her even further when one of the horses nickered softly, setting off another horse, and then one of them kicked at the post on his stall. That rattled Blayth's concentration and he loosened his grip, afraid that they were about to be seen. It was early still, and the animals were anticipating their morning meal, which would be coming shortly. Blayth didn't want to be discovered with Asmara in a compromising position by some stable groom.

Before he realized it, they were standing a few feet apart, and Blayth found himself looking into Asmara's flushed face.

"Should I apologize for forcing myself upon you?" he asked quietly.

Asmara was as close to swooning as she had ever been, but she managed to shake her head.

"Nay."

"Good. Because I do not want to."

Asmara swallowed, hard. She didn't know what to say to that. She knew she should be terribly embarrassed, or angry at the very least, but she couldn't seem to manage it. The moment he touched her, it was as if every bone in her body turned to jelly and her mind was laid to waste.

All she could do was let him kiss her.

There was fire in the man's touch that had scorched her to the bone. And because she didn't know how to reply to his statement, as romantic conversation was completely foreign to her, she simply grinned sheepishly and looked away.

Blayth's gaze lingered on her lowered head, smiling at her coy manner. He was deeply relieved that his impulsive action hadn't resulted in a bloodied nose, or worse. All he knew was that he'd wanted to kiss her, so he had. And she had liked it.

He could hardly believe it.

"Then I suppose I should find my horse so we can depart," he said. He turned to his left, realized his horse wasn't in that direction, and then quickly turned right. "Damnable animal keeps moving himself around. He is trying to trick me."

Asmara giggled as Blayth headed down a row of stalls. He was acting about as giddy as she felt, which she thought was rather sweet. She watched him pull forth a dappled gray beast with a fat rump, leading the horse from the stable and out into the stable yard.

Asmara didn't follow him, however, because her horse was still standing there, favoring his right front hoof, so she immediately set about finding a bucket to soak the horse's hoof in. Blayth had said that the grooms would do it, but she didn't want to leave it to chance. While he was preparing his horse, she would tend to hers. Finding a wooden bucket with the remains of grain in it, she blew into it, blowing out the chaff, as she headed out into the stable yard.

Blayth saw her leaving and he called out to her.

"Where are you going?"

Asmara paused, the bucket on her hip. "To find hot water to soak my horse's hoof," she said. "I will be back by the time you finish preparing your horse. Will you make sure to find a groom to tend my horse while we are gone?"

He smiled at her, a toothy grin. "With pleasure, demoiselle."

Asmara fought off a smile as she turned and headed for the keep and the kitchen yards behind it. In fact, she couldn't seem to stop smiling, thinking of Blayth and his kisses, feeling the soft warmth of his lips on hers. Lost in thought, she put her fingers to her lips as if to feel the last place he'd kissed her. She'd never been kissed by a man in her life and her first kiss had definitely been one to remember.

She was ashamed to admit there was something in her that liked it.

The Dragon Princess had a soft woman in her, after all.

The sun continued to rise overhead and the breeze was picking up, pushing puffy clouds across the sky. Somewhere to the east, storm clouds were starting to gather and it was possible they'd have a storm by nightfall, but Asmara wasn't paying any attention to that. She was thinking ahead to the trip to Carmarthen and wondering if Blayth was going to try and kiss her again. Secretly, she hoped so. As she neared the keep, she began to hear someone calling her name. Torn from her daydreams, she turned to see a most unwelcome sight.

Cader was heading in her direction.

Immediately, Asmara went on her guard, knowing that if her father had come all the way to Gwendraith, he must be very mad, indeed. She'd had almost three days before he'd shown his face, but she supposed that she knew, in the end, that he would come for her. Finding her missing at Llandarog, he probably assumed she went home, but when he didn't find her at Talley, then he came looking for her at any one of the recently captured castles. Gwendraith was closest and the logical choice.

Unfortunately, he'd caught her out in the open. There was no running and hiding now. With a heavy sigh, she turned and headed in his direction.

"Greetings, Dadau," she said evenly. "It is a fine morning, is it not?"

Cader looked weary and furious. He was in no mood for his daughter's flippant greeting. "What are you doing here?" he growled. "Why did you leave Llandarog?"

Asmara had been anticipating this question at some point and she was prepared. "Because Llandarog is dead," she said. "There is nothing happening there. The men are lazy and bored. I came to Gwendraith to see if I was needed because, certainly, I am not needed at Llandarog."

Cader's lips were set in a hard, flat line. "That is for me to decide, not you," he hissed. "I need you at Llandarog to oversee the men."

"Nursemaid them, you mean."

His eyes narrowed. "What does that mean?"

She threw up her free hand, the one that wasn't holding the bucket. "It means that an old woman could do the same job you want me to do," she said angrily. "The men at Llandarog do not need a commander; they need a nurse to wipe their noses and settle petty squabbles. I am a warrior, Dadau; I cannot sit around and tend an army of fools."

Cader sighed sharply. "I decide what you will do, Asmara," he snapped. "You do not seem to understand that. In fact, since you are so unhappy at Llandarog, you may return home to your mother and sister. I cannot use a warrior who will not follow my wishes."

Asmara paused; she could do one of two things at that moment. She could fight him, or she could try to ease the situation. Her father was as stubborn as she was and, truth be told, she'd done wrong by leaving. She knew that. But she didn't want to tell him the truth of exactly why she'd left. She would never admit that she'd come to Gwendraith because of a man. Instead, she turned the conversation to something she and her father were joined against – Morys.

"I do not think that would be wise," she said, presenting someone who was much calmer than she had been only moments earlier. "Dadau, I will truthfully tell you why I came. It was something I did not want to speak of to you, but now… now I must."

Cader had no patience for her. "What is it?"

"I am convinced something is very wrong with Morys."

He rolled his eyes. "Nothing is wrong with him," he said. "You simply want to find fault with him because you do not like him."

"Nay, Dadau, not this time," she insisted. "There *is* something wrong. He is up to something."

Cader was still irritated with her, but part of him was the slightest bit interested in what she had to say. Asmara had always proven herself wise and a good judge of character. It was true that she was rash, and bold, and that was just something Cader lived with, but she was also someone he trusted. Therefore, he was inclined to listen to her as long as she wasn't trying to stir up anything.

"*Merch*, I know you do not like your Uncle Morys," he said, less angry than he had been. "As far as him being up to something, he is *always* up to something. That is who he is."

He shook his head and lifted his hands in a futile gesture, as if he didn't quite know how to address that side of his brother's character. Asmara closed the distance between them, putting a hand on his arm.

"This is different than his usual ambition," she said, lowering her voice. "There is something going on that he is not telling anyone, and it centers around Blayth."

Now, she had her father's attention. "What do you mean?"

Asmara was very careful with how much she told him; she had a plan in mind, a plan that would allow her to remain at Gwendraith, and with Blayth, but she had to make it believable to her father or he really would make her return home. And she very much wanted to stay.

Therefore, she rolled out an explanation that was half-truth, half-speculation. She wanted her father to hear what she had heard for the most part, at least enough to convince him that she would be doing right by remaining at Gwendraith.

"I am not entirely certain," she said after a moment, "but I have had a few conversations with Blayth. Do you know he cannot remember anything before he came to live with Morys? He told me that it was Morys who told him he was the bastard son of Llywelyn. That information never came from Blayth; he does not remember if he is or not."

By now, Cader was over his anger at his daughter, listening intently to what she was telling him about his brother and the mysterious warrior known as Blayth the Strong.

"*Morys* told him who he was?" he clarified.

Asmara nodded. "Aye," she said. "I have been asking around and I believe I have the confidence of a few of Morys' men. I want to know what they know about Blayth. It's my belief that Morys is trying to use the man for some greater purpose, like a puppet. He gives orders and Blayth obeys."

Cader wasn't following her. "For what purpose?"

She lifted an eyebrow. "Think about it," she said. "What if Morys is trying to unite Wales under Blayth, but Blayth will have no real power? It will be *Morys* with the power, Dadau."

Cader was looking at her with great skepticism but, on the other hand, it sounded very much like his brother. Morys had always been extremely ambitious and with the bastard son of Llywelyn under his control, the power Morys could wield might be limitless. In truth, he couldn't put anything past the man.

"That is serious speculation," he said. "What proof do you have?"

Asmara shook her head. "None," she said. "All I know is what Blayth has told me and what Morys has told all of us. But it all seems so strange, Dadau… doesn't it?"

Cader had to admit that it did. "And that is why you came here?"

Asmara nodded, even though she was lying about it. "If Morys is trying to gain power, then we should know, shouldn't we?" she said. "And what about Rhys ap Maredudd? He is the one heading this rebellion, but Morys is telling everyone that Blayth is the only true Welsh prince and that he is the one who should lead it. Rhys will not take any of this without a fight and it is possible that Morys will lead us all into a massive civil war – Rhys against Blayth."

It was a horrific thought. But knowing what he did about his brother, none of this was far-fetched. It was not only possible, but probable. With that in mind, Cader suddenly wasn't so angry about Asmara's presence at Gwendraith. The woman had good instincts.

"Then you wish to remain here?" he asked.

"Someone should, don't you think? Someone needs to watch Morys and see what he is planning."

"You could just ask him, you know."

"Do you truly believe he would confess such a thing?"

Cader shook his head reluctantly. "Nay," he said. Then, he sighed heavily. "Very well. You may remain. But you will send word to me if you discover anything."

"I will come and tell you myself if I discover anything."

"I will hold you do that."

He was going to allow her to remain. Asmara struggled against showing the relief she felt.

"You may as well see Morys while you are here," she said. "He returned from Carmarthen two days ago, some kind of secret meetings with Howell, so you should ask him about it. He did not tell me anything."

Cader was never in the mood to speak with his brother, but he thought that might be a good idea.

"I did not know about any meetings at Carmarthen," he said.

"I did not think so."

Cader's gaze trailed up the massive keep as if to see Morys somewhere inside. "I am interested to know what was discussed."

"Then go and ask him," Asmara said. She held up the bucket in her hand. "I am going to the kitchen yard for hot water. My horse has a wound on his hoof that must be soaked. Oh… and if Morys asks you, I told him that you sent me to Gwendraith to see if I could be of any help. That is all he knows."

Cader simply lifted his hand, acknowledging the situation, before heading off to the keep. Asmara stood there a moment, watching him go, wondering what would take place in the coming discussion between her father and his ambitious brother. If Morys felt cornered, or probed, the discussion might not go well at all. Asmara was coming to think that it might be a good idea to remain at Gwendraith to make sure a brotherly meeting didn't turn into a brotherly argument.

That had been known to happen.

Not surprisingly, when she told Blayth that her father had arrived and wanted to know about the meeting with Howell, Blayth thought remaining at Gwendraith as the brothers ap Macsen held their meeting was a good idea, too. The trip into town could wait for another day.

After several long hours of arguing, Cader never did find out the details of Morys' meeting at Carmarthen, only that there was a larger meeting for all of the warlords slated several days later. That was all Morys would tell his frustrated brother, who ended up riding out just before dawn and heading back to his village.

Asmara had seen her father as he'd ridden from Gwendraith, knowing how genuinely upset he was at his brother's secrecy. It gave even more credence to her supposition that Morys was up to something, or even hiding something, and she knew without question that her father would be present at the big meeting at Carmarthen. In fact, he wouldn't miss it.

Something told Asmara that the meeting was going to be a volatile one.

In truth, she had no idea just how volatile.

It would be life changing for them all.

CHAPTER TWELVE

Rhydilian Castle
Isle of Anglesey

BUILT FROM THE black, ancient stone of Wales and rising like a dark beacon out of the forest, Rhydilian Castle sat nestled atop a wooded hill. The very green and very wet land surrounding it for miles was a marshland, and legend said that there was something evil lurking in the marsh. Many claimed to have seen it, a beast that rose up out of the swamp and fed during the full moon. Because of this rumor, no one went near Rhydilian Castle during that time.

It was a legend that made a dark and eerie castle seem even darker and eerier, and the truth was that it wasn't a legend so much as it was fact. Since ancient times, there really had been a creature, or at times creatures, lurking in the swamps surrounding Rhydilian and it was an excellent way to keep an army at bay. Rhydilian had never known a serious siege because of it, making it a rather safe and peaceful place.

Rees de Lohr had arrived at Rhydilian the night before, an exhausted young knight bearing a missive from his father. He'd handed the missive over to Bhrodi de Shera, Earl of Coventry and the hereditary King of Anglesey, and then he'd been taken into the hall where he'd promptly fallen asleep near the hearth. This morning, he was still there, now surrounded by the dogs that lived in the hall, all of them snuggling up to the knight.

This was the scene Bhrodi encountered when he entered the hall after a restless night. A big man with a tight, muscular body and eyes the color of emeralds, Bhrodi snorted when he saw that his young cousin had become the bottom of a dog pile. He'd tried to get the man to rise and sleep in a good bed, but Rees wouldn't move. Now, he was paying the price for being too weary to seek a decent bed.

He was going to smell like a dog.

Leaving the knight and his canine friends, Bhrodi headed for the solar of Rhydilian, a small, circular chamber near the entry that had been used by generations of his ancestors. His hereditary title came from his mother's side, as she was the only child of the last King of Anglesey, and his earldom came from his father's side. He had a half-dozen very close cousins on that side, men who were English to the bone and men he trusted to rule his earldom fairly and justly, because he felt it was more important to have a presence in Wales as one of the last true Welsh princes. A prince would outrank an earl every time, even an English earl, so Bhrodi remained in Wales as a beacon of hope and strength to the Welsh people.

But with that beacon of hope and strength came grave responsibilities.

The missive from Chris sat on the large, cluttered table in the solar. As soon as Bhrodi entered the chamber, he could see it. He'd left it here last night and had gone to bed, hopefully to sleep on the news he'd received and awaken with a fresh perspective. But he found that this morning his perspective wasn't any fresher or any clearer. The news from Chris was so serious that he'd not even told his wife about it, although it affected her more than it affected him. A de Wolfe brother had returned from the dead, Chris had said. Bhrodi's wife was a de Wolfe, and the missive spoke of a brother she had lost five years ago.

At least, that was what she believed.

In any case, Bhrodi needed to be very careful when he gave her the news.

He hadn't told her last night for a variety of reasons, but not the least of which was the fact that she was busy with their two children, three-year-old William and the infant, Perri, who had seen seven months. Both of them had a slight case of the sniffles, and Perri was teething, making for two miserable children. Bhrodi's wife, Penelope, had two nurses that helped her with the children, and all three of them had been up for most of the night soothing the boys, who were sleeping peacefully this morning. Bhrodi hoped his wife was sleeping peacefully, too, as he'd not seen her since he went to bed. She'd spent the night in the boys' chamber.

As Bhrodi patiently waited for her to rise, he attended to other things, including a missive he'd received from Howell ap Gruffydd several weeks earlier. Howell was a warlord in the south of Wales and a man of a minor royal Welsh family, his bloodlines diluted by generations. Even so, he held a good deal of power in the south along with Rhys ap Maredudd, another minor Welsh prince who, according to Howell's missive, was beginning to stir up another rebellion. But it wasn't the rebellion or the request for support that had Bhrodi's eye this morning – it was the mention of a bastard son of Llywelyn the Last, a man named Blayth the Strong.

Bhrodi had been shocked to see that name not only on Howell's missive, but on Chris de Lohr's. Howell spoke of Llywelyn's bastard, a man who would rally all of Wales for one final push against the English, while Chris' missive spoke of Blayth as the long-dead de Wolfe son, James. Bhrodi had read both missives side by side last night, first one and then the other, trying to figure out what was going on. Howell made no mention of de Wolfe, in any form, while Chris said he had an eyewitness who identified the man calling himself Blayth as James de Wolfe.

It was astonishing information.

Bhrodi had never met James. He had died the year before Bhrodi married Penelope. The de Wolfe family was a very close-knit group, and Bhrodi had been told how James' death had devastated the entire family. Penelope had told him that her father had never gotten over the death, so to hear that the man might quite possibly be alive was truly staggering. Even more staggering was that he was posing as a Welshman and claiming to be the bastard of the last true Welsh prince.

It was a baffling mystery.

In truth, Bhrodi wasn't entirely sure how his wife would take the information, but he had to tell her. Chris had asked for an urgent meeting, for Bhrodi to come to Lioncross, and Bhrodi was inclined to agree. This information needed an urgent meeting because things had to be clarified. If a man had returned from the dead, that was one thing. But if he was posing as a Welsh prince and inspiring a rebellion, it was quite another.

With thoughts of dead brothers and Welsh princes on his mind, Bhrodi broke his fast with some bread and warmed wine, pondering the land outside his window as the sun rose. He could smell smoke in the air, wafting in through his window, which was coming from the cooking fires of the nearby village. As he stood at the window with the warm cup in his hand, sipping on it and thinking of the chaos happening in the south of Wales, he began to hear his wife's voice.

He was surprised she was awake so early, given the sick children she had been up with the night before. But Penelope was in the hall, giving instructions to the servants and her voice grew louder as she came closer. He could hear her speaking of taking porridge up to the children and of hot water for their baths. He turned away from the window about the time she entered the solar.

Bhrodi smiled at his wife. Every time he looked at the woman, his heart fluttered anew. That had never changed, the thrill of seeing the person he loved best in the world. She was a de Wolfe to the bone, bred from excellent stock, and as beautiful as a new morning with her dark brown hair and hazel eyes that were gold in certain light. Both of their children had inherited those de Wolfe eyes.

But Penelope was no ordinary woman; because she was a de Wolfe and came from a family of great knights, her father had indulged her and she, too, was raised as a knight. As the baby of the family, William could not deny his daughter anything, so the result was a beautiful woman who could fight with the best of them.

Bhrodi had tamed the fighting streak in her somewhat, especially when the children were born, but he still wouldn't tangle with her. He was very proud of his wife who could fight as well as, if not better, than most men.

"Good morn, *caria*," he said sweetly. His pet name for her was *caria*, which meant love in Welsh. "How are the boys this morning?"

Dressed in a soft yellow surcoat, her lovely hair wound and pinned at the nape of her neck, she didn't look as if she'd been up most of the night. She came to her husband, putting her arms around him as she kissed him sweetly.

"They are perfectly fine," she said, a weary twinkle in her eye. "It is as if nothing is amiss. William is demanding his toy soldiers and the baby wants to eat, so everything is normal once again."

Bhrodi gave her a squeeze before releasing her. "And how is their mother?"

She grinned. "I am perfectly fine, too," she said. Then, she yawned. "Although I am going to sleep this afternoon when they do. Mayhap you will join me?"

He could see the suggestive expression on her face and knew exactly what she meant. He was quite agreeable. "It would be my pleasure, literally," he said, a seductive hint to his voice. "In fact, I believe an afternoon like that is how we had Perri."

Penelope giggled. "Mayhap we shall have a girl this time."

"You promised me twelve sons. We have ten more to go."

Penelope rolled her eyes and Bhrodi snorted at her, touching her hand affectionately as he made his way over to his cluttered table. Penelope followed and, seeing the remnants of bread and cheese on a plate, took a piece of cheese and popped it in her mouth. He handed her the warmed wine still in his hand, and she accepted it gratefully.

As Bhrodi reached his table, the first thing he noticed were the two missives, reminding him of the pressing matters weighing upon him.

He was aware that he had to tell Penelope what he knew, but he honestly wasn't sure where to begin. Reaching down, he picked up the missive from Howell. Perhaps it was best to start with that one before leading into de Lohr's.

"In truth, I am glad you are here," he said. "There is something I must discuss with you."

Penelope looked up from her cheese. "Oh? What is it?"

He held up Howell's yellowed vellum. "Do you remember the missive I received from Howell last month?"

Penelope nodded. "I do," she said. "He asked for your support in some rebellion. You are planning on taking your army into the south because of it."

Bhrodi looked at the vellum as he set it back to the table. "I should have already left," he said. "He asked for my support weeks ago."

"Then why have you not gone?"

He sighed faintly and sat down. "I am not entirely sure," he said. "Howell mentioned the rising rebellion, and Rhys ap Maredudd's plan to starve out Pembroke. But he also mentioned some man I have never heard of who is claiming to be the bastard son of Llywelyn ap Gruffydd, the last prince of Wales. Do you recall?"

Again, Penelope nodded. "I think so," she said. "What about him?"

That was the question he had been looking for, a way to tell her everything in a normal conversation rather than dump the information on her in a dramatic burst. This news was so shocking that it wasn't something he could just come out with. In truth, he was genuinely fearful for her reaction. With that on his mind, he rose from his chair.

"Interesting that you should ask that question," he said. "You know that there is always some fool claiming to be a Welsh prince and trying to drive rebellion, so mayhap that is why I have not been so quick to move on this. I cannot support every man that claims he is Welsh royalty, so I have been waiting to see how this new rebellion takes root. Will it grow? Or will it die? I have been waiting to see, I suppose, because the name Blayth the Strong means nothing to me. But then, yesterday, I received a missive from Chris de Lohr. His son, Rees, brought it. Did you see him sleeping in the hall?"

The light of recognition went on in Penelope's eyes. "Is *that* who that is?" she asked. "He is crammed into a corner near the hearth, with dogs all around him. I did not recognize him."

Bhrodi grinned. "Aye, that is Rees," he said. "His father has some interesting things to say about the rebellion rising in the south."

Penelope was interested. "Oh?" she said. "Has he been attacked?"

"Not yet."

"Then what does he say?"

Here it comes, Bhrodi thought. He was trying desperately to be tactful.

"Do you know a knight by the name of Corbett Payton-Forrester?" he asked.

Penelope immediately nodded. "I do," she said. "His family is close to our family."

"How *well* do you know him?"

She shrugged. "Well enough," she said. "He is older, so he and my older brothers were great friends. He and his brothers would come to our home frequently."

"Then he would know all of your brothers well?" Bhrodi ventured. "Scott? Troy? Patrick? James?"

Penelope nodded her head. "Aye, of course," she said. "Why do you ask? What is this all about?"

Bhrodi paused a moment, considering how to continue. "Payton-Forrester was a garrison commander at one of the castles that the Welsh overran," he said. "He was kept prisoner for a while before being released. He returned to de Lohr with a message from the rebellion, but he also returned with some… news."

"What news?"

With a sigh, Bhrodi reached out and took his wife's hand, caressing it. "Payton-Forrester came into contact with this man calling himself Blayth the Strong, the same man mentioned in Howell's missive," he said. "He swore to de Lohr that Blayth the Strong is, in fact, your brother, James."

Penelope stared at him. For a moment, she didn't react. But the seconds ticked away and as his words sank in, her eyes suddenly widened.

"*What*?" she hissed. "That is not possible!"

Bhrodi let go of her hand and reached over his table, picking up the missive and handing to her. He didn't say a word as she snatched it from him and started reading it, greedily, and when she came to the part about her brother, she gasped. Bhrodi couldn't tell whether it was a gasp of horror or one of delight, but he suspected the former. Her hands began to shake as she read the missive again before finally handing it back to her husband.

Bhrodi took the missive from her, watching her face, noting that she looked rather pale and sick.

"*Caria*?" he asked softly. "Speak to me. What are you thinking?"

Penelope didn't know what she was thinking, only that she was swimming in the vast and unsteady sea of disbelief.

"I… I do not know," she finally said. "God, Bhrodi, I do not know. It cannot be true!

He put a comforting hand on her shoulder. "Would Payton-Forrester have made such a mistake?"

Penelope was struggling to keep her composure. "I would hope not," she said. "But I cannot say for certain. With something as serious as this, I would sincerely hope not."

Bhrodi stroked her shoulder. "As would I," he said. "If he knows your family well, then he knows your brother was killed at Llandeilo. Was he, in fact, at Llandeilo when James was lost?"

She lifted her slender shoulders. "I do not think so," she said, "but *you* were."

Bhrodi nodded, resisting the urge to hang his head. He had, indeed, been present at Llandeilo when James had been killed. It was something he'd had to reconcile with William and the rest of the House of de

Wolfe, and no one had ever suggested he was accountable for James' death. It was simply a battle, like any other, and it had been well before Bhrodi and Penelope had married, before they had all become family. In fact, it wasn't even something that was even discussed any longer so he knew that Penelope bringing it up wasn't a malicious attempt. It was simply fact.

He *had* been there.

"I was," he said quietly, "but you know I was tied up with Gloucester's army. I never once saw the de Wolfe army until the end, when they were retreating. I had my own problems at that time, so I never saw the de Wolfe dead or wounded."

Penelope knew that. "I suppose the point I was making was that my father and brothers were forced to retreat," she said, pain in her eyes. "Papa held James as long as he could before my brothers forced him away. He said that Uncle Kieran tried to pick James up and carry him, but that he, too, was forced to drop him. I've always said that Papa never got over James' death, but the truth was that it wasn't just his death. It was the fact that he had to leave him behind. He did not have a body to bring to my mother or to Rose, James' wife. And with no body..."

Bhrodi was aware of the point she was making. No body, no confirmed death, so it was entirely possible that James had survived.

"I cannot say that I would ever get over having to leave my son behind on the battlefield," he said. "I do not know who fought against de Wolfe at Llandeilo and I do not know what would have become of your brother's body. You have never asked me to find out, but it seems now as if there is some question as to whether or not the man was even killed. You said that Payton-Forrester knew James well. If so, then surely he would know the man on sight. He would know if Blayth the Strong was, in fact, your brother."

Penelope was so overwhelmed with the thought that she could hardly think straight. "Oh... Bhrodi," she finally breathed. There was anguish in her voice as her carefully held composure began to crack. "I suppose it is possible that he did not die, since we never had his body to bury. My God… what if James did *not* die? What if Papa left him behind and he lived? Do you know how that will tear my father apart?"

She was starting to cry now. Bhrodi took a knee beside her chair and put his arm around her shoulders to comfort her. "Chris has asked that I come to Lioncross Abbey," he said softly. "He feels that it is important enough to discuss it face to face, and I agree. We must discover the truth about Blayth the Strong, one way or the other, because the man is feeding a rising rebellion against the English."

Penelope looked at him, tears spilling down her cheeks. "But what if it really *is* James?"

He kissed her on the forehead. "I swear to you that I will find out," he said. "But until I do, you must not tell your father. There is no sense in worrying the man if there is nothing to worry over. At least, not yet."

Penelope wasn't really listening to him because she was lost in a maelstrom of her own fear and speculation. "If it is my brother, why has he not come home?" she wept. "Why did he stay in Wales? Does he think we do not love him? Bhrodi – what if he thinks we do not love him because Papa left him behind?"

It was such a tragic thought, one that upset her deeply, and Bhrodi put his arms around her. He felt so very badly for her sorrow.

"There is no use in fretting until we can confirm the truth," he said again. "Once we know if it is your brother or not, then you can ask your questions."

She wiped at her wet face. She knew he was right, but she was so very upset by the entire circumstance. "When are you leaving?"

"Right away."

"I am going with you."

Bhrodi knew she might say something like that. "Nay, *caria*," he said firmly. "You must stay with the boys."

But Penelope would not be discouraged. From tears one moment to demands the next, she would not let him discourage her. "I *must* go," she insisted. "The children will be fine with their nurses. I must do this,

Bhrodi. I must see for myself if it is James."

"Do you not trust me to discover the truth?"

"Of course I do," she said. "But you do not know my brother on sight. I would recognize him in an instant."

Bhrodi sighed heavily, mostly because she was right. She would know her brother on sight, and he had a feeling she wouldn't rest until she did. This was the chance he'd taken by telling her the contents of the missives, and now he was facing that which he feared – she was demanding to come with him. He didn't want her to, but he knew he couldn't keep her away. If he denied her, she would only follow him.

Eyeing her, he stood up.

"You are not going to give me a choice, are you?" he asked.

Penelope could see that he was displeased. Standing up, she went to him, putting her hands on his arm. It was, perhaps, the most important thing that had ever happened to the de Wolfe family, and he had to know just how serious she was about this.

The loss of James was an event in her family's history that had shaped all of them and changed them forever. They'd lost James, the gentle but fierce brother, and Penelope had such fond memories of him. He would ride her around on his war horse when she was younger and receive his mother's wrath because of it. He was easily bent to her will, and would play with her or give her sweets, and then pretend to fight his brother, Patrick, for the title of Favored Brother. Penelope remembered very well that they would trade off "killing" one another for her favor. God, she had loved him. If there was even a chance James had survived Llandeilo, then she had to know.

They *all* had to know.

"I *am* giving you a choice," she said after a moment, "but I am begging you to allow me to come. Bhrodi… I loved my brother very much. He was kind and generous and humorous, and I miss him every day. Please do not deny me the chance to see him again if, in fact, it is really him. You cannot know what this means to me."

Bhrodi rolled his eyes in defeat. "As I said, I have no choice," he said, but he wasn't angry about it. Simply resigned. "You had better hurry and pack, then. We will travel light and swift, so keep that in mind. I plan to make it to Lioncross in just a few days, so the travel will be difficult."

Penelope was very eager to go and relieved he wasn't giving her grief about it. In truth, she knew he understood her need to know the truth.

"I will endure, I promise," she said.

"You had better endure," he said. "One complaint and I shall send you home."

Penelope knew he wasn't serious, but she also knew he wasn't keen on her going. Throwing her arms around his neck, she kissed him swiftly and fled the solar before he could change his mind.

Bhrodi watched her go, thinking on the journey ahead and the wife he was now bringing along. After the shock and tears had faded, he could see the hope in her eyes, hope that the rumors were true and it really was her brother.

Still, Bhrodi was leery about it. Men had been wrong before and he would hate to see her so disappointed. But something told him that in any case, disappointment would be inevitable for one very good reason – a man who let his family believe he was dead was not a man who wanted to be found.

As Bhrodi prepared the escort party for the trip to Lioncross, Penelope was doing something he'd asked her not to do. He'd told her not to tell her father about any of this until they could confirm that James de Wolfe was, indeed, alive, but all Penelope could think of was how devastated her father had been when James had been killed. Penelope knew, as the entire family knew, that it was something her father had never recovered from.

Having two small sons of her own, Penelope could only imagine how she would feel if one of her sons had been killed. She also knew that if there was even a chance he had not been killed, and that he was still alive somewhere, she would desperately want to know. It simply wasn't fair to keep her father in the dark in a matter of such importance, especially when it came to James.

Sweet James.

Therefore, against her husband's wishes, Penelope wrote a missive to her father while Bhrodi was busy with preparations for their departure to Lioncross. She paid one of the stable grooms handsomely to take the missive north to Castle Questing, and the young man was more than happy to do it, slipping from Rhydilian's postern gate, following the River Nodwydd until he came to a road that would take him towards the mainland. It was going to take him a week at the very least to reach Castle Questing, and Lady de Shera had insisted it was a matter of life or death.

When Penelope left with her husband and Rees de Lohr the next morning in the early dawn hours, it was with the knowledge that her father would soon know what she knew.

James had risen from the dead.

CHAPTER THIRTEEN

Gwendraith Castle

SHE WAS SHORT and pretty, with dark brown hair.

And she was pelting him with snowballs.

Visions of a castle he didn't know, and those same people whose names he couldn't remember, were in his dreams again. There was a pretty little girl with long hair crying about snow in her ear, and then there was a one-eyed man hugging him. He'd seen that man in his dreams many times, but he had no idea who he was. All he knew was that he loved him, but he'd stopped trying long ago to remember the man's name.

He never could.

And then he was getting amorous with the girl with the dark brown hair. He could feel her soft skin in his hands, and he had feelings for her. He wasn't sure if it was lust or love or something else, but that girl brought about arousal in him and the intense feeling of attraction. He'd dreamed about her before, too. And in his dreams, she was something special to him. In truth, she had been his only experience with a woman that he could recall, a dream lover who had captured his attention.

But the dreams with his dream lover in them turned into something else. This often happened, too – his dreams would be those of nameless people he loved and then it would shift to a battle. Or, sometimes it was just the battle and nothing more. He could hear men screaming and fighting over his head as he lay on the ground. Fighting and more fighting.

Atty!

Scott!

Names that meant nothing to him, but he felt like they should.

In his dream, he could taste fear but he couldn't move. Someone was trying to pick him up off the ground, but he fell away. He was conscious, hearing everything, but he couldn't move. He couldn't speak. But he had the greatest sense of loneliness he'd ever known, and as his dream faded into mist, all he could feel was a profound sense of loss. It left him feeling hollow and shattered, with a pain in his heart that he couldn't describe. All he knew was that he felt… lost.

And then he awoke.

His heart was pounding, and he was sitting up in bed. Blayth didn't even remember sitting up, but he was. There was sweat on his brow and he wiped at his face, trying to settle down. God, he hated these dreams. He had them frequently. It seemed that when he went to sleep, he entered another world, all his own. He spent his days in the real world and the nights in a world of people he didn't know and fearsome battles that left him breathless.

He really hated that dream world, because it left him feeling sad and worn.

Blayth knew he couldn't go back to sleep again. That was the curse of his vivid dreams. If he did, he'd fall right back into the same dream and wake up in a panic again. Therefore, he endeavored to remain awake. It was probably only an hour or two before dawn, anyway. There was no reason to return to sleep and suffer through another battle and more panic, or try to remember people he didn't know.

His chamber was just off the entry of Gwendraith's keep. It had been a guard room when they first took over the castle, but he transformed it into his bed chamber. That way, he was the first to hear of anything from the outer ward and the first man out of the keep if need be.

Climbing out of bed, he lit the taper on the bedside table. Before pulling on his leather breeches and long tunic, he headed to the basin to splash some water on his face and hair. Hair wet, he raked it back over his lumpy skull, or at least the left side of it was lumpy from the damage. There was a small piece of broken mirror that had been left behind at Gwendraith and he picked it up, gazing at his reflection.

Sometimes, he would stare at himself and wonder just who he really was. Morys called him Blayth, and although he'd gone along with Morys' explanation about his past, he wondered quite often if that was really true. Something told him that all of those people he didn't recognize in his dreams and the woman with the dark brown hair were all part of his past and had nothing to do with being a captive and tortured by the English. Something told him that his past was filled with better things than that.

The keep was quiet at this hour. He was awake, but he didn't want to go about his duties yet. It was rare when he had moments of quiet like this, to relax and ponder his thoughts. Against the wall, and piled with his possessions, was a variation on a citole, a stringed musical instrument that he'd been given. For some reason, Blayth's ability to sing and play an instrument had never left him, and it was something he enjoyed doing from time to time. He could remember so many songs and sing them quite ably. Picking up the instrument, which he hadn't played in a long while, he took it with him as he headed out to the hall.

Men were sleeping on the fringes of the great hall, along with packs of scruffy-looking dogs, but Blayth didn't pay any attention to them. His chamber was rather cramped and close, and he didn't feel like spending any amount of time there, so he'd come out to the hall where the fire was dying and men were snoring.

Sitting down at the old feasting table, he kicked back his legs and leaned against the tabletop as he began to pick at the strings of the citole. A haunting melody came to mind and he quietly began to sing.

Come roam with me, my love,
Come roam far with me,
Away from this hard world,
And love only me.

His voice was rousing a few of the men, who began stirring in their sleep. He plucked a few more chords before starting the second verse.

They said that you loved me,
They said that you cared.
They said that your strong heart,
Wasn't mine to be shared.

More men stirred, coughing as they began to awaken to the sound of Blayth's beautiful baritone singing voice. He didn't care a lick that he had awakened them, so he continued to sit there and hum the song, thinking of the coming day. He had great hopes of seeing Asmara and, perhaps, even taking that trip into Carmarthen that had been put off after the arrival of her father.

Even though there had been no great argument between Morys and Cader the day before, it was clear that not all was well between them. Cader wanted information from Morys' meeting with Howell, but Morys told him very little other than the coming planned meeting at Carmarthen Castle next month.

Frustrated, Cader finally left Gwendraith in the late afternoon, heading to Carmarthen Castle to ask Howell personally what had been discussed between him and Morys, a move that utterly angered Morys. He liked to feel special, as if he was the only one privy to such inside information, but Cader wasn't going to let him get away with it. He was part of this rebellion, too, and risking his men just as Morys was risking his. Therefore, he'd stormed off before sunset for the short ride to Carmarthen.

But Asmara had remained.

Blayth's thoughts turned to the elegant creature everyone called the Dragon Princess. To him, she was becoming so much more than that. Their kiss yesterday had been an event that had changed something within him. He couldn't believe she wasn't repulsed by his big, scarred body, or his slow and sometimes hesitant speech. She had called him handsome.

No one had ever called him that before.

She hadn't objected to his kiss, either. In fact, she seemed to enjoy it. He knew that he certainly did. She was the first kiss he'd ever had outside of his dream lover, but nothing with his dream lover had ever been so satisfying.

He knew he had to kiss Asmara again.

Kiss her and more. He'd never been one to think of marriage, but when he looked at Asmara, he was starting to think of such things. He couldn't imagine not spending his life with her by his side, that strong and beautiful woman. She had endeared herself deeply to his damaged, confused soul, so much so that he knew he never wanted to be without her.

Odd thoughts for the usually solitary man.

Sitting back against the tabletop, he continued to strum his citole and think of Asmara ferch Cader. The hall was stirring around him, with men starting to rise for the day thanks to Blayth's music. There were even a few grumbles and dirty looks in his direction. But he didn't care, lost in a world of Asmara, and wondering what she looked like under the baggy clothing she wore.

As he continued to strum and think on golden-eyed beauties, he caught movement out of the corner of his eye at the hall entry and looked over just in time to see Asmara passing by the entry, heading out of the keep.

He was on his feet in an instant.

Quickly, he made his way back to his chamber to drop off the citole before leaving the keep, following Asmara's path. It was quite early for her to be awake, with the eastern horizon just starting to lighten. There was a heavy dew in the air and the grass was wet, and his breath hung in the air in puffs of mist as Blayth continued to follow the woman from the inner ward and into the outer ward beyond.

He could see that she was heading for the stable, no doubt to check on her horse with the wounded hoof. Blayth continued to follow her at a distance. He was thinking of their kiss, of the day that followed, including sup that night where they'd sat in relative silence because Morys was upset about Cader, and Asmara didn't want to draw the man's ire.

In fact, she'd only stayed long enough to eat her meal before fleeing the hall and retreating to the chamber she'd been sleeping in. Blayth didn't go after her, though; once she was gone, Morys began talking and he didn't shut up until late in the night. After that, it was too late to see to her.

Fortunately, she was up early this morning.

The outer ward sloped downward and it was slippery from the early morning dampness, and Blayth struggled not to slip on the slick mud as he followed Asmara to the stable. He was far enough back from her that she didn't hear him, nor did she notice, as she seemed singularly focused on reaching the stable. Once she disappeared inside the darkened structure that smelled heavily of hay and animals, Blayth came to a halt just outside the door, peering inside to see where she had gone.

He was stalking her.

Inside the stable, he could hear animals stirring as daylight approached. He could also hear Asmara moving around. He remained just outside the stable entry, pressed against the wall, hearing her soft voice as she spoke to the horse. Peering around the corner again, he saw her come forth with her horse, bringing him into an open area of the stable where she could tend to his hoof. When she tied up the horse and headed back into a corner of the stable to collect a bucket, he made his move.

Blayth knew he had to be careful when he ambushed her because it was dark, and he would startle her, and he didn't want to end up missing an eye. So, he moved swiftly and quietly, and came up behind her just as she was bending down to pick something up. He tapped her on the shoulder and when she gasped and turned around, he threw his arms around her and kissed her.

But it wasn't just any kiss – it was heated and sexy, and the moment her scent filled his nostrils, it was as if a fire sparked deep inside him. Asmara's moment of surprise was quickly replaced by a response that saw her arms wind around his neck as she returned his feverish kiss. He even heard her giggle, low in her throat, and it fed his lust. Picking her off the ground, he carried her over into the last stall, which was quite dark at this hour, and pulled her down into the corner.

As he kissed her deeply, his hands started to wander. The tunic she wore was heavy against the cold morning, but he didn't try to go through it. He simply went under it, snaking his hands beneath it until he came to her warm, naked belly. She flinched when he touched her skin. But instead of pulling from him in fear, she simply let him do as he wished, as his instincts dictated. She didn't resist.

She wanted it as badly as he did.

Blayth's hands seemed to have a mind of their own. He was a red-blooded man, with all of the needs of a man, and there were appetites inside of him that he'd kept repressed. They hadn't been fed in any recent memory and now they were beginning to roar. As he suckled on her lips, he shoved her back into the corner of the stall to trap her, and his hands pulled up her tunic so that it was bunched around her waist as his hands moved to her full, soft breasts.

Both hands clamped down on her breasts and Asmara gasped. For a brief moment, she tried to push him away, unbalance by the intimate touch, but his hands were warm and gentle, and her body quickly relaxed. Blayth could feel her trembling beneath his touch as he kneaded her breasts, pinching her nipples.

All the while, his kisses were passionate and heated, and he had a raging erection that had happened fairly quickly. There was no way he could touch the woman's delicious body and not react physically to her. All he could think of was satisfying himself, and of the contentment he would feel buried within her slick folds. Somehow, he managed to pull her out of the corner and lay her down on the dried grass of the stall. When she weakly tried to protest, he buried his head beneath her tunic and, in the darkness, his mouth latched on to a tender nipple.

Asmara's protests died in her throat as he suckled her breasts, giving her pleasure that she'd never known before. In fact, she was letting him do whatever he wished and hardly uttering a word about it. Her body, young and strong and virile, was responding to his touch, and when his hands moved from her breasts and found their way into her hose, she still didn't protest. It appeared she was without thought, without any opinions whatsoever. All she wanted to do was lay there and enjoy what he was doing to her, and Blayth was more than happy to comply.

He had her where he wanted her.

The skin of her buttocks and thighs was soft beyond measure, warm and inviting. His big hands gripped her buttocks first, squeezing them as he continued to suckle on her breasts but, before long, he was moving to the intimate junction between her legs. It was warm and safe and inviting down there and she trembled at his touch, even more when he stroked her with a finger. But that touch also seemed to awaken her from her haze of passion, for the long legs started to kick and she struggled to pull away from him.

"Nay," she breathed. "We must not… you must not…"

His response was to suckle her harder. His hand was between her legs even as she tried to move away and he inserted a finger into her love-slick passage. Asmara gasped aloud at the sensual intrusion and she very quickly succumbed to his touch once more. Whatever he was doing to her was making her legs tremble, as if she had no control over them. And as his fingers probed her, the sensations he brought about dashed every thought out of her head.

She couldn't fight him off, not even if she wanted to.

As she lay there with his hand between her legs, his head emerged from beneath her tunic and he began kissing her again, oh-so-gently. Between his tender probing and his gentle kisses, Asmara was like mud in his hands. She had no bones, no will of her own. But that soon came to a startling end when voices were heard.

Men were entering the stables, preparing to feed the animals, and Blayth abruptly stopped what he was doing and quickly yanked Asmara's breeches up. She, too, was scrambling to her knees, pulling her breeches up and her tunic down, and Blayth stood up, seeing where the grooms were. Holding out a hand to Asmara, telling her to stay down and stay quiet, he headed out into the main part of the stable.

He made a preemptive move against the grooms, announcing himself as he came from the darkness. The grooms were surprised to see him but he pointed to Asmara's horse, explaining the wound on the hoof that he'd come to tend. It was a bald-faced lie, but he had to say something. He then asked for help with the animal, sending one man for hot water and salt, while the other man went to the grain stores to get buckets of oats for the horses. When the men were out of the stable as they headed about their business, Blayth quickly went to the stall where Asmara was hiding and extended a hand to her.

She took it.

Quietly, he pulled her to her feet, holding her hand in his as he led her back over to her horse.

"One of them has gone for hot water so you can soak the horse's hoof," he said quietly, looking to the entry to the stables to see if anyone else was coming in. "You can be here, ready to tend your animal, when he returns."

He turned to look at her in the growing light of morning only to realize that she was covered in hay and chaff. Swiftly, he began to brush her off, turning her around so he could sweep off the entire backside of her as she quickly moved to do the same on her front half.

"God's Bones," she muttered. "I look as if I have slept with the animals. They are going to know what we have been doing!"

Blayth shook his head to dispute her until she pointed at him and he, too, realized that he was covered in chaff. Then he started beating at his own clothing to shake it off, but as he swept and brushed and beat, he began to laugh.

"I do not mind for myself, of course," he said. "But I would hate for anyone to think ill of you. And it would not be particularly healthy to have it get back to your father."

Asmara reached out to brush off his left shoulder. "Nay, it would not," she said. "He would make me go back to Llandarog for certain if he thought… well, if he thought I was compromised in any way."

Blayth watched her as she finished brushing herself off. "I am not sorry I kissed you," he said quietly. "I very much wanted to. But the rest of it… if you were uncomfortable, then I apologize. It will not happen again."

She blushed, finding it difficult to look at him. "If my father found out what we have done, he would probably force you to marry me."

"Who says I will not?"

The coy smile vanished from her face and she looked at him, eyes wide with shock. "Marriage?" she repeated. "Who has said anything about marriage?"

He chuckled. "You just did."

"I did not mean it as an offer."

"I did."

Asmara had no idea what to say to him. Her eyes were wide and now her jaw was hanging open, genuinely astonished by the words coming out of his mouth. After a moment, she simply shook her head.

"You must be mad," she finally hissed. "Who would want to marry a woman like me? No man wants a wife who can best him in a fight."

Blayth cocked an eyebrow. "Who told you that?"

Her father had, but she didn't want to throw him to the wolves. She shrugged her shoulders. "Everyone knows that. Everyone says it."

"I do not say it," he said. "Moreover, you cannot best me."

She closed her mouth, not looking so surprised now. "Of course I can," she said. "What would make you think that I cannot?"

"What makes *you* think you can?"

She was full of outrage as he snorted, laughing at her, and she couldn't decide whether to laugh at him in return or challenge him. The warrior in her demanded a challenge.

"You have insulted me for the last time," she said. "Now I will have to challenge you to a battle since you seem so keen on offending my honor."

He wasn't finished laughing. "Is that so?"

"It is!"

"If you wish it, demoiselle," he said. "What is the weapon of choice?"

Asmara was genuinely irritated at a man who would laugh at her abilities as a warrior. "The staff," she said. "If I win, you will declare to everyone that I am the greatest warrior you have ever known so that there will be no doubt."

He nodded. "Very well," he said. "And when I win, you will marry me and stop this warrior's life. I would have you as my wife, not as a fellow soldier."

She lost some of her humor then. "But… but I have always been a warrior," she said seriously. "You cannot ask me to give that up. I do not know what I would do without it."

"I do not want my wife on the field of battle."

"Then I shall not be your wife."

"Aye, you shall."

She put her hands on her hips in growing frustration. "I do not agree to your terms."

He matched her, stubborn against stubborn. "*You* are the one who challenged *me*," he said. "I have agreed to your terms. It is very bad form for you not to agree to mine."

For the first time, Asmara began to back away, uncertain with his demands. Was he jesting? Was he not?

"Please," she said softly. "I cannot be any less than what I am. I would not be happy."

Blayth could see the genuine sorrow in her eyes and he was coming to feel badly. He hadn't meant to upset her, but he was fairly serious about not having a warrior wife. He would be worried every minute of every day if he did, worried that she might be injured or killed. He couldn't live with himself if that happened.

Faintly, he sighed.

"But you *will* marry me."

She gazed at him, her eyes like pools of undulating emotion. "If I do not have to give up what I have always known, I would be agreeable."

Blayth felt a wave of joy wash over him. The woman was actually agreeable to marrying him in spite of their different opinions on what a wife should, or should not, do. He'd never felt such elation in his entire life. All jesting aside, it was a monumental moment.

"You would?" he murmured.

She nodded. The irritation was out of her expression. All he could see was honestly in her features.

"Aye," she whispered.

"Truly?"

"Aye."

He took a step in her direction, his eyes riveted to her. "You do not care of my past?" he muttered. "You know that I do not know the truth of where I come from or who I am. This does not bother you?"

She shook her head. "Nay. I know all I need to know about you."

"And you would not be ashamed of me?"

"Never. And I will kill anyone who would say otherwise."

It was like music to his ears. He could hardly believe it. "My sweet girl," he said. "I never thought I would know a moment such as this. Now that it is here, I can hardly comprehend it."

Asmara fought off a grin, seeing her own excitement and disbelief reflected in his features. "My father will not believe it, either," she said. "All he wants is grandsons. Now he may actually have some."

Blayth smiled. "God willing," he said. "But do you still wish to fight me?"

She giggled, lowering her gaze. "I suppose it is not necessary since I have already agreed to your condition," she said. "Will I have to give up my warrior ways?"

He shook his head. "I would not wish for you to be less than who you are," he said. "But when those grandsons come along, I will ask that you do not fight whilst the child grows in your belly. Will you at least agree to that for me?"

She pursed her lips petulantly, but it was short-lived. "If I must."

"It would make me happy."

"Then I would wish to make you happy."

He simply smiled at her, joy in his heart that he could not describe. "Thank you for this honor, demoiselle," he said softly. "I shall endeavor to be a good husband and to always make you proud."

It was a sweet thing to say and Asmara was deeply touched. In fact, she was rather overwhelmed with the entire conversation, which had been quite unexpected. But nothing had ever felt so right. In her heart, it felt right and true. She'd known many men, and a few had tried to court her, but she'd never felt in her heart and soul that it was the right thing to do. But with Blayth… there was no reservation whatsoever. She cared for him and she knew he cared for her. They could have a wonderful life together.

Except for one thing.

"You know that Morys will not be happy about this," she said. "Blayth, I know he saved your life and he shall always have my gratitude because of it, but he does not wish for us to be together. We both know it."

His smile faded. "He has made that clear," he said honestly. "In fact, that is why he has kept me by his side for the past few days. He wants that my focus should be on him, and on the rebellion, and not you. I saw how he spoke to you when he returned from Carmarthen. He will not do that again, Asmara. I swear it."

Asmara. It was the first time she'd heard her name from his lips and it sounded like the angels singing. She'd never heard her name said the way he'd pronounced it. Or perhaps she'd never noticed anyone else as they'd said it. Some men had said it sweeter, some harsher… who knew? Whatever the case, to hear her name from his mouth made her feel warm and giddy all over.

"You cannot end years of animosity simply by your command," she said. "Although your desire to champion me is noble, I am afraid it may cause more problems. If Morys is already seeing me as a distraction, then it may make the problem worse if you try to intervene."

Blayth knew that. He knew how Morys was; he'd seen the petty, ugly side of the man, and he'd seen his behavior towards his brother over the past few years.

But now… things were different.

"I will speak with him," he said. "I cannot let him demean you. I *will* not. He will understand that we are to be married and if he has any respect for me, then he must respect you, also."

He was being chivalrous again. Asmara had never known a man to show her such concern.

"Since you and I have come to know one another, when you are not insulting me, you have shown me that you can be quite chivalrous," she said quietly. "It occurs to me that you must have learned that somewhere. Surely a man who has been beaten and tortured his entire life, as Morys has said, would not show the qualities that you have shown. Did you ever think of that?"

He hadn't. "Nay," he said. "I have not. I am as you see – simply me."

She smiled. "I realize that, but there are things about you that a man is taught," she said. "Your sense of chivalry, for one. And your ability to fight for another. You have tactical abilities that are learned, Blayth. I saw it when we overran Llandarog. You fight like a man who has been trained to fight, and that is not something English captors taught you. Does that make any sense?"

It did and, truthfully, he'd never thought of it that way. He knew what he knew, but he didn't know how he knew it, only that he did.

"Aye," he said. "Sometimes… sometimes I have dreams about men I do not know, and battles that I do not recognize. It is frustrating because I feel as if I should know these men. I told Morys of my dreams and he told me that I am dreaming of the men who tortured me, but I do not believe that is the case. When I am with these men, I feel… camaraderie. That is the best way I can describe it."

Asmara was listening closely. "But you do not know these men in your dreams?"

He shook his head. "I wish I did."

She pondered that. "And when the *Saesneg* knight called you James," she ventured. "You did not feel anything when you heard that name?"

Again, he shook his head "Not at the time," he said. "But it has become something of increasing interest to me. It is a feeling of curiosity and frustration – as if I should know the name, but I do not."

Asmara didn't push him, but she was glad she had asked him the question. They were closer now. And belonging to each other, she felt more comfortable with him than she'd ever felt with anyone in her life. He had been open and honest with her, and she felt as if she could be the same. She was greatly concerned with the way Morys treated him, like a possession, and the way Morys seemed to control Blayth's memories. Therefore, she ventured to say what was on her mind and prayed it didn't offend him.

"On the night Morys returned from Carmarthen, you mentioned what the *Saesneg* knight had said to you," she said. "Do you recall how angry he became? There was no reason for him to become so angry, but he did."

Blayth remembered that moment and nodded faintly. "I do recall."

"I have been concerned with the way he treats you for some time," she said. "When you told me that he gave you your memories and your name, that seemed so very strange to me. How would the man know of your past? How would he know everything about you?"

Blayth lifted an eyebrow. "I have wondered that very same thing."

"Have you asked him?"

"I did last eve, in fact," he said. "I asked him to send word to Llywelyn's *teulu*, the men he claimed brought me to him. He has agreed to do it."

"Do you believe him?"

"Until he proves otherwise, I will give him the benefit of the doubt."

Asmara could see that there was still a great part of him that trusted Morys, the man who brought him back to life. There was some loyalty there and she knew it. She didn't want to turn Blayth against Morys, but she wanted the man to know that, as an outsider, she thought the situation with Morys was odd.

Something, she suspected, that Blayth already realized.

"All I am saying is that I believe Morys knows more about your past than he is telling you," she said. "The way he reacted when you mentioned the name that the knight called you – de Wolfe – tells me that he knows more. *Much* more."

Blayth simply nodded, mulling over her words, as the groom suddenly reappeared, bearing two big buckets of steaming water. Morning was upon them and the castle was coming alive, but the private conversation they'd been able to have for the past few minutes had been priceless. Blayth thought that, perhaps, it had been the best conversation of his life.

But the first thing he had to do was tell Morys about the situation.

With the grooms around, and more people in the stable yard, his time alone with Asmara was finished. With a smile and a wink, Blayth left her to tend to her horse while he headed up to the keep to have a particularly serious discussion with Morys. Given the complexity of the situation in general, he felt he needed to be honest with Morys, most of all, and assure him that even though he planned on marrying Asmara, it did not weaken his passion for the rebellion, nor would it affect his duties in any way. Blayth hoped that those factors would be all Morys cared about, but something told him that, deep down, there was more to it. Morys could be jealous and petty, and Blayth had a feeling those particular traits of Morys might come into play.

As he headed for the keep, Blayth prepared himself for what was to come.

A showdown was on the horizon and there would only be one winner.

Blayth intended that it would be him.

PART FOUR

THE UNWANTED

CHAPTER FOURTEEN

I WILL MARRY *Asmara.*

Those words were still ringing around in Morys' head. It was still morning and he'd awoken not long before and, having eaten a leisurely meal, he'd been interrupted from disrobing the serving woman who'd brought his meal to him by Blayth, who seemed most eager to speak with him about something.

Frustrated, he'd sent the serving woman away only to have Blayth tell him, almost immediately, that he was planning on marrying Asmara.

Any good mood Morys had felt that morning crashed into a nasty heap.

In truth, he wasn't surprised to hear Blayth's declaration. Some part of him was waiting for it, no matter how hard he'd tried to separate Blayth from his niece. There were things a woman could do to a man to make him forget everyone and everything else, including things that were the most important to him. The best laid plans had often been destroyed by a woman, and now Blayth had fallen into the feminine trap.

Stupid, stupid man.

But Morys had a plan. He always had a plan, and sometimes those plans involved ugly truths and half-lies, anything to convince Blayth that marrying Asmara was not in his best interest. The man was struck dumb by a lovely woman with long legs, and she'd more than likely already spread those legs for him, but Morys wasn't going to let all of his hard work be ruined by his treacherous niece.

Perhaps his brother put her up to it, perhaps not. That didn't much matter now. What mattered was that, in the end, Morys was going to win, no matter what the price.

It was time to lower the hammer.

"Well?" Blayth said. "Did you hear me?"

Morys nodded faintly. "I hear you."

"And you have nothing to say about it?"

Morys lifted his eyebrows. "I have a good deal to say about it," he said. "You simply caught me off guard, 'tis all. I have a great many things to say about this."

Blayth held up a finger. "I will tell you this now before you say a word," he said. "Asmara will be my wife and, as such, you will respect her. No more brutal comments about her or her father in my presence. I will not stand for you belittling or insulting her. Is this in any way unclear?"

Morys had little patience for Blayth trying to lecture him. "I told you before that you will not dictate my behavior when it comes to my brother," he said. "Just as I would not tell you how to behave with yours, if you had one."

That wasn't the answer Blayth wanted. "Insult her and you shall have to answer to me," he said. "I will not be discreet about my reaction."

Morys didn't say anything. He simply looked away, plotting what he was going to say next. He knew that it had to be powerful, powerful enough to get Blayth's attention, because if he wanted to keep the man at his side, it would have to be with more power than what Asmara ferch Cader possessed.

"So you think my brother will let you marry his daughter, do you?" he said. "When Cader knows the truth about you, he will not. No man will want you for his daughter."

Blayth eyed him. "Speak plainly."

"Do you truly want me to?"

Blayth sighed sharply. "I have no time for your foolery, Morys," he said. "I came to tell you that I plan to wed Asmara, and I will. I will seek her father's permission as soon as possible and there is nothing you can say to discourage me."

Morys fixed on him. "You do not want to challenge me on this subject," he said, his voice low and threatening. "I can tell my brother every sordid detail about your past and ensure he forbids his daughter to marry you."

Blayth knew that Morys was capable of lies and venom, so he wouldn't put it past the man. "Why, in God's name, would you do that?" he asked. "Just because I marry Asmara does not mean my dedication to the rebellion is any less. I will still be at your side, fighting for a free Wales. Why should marrying her make a difference?"

Morys grunted unhappily. "You have a destiny to fulfill," he said. "You have always known you have a destiny to fulfill, but if you stray from the course, then I will see you destroyed before I see you ruin what I have worked so hard for."

Now he was speaking of destruction, harsher words than Blayth had expected. Morys was plain when he spoke and rarely used metaphors, so Blayth knew he was speaking of killing him. The reaction went beyond what Blayth had believed Morys capable of, and he was genuinely puzzled that the man should be so rabidly jealous about a woman he intended to marry.

"I told you to speak plainly," he said. "So now you intend to destroy me, do you?"

"If you do not fulfill your destiny. If you do not do as you are told."

"What, exactly, am I being told to do that I have not already done? What has you so angry that you would threaten me when I tell you that I wish to marry?"

Morys could see that Blayth was not going to be intimidated. If he had any hope of maintaining control over him, then he had to hit and hit hard. He knew that. Blayth had never shown any measure of initiative since Morys had known him, always so willing to follow, always so willing to take directions.

But now, the Blayth he'd known for five years wasn't the same man with the introduction of Asmara. She was bringing out the assertive man in him, a man no longer willing to be told what to do and when to do it. If Morys lost control of Blayth, then all of those dreams for his personal glory would be gone. It was all he wanted, this man he'd built a persona around, a man who would give him a final legacy as the man who protected – nay, *championed* – Llywelyn's bastard son.

The one who would lead all of Wales to freedom.

He couldn't lose that now!

The hammer he'd been lowering needed to hit the ground.

"Listen to me and listen well," Morys snarled. "You owe me your very life. Were it not for me, you would have been killed long ago."

Blayth remained calm. "I am aware of that."

"Nay!" Morys snapped. "You are not aware of anything. You are only aware of what I have told you. You and your feeble mind have been strengthened by me and protected by me. *What* do you remember of your life before you came into my care, Blayth?"

"You know I remember very little."

Morys slammed down the cup he'd had in his hand, spilling the contents onto the floor. He stood up by the chair he'd been sitting in, rushing at Blayth like a madman. Blayth didn't flinch, however; he was certain that was what Morys wanted. Morys was looking for an excuse to strike him and Blayth wouldn't give him one. However, what came forth from Morys' mouth after that did far more damage than any blow from a fist ever could.

"Exactly," Morys hissed. "You remember *nothing*. You do not remember when I found you on the field of battle at Llandeilo. You do not remember how I protected you from the Welsh who wanted to kill you. *Do you*?"

His words were somewhat confusing and Blayth's brow furrowed.

"Protected me from – ?"

Morys cut him off. "Aye," he snarled. "You big, foolish brute. Do you wish to know the truth of everything? Do you wish to know why my brother will never give you his consent to marry his daughter? Then I shall tell you and mayhap you will forget this foolish pursuit. You will understand why you *must* remain Blayth the Strong, the bastard son of Llywelyn the Last, and you must remain dedicated to this cause."

Blayth was watching Morys work himself up into a sweat and, to be truthful, he wasn't entirely sure he wanted to hear what would come out of the man's mouth. A distinct sense of foreboding swept him.

"So what will you tell me?" he asked. "Fabrications? More stories to enthrall the men? Your stories lost their sheen to me some time ago, so do not think to lie to me."

Morys didn't rage at that insult. In fact, he seemed to cool rather dramatically. An odd smile came to his lips.

"Is that what you think?" he said. "That I have spun fabrications to enthrall the men? In your case, I have, but I did it to save your life. If they knew who you really were, then they would kill you. You would be dead before you could draw another breath."

Blayth faced him warily. "What does that mean?"

Morys could see he had his attention. This was the moment he thought would never come, but he was prepared for it nonetheless. Blayth had to understand why he could never be anything other than what he was, and that included Asmara's husband.

"It means that I found a dying English knight on the battlefield in Llandeilo," he said, oddly calm as he faced him. "The man had the left side of his head smashed and the Welsh were beginning to strip him. They saw a target for their vengeance and intended on killing him, but do you know what I saw? An English knight of the highest order who could tell me everything I wanted to know about the English and their plans for Wales. I thought he could tell me their movements and all the inner secrets of Edward's plans of conquest. That was what I saw, and I saw it in you. *You* were that dying English knight, Blayth."

Blayth frowned. "What in the hell are you talking about?"

Morys cocked an eyebrow. "I have made it plain enough," he said. "You were not brought to me by Llywelyn's old *teulu*, a bastard of their lord whom they'd smuggled away from the English. You were a dying English knight, a man who served King Edward, and I'd hoped to learn so much from you, but you were not conscious. There were men all around who wanted to kill you, so I stripped you of everything identifiable, covered you up, and brought you home on my wagon. I kept you hidden as much as I could, waiting for the day you would awaken to reveal all of the glories of the English, but that day did not come. If anyone saw you and asked who you were, I would tell them that you were a wounded Welsh warrior. A very *special* wounded warrior. Imagine my disappointment when you awoke and did not even remember your own name. It was a bitter disappointment to realize that you could tell me nothing."

Blayth was looking at him with some horror, as if he couldn't decide whether or not to believe him. "That… that's madness," he finally breathed. "An English –?"

Morys cut him off. "You *are* English," he said firmly. "When I realized you would not be able to tell me anything, I had to come up with some explanation about you, so the story of Blayth the Strong was born. You see, all you could said was *wolf*. It was the only word out of your mouth, so you named yourself. And you were strong; God, so very strong. You survived what no man should have survived. So Blayth the Strong became a Welsh warrior."

Blayth simply stared at him. Oddly enough, he was coming to believe him. It sounded like something Morys would do and, having come to know the man as he had, Blayth believed everything he said. In fact, it was too outlandish not to be truthful. *You are English*. Blayth began to feel rather weak as shock rolled through his body, and he lowered himself into the nearest chair. He was stunned.

I am English!

"Then you do know more than what you told me," he muttered. "I will assume that there are none of Llywelyn's *teulu* to summon, then, to confirm the story you told me."

Morys was watching him closely, pleased that the defiant man who had come to his chamber minutes before was now weak and submissive. That was exactly what he wanted to see.

"Nay, there is not," he said. "That was something I had to tell you, for your own sake. Even though you could never give me the answers I sought about the English plans in Wales, I knew you could still be of use to me. That is when the bastard son of Llywelyn was born. What great irony there is in a former English knight leading mayhap the greatest rebellion Wales has ever seen. You came to my country to harness it but, instead, I have used you against your own people. It has been a greater destiny for you than I could have ever imagined."

Blayth was leaning against the back of the chair, his gaze averted as he digested everything he'd been told. Now, so much made sense to him. He'd never truly felt like the man Morys had told him he was, nor had he ever felt completely convinced of the backstory he'd been given. The "memories" Morys had planted in his mind. It was all so astonishing that his mind was swimming from it.

"Those dreams I have had," he murmured. "Dreams of men I do not know but feel as if I should. You told me that those were the men who had tortured me in captivity. I told you I never felt as if they had been my captors."

Morys shrugged. "I am sure they are simply English comrades," he said disinterestedly. "It does not matter who they are. You do not remember them."

Blayth looked at him sharply. "But it *does* matter," he said. "It matters a great deal. I *was* someone before you found me five years ago. Surely I must have had friends and family."

Morys' eyes narrowed. "If you did, then they did not care for you," he said. "You were abandoned at Llandeilo when I found you. Your so-called friends and family left you there to die, Blayth. Do not forget that. They left you behind and you surely would have died had I not come along and saved you."

His words were like a punch in the belly. Blayth's breath caught in his throat as he realized Morys was right – he *had* been left behind to die. Did he not have family or friends that cared enough about him to take him with them when the English army retreated? If he had, then they did not come back for him. No one had tried to find him after the fact.

His guts began to churn with the realization, with the sorrow that perhaps he was unloved and discarded. Perhaps that was why he'd been left behind, just as Morys said.

He was unwanted.

"It is possible they thought I was already dead," he said, trying to defend the actions of people he didn't even know. "I was badly wounded and I was told that Llandeilo was chaotic."

"It was."

"Then mayhap they had no choice but to leave me behind."

Morys shook his head. "They could have taken you with them if they'd wanted to," he said. "You must come to grips with the fact that the English do not want you, Blayth, and the only way you can remain with the Welsh and fulfill your destiny is if they believe you are Llywelyn's bastard. As Blayth the Strong, you are someone important and powerful. You are a man of respect. Why would you not wish to remain Blayth the Strong and destroy the English who cared so little for you that they left you behind in battle?"

Blayth was left feeling hollow and sick, mostly because Morys was making sense. He hated that he was making sense but, at the moment, there was so much turmoil in his mind that it was difficult for him to think clearly.

You are English, you are English, you are English…

An English knight who had been left behind to die.

But then, something occurred to him. He remembered the English commander in the vault who had called him by a name. The man had sworn he knew him and then, just as quickly, had backed off.

James de Wolfe...

"The commander of Gwendraith, the English knight I released from the vault," he said, looking up at Morys. "He called me James de Wolfe. Is that my name? James de Wolfe?"

Morys lifted his shoulders. "I do not know what your name was," he said. "You could never tell me. All you could say was wolf. I suppose your name could be de Wolfe."

Blayth pondered that possibility. "That was what the English commander said," he said. "When I said *wolf*, mayhap I was trying to tell you I was a de Wolfe."

Morys considered telling him more about that possibility, the fact that he'd found him in a de Wolfe tunic that had been half-ripped from his body. He decided to tell him all of it, hoping it would feed his hatred against the men who left him behind.

"It is not only possible, it is probable," he said quietly. "You were wearing a de Wolfe tunic when I found you, although rabid Welshmen had nearly ripped it from your body. I took it off you and hid it. It is back at my home in Brecfa, in a chest. Mayhap I held on to it for a moment just such as this – to tell you that you were left behind by the English, Blayth. They did not care for you enough to take you with them when they fled. They left you to die."

He was beating in those words, pounding them into Blayth's head, until all he could feel was abandonment and betrayal. Was it true? Was all of this really true? His gut told him that it was. Morys liked drama, and he was fully capable of lying about anything he considered important, but Blayth didn't get the sense that this had all been an elaborate fabrication. It was too detailed and made too much sense to him.

Now, he knew the truth – he'd been a wounded English knight when Morys had found him. It had been Morys who had not only saved his life by tending his wounds, but by giving him a new identity so the Welsh would not kill him.

In no way did Blayth believe Morys' motives had been altruistic. On the contrary, he knew they were self-serving. But it was done. Now, Morys and Blayth were at the head of a rebellion against the English, fighting for Welsh freedom, and Blayth was an important and respected man. The Welsh hadn't left him behind to die and they wouldn't. He knew his Welsh brothers would save him at all costs.

Unlike the English, who had abandoned him.

But he *was* English.

"De Wolfe," he muttered. "I am a de Wolfe."

Morys was watching him very carefully and he liked what he saw; a man who was once again complacent and willing to do as he was told. He was defeated, knowing he'd been abandoned.

But it wasn't enough. Morys had to ensure Blayth would never again try to leave him, not even for something as normal as marriage.

"Do you understand why you cannot marry Asmara now?" he said. "You are English, Blayth. My brother would never allow his daughter to marry a *Saesneg* and I am certain Asmara would not want to marry one, either."

Asmara. At the mention of her name, thoughts of her suddenly filled Blayth's mind and he found himself feeling a great deal of angst because of it. His natural instinct was to refute Morys, to tell the man that it wouldn't matter to Asmara. But the truth was that she had already suspected he wasn't who Morys said he was. She had made it clear that she'd always had suspicions, so perhaps telling her the truth wouldn't matter. For certain, he couldn't keep it from her.

But Morys couldn't know that.

Morys had gone out of his way to threaten him and tell him that the Welsh would kill him if they knew who he really was. Blayth suspected that was true, but he couldn't believe it from Asmara. She cared for him, deeply. Perhaps she even loved him. Surely the truth of his identity wouldn't deter her. At least, he hoped not, because he didn't feel it was something he could keep from her. He wasn't like Morys; he didn't lie to suit his needs or wants. Therefore, he had to tell her.

"I understand," he finally said, rising from the chair.

Morys went to him, putting a hand on the man's arm. "Do you?" he asked earnestly. "You cannot tell her. You cannot tell anyone what I have told you. If you do, your life is forfeit, not to mention what they would do to me. I have protected you all of these years, Blayth. You owe me that much."

Blayth just wanted to get out of there. His mind was whirling with everything he'd been told, and he simply wanted to remove himself from Morys' presence. But more than anything, he wanted to find Asmara to tell her what Morys had told him. Tactfully, of course, but he had to tell the woman she'd been right all along.

She'd known.

"I told you that I understood," he said after a moment, trying not to snap. "And I appreciate… everything you have done for me."

He started to move away, heading towards the chamber door, but Morys stopped him. "Where are you going now?"

Blayth sighed with some irritation, pulling his arm from Morys' grasp. "To think on what you have told me," he said. "I find I am quite overwhelmed by it all, as you can imagine. Do Aeddan or Pryce know any of this?"

Morys shook his head. "They know nothing."

"Then they shall not hear it from me."

Morys didn't try to grab him again as he headed for the door. "Remember," he said firmly. "You are Blayth the Strong, bastard son of Llywelyn ap Gruffydd and a great leader among our men. You are far more valuable to the Welsh than you ever were to the English."

Blayth paused before he opened the door, but he didn't say anything. He was so confused that he didn't know what to say any longer. He simply nodded his head, opened the door, and departed, leaving Morys standing in the center of his chamber, hoping his words had impacted Blayth enough so that he understood his place in the world – the unwanted English knight who had become a Welsh hero.

But even as Blayth left the chamber and headed off, something told Morys to keep an eye on the man. He was starting to get a mind of his own, something that didn't sit well with Morys. He was thinking for himself lately, and that was dangerous. It made Blayth unpredictable at best. Morys swore he would see the man dead before he saw him ruin the greatest rebellion Wales had yet to see.

But there was a bright side in all of this. If push came to shove, Morys knew what he needed to do.

Sometimes heroes made the very best martyrs.

CHAPTER FIFTEEN

IT HAD BEEN a very strange meal as far as Asmara was concerned.

She hadn't seen Blayth for the rest of the day, after they'd agreed to marry and he left her at the stable, and she knew he'd gone to speak to Morys about their betrothal. She assumed, probably correctly, that he'd been with Morys the rest of the day, because she never saw him again after that, not until the evening descended and the men gathered in the great hall for their meal.

Asmara gathered there, too, sitting on the end of the great feasting table as she waited for Blayth to appear, but he never did. Morys appeared with Aeddan and Pryce, but as the two younger men smiled and acknowledged her, Morys looked right through her as if she didn't exist. They all sat down and the meal of boiled mutton was served, but still no Blayth. Asmara ate little, keeping her eye out for him, but he never came and, eventually, she left the hall to hunt for him.

It wasn't like Blayth not to come to the hall, especially when he knew she would be there. She fought down the fear that something might be wrong, that he was sick or injured, because it wasn't like the man not to be present, especially when Morys was there. Just as she left the hall and headed for the entry, she passed by what used to be the former guard room for the keep. She almost didn't look at the door, but she saw movement that drew her attention. The door was cracked open enough so that she could see half of a booted leg.

She recognized the boot.

Blayth had distinctive boots, probably because his feet were so big, and they were made up of different pieces of leather, in different colors, creating a patch-work pattern. Asmara hadn't seen anyone else with that kind of boot, so she felt fairly confident that Blayth was inside the chamber as she knocked softly on the door. Because of the noise in the hall, she knocked again, louder. The door jerked open then and she found herself looking into Blayth's pale face.

"What are you doing in here?" she asked. "I have been waiting for you. Are you ill?"

He looked weary and emotional. "Nay," he shook his head, his voice soft. "I am not ill. I was going to find you, but…"

He trailed off, looking miserable, or so Asmara thought. She grew concerned. "But *what*?" she asked. "What is wrong?"

He motioned her into the chamber and shut the door, bolting it. It was dark inside but for a weak fire in the hearth, and he went to the hearth to throw more fuel on it. Light, and warmth, began to bloom.

"Sit, please," he told her quietly. "I must speak with you."

Asmara found a small stool near the bed and she pulled it out, perching herself on it. She watched him as he knelt by the hearth, stirring the embers and creating warmth against the cloying darkness, and she received the distinct impression that something was very wrong. His mood was almost as dark as the chamber around them. Patiently, she sat until he finished stirring the embers and stood up, brushing off his hands.

"Did you eat anything?" she asked.

He shook his head as he went to sit on the edge of the bed. "Nay," he replied. "I am not hungry."

"Why?"

He shook his head. "There is much on my mind, I suppose."

"What has you so worried that you cannot eat?"

Blayth sat on the end of the bed, his gaze falling on Asmara. He knew that if he wasn't able to marry her, his heart would break into a million pieces. It was such a fragile heart, the one part of his body and mind that he'd not yet learned to toughen up, so even as he looked at her, he could feel disappointment sweep him.

He didn't want to lose her.

He would be unwanted yet again if he did.

"I do not even know where to start," he said softly. "I have been sitting here all day, trying to think of what to say to you and how to say it. I can think of no other way to speak in such a serious subject except to be honest."

Asmara could see how troubled he was. "Go ahead," she said. "What is so terrible?"

"I am afraid I will never see you again once I tell you."

"That will not happen. Do you not have any more faith in me than that?"

He smiled faintly. "You are as strong as you are faithful and beautiful," he said. "I have every confidence in you. But the matter is quite… serious."

Asmara watched him as he spoke and a thought occurred to her. "Did you speak with Morys today?" she asked. "About our marriage, I mean."

"I did."

"What *did* he say to you?"

So she was intuitive as well as beautiful. Blayth sat forward so he was closer to her as she sat upon the squatty stool. He gazed at her a moment, watching the firelight play off her features, before speaking.

"You said something to me today," he said. "You told me that you believed Morys knew much more about my past then he has told me."

She nodded. "I did say that. I believe it is true."

"It is."

Curiosity crossed her features. "How do you know?"

Blayth smiled faintly. Closing his eyes tightly, he hung his head, so very troubled with what he was about to say. But it was necessary.

"The easy thing to do would be to keep this information from you," he said. "But I have too much respect for you to do that. I cannot start our marriage on a lie."

She cocked her head. "And I am grateful for that," she said. "But what is so terrible?"

He didn't say anything for a moment. Then, he extended his hand to her and after a moment of puzzlement, she timidly lifted her hand and put it into his big, callused palm. He brought her hand to his lips and kissed it sweetly, feeling his entire body tingle with the thrill of it. Something about the woman made him feel as if he were walking on clouds every time he touched her.

"You were there when the *Saesneg* knight called me by a name," he nearly whispered. "Do you remember?"

Asmara gripped his hand, holding it tightly. "I do," she said without hesitation. "He called you James."

"It would seem that he was not wrong."

She stared at him a moment, trying to figure out what, exactly, he meant. "What do you mean?"

He kissed her hand again. "You have expressed suspicions that Morys has given me my memories," he said. "You said yourself that it seemed strange that he should be the one to tell me of my past, to tell me what my name was and give me an identity. It seems that your suspicions were correct, Asmara. When I told Morys that you and I were to be wed, he told me that your father would never permit it because I am, in truth, an English knight. He has kept it hidden from me all this time."

Asmara's eyes widened in shock, briefly, but she didn't erupt, nor did she pull her hand from his grip. But the realization that she had been right all along was in her expression.

"You *are*?" she whispered.

He nodded. "I have been struggling with how to tell you this because I do not want to ruin what we have started," he said. "I will be honest with you; I have never been so happy in my life. My memory is brief, only since I came into Morys' care do I remember my life as it is, and in that time I have never felt truly happy. I have served Morys out of a sense of obligation, and out of my sense of duty to the *cymry*. When he told me that I was the bastard son of Llywelyn ap Gruffydd, that served as the kindling to my great sense of duty to all men of Welsh birth. But there was no real joy in any of it, not until I met you. I… I simply do not want to lose you, but I understand if your feelings have changed."

Asmara stared at him, seeing his pain and humility in the situation. But as he spoke and told her the news, she realized that it was no great surprise. She'd known from the beginning that something was odd with Blayth and Morys, so it was really a confirmation of her suspicions. After a moment, she shook her head.

"I suppose I knew you were not who Morys said you were from the very first," she murmured. "There were so many signs that pointed to something else, that you were a *tir allan*, an outlander. Somehow, I knew you were not the son of Llywelyn, but it did not change my opinion of you. If you are English, or if you are Welsh, it does not change *who* you are, Blayth. You are still a man of strength and skill and dedication. And it does not change how I feel about you."

It was the answer he was hoping to hear and he brought her hand to his lips again, pressing it against his mouth, feeling utter and complete gratitude. In fact, the relief he felt was almost more than he could bear.

"Are you certain?" he whispered, lips against her hand.

She could see how worried he was and she reached out, putting her hand on the top of his thick, blond hair.

"I am," she murmured. "Nothing has changed with me, but I must ask you – how do *you* feel about all of this? And why would Morys confess it all to you?"

He relished the feel of her hand upon his head, touching that which was so damaged as if there was no damage at all. No revulsion. He was still wanted, thank God, and wanted by the only person in the world that he cared about.

"Morys wanted to stress to me how your father would not approve of his daughter marrying a *Saesneg*," he said quietly. "He told me that so I would forget my desire to marry you, fearful my secret would be revealed. He assured me that if the truth was known, the Welsh would turn against me and kill me, which is probably true. If they discovered that Llywelyn's bastard was not Welsh at all, it would be devastating. You must not tell anyone what I have told you."

She shook her head. "I will not, I swear it," she said. "But what will you do now? Will you continue to lead the armies as if nothing is amiss?"

He shrugged. "I thought I would. But as I considered everything today, my ideals have changed somewhat," he said. "Morys told me that I had been abandoned by the English at Llandeilo, and that when he found me, I was a dying English knight and there were Welshmen swarming over me who wanted to kill me. He chased them away and brought me back to Brecfa, creating the entire persona of Blayth the Strong, son of Llywelyn. *Wolf* was the only word I could say for quite some time, apparently, which is why he gave me my name. But when I think back to what Payton-Forrester said to me, it all makes a good deal of sense. Do you recall when the man told me my family name was de Wolfe?"

Asmara nodded. "I do."

"Then it seems I was trying to say my name," he said quietly. "The House of de Wolfe was at Llandeilo. Morys said they abandoned me."

She squeezed his hand. "Mayhap they could not bring you," she said. "You were badly injured and it is possible they simply could not take you with them when they retreated. I have been told that Llandeilo was madness."

Blayth nodded. "I pointed that out to Morys, but he insists I was abandoned and the English do not want me," he said. "He says my only choice is to remain Blayth and continue as a Welshman."

"Do you believe that?"

"All things considered, I would… except for one thing."

"What is that?"

His gaze was intense. "The way Payton-Forrester looked at me when he called me James," he said, thinking back to that moment. "You were there, Asmara – you saw his face. He was almost weeping with joy when he saw me. Did that look like a man who had seen someone who was intentionally abandoned?"

Slowly, she shook her head. "Nay," she said. "He seemed most happy to see you at first. And then… then it was like he was frightened to have recognized you. I remember thinking that it was most strange."

Blayth remembered that moment clearly. Although he hadn't thought much of it at the time, because he was more concerned with Payton-Forrester delivering his message, in hindsight it did seem a bit strange.

"Indeed," he said. Then, he shook his head, a gesture of frustration. "I have been sitting here wondering if what Morys told me was true in that I was intentionally abandoned at Llandeilo. With him, there is no knowing if that is the truth. In these dreams I have, I see men that I know that I *should* know, yet I cannot recall their names. But the feelings I have for them are not those of animosity, but those of affection. I do not even know if these men are real, but something tells me that I am dreaming of memories of my past. I have always wondered, but after what Morys told me, now I am coming to think that is exactly what has happened. What my conscious mind cannot remember, my dreams seem to be able to."

She could see that he was confused and frustrated. She clutched his hand in both of hers. "It is possible," she said. "Mayhap you will never know."

He eyed her. "I think that I will. I cannot go to my grave with these doubts, wondering about my past and what really happened to me."

"Then what will you do?"

"Payton-Forrester was heading to Lioncross Abbey Castle," he said. "More than likely, he is still there. I think I should go there, too. Mayhap, he will tell me more of what he knows about me."

She looked at him warily. "Do you think you should?" she asked.

"Will it be safe?"

He shrugged his big shoulders. "If I am truly English, then I have nothing to fear," he said. "In any case, there is something burning within me that must know. I *must* know who I am and Payton-Forrester can tell me."

Asmara could see that he meant it and, in truth, she didn't blame him. The man had his whole life taken from him and now there was a chance for him to find out who he was. Certainly, the lure of truth was strong.

"Very well," she said. "When will you go?"

Blayth shrugged, averting his gaze. "Tonight," he said. "I feel as if I cannot wait. I must go and I must go now."

Asmara could feel his sense of urgency. "Will you tell Morys?"

He nodded. "I will tell him tonight."

Asmara watched him as he looked off into the darkness of the room, a man with a million different thoughts on his mind. She didn't want him to go and leave her here, a target of Morys' animosity. But more than that, she simply didn't want to be without him. She was becoming quite attached to him and the thought of him going away filled her with angst and sorrow.

"Please take me with you," she said quietly. "I do not want to be left behind. I want to go where you go and be at your side as you discover these truths about your past. Will you please take me?"

He looked at her, a faint smile on his lips. "It would be quite scandalous, the two of us traveling together and not married," he said. "I wish I had time to seek your father's permission to marry you, but I am afraid I do not. As much as I want to marry you, I feel as if this is more pressing. I hope you understand."

She nodded before he even finished speaking. "I do understand," she insisted. "I would want to know about my past, too. But you do not need my father's permission. You have mine, and that is all that matters in the end. My father will permit me to marry whoever I choose, and I choose you."

His smile grew. "Do you suppose he will see it that way?"

She waved him off. "My father will simply be glad that I am marrying," she said. "It does not matter to whom, so long as I marry and give him grandsons."

Blayth chuckled. "Then I suppose we could find a church and ask them to marry us," he said. "It would not be a grand wedding and a great feast that you deserve."

She grinned, embarrassed. "I hate parties and grand feasts. I do not need any of those things." Then, she sobered. "Will you take me with you, then?"

It was probably against his better judgement to do so, but he couldn't deny her. He wanted her with him and he certainly couldn't leave her here. After a moment, he relented.

"Aye," he said. "Go and gather your things. But what about your horse? Is he well enough to travel with that hoof?"

She stood up, quickly. "It was healed this morning," she said. "I simply soaked it again just to ensure that it was completely healed. It was not that bad to begin with."

"Then he will travel well?"

"He will be fine."

Reaching up a big hand, he swatted her gently on the bottom with a trencher-sized hand. "Then gather your things," he said. "Go and prepare your horse and I will meet you in the stable in a little while. I must speak to Morys now."

Asmara understood, feeling somewhat special and flattered with his love tap to her arse. Had any other man done that to her, she would have flattened him. But coming from Blayth, she didn't mind it one bit. From one warrior to another, she understood an affectionate touch when she felt it.

She was eager to go with him, to help him follow the trail that would lead him to the answers he sought. It was a frightening thing that he was doing, but a brave one, and she admired him greatly for it. It didn't matter to her one bit that the man was English; to her, he was simply Blayth, the man was cared deeply for. Perhaps she had even fallen in love with him, just a bit.

More than just a bit.

She knew she loved him.

Quickly, she fled his chamber, heading to the bower she had been using since her arrival to Gwendraith to collect her possessions. Her mind was on the journey ahead, a journey of a lifetime, and something she had never imagined she would ever do. She was leaving her family, and the rebellion, to chase dreams with the man she was to marry.

And the Dragon Princess couldn't have been happier about it.

CHAPTER SIXTEEN

MORYS' PLAN HAD spectacularly backfired.

He realized that as he sat and listened to Blayth tell him of his future plans. Whatever he'd hoped telling the man the truth would accomplish, those hopes were dashed.

He'd hoped that by telling Blayth of his past, and of his true identity, that it would scare Blayth into staying the course and continuing to be a beacon of hope for the Welsh. Morys had made it clear that the English had abandoned him at Llandeilo and, therefore, didn't want him. And he'd emphasized that Blayth only had value as a Welsh legend. He thought he'd made an excellent argument for everything, and he was certain that when the conversation was over, that Blayth understood his place in the world regardless of his true background.

But that hadn't been the case.

Now, Blayth wanted to find out the truth behind his past. It had taken him a day to figure that out, to decide that none of Morys' arguments meant anything to him. Blayth had pulled him out of the hall and into a small, dark chamber off the hall the smelled as if the dogs had been using it as their privy. What Blayth had to say couldn't wait, so half-drunk, Morys stood in stunned silence as Blayth explained his desire to go to Lioncross Abbey Castle to seek out Corbett Payton-Forrester, who had called him James down in the dank recesses of the vault. He was convinced that Payton-Forrester would know more about who he had once been, and Blayth expressed a very strong desire to discover what the man knew.

That hadn't been the outcome Morys had expected.

At first, he'd been calm about it. He'd explained, yet again, how Blayth had been abandoned. A loved and wanted man would not have been abandoned on the field of battle, he said. He'd tried to convince Blayth that seeking more information from Payton-Forrester would be foolish; it might even be deadly. Clearly, the English hadn't wanted him so why show them that the man they'd tried to discard was still alive?

But the argument hadn't worked with Blayth.

He was determined to go.

Slipping…

Morys could see the rebellion slipping away. The myth he'd built, the larger-than-life story of Blayth the Strong, son of Llywelyn the Last, was slipping away and the more he tried to grasp at it, the more it slipped between his fingers. The harder he pulled, the more Blayth pushed. Soon enough, Morys could see that there was no reasoning with the man. His mind was set.

Morys was losing the battle.

That was when the situation grew desperate.

Morys had considered before what he needed to do if Blayth decided to veer from the course – heroes made the best martyrs, he reminded himself, but if Blayth was going to depart this night and head into England to seek his truth, then there was no knowing when he would return, if ever. Blayth swore he only wanted to find out the truth of his past and of his true identity, but Morys couldn't be sure that the man wouldn't return to who he was before. Blayth hadn't made that very clear.

If he did, there would be no chance for a hero's death in battle.

Morys was a man who, if nothing else, had always been adaptable. He'd manipulated Blayth, lied to him, coerced him, and anything else he had to do in order to control the man. Blayth the Strong was more than a fictitious character – he had become a legend that the hope for

Welsh freedom had been built upon. Now, that legend was leaving Gwendraith. The rebels were due to return to Carmarthen Castle in several days to plan the next phase in their uprising, and Blayth couldn't confirm that he would be present at that gathering. He could be in England, still chasing after his lost past, because it seemed as if now that was the most important thing to him.

No more rebellion, no more legacy.

As far as Morys was concerned, he'd badly errored when he told Blayth the truth about his past, and now he had to remedy the situation and try to salvage what he could.

It was time to do something drastic.

Therefore, he let Blayth leave and go about gathering his things for his journey, whilst Morys went to plan for what needed to happen. Blayth would never realize what was happening until it was too late.

Dealings were about to get dirty.

"THE MOON IS so bright that it is almost like the sun," Asmara observed as she stood at the mouth of the stables, gazing up into the crisp night sky. "How far do you think we can travel tonight?"

Blayth was finishing securing his crossbow to his saddle. "To Llandovery, at least," he said. "We shall find a place to sleep outside of the town and then continue on in the morning."

She turned to look at him. "We could wait until dawn and leave," she pointed out. "We could make at least thirty-five miles in the daylight."

He pulled his horse over to where she was standing. "And we will," he said. "But we are going to do several miles tonight also. Unless you are too weak and feeble to do it."

She scowled at him although, this time, she knew the insult wasn't malicious. Insults were becoming terms of endearment these days, and she knew he was jesting with her.

"I can outride you any day," she said. "I will still be riding when you are on the ground, writhing in pain because your little onion sacks are beaten to death from the strain of travel."

He started to laugh, knowing exactly what she meant. "*Onion* sacks?" he repeated. "You mean my ballocks?"

She turned her nose up at him. "I do not use such language."

He laughed out loud. "God's Bones, woman, you just referred to them by calling them onion sacks," he said. "Whatever you call them, they are all the same – a man's balls."

Asmara couldn't stop the giggling. "Do you truly say such things in the presence of a lady?"

He eyed her. "Since when do you call yourself a lady?" he asked, watching her whirl to him in outrage. He held up a finger. "You are a woman, and a beautiful one, but you are also a warrior. I have never known the term lady and warrior to be interchangeable."

He had a point. Asmara simply shrugged and moved to mount her steed. "You have called me demoiselle since we have known one another," she said as she heaved herself up into the saddle. "Does that not mean lady?"

He mounted his horse also. "It does," he said. "It means a young, unmarried lady."

Asmara gathered her reins, pausing to look at him as he gathered his. "That is something else that told me you were not who Morys said you were," she said, watching him look at her questioningly. "You called me demoiselle."

He smiled at her under the moonlight. "What would you have me call you?"

She shrugged coyly and looked away. "That is not what I mean," she said. "I meant that no one but the English or the French do that. That told me that you were not Welsh-born or, at the very least, you did not grow up in Wales."

Blayth reined his horse over to her. "I will ask you again," he said softly. "What would you have me call you?"

That low, slow voice was purring at her and Asmara could feel her cheeks flame; she was grossly unused to the flirtatious games played by men and women.

"Whatever you wish," she said. "My name is Asmara."

"And it is a beautiful name," he said. "But I think I should like to call you something else."

"What?"

"*Cariad.*"

It meant *sweetheart* in Welsh, and Asmara's red cheeks grew redder. She'd never in her life been called anything other than her name, not even by her father, although her mother had often called her and Fairynne pet names. *Gwirion*, mostly, which meant "silly". But that was different, from a mother to a daughter. But this… this was from a man who was to be her husband.

She'd never felt so giddy in her entire life.

"If that is what you would like to call me, I will not contest," she said.

He laughed low in his throat, seeing even in the moonlight how embarrassed she was. Clucking softly to his horse, the animal began to move forward, followed by Asmara and her excitable young stallion.

"I have never called a woman *cariad*," he said. "You will be my first."

"As you will be mine."

It was a sweet sentiment between two people who were unused to such things. In warm silence, the pair headed out of the stable yard and into the outer bailey, which was mostly devoid of men at this hour. Pinpricks of light emitted from the keep, from several of the outbuildings, and from the gatehouse as men settled in for the night. With the moon bathing the land in a silver glow, Asmara and Blayth headed for the two-storied gatehouse.

There were men upon it, men with torches, and as they drew closer to the gate, Blayth called up to the men who were manning it.

"Open the gates," he boomed.

It was usual for there to be a delay of several seconds before the gates started moving. But in this case, the seconds turned into a minute and more. Blayth called to the gate guards again, thinking they might not have heard him, but then he saw Aeddan and Pryce heading towards him from the small guard room built into the gatehouse.

Curious, he moved his horse towards them to ask what the issue was, but that was when he saw Morys emerging from the gatehouse guard room as well. He wasn't a welcome sight.

Something told Blayth that the situation was about to turn.

"What is amiss that you will not open the gates?" he asked Aeddan as the man drew near.

Aeddan didn't look pleased. There were other men around, Welsh warriors, but he kept his voice down because he didn't want them to hear.

"Morys wishes to speak with you," he said as he reached Blayth. "He told us to hold the gates when you came. Blayth… he is armed."

Blayth's eyebrows lifted. "Armed? Why?"

Aeddan simply shook his head; either he didn't know, or he didn't want to say. In any case, Blayth didn't push him. Something was amiss, and Aeddan was letting Blayth know that he had to expect anything.

With Morys, that was usually the case.

Blayth kept his cool on the surface but, on the inside, his concern was mounting. He thought he'd said everything to Morys that needed to be said and couldn't imagine why the man was here… unless the words they'd spoken between them weren't final in Morys' opinion. And now the man was armed to stop him?

In truth, Blayth wasn't surprised. He wasn't surprised that Morys wasn't willing to let him go so easily, perhaps to try one more time to convince him that it would not be in his best interest to dredge up his past. But Blayth was resolute that he needed to try.

Nothing Morys could say would change that.

"Morys?" Blayth said, calling to the man with veiled impatience. "What did you wish to speak of?"

Morys came forward, out of the darkness of the gatehouse, making his way towards Blayth. It was then that Blayth saw the crossbow in Morys' hand; he wasn't pointing it at anyone, but merely aiming it at the ground. But he was carrying a weapon, as Aeddan had said he was, and the concern Blayth felt blossomed into full-blown apprehension. It wasn't for him so much as it was for Asmara; if Morys tried something, he didn't want her caught in the crossfire.

But seeing Morys with the weapon, now Blayth was coming to understand what this was all about. Morys wasn't here to talk him out of anything. Somehow, someway, Morys was going to force him into remaining because, Blayth knew, this went again Morys' plans. This wasn't want *Morys* wanted, so he was going to resort to intimidation.

Blayth braced himself.

But what he didn't know was that several feet behind him, Asmara was also reaching for her crossbow, tied off on her saddle. She, too, was watching Morys come forth with a weapon in his hand and she knew he had it for a reason. It wasn't simply to hint at threats and intimidation. Morys was aggressive, bold, and reckless, and if he felt he was being wronged, he would more than likely lash out at whoever he felt was wronging him. In this case, it was Blayth, leaving on his own quest and evidently not placing the greater priority on the rebellion and Morys' wants.

Much like Blayth, none of this surprised her. And she wanted to be ready.

"Get off your horse, Blayth," Morys said calmly. "You are not leaving. We have more important issues to deal with."

Blayth remained calm. "I will not disagree that the issues are important," he said evenly. "But I have explained that this is something I must do, Morys. It does not diminish my gratitude in what you have done for me, but surely you understand my need to know the truth."

Morys was clearly impatient. "The truth you seek will be there in a year from now or five years from now," he said. "The past cannot be changed. It will still be there in time but, for now, I need you here. You have an important destiny to fulfill at present."

Blayth eyed the man. Unless they wanted the secret of Blayth's true identity and background revealed, there wasn't more either of them could say. Blayth had said everything he'd wanted to say earlier, so Morys' attempt to force him into remaining was not sitting well with him. He honestly couldn't believe the man was threatening him, out here for all to hear where their secret could easily be revealed.

But maybe that was Morys' plan.

As Blayth contemplated how to handle Morys, Asmara didn't have quite so much patience. As she saw it, Morys was, yet again, trying to control Blayth and as the man's betrothed, she wasn't going to stand for it. She'd never liked her uncle. In fact, she'd hated him for how he'd always treated her father, and she wasn't going to let the man push Blayth, or her, around any longer.

It was time to take a stand.

The crossbow in her hand lifted.

"Get out of the way," she told her uncle as she urged her excitable horse forward. "You know why he has to leave, so get out of the way."

Morys looked up to see Asmara pointed a crossbow right at him. He wasn't all that astonished that she had asserted herself, but it did infuriate him.

"This is not your affair," he said. "Put that weapon down before you hurt someone."

It was the wrong thing to say to her. "I am going to hurt *you* if you do not get out of his way," she growled. "You have spent your entire life belittling people and ordering them around, my father included, but you are not going to do it now. You are a bitter excuse for a man, an inglorious fool who is trying to make himself feel important by pushing Blayth to do things you cannot do yourself. You are riding on his glory but, this time, he is going to choose his own path. Standing in front of these gates is only going to see you injured, or worse. I will not let you do it."

He shook his head at her as if disgusted. "Shut your ridiculous mouth, girl," he said. "My brother did not take a firm hand to you when you were younger, so you do not know your place. He let you do whatever you pleased and now you are a grotesque shadow of a female, neither a lady nor a man, but something in between. I can only imagine how you seduced Blayth because, certainly, there is nothing about you that is seductive or soft, and now you try to push yourself into business where you do not belong. Someone should have shut you up years ago."

Asmara didn't feel shame like she normally would have because her uncle was simply having a tantrum and pulling her right along with him, showing off to the men around him. Aeddan and Pryce were standing near Asmara, looking very strained and upset by what was going on, so she turned to them rather than responding directly to her uncle.

"Do you know that he has been lying to you this entire time?" she said loud enough for Morys to hear her. "He has been manipulating you and belittling you, pushing you around because he believes it is his right, as a prince of Deheubarth. Ask him why he does not want Blayth to leave Gwendraith. See if he is brave enough to tell you."

That drew a very strong reaction from Morys. "I told you to shut your lips, you stupid chit," he snarled. "You, who has sprung from the weak loins of my brother. He is so weak that he could only have females. Females he has raised as sons!"

"At least my father had children," Asmara fired back. "If I were you, I would be careful who you accuse of being weak. Coming from a man who could not impregnate his wife, I would say *you* are the weak one in the family."

Morys' featured twisted, a macabre expression of rage on his face. "Bitch," he hissed. "You will regret that."

He started to lift his crossbow but Blayth was there, putting himself between Asmara and Morys. His gaze was deadly.

"I told you that you would not insult her in my presence," he said. "And if you intend to use that crossbow on her, know that I will snap your neck before you can reload it. Make a move against her and it shall be your last."

Morys was quickly moving beyond rational thinking. He was used to being in control, always, and he looked at Blayth's words as a revolt. Now, the man was challenging him and Morys' pride took a hit. It was a fragile thing, fed by his inflated sense of self-worth and the submission of the men under his command. It was easily bolstered and even more easily shattered. If he didn't have control over all things, then he had nothing, and right now he was facing that very possibility with Blayth.

He couldn't let the man gain the upper hand.

He was going to take him down.

"Did you hear him?" he cried, raising his voice so that even the sentries on the wall could hear him. "Do you know why he is threatening me? Because I know the truth about him!"

The men began to stir in the darkness, hearing Morys' words. The general consensus believed that Morys was an arrogant man and would like to have his way in all things, but he also had that hereditary respect because of his lineage. He was followed more out of duty than out of love or respect, so when he started shouting about truths and threats, men listened but it was always with some doubt.

In fact, Aeddan and Pryce, now standing next to Asmara, listened to Morys with more doubt than most. They'd been around him far too long to believe anything he said without reservations. As the man began to cause a scene, Asmara turned to Aeddan once more.

"Get into the gatehouse and open the gates," she pleaded softly. "This is not going to end well if Blayth is not permitted to leave."

Pryce heard her. Having no love for Morys, he immediately moved towards the gatehouse, trying to stay to the shadows and trying to stay out of Morys' line of sight. As he moved off, Aeddan whispered to Asmara.

"What *is* this all about?" he asked.

Asmara kept her eyes on her uncle. Since she didn't know the man particularly well, she didn't feel comfortable telling him the truth. That would have to come from Blayth, for it would be Blayth's decision to trust his friend with such things.

"Whatever he says, it is not the truth," she muttered, avoiding the question. "All Blayth wants to do is leave Gwendraith, but Morys wants to keep him here."

"But why?"

She shook her head, unwilling to answer directly. "Just know that Morys is a liar. He will say anything to manipulate men. But I think you already know that."

Aeddan did. He'd seen it his entire life. He'd seen the man beat down and belittle his own father until the man died at an early age. Before he could question her further, Morys turned to Blayth and pointed at the man.

"We have all been cruelly betrayed by this man," he said. "I will not let him leave because he is a traitor. He is loyal to his English captors and plans to run to them and tell them of our plans. That is why I will not let him leave and why his woman is willing to kill me! She knows he is a traitor, too, and she is trying to help him!"

Asmara was infuriated as men began to grumble. Morys was collecting quite a crowd, but that was what he liked – an audience. She was shocked to hear the lies coming forth, but she also knew that there were men who would believe him without question. If Morys was able to rile them up enough, then there would be trouble.

"That is *not* true!" Asmara shouted. "Listen to me, my brothers! Morys has been lying to you from the beginning about Blayth. He has told you that he is the bastard son of Llywelyn the Last, our noble prince, but that is not the truth. He told you that so that he could control you and force you to fight in this rebellion. If there is a traitor here, it is Morys ap Macsen and not Blayth, who has also been lied to *by* him. He is a victim in all of this as much as any of you. Do not believe a word Morys has told you!"

More grumbling came from the crowd that was gathering. Furious, Morys could hardly believe that Asmara had dared to contradict him. No one contradicted him, not ever, and he was losing all control. His temper was spiraling as he realized Asmara was planting a seed of doubt among the men, a seed of doubt that could see his legacy ended. She was ruining everything.

She was going to pay.

"You would believe a woman?" he screamed. "She and her father have long hated me because I am the eldest son, the leader of all men, and she lies to erase your love for me. Blayth is a traitor and he must be stopped!"

He continued to shout venom as Asmara was turning to Aeddan, still standing next to her. When she spoke to Aeddan and Pryce in the stable those days ago, when she'd been trying to discover more about Blayth, she had seen the lack of blind respect from the brothers when it came to Morys. She could only pray that they loved Blayth more, and trusted him more, because she could no longer hold back the truth. If this situation was going to veer out of control, then Blayth would need help.

Only the truth would open that door.

"Do not listen to him," she hissed. "He has been lying to you about Blayth. You were there when he brought Blayth back from Llandeilo, were you not?"

Aeddan, greatly torn and confused by what was going on, nodded. "I was."

"Then you know that Blayth came from Llandeilo."

"Morys said he was delivered by Llywelyn's *teulu* and…"

She cut him off, shaking her head. "Blayth was an English knight, wounded at Llandeilo," she hissed. "His real name is de Wolfe, but Morys lied to you. He has fabricated everything – Blayth's name, his history – everything. He is not Llywelyn's bastard son. He is an English knight, but he did not remember that. Yet, Morys knew, and he lied to Blayth and told him he was someone he was not. Morys told him that he was Llywelyn's bastard so he could feed the rebellion. He only told Blayth tonight of his true past, and now Blayth has a chance to discover who he really is, only Morys will not let him go. If you love Blayth, you will help him. *Help* us, Aeddan!"

Aeddan was looking at her in utter shock. "He… he is *Saesneg*?"

She nodded rapidly, glancing at Morys because now he was pointing at Blayth again and shouting about his treachery. "He is," he said. "And Morys *knew*. Blayth did not, so he is not to blame. The only one to blame is Morys. Help us leave before it is too late!"

It took Aeddan a few moments to overcome his astonishment and realize that what Asmara said made a great deal of sense. Morys' story about how Blayth came into his possession never made sense to Aeddan but out of respect to Morys, he accepted it. Nay, he wasn't surprised at all to discover that Blayth, the damaged warrior, was actually an English knight.

It made all the sense in the world.

Aeddan had been there from the beginning. He'd been there when Blayth had awoken from his lengthy unconsciousness, and he had been there when the man learned to speak and walk again. Aeddan had helped him with everything, so he knew that Blayth had no memory of who he was prior to his terrible injury.

But Morys knew.

Damn the man… he *knew*.

"But where is Blayth going?" he asked after a moment, feeling her panic. "Does he even know?"

Asmara shook her head. "He is *not* going to betray the Welsh if that's what you are asking," she insisted. "You must believe me. He only wants to find out who he really is, Aeddan. He has a chance to discover his true past. And Morys does not want him to go, so he is lying to everyone, still!"

He is lying to everyone, still. That seemed to snap something in Aeddan, who could see what was happening. He could see the entire picture – Morys, caught in his web of lies, was trying to salvage the situation by turning everyone against Blayth. He didn't know why he should believe Asmara, but he did. God only knew how long he'd hated Morys and he'd hidden that hate behind obedience and forced gratitude, but he wasn't going to let the man destroy Blayth, someone he considered another brother.

He had to help.

Just as he moved to do so, the gates began to lurch open and Morys, startled by the sound, turned to look to the gates. It was a reflexive reaction, brought on by the creak of the chains. But when he turned to look, he accidentally pulled the trigger on the crossbow. The iron-tipped arrow flew right at Asmara, hitting her in the left shoulder.

As she cried out in pain and jerked back in the saddle, Asmara also squeezed the trigger of the crossbow she was holding, and the arrow went flying. By chance, it found its mark in Morys' neck, and the man collapsed into the mud, mortally wounded.

Panic ensued. Men were yelling, charging forward, and Blayth did the only thing he could do – he grabbed Asmara's reins and spurred his horse towards the open gates, trampling Morys as he went. Together, he and Asmara galloped out of the gates and into the silver-bathed landscape beyond, fleeing the frenzy of Welsh who had been both stirred up and repulsed by Morys' words.

But the chaos quickly died as Blayth and Asmara fled into the night, and men began to discuss what should be done. Some wanted to follow them, but Aeddan called them off. There would be no following, he said. Blayth had committed no crime.

The only crime had been committed by a man who was not long for this world.

So the Welsh began to disburse for the most part, milling around with some confusion on the cusp of a most confusing night. Beaten down into the mud by two fleeing horses, Morys struggled for air as Aeddan stood over him and watched him labor. He couldn't even make a move to help the man, so great his hatred and disgust. Morys had finally demonstrated what he was fully capable of, and that greed had ultimately destroyed him.

As Morys' breathing began to grow unsteady, Aeddan knelt down beside him and watched his chest rise and fall for the last time.

"I hope you can still hear me," he rumbled. "If there is any justice in this world, I have seen it served tonight. You received exactly what you deserved."

With that, he stood up and walked away, moving to the open gates to watch Blayth and Asmara as they disappeared into the night. In truth, the more he thought on what Asmara had told him, the more hope and even happiness he felt for Blayth. A man who had been the prisoner of a vile beast, fed lies and kept like a prized animal, now had the chance for true freedom. Whether or not it was at the head of a rebellion was no longer the issue.

The man had a chance to find himself, and Aeddan hoped for the best. When he told his brother what had happened, Pryce hoped for the very same thing.

They could only pray for the best for a man they looked upon as a brother, English or Welsh.

Godspeed, Blayth.

CHAPTER SEVENTEEN

Castle Questing
Northumberland, Seat of the House of de Wolfe

WILLIAM HADN'T BEEN aware of just how long he'd been staring at the missive from his daughter. The faded yellow vellum sat on his massive desk, illuminated by the light from two banks of candles, one on either side of the table. He always kept the desk well-lit because his eyesight wasn't what it used to be.

Hell, he'd lost his left eye in Wales over forty years ago, and he'd learned to compensate. But now as the years advanced and his body grew older and more tired, his one remaining eye wasn't very good. He had difficulty reading and, sometimes, difficulty seeing the smaller details in things. But he pretended like everything was fine. He always pretended that everything was fine because he didn't want his family to worry over him, but worry they did.

His family.

He'd sat staring at that vellum, pondering the contents with a mind that wasn't quite apt to believe what he'd just read. He'd had to read it four times before setting it aside and simply staring at it. He didn't want to believe any of it, but he knew that his daughter, Penelope, wouldn't lie to him and he further knew she wouldn't have sent the missive unless she had just cause.

That was what the missive was all about – *his family.*

As William pondered the contents of the missive, he realized that every part of his body was aching with stress and anxiety as a result. *Damnation!* He thought. He'd allowed the contents of the missive to get past his logical mind and into his veins, where it would pulsate through him and turn his shock into a physical manifestation. If he wasn't careful, it would tear him apart. He could already feel it, pulling at him, tugging at his arms and legs and chest, and if he allowed it… God, *if* he allowed it… it could easily destroy him.

Nay… he'd come too far in his life, and he was too happy in his legacy, to allow anything to destroy him. He was William de Wolfe, the Earl of Warenton and the man known as the Wolfe of the Border. Nothing could destroy him.

Nothing but a missive bearing one name that had nearly sent him into oblivion.

James.

It just wasn't possible. Five years after James' death in Wales, to receive a message that suggested his son hadn't died in Wales was foolish at best. Ludicrous, even, and stupid when all else failed. *Outrageous!* All of these words rolled through William's mind as he looked at the missive. But in the midst of an explosion of adjectives, one small word also filled his mind, something that had the strength to push aside all of the others.

Hope.

But he couldn't allow himself to feel any hope at all. It was preposterous. Furthermore, he couldn't, and wouldn't, tell his wife the contents of the missive because she, too, would be filled with the same stress and anxiety that he was.

William and his wife, Jordan, had ten children total, with nine living to adulthood, and only one of them lost as an adult – his beloved son, James. It was no secret in the family that William had never quite recovered from James' death, which was why the missive from Penelope had him reeling. He'd never gotten over the guilt of having left his son behind when the English had retreated at Llandeilo. He had no body to bring home for James' wife and mother to mourn, and that had made him feel so very weak and guilty.

And now this damnable missive, dredging it all up again.

He felt sick.

But he also knew he needed help. He needed the calm, rational eye of someone he trusted, so when he'd finished absorbing the contents of the missive, he stood up and collected the vellum, rolling it up tightly and holding it against his heart as if that somehow brought him closer to the son he'd lost. With the missive clutched to his chest, he quit the lavish solar of Castle Questing and headed to the upper floors of the enormous keep.

Castle Questing was William's seat, and had been for forty years. Most of his children had been born here, as had many of his grandchildren, nieces, and nephews. The keep itself was more of a rectangular building, with three floors and more than two dozen rooms. There was more than enough space for a large family or two, and he shared the home not only with his wife and two of his sons, but he also shared it with another family.

In the days long past when he had served at Northwood Castle as the Captain of the Army, he'd had a dedicated knight corps of nine men. Paris de Norville was his closest friend, a man who also became family when four of William's children married four of Paris'. Kieran Hage was also his closest friend, a bear of a man who had been third in command at Northwood, and a man who was also family by virtue of the fact that two of William's children had married into the Hage family, including James.

When William had been granted Castle Questing by Henry III, he'd taken Kieran with him to help him establish his new seat, leaving Paris at Northwood as the Captain of the Army for the Earl of Teviot. But it didn't matter that Paris was thirteen miles from William and Kieran; the men were as close as they'd ever been, and nothing could change that.

Nowadays, William and Kieran and their families still occupied

Castle Questing. Considering Kieran had married Jordan de Wolfe's cousin, Jemma, long ago, it made the families that much closer, so they were literally one giant family. William saw Kieran daily and had for the past forty years, through good times and bad, and even though William had brothers, he considered Kieran closer to him than a brother could ever be.

And that was why William was taking the missive to Kieran.

Taking the long flight of mural stairs up to the third floor of Castle Questing, William entered the east wing of the keep, a floor and section of the castle that was exclusively used by Kieran and his family. He was heading for Kieran's chamber at the end of the corridor, a room with windows that faced northeast so Kieran could watch the sunrise. He didn't move much from his bed these days, something William refused to acknowledge.

But he was the only one.

Everyone else had resigned themselves to the fact that Kieran was growing weaker by the day. His heart hadn't been particularly healthy for the past several years. But only in the past year had they begun to see a steady decline in a man William had called the strongest man in the north.

In Kieran's prime, there wasn't a man in England or Scotland who could best him in feats of strength. A massive man with a big neck, broad shoulders, and hands of steel could rip men apart without the aid of a weapon, Kieran was an immovable object on the field of battle and had survived wounds that would have killed a lesser man. But this mountain of a man had a calm manner about him and always had; he was cool in any circumstance, cooler still in the heat of battle. He also possessed an ageless wisdom, something that William now sought. He needed Kieran's level head to help him decide what to do about Penelope's missive.

There were decisions to make and William feared he couldn't be objective about them.

As he approached Kieran's door, the panel opened and a small, round woman appeared. She had a tray in her hands and she closed the door behind her, glancing up to see William approach. Lady Jemma Hage had been a lush Scottish lass in her youth, and she was still lovely even in her advanced years. The fiery woman Paris had branded a banshee those years ago had been the rock of Kieran's family, her strength beyond compare. William smiled when their eyes met.

"How is your husband today?" he asked.

Jemma's forced smile told him something he didn't want to know. "He is eating better," she said in her thick Scots accent. "He finished his entire nooning meal. He hasna done that in a while."

William looked at the tray she was carrying; there was a small empty bowl, a wooden plate with crumbs, a cup, and little else. To him, it didn't look as if there had been much food to begin with, but he didn't say anything. He simply smiled.

"Good," he said. "He shall be back on his feet in little time. May I see him?"

Jemma's smile faded. Like everyone else at Questing, she knew that William was in denial of Kieran's health. To him, Kieran was simply resting and would soon resume his place as the commander of the de Wolfe armies. But it wasn't the case, and Jemma as well as Jordan had tried to tell William that.

He simply wouldn't listen.

"Ye may," she said. "But I must speak tae ye first."

William's expression lost its warmth. If she was going to say what he thought she was going to say, then he didn't want to hear it.

"What is it?" he asked warily.

Jemma sighed faintly, seeing that William was already on his guard. "William," she said quietly. "I know ye dunna want tae hear this, but ye must know that the physic says that Kieran is growing weaker. We've been trying tae tell ye this, but…"

As she knew he would, he averted his gaze and pushed past her. "He is not," he said, cutting her off. "He is simply growing old; we are *all* growing old. It is age and nothing more."

Jemma reached out and grabbed his arm before he could get past her. "Would ye stop?" she hissed. "I know ye dunna want tae hear such things and surely, I dunna want tae say them, but Kieran will not rise from his bed as ye hope. The physic says his heart… ye know he has a bad heart. It is only a matter of time now before…"

William cut her off again, yanking his arm out of her grip. "It is not true," he said, moving to the door. "I cannot believe you."

"William," Jemma snapped as he put his hand on the door latch. "Ye're only making this harder. Ye need tae accept that Kieran is dying. Do ye think it doesna pain me tae say so? Do ye think I want tae lose the man I've loved most of my life? For my sake, ye must stop pretending everything will be okay again. Ye drive a stake through my heart every time ye do."

William paused at the door, his jaw ticking faintly as he listened to Jemma spew things he refused to believe. His hand was on the latch but he didn't open it. Gradually, his hand came away and he turned to Jemma.

"Please, Jemma," he said hoarsely. "I cannot… I cannot face this."

"And ye think I can?"

William's jaw continued to flex. "You are giving in to the physic's opinion. He is not God. He does not know everything."

"He knows enough tae know that my husband is dying."

William's jaw stopped flexing as she laid bare the truth of the matter. It was so very difficult to hear. "I… I simply cannot believe it."

Jemma understood. William was very attached to Kieran, and Kieran to him. The older the two became, the deeper their connection.

"Ye must," she said quietly. "Not facing the truth will not change things."

William closed his eye as if to ward off what she was saying. He knew she was right, but he didn't want to agree. He simply couldn't.

"I met Kieran when I was quite young," he said after a moment, realizing there was a lump in his throat. "I am sure you have heard the story. He and Paris and I were all fostering together at Kenilworth, with the same master, before our master moved to Northwood Castle to serve the Earl of Teviot. We all came to Northwood together, including Kieran's brother, Christian. I think I was ten years and four; so was Paris. Kieran was a year younger, and Christian was not quite nine years of age. Even back then, Kieran was a lad of considerable strength. Paris and I would go around making bets with the other squires that Kieran could wrestle them to the ground and we made a good deal of money off of Kieran's strength. But then, our master heard what we were doing and punished us. He took all of the money we had earned from the bets, telling us that the money belonged to him and not to us. Did Kieran ever tell you about that?"

Jemma was listening to the story with a faint smile on her lips. "He has told me some of it, but not all of it," she said. "He said ye whored him out."

William burst into soft laughter. "We did," he said, his white teeth flashing. "God help us, we did. And he went along with it, the big dolt that he is. But even then… even then, Jemma, I knew that Kieran and Paris and I would be friends forever. There are some people who mark your heart like that. Kieran has always been the brother I wish I had and the thought of losing him… I cannot face it."

Jemma's smile faded as she saw William tear up. He was emotional in his old age. "I cannot pretend tae know the bonds of men who have faced life and death together," she said quietly. "All I know is that the bond they share is as strong as anything I've ever seen, and I know Kieran feels the same way about ye. If avoiding the truth is the only way ye can deal with the situation, then I'll not fault ye. But Kieran knows his time is limited and he worries about what will happen when he leaves us all behind. All I ask is that ye dunna worry him needlessly about it. If he sees that ye're strong and accepting, it willna make him so anxious."

William sighed heavily and hung his head for a moment. There was a simple but powerful truth in her words. Finally, he nodded.

"I understand," he said softly.

Leaving Jemma standing in the corridor with her tray of dishes, William opened the chamber door and stepped inside. He immediately spied Kieran, lying on a very large bed that faced the windows, and he could see three small boys crowded up on the side of the bed as they spoke to Kieran.

William forced a smile, seeing three of his grandsons. They were also Kieran's grandsons, as William's daughter, Katheryn, had married Kieran's son, Alec. Edward was the oldest, at nearly ten years of age, followed by Axel, who was eight, and Christoph, who was five. Edward was the spitting image of William, while Axel and Christoph looked much more like Kieran's side of the family. As William approached the bed, Christoph ran towards him.

"Poppy!" he cried. "They have my sword and will not give it back!"

William took Christoph's hand as he came next to the bed to see, exactly what was going on. Kieran was holding a small sword, very dull, with Edward and Axel looking at William quite innocently.

"We were showing it to Kee," Edward insisted. They called Kieran "Kee", something Edward had called him when he'd been very young because he could not pronounce his grandfather's name. It was a pet name that all the children called their grandfather. "Axel gave Christoph the sword, but Kee thinks it is too heavy for him."

William recognized the sword he'd had made for Edward when the lad was quite young, something Edward had given to Axel, and now Axel had given it to Christoph. He held a hand out to Kieran, who handed it over. He pretended to feel the weight of it.

"It is rather heavy for a young lad," he said to Christoph. "Axel, why did you give this to your brother without permission?"

Axel frowned, looking very much like Kieran in that gesture. "Because I want a new one," he declared. "Edward got a new sword, so why can I not have a new sword?"

William looked at Kieran, who simply shook his head. "All young men want the latest and finest weaponry," he said. "We did."

It was true, but William didn't want to get into an argument with his grandsons, not when he needed desperately to speak with Kieran. He handed the mock weapon back to Axel.

"You will not give this to your brother without permission," he said. "If I find Christoph with it, I will take it away from you both. Is that clear?"

Axel nodded solemnly, as did Christoph, but Christoph was starting to cry. He began to wipe his eyes furiously.

"Can I not have it, Poppy?" he asked, rather pathetically.

William was quite a pushover for his grandchildren, so it was difficult to stand tough against them. He had to force himself.

"Not that one," he said. "Mayhap I shall commission a new one for you, one that is not quite so heavy for you." When Christoph's tears instantly disappeared, William motioned to the door. "Go, now. I must speak with Kee."

There was grumbling all the way to the door as Axel wanted to know why Christoph would get a new sword, but not him. *He* was the one who wanted a new sword, anyway. When they started squabbling next to the door, William cleared his throat loudly and pointed to the door again, and they quickly disappeared through it. As the door shut on the complaining grandsons, William turned to Kieran.

"I told you not to spoil them so much," he said. "Now they all want swords?"

Kieran grinned. "Doesn't every man?"

"They are not men yet."

"They have Hage and de Wolfe blood. They were men the moment they were born."

William cocked an eyebrow. "And excellent point," he said. Then he paused a moment, scrutinizing Kieran. The man looked pale and his breathing was labored as it always was these days, but the dark eyes were still bright. "Your wife says you have had a good day today. How do you feel?"

Kieran shrugged. "The same," he said. He pointed to a stool near the bed. "Sit down. Visit with me a while. All I have had is children and women to talk to this morning."

William snorted as he pulled up the stool and planted his big body on it. "I have actually come on business," he said, his humor quickly leaving him. "Serious business, Kieran. I received a missive from Penny today."

Kieran's eyebrows lifted. "Lady de Shera? What does she have to say?"

William thought to tell him, but he couldn't quite put it into words. Instead, he handed over the missive to Kieran, who took it curiously. William sighed heavily and averted his gaze, so Kieran unrolled the missive, turned it towards the light, and began to read.

William dared to look up a few moments later, when Kieran was about halfway through, and he saw the man's eyes widened. It was Kieran's daughter, Rose, who had been married to James at the time of his death, so Kieran had a stake in this almost as much as William did. Kieran read through it once and then started a second time, now reading the missive aloud.

"… the utmost importance that I relay to you the following information told to Chris de Lohr by Corbett Payton-Forrester, who was the garrison commander for William de Valence at Gwendraith Castle until the Welsh captured it. Corbett has told Lord de Lohr of a new wave of Welsh rebellion moving through Southern Wales, led by a man who is rumored to be the bastard son of Llywelyn the Last. He is rallying the Welsh and already several castles have fallen to the rebels. Upon the capture of Gwendraith Castle, Corbett was taken prisoner by this son of Llywelyn. He has met the man, and seen his face, and has told Chris that he believes this new Welsh leader to be none other than my brother, James. He has begged Bhrodi to come to Lioncross Abbey to discuss this new threat and Corbett's assertion that the new Welsh leader is my brother that we believed dead. We are leaving on the morrow, but you must come to Lioncross, too, Papa. If this new Welsh leader truly is my brother, then you must come immediately. My love to you and Mama, Penelope."

Hearing the missive read aloud did something to William; the shock he'd experienced after reading it for himself was replaced by a massive measure of apprehension. There was something about hearing it in Kieran's calm, deep tone that sent bolts of anxiety through him and he stood up, unable to sit because his body was beginning to twitch. He began to pace over towards the windows.

"It must be a ghost," he finally said, "a phantom dredged up by the Welsh to throw the English off-balance. It is no secret that James died in Wales. We were all there, Kieran. I held him and you held him. He *was* dead."

Kieran could hear the edginess in William's voice, the uncertainty as well. "We certainly thought he was," he said. "Paris said he was."

William made it to the windows, looking out over his beloved Castle Questing. "Christ," he finally hissed. "The guilt I felt at leaving James behind. The anguish I went through, that I still go through, not having brought my son home. You know this to be true, Kieran, and now this? Why would Corbett Payton-Forrester, whose father is a good friend of mine, say such a thing? Has he no idea how this will hurt my family?"

Kieran's gaze moved back to the yellowed parchment. "William Payton-Forrester is a man beyond reproach," he said. "He has raised his sons in the same way. You know Corbett; he is a good man. He knew all of your sons, including James. I do not think he would make a mistake on a subject as fragile as this one is. If he says that he has seen James, then mayhap you should take him at his word."

William whirled around to face him. "This is madness. My son is *dead.*"

Kieran met his gaze. At the same time, he lifted up the parchment. "Is he?"

William stared at him. Then, the tears began to come as his mind allowed the possibility that what Corbett said was true. *What if… what if… what if?* With a growl, he closed his eye, warding off something that was both impossible and painful.

"Nay," he hissed. "It cannot be. It is a mistake. James died in Wales five years ago. We all saw it; we saw it when we fled like cowards and the Welsh stripped my son of his de Wolfe tunic, waving it in the air like a victory banner as we left him behind. We *saw* it. I even went back to look for his body a year after the battle, and there was nothing. You know I went back for him, Kieran. I could not leave my boy there."

Kieran could see the anguish in William's expression. "I know you did," he said. "You did all you could to recover him, but you were unable to. William, no one wants this to be true more than I do. You know I loved James like he was my very own son. When he married Rosie, I was overjoyed. No one understands your pain more than I do."

"And now?" William demanded as he moved away from the window, coming towards Kieran. "Now what? I am so angry that I want to kill but, in the same breath, I feel such… such *guilt.* Christ, Kieran; what if he wasn't dead when we left him in Wales? That very possibility has filled my nightmares and has left me sickened with the thought that I'd left my wounded son in Wales. I abandoned him. And now? My God… now, is it *true*?"

Kieran could only shake his head. "There is but one way to find out," he said quietly. "Do as Penny asks. Go to Wales and see for yourself."

William seemed to calm unnaturally fast at the simple, but truthful, words. He stared at Kieran a moment before retracing his steps back to the bed, sitting heavily once again on the stool. He suddenly looked very old and very weary.

"I knew that was to be my destiny the moment I read the missive," he muttered. "If James is alive, *really* alive, then I must know. But… God, Kieran, what if he hates me for leaving him there? I do not know if I can survive such hatred from my sweet James."

Kieran reached out, grasping William's hand. He squeezed it tightly. "You must remember who you are speaking of," he said. "We are speaking of a man who loved you more than anything on earth. He would understand why you left him behind."

"Then why did he not come home?" William asked painfully. "If he did not die, and has survived these years, why did he not come home?"

"I do not know."

"He had a wife and children here. Surely that would be enough to bring any man home."

Kieran let go of his hand and sat back in his bed. "And that is another issue," he said. "Rosie. She has since remarried and is very happy. I do not know how she is going to take this news."

William shook his head. "Do not tell her, not until we know for certain," he said. "Until I discover the truth, there is no reason to tell her. Right now, there are far too many questions with no answers. But should any of this be true, my fear of James' hatred is all too real."

Kieran sighed heavily. "You will not know anything until you go and discover the truth for yourself," he said. "But whatever happens, William, know that you did all you could in Wales. Had there been another way not to leave James behind, we would have taken it. You cannot shoulder any guilt for that."

William lifted his eyebrows, a gesture of resignation. "And yet, I do," he mumbled. "I always will. But you are correct; I will not know the truth of Corbett's report until I go to Lioncross and speak to him. Then I shall go to Wales and see for myself."

Kieran squeezed his hand again. "And I wish I could go with you, with all my heart," he said. "But alas, I am afraid I cannot make the journey. It is difficult for me to admit that, but it is the truth."

Now they were on the subject of Kieran's failing health and William exhaled sharply; he didn't want to hear the defeatist tone in Kieran's voice. "Mayhap you cannot make the journey, but you will be here when I return," he said. "And if James is alive, I will not return without him."

"When will you leave?"

"Immediately. As soon as I tell Jordan. I fear that my wife must be told of this."

"Who will you take with you?"

William thought on his sons, men who were finer and stronger knights than he could ever hope to be. Each one, great in his own right.

"Scott is south, at his holding of Castle Canaan," he said. "Troy is in Scotland, but he is not too far away should I need him. Patrick is at his garrison of Berwick Castle and Thomas is at his garrison of Wark Castle."

"Thomas has not been there very long. How is he faring?"

William shrugged. "Well, from what Troy and Paris have told me," he said. "I do not want to check on him for fear he will think that I do not trust him, so Troy and Paris have looked in on him. They say he is doing quite well, surprising from my youngest and sometimes grossly irresponsible son."

Kieran smiled faintly; Thomas de Wolfe was the youngest son in a great family of knights and he had, indeed, been grossly irresponsible for much of his young life. But that had changed a few months ago when William finally gave him a command. For Thomas, it had been his moment to grow up, so the news was hopeful that he finally had. With the de Wolfe name, there was little choice.

"He's had much to live up to, William," Kieran said. "He just needed his moment to shine."

"He will, I am sure."

Kieran fell silent for a moment as he further pondered William's coming journey. "When you go to Wales, take Scott with you," he said. "Troy and Patrick have their hands full with Scots raids at the moment and should not leave their garrisons. Scott is the only one who could possibly spare the time, and you should not go alone to face this. Take Nathaniel, too. My youngest son knew James well, and I am sure that he would like to accompany you. Will you take him?"

William nodded faintly. "Nat is an excellent knight, like his father," he said, "but I cannot take him with me. I will send him to Scotland to take over Troy's garrison while Troy comes with me. Troy would never forgive me if I did not bring him with me."

Kieran understood. The de Wolfe brothers were very close-knit. "And Patrick? If you take Troy, then you must take Patrick. He would be hurt if you did not."

William knew that. "Alec is at Berwick," he said, referring to Kieran's eldest son. "He is perfectly capable of handling any situation while Patrick is gone."

The situation was settled. "Very well," he said. "Send Nat to Scotland and leave Alec at Berwick. But take a contingent of men with you when you go south. Eight hundred, I should think. You are heading into Wales, after all, and you do not want to go undermanned."

William knew that. "I will," he said. "Anything else, General?"

There was a twinkle in his eye when he said it. Kieran had been his second in command for a very long time, and he was the great organizer in such matters. William never had to worry with Kieran in charge of mustering the army.

But there was something more to that question, at least in Kieran's view. He'd been watching his dear friend deny his health issues for several years, but never more strongly than he had as of late. Kieran was growing worse, but William refused to admit it. Now, with a months-long trip impending, they were reaching a crucial point in their relationship and, fearing that he might not be around when William returned, Kieran knew he had to speak what was on his mind and in his heart.

The time had finally come.

"Aye, there is," he said. "I want you to listen to me without arguing. Will you at least do that?"

"I never argue with you."

"You are doing it now."

William chuckled. "Very well," he said. "I will not speak another word. What else will you say?"

Kieran's good mood faded. "What I am to say is very important," he said. "There is a very good possibility that I will not be here when you return, William. The physic says my heart is growing worse by the day and there are times when I can hardly breathe. You know this. I know you do not want to acknowledge this, but you must. I have things that I need from you and I want to be assured that you will do them."

William was looking at him with an expression of great sorrow. "Kieran…"

"William, *please.*"

William sighed heavily; he was cornered, and he knew it. "Very well. Continue."

Kieran did. "I do not know what the future brings, so I must have my say," he said, lowering his voice. "I have imagined this moment many times and thought of what I would say to you. What do you say to someone who has been closer to you than a brother? What do you say to someone who has meant everything to you, as much as you and I have meant to each other?"

William couldn't help it; his eye began to fill with tears. "I do not know," he said. "I have been asking myself the same thing."

Kieran's eyes began to grow moist and he reached out again, taking William's hand and holding it tightly.

"I want to take a good look at you," he said. "It will more than likely be my last look. And I want you to know that the day I met you was the best day of my life. I have watched you become the greatest knight England has ever seen, but your greatness as a knight cannot compare with your greatness as my friend. Nay, as my *brother.* You have always been my brother, William, and I want to thank you for everything. Life with you has been quite a journey."

William's tears were beginning to spill over, his head bent over his hands as he clutched Kieran's fingers. "And I cannot imagine completing this journey without you," he whispered. "I knew this time would come but I supposed I'd hoped we would die at the same time. I do not know what I am going to do without you, Kieran."

Kieran put a big hand on his lowered head. "You will have Paris," he said. "I realize that is a poor substitute for me, but he will have to suffice."

William grinned through his tears. "A poor substitute, indeed," he said. "He loves you almost as much as I do. He will miss you very much."

Kieran smiled weakly. "He will not admit it," he said. "But there is something more, William, something that is most important to me."

"Name it and I shall make it so."

"My wife. My passing will destroy her even though she pretends to be strong. You will make sure she is taken care of, please."

"She is family. Of course I will take care of her; you need not ask."

"And our grandchildren – you and I share several. In the years to come, make sure they remember me from time to time. Tell them… tell them how much I loved them."

William's tears flowed like rain. "I will, I swear it," he said. "They will know how great their Kee was."

"Kee," Kieran chuckled softly. "I remember when Edward first called me that and it stuck. I hated it, but I could not shake it. Now, I love it. I want it to be the last thing I ever hear."

William simply nodded, squeezing the man's hand. "My tears are selfish tears, you know," he said, wiping at his face with one hand. "I do not cry for you. You will go to sleep and when you awaken, you will find yourself young and strong again, and I envy that. I cry because I will be without you, and I will miss your quiet wisdom and your great strength. I do not know if I have ever told you that I love you, Kieran, but I do. I love you as deeply as a man has ever loved his brother and I swear to you that our grandchildren, and their children, will know of you. You will be well-remembered."

Kieran's dark eyes glimmered. "Thank you," he murmured. "I am grateful."

"Is there anything else?"

Kieran nodded. "Kevin," he said. "I've not seen my son in quite some time, ever since he left for The Levant."

William knew that. Kevin Hage, Kieran's beloved son, had left England for The Holy Land because the woman he loved, William's youngest daughter, Penelope, had married another man and Kevin had been unable to cope with the loss. He'd left for The Holy Land with

Kieran's blessing, but William knew how hard it had been for Kieran to let his son go.

"I know," he said after a moment. "What would you have me tell him when I see him?"

For the first time, Kieran seemed to grow quite upset. "I never imagined that I would not speak with my son ever again in this life," he said, fighting off tears. "Kevin is special to me. I love all of my sons very much, but Kevin… I understand him. He has a tender heart, something he tries so hard to protect, but he is simply incapable of hardening. I suppose that is what I love so much about him. William, when you see him again, will you tell him… tell him how much I loved him and how proud I was of him. No matter what, I was proud of him. I want you to tell him that my last thoughts were of him. Will you do this?"

William nodded. "I will."

"Thank you."

There wasn't much more to say after that. They'd said everything they needed to. Kieran finally let go of William's hands and opened up his arms, embracing William as they both found an outlet for their quiet tears. It was an embrace of everlasting friendship and of the bonds of brotherhood that could never be broken. When William finally released him, he kissed him on the forehead and stood up.

"You must know I have been dreading this moment," he said. "I suppose that is why I have been avoiding this. I did not believe I could face it. But now… now I feel as if I have said what I needed to say. I am content, but I will say again how much I will miss you. I do not want to let you go."

Kieran smiled weakly. "I know," he said. "But I am tired, William. I am tired of being ill, of not being able to function as a normal man. I spend my days in this bed, remembering when I was young and strong and healthy. I do not like my family seeing me this way. It is no way for a knight's life to end. I had always imagined that I would die a glorious death in battle, but it seems as if I am to die an old man in my bed."

William was struggling not to weep again. Kieran had never spoken of his personal feelings on his health woes, so to know how much they affected him was difficult to hear. The powerful knight was no longer powerful; he was trapped by a dying body and deeply saddened for it.

"Is that so bad, dying in your bed?" he asked. "You have lived a full and wonderful life, Kieran. I do not mind the notion of dying in bed, with my wife by my side. I always thought the only glorious death would be the one in battle, but I have since changed my mind. A peaceful death, surrounded by my family, is more glorious to me. Mayhap it is the mark of a truly loved man."

Kieran's gaze moved to the windows that faced northwest. There was blue sky beyond in a warm autumn day. Memories of the years flashed in his mind, of him when he was young, and of William when he was young. They had, indeed, been glorious days, but what William said resonated with him – he was more content now than he'd ever been. And he had been fortunate enough to have loved deeply. After a moment, he tossed back the coverlet and put his feet on the ground.

As William watched, Kieran stood up, slowly and laboriously, and began to walk towards him. It wasn't the usual proud gait that William remembered, but more of a shuffling gait from a man who shouldn't even be out of bed. But William stood his ground as Kieran approached, looking the man in the eye when he came close. Kieran smiled faintly.

"I did not want your last memory of me to be as I lie in my bed," he said, taking a deep breath to steady himself since his heart and lungs didn't work well these days. "Remember me as I was, William. Remember me as the powerful knight who was honored to serve with you."

William lost the battle against the tears once more. They streamed down his face. "I will," he said. "It has been an honor to serve with you, also, Kieran Hage."

Kieran nodded, feeling rather proud that he'd been able to face his friend on his feet one last time. "Now," he said huskily. "Go to Wales and find your son. I will try to be here when you return, but if I am not, then this parting was well-made."

William was trying to be brave about this, but he couldn't seem to be. He couldn't speak for the lump in his throat. Lifting his hand, he touched Kieran on the cheek.

"You will always be young and strong to me," he whispered. "Godspeed, Kieran Hage. I will look forward to when next we meet again, in this life or in the next."

With that, he turned and left the chamber, feeling more sorrow and anguish than he could imagine. It was true that all of the denial he'd had about Kieran's health had hit him hard but, in the same breath, there was a satisfaction to the conversation. They'd said everything that needed to be said, and William could go forward now with his friend's wise counsel. But, God, he missed him already.

Farewell, Kieran…

PART FIVE

DRAGON TAMER

CHAPTER EIGHTEEN

Wales

THE ARROW WASN'T sticking out of her shoulder any longer, but Blayth knew that she must have been in a good deal of pain.

They were riding northeast beneath a dark pewter sky and a great silver moon that was beginning to set. Soon enough, it would disappear in the west and then the land would be as dark as pitch. Blayth knew they would have to find shelter before that happened, a place to tend Asmara's wound.

He'd tried to do it as soon as they'd left Gwendraith, but Asmara was a strong woman. She'd ripped the arrow out of her shoulder and kept her hand against the wound, pressing it with the material from her tunic to stop the bleeding. She wouldn't even let him stop so that he could get a look at the wound. She was concerned that men from Gwendraith might try to pursue them and she didn't want them to catch up, so it was best to put as much distance between them and Gwendraith as possible.

Arrow wound be damned.

Therefore, they raced off into the night. Asmara's young stallion was very fast, taking the lead as Blayth's horse tried to keep up. To the south, they could see the rise of ghostly hills and to the north, it was mostly flat lands and forests. All of it was bathed in moonlight, which made the road easy to see. They were able to dodge things that, had it been a darker night, they would have tripped over.

Blayth mostly tried to stay on Asmara's tail as she rode the horse at breakneck speed. She was only holding on with one hand as it was, the other one pressed tightly to her left shoulder, and he was genuinely fearful that she was going to fall off at some point, but his Dragon Princess remained strong. She held tight as they headed north, passing through smaller towns, and then letting the horses have their head on the long and barren stretches.

On they went, into the night.

Blayth wasn't entirely sure how long they'd been running, but by the position of the moon, he guessed that it had been at least a couple of hours. The moon was so low now that it was beginning to dip below the horizon and he knew that they had to find shelter fairly quickly. On the road ahead, they could see a small village and they could smell the smoke from the dying fires. He managed to get his horse up next to Asmara's and grab hold of her reins.

"We must stop," he yelled over the rush of the wind. "Look; the moon is setting. We must stop for the night."

Asmara looked pale and frightened. She was in panic mode, fleeing Gwendraith, fearful for her very life. They both knew what Morys was capable of and even though she'd hit the man with an arrow, she hadn't really noticed where she'd hit him other than it had been up around his shoulders. After that, everything was a blur. As Blayth slowed the horses as they neared the edge of town, Asmara was very much starting to feel the pain of her wound. Now that the rush of fear had settled, the agony of a pierced shoulder was coming to the forefront. She groaned, leaning forward in the saddle as Blayth looked at her with concern.

The town was very small and Blayth was somewhat familiar with it since Brecfa, Morys' stronghold was several miles to the west. He knew that there wasn't a tavern to be found, but there was a church at the other end of the town, one that had been there since the Normans first came to Wales.

He led Asmara's horse through the streets at a clipped pace as she increasingly gave in to the pain in her shoulder. Up ahead, illuminated by the setting moon, they could see the tower of the church, which was situated on a small hill. The tower itself was at least four stories, soaring above the countryside, while the church attached to it was long and rectangular, built from local stone and rubble.

As they drew closer, Blayth could see the churchyard with the stones atop the graves, a superstition to keep the dead from rising. There was a small structure to the rear of the church, housing of some sort, and Blayth took the horses into the churchyard and headed for the small house. Once they reached it, he slid from his horse and pounded on the door.

He had to pound on it at least four more times until he heard someone on the other side of the door. By this time, the moon was nearly down and the gnarled oak trees were casting great shadows, nearly blacking everything out. There was a small window in the heavily-fortified door that slid open.

"What's wanting?" came a voice.

Blayth could hardly see anything as he peered at the small hole. "My lady has been injured," he said. "We seek your help."

There was no immediate reply and Blayth couldn't tell if the person was looking at him or not. He leaned closer to the door, trying to see in the small window.

"Please help us," he said. "My lady has a wound that needs tending. We… we have been attacked. Won't you please help?"

More dead silence. As Blayth pondered what more to say, as he was trying not to frighten the person on the other side of the door, Asmara slid off her horse and marched up to the door.

"You are a priest," she said irritably. "You cannot refuse to aid us. Open the door or I will start screaming. That will rouse everyone in town and they will wonder what you are doing to a woman that is causing her to scream. Is that what you want?"

As Blayth looked at her, shocked and amused, the small panel jerked shut and, suddenly, the door was being unbolted from within.

When it lurched open, they found themselves looking at a small man with a care-worn face, wrapped in heavy woolen robes.

"A lady with a tongue of fire," he said unhappily, looking at Asmara. "Who are you, girl?"

Blayth pushed into the small structure before Asmara could answer. He shoved the man out of the way, pulling Asmara along with him, and they found themselves in a two-room hut, dark and cold. The man, regaining his balance after being pushed aside, scurried after the pair.

"See here," he said angrily. "What's wanting?"

Blayth found a chair in the darkness and pushed Asmara down onto it. "I told you," he said. "My lady has been injured in an attack. I would like hot water and wine if you have it, and bandages. I swear to you that we mean you no harm, but I must tend her wound."

The man appeared quite put out. He frowned at the pair and prepared to order them out, but then he realized that would be futile. They were inside now, and it was clear that they intended to remain, so he had little choice. Angered, he shut the door and threw the bolt. Then he pointed to the hearth with just a few burning embers in it.

"Well?" he said. "If you want hot water, then put fuel on the fire. It'll not burn all by itself."

Grumbling to himself, the man went into the second room, pushing back heavy curtains that covered the doorway, and disappeared inside. Asmara looked up at Blayth, who wriggled his eyebrows in silent commentary of the irritated man, before turning for the hearth. He found the kindling right away, as it was scattered by the hearth, and he carefully placed it on the low-burning coals, blowing on it until the blaze began to take off. By the time the man returned from the other room, a decent fire was beginning to roar.

"Water is outside," the man told Blayth snappishly. "Bucket is next to the door."

As Blayth stood up from the fire, the man lit two fat tapers and a soft golden glow began to fill the room. Now that there was some illumination, Blayth could see that the room was packed to the ceiling with items – pots, clothing, broken pieces of furniture, and more. It took Blayth a moment to realize that among the clutter, he saw shields – English shields – as well as pieces of armor, satchels, saddlebags, and in one corner he saw a stack of weapons. Pikes, poles, and broadswords. He most definitely saw an array of English broadswords, more than likely worth a fortune, wedged into a corner and suffering from neglect.

It was an astonishing sight and he very nearly forgot about the water, but Asmara groaned when she shifted on the chair and leaned on the table that was next to her, so he quickly went about his tasks.

But those broadswords had his attention.

As Blayth ran out, Asmara tried to find a comfortable position leaning against the table but it was nearly impossible. Her left shoulder and entire arm were aching painfully, and she kept her hand over the wound area simply because she was afraid to ease the pressure. It seemed to feel better when her hand was firmly against it. She didn't know how badly she'd been hit, but she knew it hurt a great deal.

As the fire in the hearth began to burn brightly and the tapers lit up the chamber, Asmara began to see what Blayth had seen. More clutter and possessions and weapons than she'd ever seen outside of an armory; there were several big shields stacked up, partially covered by what looked to be tunics or banners, and the broadswords in the corner glistened weakly in the light. The sight was almost enough to distract her from her pain.

"What *is* this place?" she asked the man, who was fumbling with something over by another table. "Why do you have all of these… these *things*?"

The man didn't answer her directly. He glanced over his shoulder at her. "They are mine," he said. "Tell me your name."

Asmara hesitated. "Morwenna," she said, giving him the name of her mother because it was the first thing that came to mind. "Who are you?"

"I am Jestin."

"Are you the priest here?"

He nodded. "Aye," he said. "Who is your man?"

Asmara didn't want to give Blayth's name away, either. "James," she said, wincing as she spoke because it was also the first name that came to mind, and probably not the best name to give. In order to head off any further questions, she pushed forth with an explanation. "We were traveling north to… to see his family and we were attacked."

Jestin had things in his hands as he headed over to the fire and pulled forth one of the iron arms that were used for hanging pots over the flame. He had a small pot in his hand and hung it on the arm, but Asmara noticed that he was also holding a small sack of some kind. There was already something in the pot, but she couldn't see what it was, and she watched curiously as he sprinkled something from the little sack into the pot. Using a stick leaning on the wall next to the hearth, he stirred whatever was in the pot.

Asmara couldn't help but notice that the man really didn't have much to say. He seemed very annoyed with their intrusion, but that couldn't be helped. Unsure of what more to say to him, her attention inevitably returned to the beautiful broadswords pushed into the corner. Dusty, and dulled with neglect, there was no mistaking their beauty.

"Did someone give those for safekeeping?" she asked. "Those weapons, I mean."

Jestin was over at his table, his back turned to her as he ripped up material. Asmara could hear him tearing at it.

"You might say that," he said. "Tell me why you were attacked."

He was deliberately changing the subject, the second time she'd asked a question about all of the things he had stacked up in the corners, and the second time he avoided giving her an answer. Asmara was coming to think he simply didn't want to speak of it, and the truth of the matter was that she and Blayth had barged in on the man, and threatened him, so she didn't blame him for not being friendly.

But she really didn't care. As long as they had some shelter, and she was able to tend her wound, that was all that mattered. They'd be gone in the morning, anyway, and their whole visit would have been forgotten.

"I do not know why we were attacked," she said after a moment. "An arrow hit me. That is all you need be concerned with."

Jestin glanced over his shoulder again, his dark eyes appraising her, but Asmara looked away, gazing into the fire. Much as he didn't want to speak on his massive collection, she didn't want to discuss why she'd been hit with an arrow, so silence seemed best at this point.

They'd come to a stalemate.

The entry door burst open and Blayth appeared, lugging a big bucket of icy water from the well. He headed straight to the hearth, taking a knee beside it and looking at all of the cluttered mess around the hearth until he came to an iron pot that was sitting off to one side.

He pulled it forth, peered inside of it, and then took the hem of his tunic to wipe it clean, again and again. When he was satisfied that it was clean enough, he poured the water into it and set it upon the coals.

"I am sorry I took so long," he said, "but I took a few moments to tend to the horses. While the water is warming, I should take a look at your shoulder. Does it hurt very much?"

Asmara looked up at him and he could see the answer to his question in her eyes, even though he knew she would never admit it.

"Nay," she lied. "Not very much."

He didn't contradict her. The Dragon Princess was strong in so many ways, and he would not diminish that strength, but he watched her grimace as he moved her hand away from the wound. Then he began peeling back the fabric of her tunic, getting a look at a puncture wound that was just below her left collarbone. She turned her head away as he bent lower to get a good look.

"It does not look as if it is too terribly deep," he said, "but it needs to be cleaned out."

Gingerly, he pulled out a piece of fabric from the surface of the wound, part of her tunic that was torn off when the arrow pierced her.

As he looked closer, he realized there was another head close to his and he looked to see their host standing next to him, also peering curiously at the wound. He could feel the man's hot breath on his neck as he scrutinized the wound quite closely.

"We will need the wine to wash the wound clean," the man finally said. "I have brought all that I have. We will also need to stitch it closed. I have is sewing kit."

Blayth didn't like the fact that the man was so close to Asmara, but he tolerated it for the moment. "I agree," he said. "What is your name?"

"Jestin," Asmara said; her head was turned and her eyes were closed because she didn't want to see the gaping hole in her shoulder. "This is Father Jestin. I have introduced us as Morwenna and James."

Blayth looked at her rather curiously for a moment, realizing she had given the priest fake names. Still, he understood why; she didn't want to involve the priest in their troubles and she didn't want the man to be able to give their true names if Morys and other Welshmen came looking for them. That seemed dangerous. Therefore, he kept that in mind as he watched the priest scrutinize Asmara's wound.

The man who could help them… or very well condemn them.

But he didn't seem like he was in the mood to condemn. In fact, after his initial irritation at their intrusion, he'd settled down dramatically. Now, he seemed very interested in Asmara's wound.

"I have something to help her," he finally said, rushing off to another cluttered corner of the chamber. "I read a treatise on Arabic potions and it had the knowledge of a healing mixture that keeps away fever and disease. A rotten brew, it is called. I have made it before."

Blayth didn't like the sound of that. "Rotten?" he repeated. "And it is supposed to help?"

Jestin nodded eagerly. "Aye," he said. "It cures all ailments, or at least most of them. I have given some to the people of the village who were in need and the results are miraculous."

Blayth was leery but, at this point, he was willing to allow it. He and Asmara had a long journey ahead of them and he didn't want her suffering or ill along the way. He couldn't bear it if something happened to this brave woman because of him.

As Jestin fussed over in the corner by the light of a single taper, Blayth turned to Asmara as she sat, still leaning against the old table. He felt extremely guilty about what had happened and, in truth, he hadn't really thought about it until now. He'd kept the visions of Morys' actions pushed aside because the more important task had been to reach safety. But now, he had time to think about it. They were safe for the time being, Asmara was about to be tended, and he struggled not to let the guilt of it all consume him.

"You were very brave, *cariad*," he finally said, kneeling down beside her. "It is strange... I am not accustomed to anyone fighting my own battles, but that is what you have done. You stood up to Morys in my defense and I am both awed and grateful. But please know how sorry I am that it ended with an arrow in your shoulder."

Asmara turned to look at him, feeling the warmth from the man. There was so much warmth between them now that it was present every time they looked at each other, in their expressions as well as in their touch. She could see in his expression how grateful he was and she put her hand up, cupping his bearded jaw.

"I would do it a thousand times over," she murmured. "He was trying to turn the men against you and I would not let him do that."

He put his hand over hers, turning to kiss her palm sweetly. "You are my champion," he said softly. Then, he eyed the priest over in the corner. "What did you tell him?"

Asmara turned as well, her gaze falling on the man who was busily doing something. "Not much," she whispered so the priest couldn't hear. "I did not want to give him our real names for fear that Morys might be tracking us."

Blayth thought back to the moment he saw Asmara's arrow hit Morys in the neck. "I do not think that will be possible," he muttered. "Your aim was true."

"What do you mean?"

"I believe you killed him. If the arrow did not, then we certainly did when we fled and trampled him."

Her eyes widened. "I… I did not see," she said. "The arrow was in my shoulder and that was all I was concerned with. I did not see what happened after it hit me."

He kissed her hand again. "He would have killed us," he said. "I have no doubt. What you did, you did to protect our lives. There is no dishonor or shame in that."

Asmara thought on the moment she was hit with Morys' arrow, the moment that her own arrow was accidentally released. She really hadn't been aiming at the time, but if she hit her uncle, she realized that she did not regret it. Blayth was right; Morys would have killed them both.

"I never thought I would see him do such a thing," she said truthfully. "I do not understand why he would… wait… that is not true. I *do* understand. Morys has always been selfish and deceitful. My own father will not speak ill of his brother, but I do not have such restraint. He was going to kill you to keep you from leaving him."

"I know."

"I would not have believed it had I not seen it for myself."

Blayth simply nodded, thinking on Morys and how the man had been both a blessing and a curse to him. "It occurred to me that he started seeing me as a possession," he muttered. "He saved my life. Therefore, it was his view that I should belong to him. I suppose I have always seen that in him, but never more so when you and I were coming to know one another. He did not like that my attention was somewhere other than on his goals."

Asmara could see some regret in his expression. "The only decent thing my uncle ever did was save your life," she said. "But even then, it wasn't with altruistic intentions. Still… for the fact that he did save your life, I cannot hate him completely. But for what he tried to do tonight – I can never forgive him."

Blayth simply kissed her hand again, catching sight of Jestin as the man came away from his table and moved in their direction. Blayth stood up, Asmara's hand still in his, protectively, as he looked curiously at the things the man was carrying with him.

"What do you have?" he asked.

Jestin had quite a few items which he began sitting down on the table – an empty wooden cup, a half-full wooden cup, a wad of linen rags that he'd torn up for bandages, an earthenware bottle of wine, a slender iron bar that was several inches in length, and a sewing kit with needle and thread. All of these things ended up on the table beside Asmara as Jestin went to the pot he'd put above the flames, which was now beginning to steam. Removing the pot, he carefully poured the milky contents into the empty cup he'd brought with him.

"Now," he said, handing Blayth the cup. "Have your woman drink this. Quickly, now – she must drink it all."

Blayth eyed the cup. "What is it?"

"Something for the pain."

Blayth continued to eye the cup. After a moment, he looked up at the priest. "Tell me what is in it. I will not give her an unknown potion."

Jestin glanced at him. "Poppy," he said, his annoyance returning. "There is poppy in the goat's milk. Make her drink it. It will take away her pain."

Blayth still didn't like it. He extended the cup back to him.

"Take a sip from it," he growled. "Prove to me that there is no poison in it."

Jestin sighed sharply, took the cup, and promptly took a sip. Then he shoved it back at Blayth.

"You came to me for help," he said. "If you did not want it, then I can just as easily sit by and do nothing."

He had a point. Trust didn't come naturally to Blayth, but he had little choice because he needed the help. Moderately convinced that the priest wasn't out to harm Asmara, he turned and gave her the cup.

"Drink this down," he said, putting it in her right hand. "He says it will help your pain."

Asmara had been watching the entire exchange, including the moment when Blayth forced the priest to drink the goat's milk potion. She was very touched by the way Blayth was watching out for her and she took the cup and drained it. The milk was warm and lovely, but she could taste something in it, something bitter. Licking her lips, she handed him back the cup.

"Why should he have poppy on hand?" she whispered. "Is he a physic also?"

"When the town's folk need help, they come to me," the priest said. He'd heard her question. "Either they need my prayers or my potions. Surely that is why you were sent to me, isn't it?"

Blayth shook his head. "We were not sent to you."

That seemed to surprise Jestin. "You weren't?"

"Nay."

"Then… you simply *found* me?"

Blayth nodded. "There is no tavern in the village and with the lady being injured, this was the most logical place to come."

Jestin's gaze lingered on him for a moment. "Then God must have been speaking to you," he said. "He has brought you here, to me, because He knew I could help the lady."

Blayth wasn't so sure why that seemed like such a miracle that they should have come to the church in their hour of need, so he didn't reply. He was simply glad that Asmara was receiving care.

In fact, for a man who had reluctantly admitted them into his residence, the priest had moved past that annoyance and was taking charge of Asmara's care. He seemed very confident about it. After ensuring she drank the milk with the poppy in it, he approached her with a small dagger and tore away the tunic around the wound.

"Ah," he said as he inspected the puncture. "It is not too deep, but it must be cleaned. Be still, lady, and this will go quickly."

Asmara looked at him warily. "What are you going to do?" she demanded. "And why are *you* doing this? I did not give you permission to touch me."

Jestin immediately stood up, looking at Blayth and pointing to Asmara. "Then *you* tend this ungrateful woman," he said. "I can promise you have not tended nearly as many wounds as I have, but go ahead. Make a mess of her and I will not stop you."

Frankly, Blayth wasn't very good tending battle wounds. He'd seen many, of course, and could make do in rendering basic aid, but the tending of the wounded had always fallen to other men who were more specialized in it. In spite of his brusque manner, Jestin seemed much more comfortable around potions and needles. Blayth was confident in many things, but healing wasn't one of them.

"Were you once a physic?" he asked. "Is that why you have potions and know so much about healing?"

Jestin lifted his skinny shoulders. "I read," he said. "I read a great deal. I have treatises and books and documents from all over our world that tell of many things, so I have learned much. You have seen my collection of treasures; there is a good deal of information in these treasures and I have memorized it all. When anyone is wounded in the village, they come to me because they know I can heal them. That is why I asked if you had been sent."

Blayth shook his head. "As I told you, no one sent us," he said. "If you have knowledge on healing, then I would ask you to tend the lady. She will be still for you, I swear it. But know that I shall be watching everything you do and if I am not satisfied, you will not live to see the dawn."

Jestin gave him an expression that suggested he wasn't intimidated by the threat. "You will be satisfied," he said. "And then you and your ungrateful wife will leave me and never return."

It seemed like a fair deal, so Blayth nodded and Jestin returned to his position over Asmara. She didn't seem thrilled by it, but she had little choice. She turned her head and closed her eyes as Blayth came up beside her, taking her good hand and holding it tightly as Jestin went to work.

Asmara did a good deal of grunting and wincing as Jestin picked bits of cloth from her wound, carefully, and periodically cleansing it with the wine. That seemed to hurt the most and she gasped whenever he poured the alcohol into the wound. Blayth held her hand tightly and had his arm around her shoulders, preventing her from moving around too much, as Jestin cleansed and picked. He took the iron stick-like implement and used the flat end of it to scrape out whatever debris he hadn't been able to pick away. It had been excruciating for Asmara, who had her face buried in Blayth's chest.

The cleansing and scraping seemed to go on for quite some time. Blayth was torn between anger that Jestin was causing Asmara pain, and gratitude that he was being so thorough. When the priest had finished picking and washing and scraping, he finally took a bone needle and fine silk thread and put six quick stitches in Asmara's shoulder. She yelped a little, for it was clearly painful, but that was the extent of her visible pain.

When it was finally over, Jestin took the bandages he'd made and wrapped her shoulder up in them. The last step was to hand Blayth another cup that was half-full of a dark liquid that smelled horrific. He wanted Asmara to drink it, which she did, choking it down miserably because it tasted so badly. When Blayth handed the empty cup back to Jestin, the priest pointed towards the doorway to the second chamber.

"In there," he said quietly, gathering his things. "There is a bed in there. Put her there to rest."

Blayth obeyed. Asmara was exhausted and in pain, and the poppy potion had made her extremely sleepy. Bending over, he swept her into his arms and carried her into the second chamber, which was far more cluttered than the first, but there was, indeed, a small cot shoved against the wall. A cat was sleeping on it and he swept the cat away with his foot, depositing Asmara onto the straw mattress. She was nearly asleep when he pulled the rough woolen blanket over her.

"Sleep now," he whispered, kissing her on the forehead. "I shall be nearby should you need me."

Asmara didn't respond. Her eyes were closed and she was asleep already. Pain, exhaustion, and the poppy had seen to that. Blayth's gaze lingered on her a moment before wandering out into the main chamber.

Jestin was wiping out cups and cleaning the iron implement with wine as he emerged and headed over to the blazing fire. Now that Asmara was tended, he hoped to get some sleep before the night was through but, upon reflection, he thought that was a ridiculous hope. He'd be awake all night in case Asmara needed him. He and the surly priest were about to keep each other company.

"I will pay you for your services before we leave," he said. "I am grateful for your assistance."

Jestin snorted as he wiped the iron implement. "As if I had a choice," he said. "You burst in without invitation."

Blayth couldn't disagree. "You are fortunate that is all I did, considering you called the lady fire-tongued."

"Well... she *is*."

"She most certainly is, but that is not for you to say."

Jestin continued to snort as he put his things away. "I will grant you the husband's privilege of insulting your wife, but I will not apologize for what I said," he replied. "She said you were attacked. Where did this happen?"

"Gwendraith," he said. It wasn't a lie, after all. "And before you ask me why we came so far before seeking help, we feared that we were followed."

"Were you?"

"I do not believe so."

Jestin began pulling out other things. It seemed as if the man was constantly busy, unable to remain still. The cat that Blayth had swept from the bed came slinking into the chamber and the priest petted the cat, putting it up on the table and pouring it some goat's milk.

"She also said that you were going to visit your family," he said. "Where are you from?"

Blayth didn't know how to answer that, considering he didn't really know himself. "North," he said, simply because that was the direction they were traveling. He found his attention turning towards the broadswords in the corner again and he meandered in that direction, hoping to change the subject away from him. "How did you come by these swords? They are quite beautiful and expensive, I would imagine. Did someone give them to you?"

Jestin came away from the table in the shadows where he had been standing. He had two cups in his hand and held one out to Blayth as he approached. "Go on," he said. "Take it. It is cider."

Blayth complied. He sniffed it before taking a drink of quite possibly the most potent alcohol he'd ever had the misfortune to drink. It was like a stream of fire going down his throat.

"God's Bones," he muttered. "*That* is cider?"

Jestin nodded. "I make it myself from the apples in the orchards surrounding *Sanctiadd*."

"What is *Sanctiadd*?"

"My church."

"I see," Blayth said, taking another sup of cider and trying not to cough. "You make liquid fire from those apples."

Jestin gave him a lopsided grin. "Mayhap," he said. "Usually, I drink alone. It is rare I have someone to share it with. Even though you barged into my home and were rude, I forgive you. Now you will sit down and tell me of your journey. Your lady will sleep for a long while, so we will have time to converse."

Blayth planted himself on a stool near the hearth, a small thing against his considerable size. "There is not much to tell of our journey, other than the attack," he said. "I am more interested in knowing about all of these things you have collected. If I am not mistaken, you also have English shields against the wall."

The potent liquid fire had the effect of loosening Jestin's tongue because he had already downed nearly his entire cup, indicative of a man who was used to the strong drink.

"They are indeed English," the priest said, moving to pour himself more of the cider. "You could say that I am the Keeper."

Blayth looked at him. "The Keeper of what?"

Jestin glanced at the man. "Of what you see," he said. "I am the Keeper."

"But where do you get it?"

Jestin brought the pitcher over to Blayth and poured more into his cup. From the tension they'd endured since pushing their way into the residence to the relative peace of the moment, it seemed rather strange to Blayth that they were now drinking together like old friends, but he went along with it. He was glad he didn't have to spend the entire night protecting an injured woman from an irate priest.

"I get it from the battles in this valley and others," Jestin said as he plopped down onto a chair that nearly gave way because he sat down so hard. He steadied the chair and himself before continuing. "This entire valley has seen many battles and there are always things left behind. Sometimes there are battles to the south, at castles along the southern hills, and sometimes I go there, too. When I hear of them, I go. I gather what I can and bring it back here for safe keeping."

Blayth thought that was an extremely odd thing to do. "But why?"

Jestin pondered the question as he slurped his cider. "Why not?" he said. "These are the fragments of men that must be guarded. These represent men who have died in senseless ways. These are the remnants of lives and, in God's eyes, they must never be forgotten."

It was a touching thing to say and, in a sense, Blayth could understand. "So… you keep these to remind God of the men who owned them? Of the men who died?"

Jestin nodded. Then, he peered more closely at Blayth, studying the man in the firelight. "You look as if you have been badly wounded in battle," he said, gesturing to the left side of his head. "You speak slowly, as if the damage is lasting. What happened to you?"

Blayth wasn't sure how much to tell him. "I do not remember," he said honestly. "It was a terrible battle and I was wounded, but I was eventually healed. It took time."

"Then you understand when I say that these remnants of battle must be preserved. They are tributes to the dead."

Blayth nodded slowly. "I understand," he said. "There are a good many English remnants here as well as Welsh."

Abruptly, Jestin stood up and went over to the great clutter against the far wall. He began to rummage through the wooden shields, once proud symbols of the men who had owned them, and he pulled one shield out to hold it up.

"Do you see this?" he said, displaying a blue and white striped tri-cornered shield. It was beautiful and well-made. "This is from Llandeilo. There was a great battle there a few years ago and the English army was badly destroyed. I found this near a dead de Valence knight. That is the Earl of Pembroke, you know."

Llandeilo. Blayth's heart began to pound when Jestin brought up that fateful battle, the one that had changed the course of his life. God, he knew so little about it, but hearing the priest speak of it, he was almost frantic to know what the priest knew. Had he seen anything? Did he witness the carnage?

What did the man *know*?

"I am aware of Pembroke," Blayth said, sounding surprisingly calm. "You… you were at Llandeilo?"

Jestin carefully set the shield against the wall. "It is not far from here," he said. "Panicked men came to tell me about it, so I took my cart and went to the battlefield."

"Did you see the battle?"

He shook his head. "Only the aftermath," he said. "Only when the English wounded were being killed and the Welsh were stripping the dead."

Blayth wasn't sure what more to ask the man even though he had a thousand questions on his mind. His speech simply wasn't swift enough to keep up with them, so it was better if he kept his mouth shut and didn't sound like a fool. But one prevalent thought came to the forefront – if the priest came after the battle, then the armies were already gone at that time. That meant the House of de Wolfe and the other English had retreated.

They would be heading north whilst the priest was heading south along the same road.

Did he see them?

"If you were heading to the battle when the English were retreating, the surely you saw their armies," he said, feeling anxious and curious. "They must have come this way, heading to the Marches."

Jestin was pulling forth another shield. "I saw them," he said. "They were fleeing quickly. They left their wounded; I know because I saw them. It was a slaughter, I am afraid. The English were ambushed, you see, and they could not take the dead."

Blayth stared at him. *They could not take their dead.* He had no idea that just those few words could mean so much to him. Morys had told him that he'd been abandoned and unwanted, cast aside by the English, but the priest was telling him otherwise. A man who had been there, and who had seen the carnage, was telling him something completely different.

So Morys had lied to him yet again.

"You are certain of this?" he found himself asking.

"There is no doubt," Jestin said. "I saw them fleeing and they could only take what they could carry. They left wagons behind, animals, and the dead and wounded. I was able to save some of the wounded from the Welsh, who were killing them all, but there were so many more I could not save. So… I brought their fragments back with me to preserve them. With me, they are protected, and they are remembered. They are not the lost dead."

He sounded sorrowful as he said it, a man who seemed to have no country boundaries. He was a man of God and that was all that mattered to him. Before Blayth could respond, Jestin held up a big shield, tri-cornered, with a dark green background, gold around the edges, and a black wolf head in the middle. The wolf had its mouth open and big fangs, a very fearsome head, indeed.

"See this shield?" he said. "Someone told me this is the House of de Wolfe. This is one of the greatest families in England. I have one of their tunics here, somewhere. They left a good deal behind when they fled."

Blayth stared at the shield, feeling something strange wash over him. He couldn't stop looking at the shield because there was something oddly familiar about it. He was certain he'd never seen it before – or had he? Either way, he had a very strange feeling when he looked at it, as if he knew it but didn't know it. It was both confusing and mesmerizing. Before he realized it, he was on his feet, moving to the shield even as Jestin set it down. Blayth took the shield from him and held it up in front of his face, looking at it, feeling oh-so-unsteady as he did.

And then it hit him.

He'd seen the shield in his dreams.

When he realized that, he almost dropped the thing. It was the strangest sensation he'd ever known but, as he continued to stare at the shield, he knew for a fact that he recognized it now. He *had* seen it in his dreams.

A de Wolfe shield.

Oh, God.

"What you have done," he said, his voice trembling, "is noble. That you would remember men who have been left on the field of battle is one of the greatest acts of kindness I have ever heard. I am sure that if their families knew, they would thank you."

Jestin could hear the quiver in his tone and turned to see that he was still looking at the de Wolfe shield. He seemed oddly awestruck by it.

"Sometimes, they do thank me," he said.

Blayth was still looking at the shield. "What do you mean?"

Jestin began to look around at the other things in his collection. "Sometimes the fathers come looking for their sons," he said. "In fact, a year after the battle, an older knight came looking for his son. Some of the villagers had told him that I collect things from the battlefield, so he came to see if I knew of his son. Unfortunately, I did not. It has happened before, you know, men looking for their sons. But so far, I have never been able to help them. What I keep here with me are the bones of what once was. I do not deal with the living, or even the bodies of the dead. Just the bones of battle."

Blayth set the shield down, feeling more emotion than he'd ever felt in his life. It was such a monumental moment to him in such an unexpected place. But something Jestin said stuck with him and the question that was poised on his lips was something he could barely force himself to ask.

But he had to.

For the sake of his soul, he had to.

"This older knight," he whispered. "Who was he?"

Jestin was over by the broadswords now, pulling one forth. "He did not give his name," he said. "But he asked if I knew of his son."

"What was his son's name?"

Jestin snorted, an ironic sound. "Your name, in fact," he said. "James."

Blayth's breath caught in his throat. "Was… was he English?"

"He was," he said. "He did look at my collection, in fact, and he saw the shields. He seemed to look at the one you were looking at, but he did not say anything about it. He did not ask to take it. I could not tell him about his son, so he simply went away."

The de Wolfe shield. The old knight had been looking at the de Wolfe shield. Was it a sign that he was from the House of de Wolfe, looking for a lost son? Blayth closed his eyes, struggling with all his might not to weep because his eyes stung with tears. He turned away from the shields, the swords, and sat back down by the fire, laboring with everything he had not to break down.

You were left behind, Morys had said. *You were unwanted.* Was it possible that the older knight had been his own father, coming to look for the son he'd lost? How many other knights named James were at

Llandeilo?

Something told Blayth that his father had, in fact, returned for him. He didn't know why he should think so, out of all the men who had fought at Llandeilo, but his gut told him his father had returned.

My God, Blayth thought to himself. *He came back for me.*

Opening his eyes, he blinked away the tears, noticing his cup of cider nearby and he snatched it, draining it and feeling all of that liquid fire course into his belly. Jestin, however, was oblivious to his emotional turmoil, still rifling through the clutter he had in neat stacks against the wall. He had absolutely no idea that this conversation, and those few words he'd delivered, had such an impact on the man seated before his hearth. The clouds had parted, and the sun shone brightly now, the light of understanding and realization in that he hadn't been abandoned.

He wasn't unwanted.

Blayth poured himself another full cup of cider.

"Even if you could not help him find his son, I am certain that the families of the men who once owned these possessions appreciate what you have done," he finally said, his throat tight with emotion. "I am sure it means more than you know."

Jestin carefully replaced the broadswords, inspecting his collection before heading back to the hearth and his fire-breathing cider.

"I do it because there is something in me that demands it," he said. "I do not do it for the men who war monger. I do it for their souls, so that in death, they will know some peace. But the bones of war are not all I gather – I collect a great many things, as I told you. I have collected many documents over the years, and many items in general. You saw that the other chamber is full of such things. I even write down legends and stories that I have heard, local stories told to inspire or frighten the children. I record them so that someday, men will know of the legends of our land and they will know of our greatness."

Blayth cocked an eyebrow. "Then you are a scholar as well as a priest and a healer?"

Jestin nodded. "When I told you that I was a Keeper, I meant it. I keep many things."

Blayth downed his second cup of cider, finding that it went down easier the more he drank.

"You are like the birds that collect food and twigs to build their nests," he said. "You feather your nest with anything you can get your hands on, including the bones of war, as you have put it."

Jestin nodded. "Now you see why I did not unbolt the door for you at the first. I have much to protect."

"I do not blame you."

Now, they both had at least two cups of the potent cider in them and tongues, as well as everything else, were loosening. Whatever defenses they'd had up between them were melting away as Jestin poured himself more liquor.

"I am sorry if we started out badly," he said as he poured. "I am not the rude sort, but I am careful. These days, we must all be careful."

Blayth nodded, his head buzzing with drink. "That is very true," he said, thinking of Morys and how the man had lied and manipulated him. "We must be careful even with those we are close to."

"You speak as if you have known betrayal."

Blayth sighed heavily. "You could say that."

Jestin studied him carefully for a moment, the enormous man with the scarred and damaged head.

"Tell me of yourself, James," he said. "You seem to me like a man who has seen much in life. What great stories can I write about you?"

Blayth lifted the cup to his lips, but he was grinning. "You would not believe me if I told you.

"Try me."

Blayth took a long drink of cider before looking at the man. Truth be told, the story of his life, or at least what he remembered of it, was something that folktales were made of. Morys had always insisted that he would be a legend in his own time, but Blayth didn't really believe it. Perhaps as the real bastard son of Llywelyn, he might have been, but as

James de Wolfe, an English knight who'd been used and manipulated by an ambitious Welsh lord, he really wasn't anything at all.

But the tale of Blayth *was* a fascinating story.

Perhaps it was something worth remembering.

More cider, and a bit more prompting, and Blayth told Jestin the tale of Blayth the Strong, the bastard son of the last Welsh prince, and the greatest hero of all.

It was a story worthy of a legend.

CHAPTER NINETEEN

ASMARA AWOKE TO the sounds of snoring.

It took her a moment to realize what she was hearing and when her eyes opened, she had no idea where she was. Nothing was familiar. It was a badly cluttered chamber, with dust everywhere, and sunlight was streaming in from the cracks in a shuttered window.

Turning her head slightly, she realized that she was drooling. Wiping at her chin in disgust, she lifted her head, trying to determine where she was. More snoring drew her attention and she looked down to see Blayth sleeping on the floor next to her bed.

He was sleeping on his back, his mouth hanging open as he snored loudly enough to rattle his teeth. Then, he'd stop, as if he'd awoken himself, and shift around before falling into a deep sleep again. The snoring came back. Asmara watched this cycle go on for a few minutes, enough to bring a smile to her lips.

In truth, it was rather fascinating watching him sleep.

Moving around in the bed, she could feel the pain in her shoulder, but it wasn't too terribly bad. Cautiously, she sat up, waiting for a great stabbing pain, but there was none. Sore, yes, but no agony. She sat all the way up, gingerly moving her left shoulder as much as she could, thinking she felt much better than she should given the seriousness of the wound. Swinging her legs over the side of the bed, she saw that she couldn't get to the floor without stepping on Blayth.

The man would have to move.

He continued to snore and every time he did, she tapped him on the belly with her foot. He'd stop, shift, and then start snoring again. Finally, after five or six taps with her foot to his belly, he opened his eyes and just stared at the ceiling. Asmara wondered if he was even awake. But then, his eyes moved to her, slowly, until their gazes met. She grinned.

"You snore like an old dog," she said.

He blinked and licked his lips. "Is that so?" he said hoarsely. "And you talk in your sleep."

Her smile vanished. "I do *not*!"

"How do you know?"

She didn't have a snappy retort for him so she turned her nose up. "That is not a nice thing to say."

He grinned, pushing himself up so he was still lying back but braced up on his elbows. "You cannot imagine the things you said in your sleep," he teased because she was fun to tease. "Scandalous things. I never knew you had such thoughts."

She scowled. "I did not."

"Of course you did," he said. "But you spoke of your undying love for me, mostly."

She looked at him, aghast. "I did no such thing!"

His face fell. "Then you do not love me?"

Her shocked expression transformed into something thoughtful, then embarrassed, then warm. The jesting mood of the conversation faded as something quite real took hold.

"I told you that I would marry you, did I not?" she said softly.

"That does not mean you love me."

"Do you love *me*?"

She had turned it around on him but rather than get defensive, he smiled. "There is nothing about you that is not to love," he said quietly, his sleepy eyes glimmering at her. "How do you feel?"

Asmara was touched by his words, warming her in ways she could not have imagined. His question had caught her off guard at first, but his reply had been honest and sweet. That giddy feeling swept her again, so strongly that she was nearly lightheaded with it.

"I feel wonderful," she said. "And there is nothing about you that is not to love, either."

It was a bold statement from a woman who was unused to speaking on her feelings. With a massive grin on his face, Blayth sat up all the way and reached out, cupping her face and bringing her lips to his for a sweet kiss. But their lips against one another sparked an immediate blaze, one that roared for a few seconds until Asmara lifted her left arm to put it around his neck. The moment she did so, a great pain bolted through her shoulder and she immediately gasped, dropping her arm.

"Are you well?" he asked, great concern on his features as he helped her hold her arm and shoulder still. "I did not mean for a kiss to injure you."

Asmara shook her head. "It did not," she said, holding her left arm against her chest. "I simply did not think. It really does not feel too badly, so long as I do not move it too much."

He began to peel back the bandages to see if she tore the stitches. "Then we must make sure you do not move it until it heals," he said. "It does not look like the stitches are torn. Jestin did an excellent job of tending the wound because it is healing very well already."

Asmara was relieved to hear that. "That is good news," she said. Then, she looked around the cluttered, dusty chamber. "Where *is* Jestin?"

Blayth yawned and stood up, scratching his head. "Probably in the church," he said. "That seems to be where he goes in the morning."

Asmara looked up at him. "How would you know that?"

"Because he went there yesterday morning."

She frowned. "Yesterday?" she said. "How long have we been here?"

He looked at her. "This is the second day," he said. "You have been asleep for two nights and a day. The poppy potion he gave you must have been potent."

Asmara was surprised to hear that. She felt groggy, that was true, but she didn't feel terrible. But then, a thought seized her and she reached up, grasping Blayth's hand.

"No one has come looking for us, have they?" she asked anxiously.

He patted her hand. "Nay," he assured her. "Not that I have seen. Even so, the horses are tucked away where they cannot be easily seen. When you feel better, we shall leave."

"I feel better now," she insisted. "We can leave today."

He eyed her. "There is no great rush," he said. "We can afford the time for you to heal."

She shook her head and stiffly stood up from the bed. "We cannot," she said. "Every day that we delay is another day that Payton-Forrester might leave Lioncross Abbey. If we want to catch the man, then we must hurry."

She had a point, but Blayth wasn't going to insist they depart for Lioncross sooner than she was ready. He might push his men like that, but he wasn't going to push her like that.

"And we will," he said. "But it is my suspicion that he will be there for some time. When we released him from the vault, he had been starved and tortured, and I can imagine the ride to Lioncross must have taken a lot out of the man. Therefore, I would wager to guess that he will be at Lioncross for a time until he has sufficiently recovered his strength. I think he will be there for at least a few more days, certainly enough time for us to make it to Lioncross, too. Besides… given that we have stopped at a church, I had an idea."

She wasn't following his train of thought. "What idea?"

"You said you would marry me, and we have a priest at our disposal," he said, his eyes twinkling. "Mayhap we should take advantage of the situation."

Asmara quickly knew what he meant, and her cheeks flushed, feeling her excitement. "I think he believes that we are already married," she said. "When we first came here and he asked our names, I never told him that we were not married."

Blayth snickered at the thought of duping the priest. "He did let us sleep in the same chamber," he said. "He must believe we are married. I hope he is not too angry to find out that we are not."

"I suppose there is one way to find out."

Blayth shrugged. "True enough," he said. "I will find him. Meanwhile, you can change out of your torn and soiled clothing if you wish. I will bring your satchel to you so that you can clean up."

Asmara thought that sounded like a wonderful idea." I would be appreciative," she said. "And mayhap some water? I would like to wash my hands and face."

He put up his hands. "Remain here," he said. "I will bring you everything. You do not need to move around overly with that shoulder."

Smiling faintly, Asmara sat back down on the bed, watching him as he quickly headed into the other chamber. She realized that she could get very used to the man's chivalry, something that had endeared her to him from the start. He was kind, gentle, and thoughtful. As she'd told him – what wasn't there to love?

She patiently waited for him to return with her satchel, and he did so quickly. The sun was becoming brighter now, sending long beams of yellow light into the room from the cracks in the shutters. Once Blayth brought her satchel and a bowl of cold, clear water from the bucket near the hearth, he went to the window and pulled back the shutters, letting the daylight in.

From the window, he could see the vibrant green landscape beyond. There were trees in the way, but he could see the meadow across the road and the white flowers that grew there. There were some clouds in the sky but, to him, he'd never seen a more beautiful day. With Asmara by his side, every day was beautiful.

"It looks to be good traveling weather," he told her. "I shall go find you something to eat and then I shall speak with Jestin. Do you require anything else?"

Asmara had untied her bag and was pulling forth items, trying not to use her left arm as she did it.

"I do not believe so," she said. "But I am rather hungry."

"I would believe that."

"What did you do all day yesterday while I slept?"

Blayth made a funny little laugh, scratching at his temple as he turned to look at her. "Suffered through one of the worst aching heads I have ever had," he said. When she looked at him curiously, he explained. "Jestin makes cider from the apples in his orchard that is like drinking lightning. It is potent enough to get a man very drunk if he is not careful. Unfortunately, I was not careful."

Asmara laughed at him. "Let that be a lesson to you," she said. "Beware of priests and their ciders."

He wriggled his eyes in agreement. "In the future, I certainly shall," he said. Then, he turned away from the window and headed towards the chamber entry. "I will leave you to dress. Or would you like for me to stay and help you?"

Asmara looked at him, feeling her cheeks flush as she fought off a self-conscious smile. "Once we are married, I shall gladly accept your assistance."

He could see that she was sweetly embarrassed by his offer. "Then I shall hurry and get the priest *now*."

She laughed. "I will be dressed by the time you return." He was almost through the doorway when she called to him. "Blayth?"

He paused and looked at her. "Aye?"

Her smile faded. "When we are married, what shall I be known as?" she asked. "What I mean is that wives assume their husband's name. What shall I be called?"

It was a very good question but one he'd not really considered until now. After a moment, he shook his head. "Ap Llywelyn is not my name," he said quietly. "That has been established. Until we can establish *what*, exactly, my name is, then you shall be addressed as My Lady Wife, Lady Blayth."

"But… your name is James."

"What would you prefer to call me?"

"What are *you* comfortable with?"

"As I said, until my identity can be established without question, I shall continue to go by Blayth. It is the only name I remember."

Asmara nodded, an acknowledgement of a most confusing issue. Blayth gave her a smile, and a wink, before leaving the chamber in search of Jestin.

As Asmara cleaned up, Blayth nosed around the main chamber for food and came across a half of a loaf of brown bread, covered up with cloth, and some hard, white cheese. He took it back to Asmara for her to eat before heading out of the small residence and into the cold morning beyond. The grass was wet with dew and moisture hung from the trees. He headed for the church, with its enormous tower and chapel attached, and entered through a side door.

Inside, it smelled of earth and incense, and he looked up at the heavy crossbeams across the ceiling, supporting the pitched roof. It was the first time he'd been inside the church because yesterday, as he'd told Asmara, he'd spent most of the day nursing a horrific headache, which meant he'd spent his time mostly lying down because it was more comfortable. He'd wanted to inspect the broadswords of Jestin's collection, but he didn't quite make it. He'd slept heavily last night only to be awakened by Asmara's smiling face and blatant insult.

He wanted to wake up that way for the rest of his life.

In truth, he really didn't know if Jestin spent his days here in the church. He'd only said that because the man left early yesterday morning, and this morning he'd also left early and had headed in the direction of the chapel. Therefore, Blayth could only assume the man was somewhere in the church and he found himself heading for the big tower, plainly seen through an open door on the west end of the chapel.

"Jestin?" he called.

He thought he heard a muffled reply coming from the tower so he continued on, entering the low doorway that led into the great stone turret, and he immediately saw Jestin sitting to his right, hunched over a table that was positioned below a window. The effect was such that there was light on the table, illuminating vellum, something Jestin appeared to be writing on. The table was crowded with pieces of vellum and writing instruments. The priest lifted his quill when he saw Blayth enter, turning towards the man.

"Ah," he said. "So you have escaped the clutches of the demon cider?"

Blayth gave him a lopsided grin. "If you know it is sanctioned by Satan, then why do you make it?"

Jestin laughed softly. "Because I like it," he said. "That must mean that *I* am sanctioned by Satan. But let us not discuss my immortal soul; let us discuss you and your lady wife. Has she awakened yet?"

Blayth nodded; he was coming to like this irreverent priest, just a little. "She has, indeed, awakened," he said. "And I have a confession."

"Then you have come to the right place."

"She is not my wife. We would like for you to rectify that situation."

Jestin lowered his quill completely. "I see," he said thoughtfully. "Well, I suppose nothing untoward has happened since you have been here. But why did you not tell me the truth?"

Blayth shrugged. "There was never really the opportunity, I suppose," he said. "She was injured and I was only concerned with her care. We did not intend to be deliberately subversive."

Jestin really didn't seem to mind. "And I did not ask you if you were married; I only assumed," he said. "No harm done, I suppose. But we shall remedy the situation. I would be pleased to perform the rite."

Blayth cast him a long look. "I am not so sure now," he said. "I cannot have my marriage rite performed by a priest who is sanctioned by Satan."

Jestin chuckled. "I promise that Satan will not enter into this," he said. "I am glad you wish to marry the lady, even though she has a tongue of fire. You will have to douse that fire, Blayth."

Blayth shook his head. "I do not want to," he said. "What that woman has done in her life… she is fearless and brave as few men are. She is as strong as the mountains and then some. Nay, I would not douse her fire. I worship it."

Jestin thought it was a rather sweet sentiment, something rarely heard these days. He'd not often come across men who spoke so highly of their women. He pointed to the vellum on the table, with his neat writing on it.

"You told me the story of Blayth the Strong on the evening you arrived, when the demon cider loosened your tongue," he said. "I am writing it all down, by the way. It is a tale of great heroics. But you shall have to tell me the story of your lady if she is so fine and strong."

"She is," Blayth said. "But I am not sure I want to share that story. Mayhap the story of the Dragon Princess is just for me."

Jestin's eyebrows lifted. "The Dragon Princess?" he said. "I am intrigued. Then that would make you something of a dragon tamer."

Blayth shook his head. "Do not let her hear you say that," he said. "She would not like it."

Jestin lifted his shoulders carelessly, as a man does when he is too foolish to be frightened by a woman. "It is not for her to know, is it?" he said. "She is brave, you say?"

"Like you have never seen."

"She does not dress like a lady. She dresses more like a warrior."

"That is because she can fight better than most men."

"But she is a princess?"

"Rhys Gryg is her grandfather," he said. "Her great-grandfather was the last King of Deheubarth."

That meant something to Jestin, who was suitably impressed. "Then she is, indeed, a Dragon Princess," he said. "And you wish to marry her?"

"Aye."

"What of her father? Does he give his permission?"

Blayth didn't want to have to explain the entire situation, so he lied about it. "He is dead," he said. "She has no one but me, and I intend to marry her. She deserves to be worshiped and tended as only I can."

Jestin didn't push him on the subject; he was coming to like this slow-speaking but witty man who spoke so fondly of his lady. "Very well," he said. "When do you wish to marry her?"

"Today. Now, if we can."

Jestin nodded thoughtfully. "Two acolytes will be here at noon to help me with Sext, the mid-morning prayers for the faithful," he said. "I will perform the marriage rite before Sext and they shall witness the ceremony."

Blayth was satisfied. "My thanks," he said. "I shall pay you for your service."

Jestin turned to him, a shrewd twinkle in his eye. "I do not want your money," he said. "I want you to tell me of the story of the Dragon Princess."

Blayth had to grin at the man; he was persistent. After a moment of debate, he finally relented.

"If I do this, you cannot tell her," he said.

"I will not say a word."

"Are you going to write her story down as you've written mine?"

"Of course I am. I told you that I am the Keeper of legends."

"Then do it after we have left, please. I should not like for her to know."

Jestin agreed. For the next two hours, he heard Blayth tell him what he knew of Asmara and of her brave breach of Llandarog Castle.

It was everything Jestin hoped it would be.

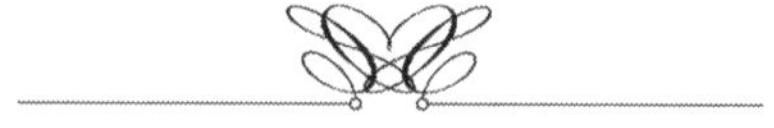

DRESSED IN A dark green woolen tunic that went to her knees, with her leather breeches beneath it, Asmara became Blayth's wife as they both stood at the entry to Jestin's church beneath a canopy of oak branches, swaying in the gentle wind.

It was right before the noon prayers and two boys from the village were witnesses as Jestin performed the marital rite. The younger of the boys picked his nose through the entire ceremony, right in Blayth's line of sight, and he found it very difficult not to make threatening faces at the child at the terrible display of manners.

He focused on Asmara instead, on her lovely face as she gazed up at him with a mixture of adoration and excitement. Her pretty hair was braided and draped over her right shoulder. Even though she wasn't dressed in fine clothing, she couldn't have been more beautiful to him had she been wearing silks and jewels. He smiled at her the entire time, taking his vows, feeling his connection with her down to his bones. She was embedded in him, the strength of their feelings for one another more powerful than anything he'd ever known.

The day he realized she meant something to him was the day he began a life he never thought he'd have, something sweet and loving and kind. He was a man who had been born at least twice in his lifetime, but with Asmara in his life, he felt as if he was being born yet again. When the rite was over, and Jestin finished praying, Blayth took Asmara in his arms, being very careful of her left shoulder, and kissed her.

It was the best kiss of his life.

Shortly after the kiss, they could see villagers arriving for the nooning prayers, so he took Asmara back to the residence and closed the door, bolting it. He was fairly certain that Jestin wouldn't disturb them, at least for a couple of hours, and he very much wanted that time alone with Asmara. Once he finished bolting the door, he turned to find her standing behind him rather expectantly.

He grinned sheepishly.

"I have good news," he said.

She cocked her head curiously. "What is it?"

A somewhat seductive expression spread across his face. "I have taken a wife," he said, "and I am a better man for it."

She laughed softly. "And I have taken a husband," she said. "To be truthful, I never thought I would. I still can hardly believe it. What man wants a wife who can best him in a fight?"

Blayth went to her and put his arms around her, kissing her soft mouth. "Me," he whispered. "Let me prove it."

Asmara could only nod her head, the flames of lust consuming them quickly as they so often did when they touched. But this wasn't the stables of Gwendraith, where they had to hide in the darkness, concealing their desire from others. Now, they were in the proper place at the proper time, and nothing was going to stop their passion.

Now, they could explore their feelings for one another without reserve.

Blayth could think of nothing else. Although extremely mindful of her wounded shoulder, he wasn't going to let it get in his way of expressing his love for his new wife. God, he loved her with everything he was, with every heartbeat that pulsed through him. She was like air and water to him; he needed her to survive. Now, she was finally his.

He would wait no longer.

His kisses were tender at first, gentle upon her lips and jaw. He was so very gentle with her. But quickly, they grew heated, and more powerful, and he swept her into his arms and carried her into the chamber with the tiny cot. It was all they had for what they needed to do, but it would be enough.

Carefully, he began to remove her from her clothing, untying the fastens on her tunic as his kisses distracted her from the fact that he was slowly undressing her. As he'd discovered in the stable of Gwendraith, she was easily distracted by his kisses and he used that to his advantage. All he wanted to do was get the woman naked and beneath him where he could feel their flesh touching. Nothing else seemed to matter. He had to claim her in every possible way.

But she seemed to be hesitant even though his kisses were powerful, and he remembered from their time in the stable that it had been dark then, perhaps somehow giving her a false sense of modesty. Quickly, he left her and went to the only window in the chamber, closing the shutters so that it was darker in the room and they had more privacy. He wanted her to be comfortable and that action seemed to ease her a great deal. In the dim light, he lay her down on the small bed and continued.

There wasn't much room for him to lay beside her so he had to half-cover her with his body. For a man with no real memory of ever having coupled with a woman, because he'd never bedded one in the time he had been with Morys, he was acting purely on instinct, or so he thought. Perhaps there were some latent memories driving him, because he seemed to know exactly what to do. In the shadowed room, he resumed his kisses as his hand snaked underneath her tunic and onto her warm, soft belly. He remembered that belly, silky and smooth, but his hand immediately went to her breasts as his mouth found her sensitive earlobe and suckled.

Asmara gasped at the overload of sensations, something that turned her limbs to mush. Blayth felt her relax and he was able to lift the tunic over her head, immediately moving to strip her of her breeches as well. In nearly the same motion, he ripped off his own clothing, tossing it into a heap on the floor.

The moment his naked flesh touched hers, he knew he was lost.

Blayth wedged his knees between her slender thighs, his fingers moving to the dark curls between her legs as his lips found a tender nipple. Asmara twitched and groaned as Blayth suckled strongly, reacquainting himself with her delicious body. When his finger slipped into her, there was no discomfort; she was slick, her young and powerful body ready for his throbbing member, ready to accept the destiny of a woman.

There was no pain and no fear… only passion.

Asmara's pants of pleasure were beginning to echo off the walls. Blayth inserted another finger into her, listening to her groan as she lifted her pelvis to him, seeking more of his touch. His tongue lapped at her nipples and he could feel her slick passage contracting around his fingers, a physical response to the ritual of mating. It was her body demanding his, whether or not she knew it, and he would answer the call.

Blayth removed his hand from her, no longer capable of pacing himself. He was trying; genuinely, he was trying, but her soft body was demanding him and he shifted his bulk, placing his heavy arousal against her and thrusting gently. He slipped into her without effort.

Her body was drawing him in, deeper by the moment. Asmara gasped at his intrusion, her pants of pleasure less evident as he gained headway. Blayth kissed her deeply, murmuring against her mouth and promising the pain would only be momentary. The further he moved into her, the more uncomfortable it was becoming, and he knew he could wait no longer.

Gathering her tightly against him, Blayth drew back and coiled his buttocks, driving into her. He couldn't be sure he breached her maidenhead, because Asmara had spent her life in strenuous activity, including riding horses astride, so it was quite possible that she didn't even have one. But it didn't matter; from her reaction, he knew she was virgin. There was no doubt. When she yelped into his mouth, it only confirmed what he already knew. Holding her close and seated deep inside her, he could hear his own gasps echoing off the walls.

Blayth didn't wait to give her pleasure. Cupping her heart-shaped bottom with one hand, he began to move. Within the first few thrusts, Asmara groaned, feeling uncomfortable and overwhelmed. But his gentle whispers broke through her haze and she instinctively began to respond to him, experiencing the friction of his manroot as he penetrated deep. The discomfort soon gave way to a blossoming fire that grew brighter by the moment.

Now, the spark that had existed between them from the beginning was finally allowed to blaze.

Asmara lay beneath him, her long legs parted and his big body pounding into her, experiencing every thrust, every withdrawal, with a pleasure she could never have imagined. There was something so deeply intimate about it, yet so deeply strong. He never stopped kissing her, or gently touching her with a free hand, the entire time, as if worshipping everything about her in the most powerful way possible. Every time their bodies came together, Asmara swore she could feel the sparks shooting up into her belly. The harder he drove into her, the more brilliant the sparks.

Blayth, too, was feeling the sparks shooting through his body as he felt his climax approach. She was so tight around him, so slick, that it was pleasure beyond all human comprehension. It felt like seconds, but it was actually several long minutes before he finally reached his peak, breathing her name as he released himself deep. Even so, he continued to move, feeling the slippery wetness he had put into her.

It was heaven.

Asmara felt his spasms, hearing her name in his strangled groan. But his thrusting continued as he reached between their bodies, his fingers probing her wet curls. A gasping scream erupted from her lips as he gently pinched her pulsing nub of pleasure, bringing her to the first release she had ever experienced. Waves of pleasure consumed her as her body twitched and rocked, and Asmara was vaguely aware of Blayth's soft laughter.

"So you like that, do you?" he breathed, his fingers still between her legs, touching her where their bodies were joined. "I shall have to remember that."

Whatever he was doing to her caused her to climax twice more, her entire body bucking with the pleasure he was bringing her. He was still embedded in her, still moving, stroking in and out of her as she experienced something more intimate and glorious than she could have ever dreamed.

The mating of a husband and a wife.

Finally, she put her hand between her legs to stop him because she was growing flushed and faint. It had all been so terribly overwhelming. When her fingers stilled his, he laid his head on her shoulder, dropping gentle kisses on her flesh.

"What is not to love about you, my lady?" he whispered. "From now until the end of time, I will love you and only you."

Asmara's breathing slowed and she opened her eyes, staring up at the ceiling and feeling Blayth's weight on top of her. He was still in her, too, for she could feel his male member twitching and throbbing, as if it had a life all its own. It had been such a beautiful and overwhelming experience that tears trickled down her temples. Bringing up her legs, she wrapped them around him, holding him tightly against her.

"And I shall love only you," she murmured. "You are my husband, my love, the man I adore. Tell me that this is only the beginning, Blayth. Tell me that our life will always be filled with such wonder."

He lifted his head to look at her, seeing the trail of her tears down to the bed. Gently, he wiped them away.

"It will always be filled with such wonder," he promised.

She turned to look at him. When their eyes met, all the words in the entire world weren't enough to describe the beauty of the moment. What they were feeling went beyond words.

It went beyond love.

Finally, they were one.

WHEN JESTIN FINISHED with the noon prayers, he never even tried to return to the residence where the newlywed couple had retreated. Something told him he wouldn't get past the door, anyway.

Heading to his tower room, he sat down at his table beneath the window and continued his story about Blayth the Strong, finishing the legend as told to him by the very man it was based upon. Only in this legend, he added the tale of the Dragon Princess and how she and the Welsh hero had fought for freedom against the English in a small valley in southern Wales.

By the time he finished the tale, even he was coming to believe that the two of them were something beyond heroic.

They were the stuff of legends.

CHAPTER TWENTY

Carmarthen Castle

"PAPA, PROMISE ME that I can go with Asmara," Fairynne begged. "You sent me home after Llandarog and it simply wasn't fair. Why should I have to go home while Asmara is allowed to fight?"

It was the gathering of the great houses once again at Carmarthen Castle, with Howell calling forth those who had taken the castles of Idole, Gwendraith, and Llandarog because there was a new push coming, something he needed all of his men for. It was the moment Morys had spoken of, and that had been planned for, and Cader was there, as was Fairynne, mostly because her father couldn't keep her away. She'd followed him – again – and now she stood next to him, as annoying as a gnat.

When she buzzed too much, he swatted her, which was what he did when she started begging him about being allowed to return to Gwendraith with her sister. Fairynne yelped and rubbed at her bum unhappily, but she shut her mouth. Swats from her father weren't meant to be disobeyed.

As Fairynne stewed, Cader was keeping an eye out for his eldest daughter with the party from Gwendraith. It was later in the afternoon, and most of the larger houses had already arrived, but Morys and the men from Gwendraith hadn't yet appeared. When the Brondeifi men from Lampeter arrived, men who had served directly with Rhys ap

Maredudd, Cader decided to retreat into the great hall of Carmarthen where the men were starting to gather.

Howell was in the hall, as were his *teulu*, and at some point, the discussions would begin, if they hadn't already. Not wanting to miss anything, Cader headed for the gathering, but he was quite sure Morys would be very loud when he arrived and upset if the discussions started in earnest without him.

With Fairynne tagging after him, Cader entered the cold, dusty great hall and skirted the edges of it, making his way around the gathering groups and towards Howell, who was near the feasting table, in nearly the same place he'd been in the first big meeting they'd had those weeks ago.

The hall looked the same, only more run-down and dirty, and the broken feasting table was still broken. Even so, as Cader moved around the side of the hall, now holding Fairynne by the hand so she wouldn't get separated from him, Howell climbed up onto the table and lifted his hands for silence.

"My friends, my allies, you honor me with your presence yet again," he said. "We have much to discuss, so please quiet your conversations."

The buzz in the hall died down as men began to turn in his direction. Cader came to stand next to Hew, and the two men acknowledged each other silently before turning their attention to Howell, who seemed to be looking around the chamber as if counting heads. In fact, that was exactly what he was doing, making sure everyone of importance was present, but he seemed rather confused. When he noticed Cader standing below him, he spoke.

"Where is your brother?" he asked.

Cader shook his head. "I have been wondering the same thing," he said. "I have not seen him in some time, but I am sure he will be here. He would not miss it."

Howell knew that about Morys. If there was battle and glory to be had, he wanted to be in the middle of it. "Strange," he said. "He should have been one of the first to arrive. He has known of this meeting for several days."

"Gwendraith is not far from here," Cader said. "Shall I send a rider?"

Howell looked to Hew. "Will you go?"

Hew didn't want to leave the meeting, but as Howell's *teulu*, he didn't have much choice. If his lord needed him, then he would go.

"If you wish it, lord," he said.

Howell nodded. "Be quick, then," he said. "If you see Morys on the road, tell him to hurry. Everyone has gathered and he must not delay."

Begrudgingly, Hew turned for the hall entry, very put out that he should have to go and hunt down Morys ap Macsen, a man he didn't even like. The man was arrogant and nasty. Several days ago, he'd come to Carmarthen to discuss this very meeting with Howell and he'd been quite pushy about it. Hew was starting to think that Morys had a rebellion of his own in mind, something led by the man he claimed to be Llywelyn's bastard, and they were thoughts he'd relayed to Howell, but the man didn't seem too concerned about it. Morys dreamt big but, in Howell's opinion, much of it was just talk.

But he was still an important part of this rebellion and as Hew headed from the hall on the unhappy task of tracking Morys down, he ran headlong into two of Morys' men as they entered the hall.

Aeddan and Pryce had arrived and Hew recognized them immediately. He went to the pair, curiosity in his expression.

"I am glad that Morys has arrived," he said. "Howell has sent me to find him. Where is he?"

Aeddan looked at Hew, a man he had known for years but didn't know particularly well. He stuck by Howell's side and rarely ventured far from it.

"He is not here," he said, his voice low. "I must speak with Howell immediately. It cannot wait."

Hew sensed something urgent in his voice. He looked more closely at the man to see that he looked weary and strained.

"God," he hissed. "What has happened?"

Aeddan simply shook his head, pushing through the crowd of men with his brother in tow, away from Hew, who began to follow. Aeddan pushed all the way to the broken feasting table and when Howell saw him, he recognized him.

"Ah," he said. "Morys has arrived. Where is your lord?"

Aeddan saw Cader next to the table Howell was standing on. The question had been asked and although Aeddan had hoped to tell Cader privately the fate of his brother, he knew that any delay would upset the entire meeting. Men would be on edge, and rumors and speculation would run rampant if he were to take Cader aside.

Therefore, he knew he had to speak to all of them, as cruel or as harsh as it might seem, because he'd been planning for two days what he was going to say at this meeting. It was the meeting Morys had spoken of, knowing this would be where they decided the details for the second wave of conquest. But now, Morys would no longer be part of those plans.

And Aeddan wasn't sorry in the least.

He'd spent the past two days in turmoil, having his lord buried and hating the man with all his heart. Everything he'd suspected about him had been true, about his lies and manipulation, and to realize that his faith in the man had been misplaced had been a bitter seed to swallow. Aeddan's father had served Morys, and he and Pryce owed the man a great deal, as they'd once told Asmara. They'd often remained blind to Morys' greed and conceit, but what happened two days ago at Gwendraith erased every bit of gratitude they'd ever felt for Morys. In those brief few moments when Morys had challenged Blayth, they saw the man for what he truly was.

A devil.

Therefore, when Aeddan answered Howell's question, he was looking at Cader.

"Lord," he said steadily, "I regret to inform you that your brother, Morys, has been killed."

A collective gasp went up, followed by dead silence. Cader's expression didn't seem to change much other than his eyes seemed to narrow in disbelief.

"What?" he finally hissed.

Howell came down from the table, putting a hand on Aeddan's arm to force the man to look at him. "Is this true?" he gasped. "What happened?"

Now, the real story was about to unfold. Aeddan didn't want to speak ill of the dead, no matter how much he despised the man, but he had to speak the truth. To a roomful of men who looked to Morys as a leader, they were about to receive a shock as to who Morys really was.

He braced himself.

"There is no way I can tell you what happened without telling you of everything surrounding his death," he said. "I will tell you the truth from my own experience, and from what I was told by both Blayth and Asmara ap Cader."

Cader's features paled. "Asmara?" he repeated. "What does she have to do with my brother's death?"

Aeddan could see that Cader was already quite upset and he tried to be careful in how he delivered the news. But no matter how careful he was, the end result would be the same.

Shock.

"I will tell you, great lord," he said. "But first, you must know that what Morys told you of Blayth the Strong was a lie. He is not the bastard son of Llywelyn the Last. He is an English knight who was gravely wounded at Llandeilo. Morys saved his life, but only to use him. He fabricated his history, and his name, because Blayth did not remember who he was. He accepted what Morys told him because he did not know any differently, but Morys knew the truth. He was using Blayth to spur this rebellion so that he could seek the glory of it."

Cader was ashen as he listened to what his brother had done. "My… God," he whispered. "Is this true? Did he really do this?"

Where Aeddan was trying to be tactful, Pryce would not make that mistake. He hated Morys and he didn't care who knew it.

"Of course he did," he said loudly, angrily. "He used Blayth and he lied to him, but that lie came to light when we took Gwendraith from the *Saesneg* because the garrison commander knew Blayth in his former life, when he was a *Saesneg* knight. He called Blayth by name, and Blayth asked Morys if it was true. Morys lied to him again. I do not know exactly what happened after that, but Morys finally told Blayth the truth of his origins and when Blayth tried to leave Gwendraith to seek answers of his past, Morys turned on him. He told the men that Blayth was really a *Saesneg* traitor and he tried to turn us all against him, but it did not work. Lady Asmara defended Blayth and Morys hated her for it."

By now, the hall was beginning to rumble with men repeating the story and discussing it, shocked and angered at what they were hearing. Aeddan tried to raise his voice, to calm them down, but the buzz was too strong. It was Pryce who finally leapt onto the dilapidated feasting table and began shouting.

"Morys threatened to kill Blayth if he tried to leave him," he boomed. "At the gates of Gwendraith Castle, he had a crossbow in his hands and he threatened the man, who was determined to leave. Morys finally tried to kill him, but he hit Lady Asmara instead. She, too, was armed, and she fired back to Morys, striking him in the neck. And that is what killed him, good lords. He deserved it!"

The roar in the hall reached a splitting capacity as men shouted their support of Morys' death, while still more were shouting about the entire situation. Above all of the shouting, Cader sank down into a chair, his face in his hand, while next to him, he heard sobbing and turned to see Fairynne weeping.

"Is my sister dead, too, Papa?" she sobbed. "What happened to my sister?"

Cader was wondering that very same thing, completely overwhelmed with what he'd been told. Standing up unsteadily, he pushed his way through a few men until he came to Aeddan. Cader grabbed him by the arm.

"What of my daughter?" he demanded. "Did she survive?"

Aeddan turned to him, looking into a father's worried face. "Morys hit her in the shoulder," he said. "I do not know how bad it was, but she rode from Gwendraith with the arrow in her shoulder. It was not bad enough to topple her from her horse. Great lord… she went with Blayth to discover the truth behind his past. I cannot believe that she succumbed to Morys' arrow. She is too strong for that, and God is not so cruel."

Cader was relieved, but he was still very concerned. "But where did they go?"

Aeddan shook his head. "I wish I could tell you, but I do not know," he said. "All I know is that Asmara told me his real name was de Wolfe, so mayhap they have gone to find the House of de Wolfe. I wish I could tell you more. But I can tell you this – I do believe that Blayth was in love with her, and she with him. No one told me, but you could see it in their eyes. There was something between them that was very special, indeed."

Cader was struck by his words; Asmara in *love*? He'd never heard anything so foolish. Asmara wasn't the type. He pondered the information, struggling not to be overcome by it.

"What of my brother?" he asked. "What became of his corpse?"

Aeddan paused, wondering if he should tell the man about his brother's grisly end, being trampled by horses, his body broken and smashed. Ultimately, he decided against it; it didn't matter in the end, anyway.

"I gave him over to St. John's Church in Llanegwad for burial," he said. "Forgive me, great lord, but after what I witnessed, I wanted nothing more to do with him."

Cader accepted the statement without judgement. Perhaps there was none to give. In any case, Aeddan watched the man struggle with what he'd been told, but he didn't sense any animosity because of it. Simply resignation. Cader finally turned away from him and put his arm around Fairynne, who was still sobbing her eyes out.

With his gaze lingering on the pair, Aeddan leapt onto the table beside his brother and emitted a piercing whistle between his teeth, loud enough to shock the room into silence.

He had more to say and he wanted men to hear it.

"Listen to me, please," he said. "I did not tell you all of this to turn you against Blayth, who was lied to. I told you all of this because you needed to know that there was subversion going on, perpetrated by a man you trusted. Although I know Morys was self-serving, and his reasons for the most part were selfish, we must all remember one thing – Blayth was a leader in our fight for freedom. Whether the man was real, or a myth, the fact remains that his name means something to the *cymry*. Morys built up a Welsh hero in his lies and it is something we must not take away from those fighting for our freedom. Mayhap, it will be an even greater inspiration now that he has left us. This is a gift, good men. The myth of Blayth the Strong is *our* gift. We should not waste it."

The young Welshman had a point. It was possible to turn such a shocking situation into something positive, by using Blayth as a martyr in their question for freedom. As Morys himself had once considered, martyrs made the very best heroes of all.

Aeddan climbed off the table, followed by his brother, only to be faced with Howell. The older man looked particularly worn and weary. He was having a difficult time accepting what had happened. But in Aeddan's final words, he found hope that it would not be as devastating as he originally believed.

"Morys built up an elaborate web around Blayth," he said. "It is something that has indeed given the *cymry* great inspiration. You are correct – mayhap it is a gift we should not waste. Sometimes the myths are even greater than our realities."

Aeddan nodded. "That is very true," he said. "But there is something else to consider – when Blayth fled Gwendraith, Lady Asmara went with him. The rebellion has also lost the Dragon Princess, as great a legend as there ever was. Her memory should not be forgotten, either."

Howell thought on that. "It is difficult to lose such strong warriors," he said. "You said that you saw them leave together?"

"I did, great lord."

"You do not know where they went or if they will return?"

Aeddan shook his head. "Lord Cader asked the same question," he said. "All I know is that Blayth went to discover his true past and Lady Asmara went with him. Whether or not they will return, I cannot say. But if I could speculate, I would not think so. Blayth was living a lie here in Wales, and a man cannot live a lie forever. Even so, what he has left us is a gift, as I have said. The memory of Blayth, and of Asmara, shall fuel this rebellion, mayhap stronger than before."

Howell was willing to accept that. With Morys dead, and Blayth vanished with the lady warrior known as the Dragon Princess, the rebellion led by Rhys ap Maredudd had lost three very strong patriots. But it was true what Aeddan had said – sometimes myths were stronger than truth, and Howell was willing to use the memories of Blayth and Asmara to inspire those fighting so hard for their freedom.

Perhaps the rebellion would find new life from it, after all.

As Howell went to gather his thoughts and continue the discussion that needed to be pursued at the gathering, the next phase in the rebellion, Cader was still reeling from the news of his brother's death and Asmara's disappearance. He found a chair against the wall and sat down, pulling Fairynne with him as she wept over her sister.

In truth, Cader didn't know what to say to her to give her comfort because he had no idea if Asmara was dead or alive. Aeddan's words had given him some hope that she'd survived, but he still didn't know for certain. It was going to be a difficult thing to tell Asmara's mother, but Morwenna was a strong woman. That was where Asmara got her strength from. Morwenna would be philosophical about the situation and she wouldn't let her husband know how worried she was. That was simply her way. But through the chaos, something Aeddan said stuck with Cader above all else.

I do believe that Blayth was in love with her, and she with him.

That was something Cader never thought he would hear and reliving those words in his mind brought a smile to his lips. At first, he hadn't believed it, but now that the news had time to sink in, he was willing to believe anything. Asmara? In love? How many times had he scolded her for having no marital prospects, and for not allowing him to find her any? Too many times to count. Every time he'd bring up grandsons, she would say "*someday, Dadau, but not today*". That was her standard answer to about anything he said to her regarding marriage and children.

Now, he was told that she'd fallen for Morys' silent warrior, a man who wasn't even Welsh, so they had discovered. But Asmara was an excellent judge of character, and Cader had always trusted her instincts, so he couldn't imagine that she'd put herself in a stupid situation with a man who wasn't everything she thought he was. Cader hadn't really known the man, or shared more than a few words with him, but he saw the warrior as a scarred, nasty brute who was fearless in battle. Surely Asmara saw the same but, clearly, she saw even more than that.

Finally, she'd found a man who didn't mind that his woman could fight.

More and more, Cader pondered that very thing. The death of his brother was fading; he was distressed by it, but not overly. Given Morys' ambitions, it was only a matter of time before he got himself killed or someone killed him, so Cader simply accepted what had happened. It was done.

But Asmara – that had his attention far more than his brother did. His long-legged, beautiful daughter who had lived the life of a warrior had actually fallen in love, and now she was with the man she loved helping him seek out what was important to him… *who he was.*

It was a noble quest, Cader had to admit, and he didn't feel one bit of disapproval for what Asmara had chosen to do. In fact, he was glad – she was no longer fighting in a rebellion meant for men as she found her place alongside the man she loved.

That was noble, indeed.

It would take some time for Cader to accept her absence, but he refused to accept her loss. Somehow, he suspected he would see her again. He couldn't believe Morys' arrow had killed her and he refused to believe that she would never return to see him, perhaps with those grandsons he so badly wanted.

Someday, Dadau, but not today.

It seemed that someday had finally come.

As Cader sat back in the chair and thought of Asmara and her adventure of a new life, he happened to glance over to check on Fairynne and saw her talking to the younger of the ap Ninian brothers, Pryce. She was no longer weeping as he held her hand and seemed to be gently explaining things to her. Fairynne, his flighty, silly, and sometimes rebellious daughter, was listening to him intently, wiping away her tears, and then finally smiling at him.

Pryce smiled back.

That was when Cader chuckled, shaking his head at his daughters, warrior women who were tough and skilled in battle yet, at heart, they were women just like all the rest, women who were the happiest with a good man by their side. As much as Asmara and Fairynne pretended otherwise, the devotion of a good man was perhaps the greatest achievement they could both find. For their father, it was the thing that gave him the most peace of mind. His gaze lingered on Fairynne as she let Pryce hold her hand, and it was bittersweet to realize that she, too, might soon be leaving him.

Glancing up to the heavens, Cader said a little prayer for Asmara.

Fair winds and fortune, my daughter, wherever you may be.

Somehow, he knew God heard him.

CHAPTER TWENTY-ONE

Six Days later
Lioncross Abbey

THE SKY WAS crowded with gray-tinged clouds, blown about by a blustery wind.

Asmara and Blayth were nearing Lioncross Abbey Castle, perched on the rise in the distance like a great crouching beast. It had massive towers on the corners of the curtain walls, and the mass of it was bigger than anything either of them had ever seen. The small Welsh castles had nothing against this enormous Norman monstrosity, at least from their limited experience. As they drew close and the wind whistled and howled, Asmara was beginning to feel a distinct sense of foreboding.

But they couldn't turn back. She knew that. Her young stallion had come up lame again and she needed to find a safe haven to tend the horse. In fact, that had been their delay in leaving Jestin – the abscess in the hoof had returned and they had taken two precious days to try and ease it. When the horse seemed healed, they departed for Lioncross but the second day of their journey, the horse came up with a limp, so it had been slow going for the rest of the trip, which was fortunately almost over.

Now, Lioncross was on the horizon.

"How do you feel when you see the castle?" Asmara asked Blayth as they plodded along on the road, which had wound its way around the small hills of the Marches. “Are you still as determined as ever to do this?”

Blayth could hear the doubt in her voice. She was fearful of what was to come and, truth be told, so was he. But it did not diminish his desire to know the truth.

“I am,” he said, turning to look at her. “You should not worry. All will be well.”

Asmara tore her gaze away from the distant fortress, smiling weakly at him when their eyes met. “I am not worried for me,” she said. “Only you. De Lohr is the heart of the Marcher lords and he commands thousands. I feel as if we are walking into the belly of the beast.”

Blayth didn’t blame her for her apprehension. She’d spent her life fighting against men like the de Lohr. He was her enemy.

“You needn’t worry,” he said. “If I am really a de Wolfe, then I will be welcomed.”

“And if you are not?”

He cocked his head thoughtfully. “I have been thinking about the situation,” he said. “I would assume all English know one another, especially if they have fought in Wales, which the House of de Wolfe has.”

“We know that.”

“So has de Lohr.”

“Do you think they know each other, then? The House of de Wolfe and the House of de Lohr, I mean.”

He nodded. “It would make sense, would it not?” he said. “De Wolfe was at Llandeilo and we know that de Lohr has been involved in Edward’s conquest of Wales. Surely they know each other.”

“And if they do?”

He looked at her, then. “Then mayhap de Lohr will know me, as a de Wolfe,” he said. “I have been thinking he might. If Payton-Forrester is no longer here, then mayhap the earl will know me, or at least of de Wolfe. If I tell him my story, mayhap he will help.”

Asmara didn’t say what she was thinking, which was something not quite as optimistic as he was. She didn't want to discourage him, not when they'd come so far and this was something he felt strongly that he needed to do, but the sight of the mighty bastion suddenly had her questioning the sanity of all of this. The English were something to be feared, and other than Pembroke Castle, this was the closest she'd ever come to an English stronghold.

The Welsh in her was naturally apprehensive.

"We can only pray," she finally said. "But they will know we are Welsh. They will hear it in our voices when we speak their language, and it will not sound English. What if they do not believe your story?"

"We shall soon find out."

Those were words of reason, not of comfort, and Asmara made a face at him when he couldn't see her. They continued along the road, passing through the small green hills and coming up on the south side of the castle. There was a village to the east, and a fairly large one, but the road to the castle from the south didn't pass through the village, it only skirted it. Soon enough, they saw the great lion-headed gatehouse of Lioncross looming before them.

The gates were open and people were passing in and out, going about their business, but there was a gang of heavily-armed de Lohr soldiers at the mouth of the gatehouse to ensure against any unsavory characters. Blayth had his eyes on the soldiers as he climbed down from his horse and with a hand gesture, asked Asmara to do the same thing. He was cautious as he approached, leading his horse, planning to say what he'd rehearsed in his mind a thousand times on their journey north. Now was the moment.

He prayed it went in his favor.

Approaching the group of armed soldiers as they watched peasants go in and out of the castle grounds, he was polite in his greeting.

"My name is Blayth," he said. "This is my wife, Asmara. We seek Sir Corbett Payton-Forrester. Is he here at Lioncross?"

The soldiers looked at him curiously. There was no real hostility, merely interest. They began looking at each other.

"He was here," one of them said. "I don't know if he's gone. Does anyone know?"

The soldiers began shaking their heads at each other. The younger soldier who had spoken first looked at Blayth.

"Do you know him?" he asked. "What do you want with him?"

Blayth could see that the soldiers were looking at the badly damaged left side of his head, and looking him over in general. He was an enormous man, and heavily scarred, and clearly something of interest.

Blayth could feel their scrutiny but he wasn't self-conscious about it. As long as they weren't being openly hostile, he could accept their curiosity.

"I have… unfinished business with him," he said. "He was a prisoner in Wales. It was I who released him so that he could escape. I would like to speak with him."

That brought a reaction of surprise from the soldiers, one of whom called for his commanding officer. An old soldier emerged from the guard room, speaking to another soldier and sending him off running before turning for the crew at the open gates. The soldiers were waving him over and he moved, rather slowly, until one of the men spoke to him and pointed at Blayth. That seemed to get the old soldier's attention, and he moved among the men at the gate until he was in front of them, now with a clear view of Blayth.

Like the soldiers, the commander was now looking over the enormous, scarred warrior. He was definitely a curiosity, for all of them. It wasn't often one saw a man that badly damaged and still standing, so that brought some respect from the old soldier. He approached cautiously.

"I understand you are looking for Corbett Payton-Forrester?" he asked.

Blayth nodded. "I am," he said. "We have unfinished business. Is he still here?"

The old soldier started to nod, but suddenly, he came to a halt. He blinked his eyes as if he wasn't sure what he was seeing and took a couple of steps in Blayth's direction. His eyesight wasn't very good at a distance, anyway, so he had to get closer in order to see the man more clearly and when he did, his eyes widened.

"What… what did you say your name was?" he asked, sounding startled.

"I am Blayth," Blayth replied. "This is my wife, Asmara."

The old soldier looked at him a moment longer before drawing back, a look of utter shock on his face.

"*Blayth*?" he repeated. "Is… is that what you said?"

Blayth wasn't sure why the man seemed shaken up. In fact, it made him just the slightest bit wary. "Aye."

The old soldier began to back away, but he was still looking at Blayth. He held up a hand to him. "Come with me," he said, urgently. "Come into the ward with me, please. Bring your wife."

Blayth thought the old man sounded rather odd, as if he were either very excited or very frightened about something. His voice was trembling. But Blayth obliged, motioning to Asmara, who followed him cautiously. She was still unsure about the entire situation, now being invited into what she had termed the belly of the beast. They entered the grounds of Lioncross Abbey Castle, passing under the enormous gatehouse with the lion's head on it, and into a ward that was larger than anything either of them had seen inside of a castle.

The bailey was divided up into sections, with great stone walls creating the barriers, and the old soldier motioned them to a yew tree that was over near a wall that had a soldier's training area beyond. The tree had wooden benches built around it and the old soldier pointed to it eagerly.

"Remain here," he told them. "I will return."

He started to walk away. "Are you going to tell Payton-Forrester than I am here?" Blayth called after him.

The old soldier didn't reply. He simply kept walking, very quickly in fact. Blayth watched the man as he headed for the enormous, multi-leveled keep. When the man disappeared through the arched entry, he took a few steps towards Asmara, who was standing beneath the tree.

"That seemed odd," he muttered to her. "I wonder why he was running like that."

Asmara was leery about the entire circumstance, more so now with the soldier's reaction. "I do not like the way they are looking at you," she said. "Why did he run like that?"

Blayth shook his head slowly. "I do not know," he said. "But I am sure we will find out."

It was just a feeling he had.

CHAPTER TWENTY-TWO

IT HAD BEEN a very long trip from Wales.

At least, it felt like that. The weather had been excellent and they'd made astonishingly good time. But even so, it had been a long trip for one very good reason: life-changing news was awaiting them and they couldn't seem to get to Lioncross fast enough.

Bhrodi and Penelope had been at Lioncross ten days now, and it had been ten days of excitement, sorrow, and exhaustion. Even though neither of them had gotten much sleep on the trip from Wales, there was no possible way that Penelope was going to rest once they arrived, and she hadn't. She wanted answers, as she'd had the entire journey to think about de Lohr's missive, and what Corbett Payton-Forrester had said about her brother. So by the time they arrived at Lioncross, she was full of questions and nearly frantic about it.

As fortune would have it, Corbett was still at Lioncross, still recovering from his harrowing ordeal. He'd lost a good deal of weight and was fairly weak, so a diet of good food and regular attending from Lioncross' physic were needed to nurse him back to health.

But that didn't stop Penelope from interrogating the man until she could interrogate him no more. She'd asked the same questions a hundred times, always with the same answer, and within a day of their arrival to Lioncross, Penelope was convinced that her brother, James, was alive and leading a rebellion.

So was Corbett.

It was problematic even under usual circumstances, but these were *un*usual ones. A dead man was leading the Welsh against the English, and Bhrodi knew that, at some point, Penelope was going to want to go to Wales to see for herself. He had been preparing himself for the showdown to come, ten days of discussions and intimation from his wife that the next step would, indeed, be heading for Wales.

Of course, he wasn't going to take her into Wales and that wasn't going to sit well with her once she came right out and asked him. Bhrodi never denied her anything, nor had her father or her many family members, so a denial to Penelope wasn't something she was accustomed to. He was going to have to watch her very closely because the woman wasn't beyond sneaking out when her husband wasn't looking. She knew that her brother was most likely at Gwendraith Castle, because that's where Corbett said he would be, and she knew that if she headed southwest, she would eventually be able to find it.

Bhrodi knew he was going to have to keep an eye on her.

The showdown that he feared came on the afternoon of their tenth day at Lioncross. Penelope had spent the morning with Kaedia, Chris' wife, in the garden of Lioncross, tending the smaller animals that they kept for food and as pets. There was an astonishing bank of rabbit cages, containing more rabbits than Penelope had ever seen, and she was fascinated by the rabbits that were about as large as a small dog. They were friendly, and soft, and she was growing quite fond of them.

But she had also been talking to Kaedia as the woman tended to the hare collection, and Kaedia had strong opinions about family. She knew about the situation with Penelope's brother and she had told Penelope that she would let nothing stop her from discovering the truth about a long-lost brother. It was an opinion Penelope shared. Therefore, after her visit with Kaedia, Penelope wandered into the stables of Lioncross, near the soldier's training field, to find her husband tending to his horse.

And that's when it began.

It was quite innocent at first.

"I was told you were here," she said, leaning in to Bhrodi as he put his arm around her shoulders and kissed her on the forehead. "Is something wrong with your horse?"

Bhrodi shook his head as he watched the smithy file off some of the big, black beast's hoof. "Nay," he said. "He has a loose shoe that must be fixed."

Penelope watched the smithy working on the horse. "His gait was strange on the trip, wasn't it?"

Bhrodi nodded. "It was, indeed," he said. "The shoe did not seem loose to me, but the smithy assures me that it was."

The conversation died as they both watched the man work on the horse until Penelope changed the subject.

"Do you know where I have been?" she asked.

"Where?"

"With Kaedia as she tended the rabbits."

"I would have never guessed."

He was jesting with her since she spent so much time at the hutches. She grinned at him. "Kaedia and I were talking," she said. "Did you know that she has thirteen brothers?"

Bhrodi's eyebrows lifted. "Then her father has his own army."

Penelope laughed softly. "I have six," she said. "That is plenty."

"Your father would have been happy with thirteen, too. Imagine the damage he could have done with that bunch."

She grinned at the comment, but that smile soon faded. "Now he has a chance to have a son returned to him," she said. "Bhrodi, I cannot sit here any longer while James is in Wales. I must go to him; I *must* see him."

The hammer had been lowered, just like that. Bhrodi didn't want to argue in front of the smithy and he could sense that such a conversation was coming. With his arm still around her shoulders, he turned around and pulled her out of the stable with him.

Now, the battle could begin in earnest.

"I understand that you wish to go," he said patiently. "Truly, *caria*, I do. But you know what Corbett and Chris have said – it is very possible that James is an agent for Edward and if you go running into Wales to save him, you may ruin everything he has accomplished. Do you understand that?"

"Of course I do," she snapped softly. "I am not daft. But I cannot believe that he is on any special mission for Edward. Surely, if Edward had any mission in mind for my brother, he would have told my father, and I am positive my father knew nothing. You were not there when he returned home from Wales without James; you have never seen anyone so broken."

Bhrodi faced her, putting his hands on her shoulders. "It is possible that Edward did not want your father to know simply to protect him," he said. "Even if your father did not know, and James truly is an agent for Edward, what will rushing into Wales accomplish? What do you intend to do?"

She was growing upset. "I must *see* him," she said. "I simply want to see if it is him."

"And then what?"

"Then I will know that he is not dead!"

He was trying not to become irritated with her. "And *then* what?" he asked. "Will you tell your father? Because you know he will go running right into Wales to see for himself, and that will probably get him killed. Is that what you want?"

She frowned. "Then why did you let me come to Lioncross if you were not going to let me go into Wales to see for myself whether this Blayth is my brother?" she asked. "Your plan was to come here and not take any action?"

He cocked an eyebrow at her. "I am going to take some action," he said. "You already know that Howell has sent a missive, requesting my support for Rhys ap Maredudd's uprising. I intend to go to Howell and size up the situation before I allow you anywhere near the Welsh rebellion."

"But…"

He held up a finger, cutting her off. "When we came to Lioncross, we did not know that Corbett suspected your brother might be an agent for Edward," he pointed out. "Now that we know, the situation has changed. I cannot allow you to go charging in and possibly give him away to the Welsh. That is why I must size up the situation first before I permit you anywhere near him. Surely you understand that, Penny. This is a very delicate situation and it must be handled carefully."

Although it didn't make her particularly happy, she understood. "I do not want to ruin whatever James has been working towards if, in fact, he is an agent for Edward," she said begrudgingly. "But there is also the possibility that he is not an agent for Edward. What then?"

"Then we shall decide what needs to be done," he said quietly. "As Chris mentioned, we cannot allow your brother to bring down the entire de Wolfe legacy. It is a very delicate situation, *caria*. We will do our best to deal with it."

Penelope was deeply unhappy that he wasn't going to let her go into Wales right away. "When will all this be?" she asked. "When do you plan to tell my father?"

"As soon as he arrives."

She looked at him curiously. "Is he coming here?"

He shrugged. "He should have received your missive six or seven days after you sent it from Rhydilian," he said matter-of-factly. "Based upon the content of the missive, I would not imagine that your father would wait to come to Lioncross, meaning he has already been on the road for several days. I expect he should arrive any day now."

Penelope was looking at him, her mouth hanging open. "How did you know I sent him a missive?"

He cast her a sidelong glance, a smile playing on his lips. "Rhydilian is *my* castle, Penelope," he said with some irritation. "There is nothing that goes on at my castle that I am not aware of. You paid a stable groom to ride to Castle Questing to tell your father about James after I specifically told you not to."

She was both defiant and contrite. "I did," she said, thrusting up her chin. "I could not, in good conscience, keep such information from him. How would you like it if someone kept information about William or Perri from you? They are *your* sons, Bhrodi. You would have a right to know. So does my father. It simply wasn't right not to tell him."

He really wasn't angry at her and even if he was, it never lasted long. He sighed heavily. "As I said," he muttered as he turned back for the stable, "your father should be here any day now. We can discuss the situation with him, but I have a feeling he will want to go into Wales to see for himself and if that is the case, I cannot stop him. You know I cannot stop him. And I have been afraid all along the man is going to go charging into Wales and get himself killed."

Penelope shook her head. "He will not do anything so foolish," she said. "But you are correct when you said he will want to see for himself. I do not know what we can do about that."

"You de Wolfes are a foolish bunch."

"Foolish and loyal. When we love, it is deeply, and it is for life. Much as I love you."

Bhrodi just shook his head and Penelope received the impression that he was greatly distressed that William de Wolfe should want to go into Wales at all. The last time the man had been in southern Wales, he'd lost a son, or so he thought. Bhrodi couldn't even fathom what would happen this time around.

As Bhrodi blew his wife a kiss and meandered back into the stable to see to his horse, Penelope was lost to thoughts of her own. Her father would soon be here, and they would decide what to do about James and the rising rebellion. She had quickly come to learn that the case of her brother returning from the dead wasn't simple in the least. Speculation on him being an agent for Edward had entered the situation, making it more complex than ever.

As Penelope wandered along the edge of the training ground, heading for the main portion of the bailey and the gatehouse, she thought back to the day when her father had returned from Wales with only three sons and not the four he'd left with. She remembered the army returning, the massive de Wolfe army coming in through Castle Questing's three-storied gatehouse, and she remembered distinctly when her father went to her mother, who was waiting patiently for her husband, and threw his arms around her. She also remembered watching him whisper something in her ear, and she heard her mother wail.

It had been the beginning of a horrible day, one that none of them would ever forget. As her mother had wept in her father's arms, Kieran had approached Rose, who was James' wife. She had given birth to a girl while the army was in Wales, and she'd been standing with the infant in her arms and a small boy standing beside her. Kieran had taken the child out of her arms, handed it over to Rose's mother, and then calmly informed Rose that her husband would not be returning home.

The news must have confused Rose because she tried to run away. She tried to run right into the returning army and she would have had Patrick not grabbed her. She fought Patrick viciously, howling and screaming that they were all lying to her and that James was somewhere in the army. She simply had to find him. It had been a chaotic scene as Rose's mother had taken Rose's children back into the keep, struggling to keep everyone calm.

But Rose wouldn't be calm. She'd been hysterical until she abruptly fainted in her father's arms.

After that, the news had spread.

James de Wolfe had died at Llandeilo.

Penelope sighed heavily as she still remembered that day. It still brought tears to her eyes to think of it and the anguish they'd gone through. Life had gone on, and Rose had eventually married a fine young knight who accepted James' children as his very own, but life had never been the same for the House of de Wolfe. They had lost one of their own, and that hole would always be there.

That was why she was so determined to go to Wales.

What if the hole could be filled? What if the belief of James' death had been some horrible mistake?

The wind was picking up now as Penelope crossed from the training area and into the main part of the bailey. Almost immediately, she saw a couple sitting beneath the yew tree that had grown into a monstrosity of a tree. There were benches beneath it, and it was a good resting place with lovely shade, and she passed close to it as she emerged into the bailey. She could see a man sitting on one of the benches, his back turned to her, but the woman was fairly close, checking the hoof of a gorgeous young stallion. Appreciative of horseflesh, Penelope moved closer, noting the fine lines of the animal.

"What a beautiful horse," Penelope said. "How old is he?"

The woman's head came up as she was addressed in the language of the Normans. She looked over to see a lovely young woman with hazel eyes approach, her focus fixed on the horse. A little startled at the attention, she was hesitant in her reply.

"He has seen three summers," she replied. "He… he is still quite young."

Penelope recognized her Welsh accent and she switched to the Welsh language, something she had learned from her years of marriage to a hereditary Welsh king.

"You are Welsh?" she asked.

The woman nodded to the question, perfectly spoken in her language. "Aye."

Penelope smiled. "So is my husband," she said. "My name is Penelope. Who are you?"

"Asmara ferch Cader."

Penelope continued to smile as she reached out to pet the horse. "He is so very beautiful," she said. "Did you raise him from birth?"

Having been a warrior for most of her life, Asmara wasn't very good with social skills when it came to other women, but she wanted to respond to this friendly young woman.

"I was there when he foaled," she said. "I watched him take his first steps and since that time, he has always been with me."

"What is his name?"

"Storm."

Penelope continued to pet the horse, noticing that Asmara was still holding the animal's hoof. She pointed.

"Is he injured?"

Asmara looked back to the hoof with the abscess that wouldn't heal properly. "He has been bothered by poison in it," she said, pointing to the area when Penelope looked closer. "I must tend to it as soon as possible."

Penelope looked at her. "Then why are you here?" she asked, indicating the training area she had just come from. "The stables are through there. The grooms will help you tend to your horse. Would you like me to show you were to go?"

Asmara shook her head. "Nay, but I thank you," she said. "The soldier told us to wait here, so we are. I should not like to leave or it might anger him."

Penelope frowned. "What soldier?"

"The commander at the gatehouse."

She understood, somewhat. "I see," she said. "Are you here to visit someone, then?"

Over on the bench, the man was listening to the conversation but Penelope couldn't quite see him. When he heard the question, he stood up, his head popping up over the back of Asmara's stallion.

"We are here to see a knight," he said in his slow, deliberate speech. "We must wait here until the soldier returns for us."

Penelope looked at the man, heard the voice, and time seemed to stop. A buzzing filled her head because she honestly couldn't hear anything else around her, nor could she see. The entire world could come crashing down around her and she would still be standing there, still looking into the face of the man who had just spoken to her. He was older, scarred, the sides of his head were shaved, he was missing his left ear, and a beard covered the lower part of his face. He had the look of a barbarian.

But… by God, she knew him.

She'd seen him a million times, in her dreams and in her heart, as a child, as a girl, and as a young woman. The face had changed slightly from what she remembered, and the left side of his head was badly damaged, but it didn't change the facts. It didn't change what she knew in her heart.

The ground seemed to rock as she stared at him and her breath caught in her throat. She thought she might faint until she realized that she wasn't breathing, so she forced herself to take a gasping breath.

A hand flew to her mouth.

"It… it…" She breathed, hardly able to speak. "I… you are…"

She couldn't finish because it occurred to her that he wasn't running at her with joy. He was simply looking at her with some confusion, as if she were a stranger. There was no light of recognition in his eyes, no warmth of realization. He wasn't seeing what she was seeing.

But she was seeing it all.

My God… *it was James.*

"You're here," she finally gasped.

It was all she could think to say. Asmara, seeing that the friendly woman looked as if she'd seen a ghost, suddenly began looking between the pair. Blayth was looking at the young woman with some concern, as if he'd said something wrong, but the young woman was ashen white and breathing unsteadily. She was looking at Blayth the same way Payton-Forrester had, and it occurred to her that this young woman might recognize him just as the English knight had.

Her heart began to pound, just a little faster.

"Lady?" she said to Penelope. When the woman didn't respond, she said it again, louder. "Lady Penelope? Do you know him?"

Penelope snapped out of whatever trance she was in, looking to Asmara as tears filled her eyes. All of those things that Corbett and Chris had said, about James being an agent for Edward, filled her mind and the world began to spin. Before she said something that would ruin whatever James had been trying to build, because Bhrodi had warned her about wreaking such havoc, she simply looked back at James, her beloved brother, and could only think to say one thing to him.

"Do… do you know me?" she whispered.

Blayth found himself staring at her, hard. As she said that, he realized there was something familiar about her, but he couldn't quite place her. It was mostly in her eyes – he knew those eyes, now filled with an ocean of tears. Clearly, seeing him had her shaken and he had no idea why. But when she asked that question, he, too, realized that she had the same expression that Payton-Forrester had when he'd first looked at him.

It was the light of recognition.

He sighed sharply.

"I… I don't know," he said. "But I know I should. Do you know *me*?"

Penelope blinked and the tears splattered. She suddenly didn't care what Chris or Corbett or even Bhrodi had said. This was her James, the brother she thought she'd lost, and she could hardly believe it. Every fiber in her body screamed with disbelief, while her heart began to leap with joy.

It was him!

"Aye," she finally said, breaking down into tears. "I do. I know you."

Asmara rushed to her side, seeing how overwrought she was. "You *do*?" she asked in disbelief. "Who is he to you? Please tell me. Do not be afraid."

Penelope was beginning to sob. Her hands were over her mouth as she took a few halting steps in Blayth's direction, her eyes drinking in a sight she never thought she'd see again in this life. She couldn't even answer Asmara's question as her teary gaze held her brother.

"You were dead," she sobbed. "We were told you were dead. But you are not! You are alive!"

Asmara was following her, genuinely trying to find answers from the woman. "Who is he to you?" she begged. "Please tell me."

Penelope heard the question and she swallowed, wiping the tears that were coursing down her cheeks. "My brother," she whispered. Then, she looked at Blayth, who was looking at her in astonishment. "Don't you know me? I'm Penelope. I am your sister. James, we thought you were dead!"

She was off sobbing again, hands over her mouth to stifle the noise. Asmara looked to Blayth in shock.

"James," she said to him. "She called you James."

Blayth was nearly as stunned as Penelope was, only marginally better at keeping his emotions in check. But it was a hard-fought battle. Everything he'd come to Lioncross to discover had happened right here, right now, in the most unexpected of places. It had happened so swiftly that he could hardly believe it. Reaching out, he grasped Penelope by both arms, his expression beseeching.

"I am sorry," he said hoarsely. "I do not remember you. I do not remember anything. I was badly injured at Llandeilo and lay unconscious for weeks. When I awoke, I had no memory of who I was, so I do not remember you. I wish I did. God, I wish I did. Am I *truly* your brother?"

Penelope nodded. Then, she threw her arms around his neck, nearly knocking him off-balance as she sobbed her heart out.

"James," she wept. "I have missed you so terribly. We have *all* missed you so terribly. I never thought to see you ever again!"

Blayth didn't know what to say or what to do. He kept from putting his arms around her because she was essentially a stranger, and he was quite uncomfortable with her display of emotion. But when he looked at Asmara, he could see the tears in the woman's eyes. Tears of joy, he thought. But he, too, was beginning to feel tears.

He felt as if a large piece of a larger puzzle had just come to light.

She knew him.

You are my brother!

"Please," he begged her, trying to pull her away from him. "Please tell me; are you certain I am your brother?"

Penelope nodded, struggling with her hysterics, but she genuinely couldn't help it. "Aye, of course," she said, releasing her death grip on him. "I came here to find you and I did!"

Blayth was beside himself with the situation, trying to think of what to ask her. There was so much he wanted to ask. But he could only think of one thing at a time. He couldn't speak as quickly as his mind worked, so it was a struggle to get the words out.

Asmara could see that. His face was turning read, overwhelmed with the situation. So she went to stand beside him, her hand on Penelope's arm because the woman was still so upset.

"You called him James," she said. "Can you please tell us your family name?"

Penelope wiped furiously at her eyes, taking a deep breath to steady herself. "De Wolfe," she said. "My father is William de Wolfe, the Earl of Warenton. In his youth, he was called the Wolfe of the Border. There is no greater knight in all of England than my father. *Our* father."

Asmara looked at Blayth to see how he was taking the news; his eyes were wide, staring at Penelope as if she alone contained all of the answers he'd ever wanted to know. The key to his past was standing right in front of him and he was so stunned that he couldn't even speak. She could see his mouth moving, but nothing was coming forth.

Now, at this moment, his limited power of speech had failed him.

"My husband knows nothing of his past," she told Penelope. "As you can see, he is having a difficult time speaking. He was badly wounded at Llandeilo, smashed in the head, and there have been some things that have been slow to recover. His ability to speak has been one of them, but the only memories he has are of those since Llandeilo. His only memory is as a man of Wales. That is all he has known these past five years."

Penelope listened carefully to what she was being told and it was starting to occur to her what had happened. The explanation was perfectly clear. James' memory had been erased from the terrible wound to his head, the evidence of which was right before her. The left side of his head was in ruins. Without the ability to tell anyone who he was or return home, he'd simply remained in Wales because it was all he knew.

It was all he could do.

Dear God… so many things became clear in that brief explanation and she looked to her brother, feeling more disbelief and sympathy than she ever thought possible. Reaching out, she took one of his big, callused hands.

"You are my brother, James de Wolfe," she said, her voice tight with emotion. "You are the fourth son of William de Wolfe and his wife, Jordan. You have three older brothers – Scott, Troy, and Patrick. You have a twin sister, Katheryn. You also have another sister, Evelyn, and two younger brothers, Thomas and Edward. And then there is me, the baby of the family. You used to bring me sweets when I was a child and I would call you my favorite brother. Then, Patrick would bring me sweets and I would call him my favorite brother. You would challenge Patrick to a duel for the title of Supreme Favorite Brother, and I would demand a long and drawn-out death from the loser. You don't remember any of this?"

Blayth was listening to her, his eyes filling with tears. He simply couldn't help it. He had so many brothers and sisters, and he didn't even remember them. It was tragic beyond words.

"I wish I did," he whispered. "I wish I remembered it all."

Penelope could see that, and it was a struggle for her not to burst into tears again. Reaching up, she put her hand on his damaged face, tears spilling down her cheeks when she saw the tears coming from his eyes. The man wanted so badly to remember what she was telling him.

"We had such wonderful times as a family," she said haltingly. "We were very much loved by our parents, and we loved each other. Above all, know that you were happy and that you were loved. When Papa returned to tell us that you'd been killed at Llandeilo, it was a great loss for us all. Papa has never recovered from it, James, not ever. He never got over the guilt of having to leave you behind."

Blayth's lower lip was trembling. "I was told that the English left me behind," he murmured. "I was told that I was unwanted."

Penelope was shaking her head before he even finished. "That is not true," she said. "I was told that Llandeilo was chaos. The English were outmanned and ambushed, and they had to leave their dead behind in the retreat. Believe me; if Papa could have taken you with him, he would have. He told me that Uncle Kieran tried to carry you out, but that he had to leave you, too, or risk being killed. They *tried* to bring you, James, but it simply wasn't possible. Please don't think you were left behind because you were unwanted. Papa even went back to find you, once, but no one could tell him what had become of you."

Blayth closed his eyes, the tears falling as he turned away from her. Asmara went to him, putting her arms around him as Penelope stood there and watched the pair. Her hysteria had eased, but her tears hadn't. She was still weeping silently, watching her brother as he was comforted by a woman who called herself his wife. As she stood there, wiping the constant flow of tears from her face, she heard a voice behind her.

"Penny?" It was Bhrodi. "What is happening here?"

She turned around to see her husband standing behind her, looking quite confused and concerned. She rushed to him, throwing her arms around him as the sobs came again. She wept against him as he held her, but he didn't hold her for long. His concern had the better of him.

"Penny, what is the matter?" he demanded. "Why are you crying? And who are they?"

He was indicating Blayth and Asmara, and Penelope labored to stop weeping so she could explain.

"It's him," she whispered tightly. "It is my brother, James. He… he is here. I do not know how he is here, but he is. It is *him*!"

Bhrodi's eyes widened. "What?" he hissed. "Are you serious?"

Penelope nodded fiercely. "Very," she said. She tried to explain something that even she herself didn't quite understand. "When I left you in the stable, I walked out here and there he was, sitting under the yew tree. I started talking to the woman about her horse and then I saw him… he said that he was waiting for someone. Bhrodi… it is a miracle!"

Bhrodi was astounded. He turned to look at Asmara and Blayth, who were now turning around to look at him. Greatly shocked, Bhrodi took a few steps towards them, inspecting the big, blond warrior with the scarred head. He couldn't take his eyes off the man as Penelope walked beside him, her hands wrapped up in his big palm.

It wasn't that Bhrodi didn't believe Penelope because, clearly, something had happened. Everyone was in tears, their features ashen, as if they had all just had a great shock. But Bhrodi didn't have an emotional stake in this, other than his wife, so he could be a little more objective. He looked closely at the big warrior with the beard and in looking into the man's eyes, he could see the faint resemblance to his wife. They both had the same eyes.

His jaw dropped.

"What is your name?" he asked.

"Blayth," the man responded without hesitation.

Blayth. The man mentioned in Howell's missive, Bhrodi thought quickly. He wasn't only astonished by the man's appearance, but quite curious about it as well. The man was supposed to be in Wales leading a rebellion, wasn't he? So why was he here at Lioncross Abbey?

"Why are you here?" he asked in his perfect Welsh.

Blayth didn't know who the man was other than the fact he must have been Penelope's husband. *His sister*. He was big and dark, and had the look of a warrior about him, but Blayth wasn't going to answer any questions until he knew who, exactly, he was.

"Forgive me," he replied. "I do not know you. What is your name?"

"Bhrodi de Shera."

Blayth knew that name; he'd heard it a thousand times, a name revered by the Welsh. The man was the hereditary King of Anglesey. He remembered hearing that Bhrodi had married a *Saesneg*, but he had no idea that the man's wife was Penelope de Wolfe.

It seemed it was a day full of surprises, and things were coming full circle, but Blayth was still cautious. He wasn't sure just how devout, or rabid, Bhrodi might be about the Welsh rebellion, so he wasn't sure how much he wanted to tell the man.

He would proceed cautiously.

"Great lord," he said, bowing his head respectfully. "I have heard of your greatness. It is an honor to meet you."

Bhrodi was watching him like a hawk. He kissed Penelope's hand before letting it go, taking a step away from her and crooking a finger at Blayth. The man immediately obeyed, and Asmara tried to follow, but Bhrodi held up a hand to stop her, so she didn't go any further. She stood there, concerned, as Bhrodi pulled Blayth with him into a private conference.

With the women looking after them rather anxiously, Bhrodi came to a halt and turned to Blayth. He took a moment just to look the man over again, now that he was at close range, and he could see every detail of him from his damaged head, to his wife's eyes, to the shape of William de Wolfe's face. Beneath that reddish-blond beard, he suspected the man looked a great deal like William. He folded his big arms over his chest.

"What are you doing here?" he asked quietly. "I received word from Howell ap Gruffydd that you were helping drive Rhys ap Maredudd's rebellion in the south. You are aware that Howell has asked for my support."

"I am, great lord."

"Then if you've come to Lioncross to create some sort of a ruse or betrayal, I am going to tell you to go back to Howell. This is no place for you."

Blayth understood his concern but, in explaining his presence, he was going to have to tell Bhrodi things he wasn't so certain he wanted to tell him. He wanted to proceed cautiously, but it may not be possible.

The truth was the only thing he could give the man.

"I am not here to create a ruse, great lord," he said. "I am not sure how to explain this to you without telling you everything, so suffice it to say that I am no longer part of the rebellion."

Bhrodi's brow furrowed. "Why not?"

"Because I am English. I have come to Lioncross to discover who I truly am."

Bhrodi cocked his head curiously. "I do not understand."

Blayth conceded the point. "I know," he said. "I was discussing it with your lady wife before you came. You see, I was badly injured at Llandeilo five years ago. You can see the damage on my head. When I awoke from this wound, I had no memory of who I was. I was taken in by Morys ap Macsen, who told me that I was the bastard son of Llywelyn the Last. Without any knowledge of my past, I trusted him. I believed him. But recently, Morys told me the truth of who I am, and I have decided that discovering my true past is more important than fighting in a Welsh rebellion when I am not even Welsh. If that offends you, great lord, then I beg your forgiveness. But that is why I have come to Lioncross – to find out who I really am."

It was an astonishing story, but one that made sense to Bhrodi. He was sure there was much more to it but, in that brief explanation, he didn't sense lies or deceit. He sensed that Blayth truly meant what he said and, clearly, his reaction to Penelope and hers to him were genuine.

"Then… you are not here to try and wreak havoc?" he asked.

Blayth smiled thinly, shaking his head. "Nay, great lord," he said. "The only havoc I seemed to have wrought is upon your lady wife when she told me who I was."

It all seemed honest enough, but there was one more thing on Bhrodi's mind. "I will ask you a question and you will tell me truthfully," he said. "Know that I will not punish you in any way, but I must know the truth. Will you do this?"

"If I can, great lord."

"Are you an English agent for King Edward, sent to destroy ap Maredudd's rebellion?"

Blayth looked at him in surprise, such a genuine reaction that

Bhrodi knew right then that the man wasn't who he'd been suspected of.

"Nay, great lord," he said, perplexed. "Have men been saying that about me?"

Bhrodi shrugged. "I heard someone say it," he said. "Then it is not true?"

"Nay, great lord, I swear with all my heart it is not."

Bhrodi believed him. "That is good," he said. "Because that has been something of a concern. For your father's sake, I was hoping that your reported death wasn't some elaborate hoax."

Blayth shook his head as if the entire concept baffled him. "Not at all, great lord," he said. "It seems like something terribly cruel to do. I hope my father did not think that."

"He does not know. And he never shall from my lips."

Blayth understood. "Nor mine," he said. From the corner of his eye, he could see Penelope and Asmara standing together, now in quiet conversation, and he was drawn to the woman who had identified herself as his long-lost sister. He very much wanted to be part of that conversation, too. "Now, if I may have your permission to speak with your lady wife and find out about my family, I would be grateful."

Bhrodi simply nodded and Blayth smiled, a genuine gesture. But before turning to the women, he paused one last time.

"I have been told that I am a de Wolfe, but you must understand that being *cymry* is the only thing I remember," he said. "I find myself in a very strange position now, a *Saesneg* by birth, but a Welshman by heart. I would be proud to call you brother in any case. But knowing what I do about you, and how the Welsh feel about you, I hope that from time to time you will permit me to speak to you of the Wales I remember."

For the first time, Bhrodi smiled at the man. He could sense a kind man, perhaps even a gentle nature, which seemed odd considering the reputation Blayth the Strong had amassed as a warrior.

"I would be honored," he said. "But remember this – the English heritage you have and the love of your family are as strong as anything I have ever seen. They adore you, James. Do not be afraid to embrace that. It is something few men ever know."

Blayth simply nodded, perhaps lingering on the thought of being loved beyond measure, before turning for the women and making his way over to them.

Bhrodi simply stood there and watched as Penelope pulled the man over to the benches beneath the yew tree, where Blayth the Strong would learn about James de Wolfe from one of the people who had loved him best.

A sister who had once called him her Favorite Brother.

Truth be told, he still was.

CHAPTER TWENTY-THREE

"GOD, I NEVER thought we'd get here," Scott muttered. "That must have been the fastest trip from northern England that I have ever had the discomfort of participating in. Papa, how is your backside?"

William de Wolfe grunted as he glanced up at the massive gatehouse of Lioncross, feeling an extraordinary amount of relief.

"Painful," he muttered. "As if it has been spread a mile wide by all of the time we have spent in the saddle."

"You have no right to speak on such things," Patrick said, reining his enormous red beast in behind his father. "I have been in the saddle longer than any of you. All the way from Berwick, for Christ's sake. If I can no longer have children, you are all to blame."

As Scott snorted at Patrick's misery, Troy chimed in. "I am surprised the horses are still standing," he said. "We must have done forty miles a day at times. Thank God these beasts are as strong as they are, or we would still be up in Manchester somewhere."

As William listened to his sons bicker back and forth, men who were exhausted by the pace their elderly father had set, his focus was on the wide bailey of Lioncross as it opened up before them. He had his three eldest sons with him along with eight hundred men and three wagons, as he'd promised Kieran. An entire army was rolling in with him and he could hear the sergeants organizing the men, pulling them into the bailey that could easily accommodate a thousand men or more.

It was mid-morning on the eleventh day since leaving Castle Questing to come to Lioncross. With every mile they drew closer to the Marches, William's anxiety had grown. His sons surely must have felt his mood, but they kept the conversation as normal as possible, trying to keep their father sane as he entertained the hope of recovering a dead son.

It was a like a massive weight hanging over them all.

In truth, Scott and Troy and Patrick thought it was a false hope. They, too, had read the missive from their sister, but they had been tactful in pointing out that what Penelope had given them was at least third-hand information. Corbett Payton-Forrester "thought" he'd seen James and although it was cruel to make such a mistake, it was true that mistakes like that had been made before. Still, William was determined to come, and they would come with him. So, four big de Wolfe knights entered Lioncross' bailey, all of them hoping beyond hope that Penelope's missive hadn't been wrong.

But the moment the army began entering the gates was the moment the chaos really began.

First, it was Chris de Lohr emerging from his keep along with his sons, Morgen and Rees. William saw them coming and he reined his horse to a halt, stiffly dismounting as Corbett suddenly emerged from the keep as well, coming up behind Chris and his sons as they made their way across the bailey.

Scott, Troy, and Patrick saw the onslaught of knights rushing from the keep so they, too, dismounted, coming up behind their father like a great line of support, wondering why everyone seemed to be running at them.

It was something that filled William with great apprehension. He had been prepared for polite greetings and small conversation before delving into the meat of the situation. But when he saw all the rush of de Lohrs coming at him, his tactics changed. He'd come a very long way and there was only one question he wanted answered.

As Chris came near, William held out his hand to the man.

"Is it true?" he demanded. "Is my son alive?"

Chris heard the father's plea and it was heartbreaking. He grabbed William's outstretched hand, taking it tightly as he hugged the man.

"My lord," he breathed. "It is true. James is alive."

William simply stared at him, letting the words sink in. But behind him, his sons' reactions were varied – Patrick's eyes widened, Troy hung his head as if he'd just been dealt a great shock, and Scott put his hand over his mouth in astonishment.

The most emotional of the brothers, Scott could hardly hold back the tears.

"He *is*?" Scott asked hoarsely. "Dear God… it's really true? James is alive?"

Chris nodded, seeing the wild range of emotions running through the de Wolfe men. He still had William in his grip and he could feel the man trembling.

"It is," he said evenly. "Truly, he is. I have seen him. I have spoken with him. But that is why I have come to greet you in the bailey – there is something you should know before you see him."

William was quivering so badly that his knees were beginning to give way. "Where is my son?" he breathed. "I must go to him. Where is he, please?"

"He is inside," Chris said. "He came yesterday. Penelope and Bhrodi are here, too, and they are all inside. I told my men to be discreet when they saw your army arrive so that I could have a chance to speak with you first, but your daughter is very nosy. I am sure she has been watching the horizon for you, so my time with you is limited before she interrupts. My lord, you must listen to me about your son. There is much you must know."

William was holding on to him with two hands now. "He is *here*?" he asked, incredulous. "James is at Lioncross?"

Chris nodded. "He does not go by James any longer," he said. "His name is now Blayth. As his story goes, he was badly wounded at

Llandeilo, as you know."

"He *was* dead!" William hissed. "I held him in my arms and he was *dead*!"

He was starting to grow upset and Scott came up beside his father, putting his arm around his broad shoulders. "We all thought he was, Papa," he said steadily. "I thought he was and so did Uncle Paris. You cannot blame yourself in that you thought he was dead."

William closed his one good eye, the tears coming. "God," he gasped. "How he must hate me for having left him behind. I did not want to."

"You had no choice," Scott said again, growing concerned over his elderly father's mental state. "You cannot blame yourself. We will tell James the truth."

"Nay," Chris said, interrupting them. "William, he does not remember *anything*. His head wound was so terrible that he lay unconscious for weeks and when he awoke, he had no memory of who he was. A Welsh warlord took him in, healed him, and told him that he was the bastard son of Llywelyn the Last. Do you hear me? James' only memory is of being told that he was a Welshman with a great legacy, and that was why he was part of Rhys ap Maredudd's rebellion. He does not remember you at all."

By now, William, Scott, Troy, and Patrick were looking at Chris in astonishment. "Is this true?" William said with awe. "He… he did not know who he was?"

Chris shook his head. "Nay," he said. "He only came to know his true identity a few days ago and he set out to discover the truth about his past. He knew Corbett was here and he came to find him, because Corbett saw him when he was in Wales. Corbett recognized him, but James did not return that recognition."

Chris turned to look at Corbett, who stepped forward when he saw that the attention was on him.

"It is true, my lord," he said to William. "James commanded the Welsh rebels who captured Gwendraith Castle, where I was the garrison commander. They managed to capture me, too, and I was in the vault for a month before James came to question me. I recognized him, but he did not recognize me, and then I thought… I thought that, mayhap, he was only *pretending* not to recognize me."

William wasn't following him. "What do you mean?"

Corbett felt somewhat foolish for ever suspecting such an elaborate scheme. "Because I thought, mayhap, that he'd meant for everyone to think he was dead because he was an agent for King Edward."

William was thoroughly confused now. "An *agent*?" he said, aghast. "For what purpose?"

Corbett was feeling foolish. "To infiltrate the Welsh resistance, I thought. James is a de Wolfe, after all, and the de Wolfe connection with the crown is very close. I thought that he might be a spy."

William glanced at his sons, who had a variety of shocked and confused expressions on their faces. "James?" he said as he turned back to Corbett. "My son a spy?"

Corbett shook his head before William finished speaking. "He is not, my lord, I assure you," he said. "It was simply a wild idea I had, but James is no spy. Lord de Shera is convinced of it. In any case, James knew that I recognized him, and it was he who released me from Gwendraith. So when he came seeking the truth behind his past, he came to Lioncross because he knew that I would be here. He came to find me."

"It is true," Chris said, seeing the bewilderment settling over the de Wolfe men. "All of it is true. But what James did not know was that Penelope would be here, also. Penelope has spent every second with him since yesterday. She has told him so many things, things he does not remember, so do not be disheartened if he does not know you, William. He does not know anyone."

William stared at him a moment before hanging his head, processing what he'd been told. His beloved boy, his sweet James, had no memory of who he was and would therefore treat him like a stranger. William didn't know if he could take that, not from James. The young man he so clearly adored, a young man he'd been so very proud of. He'd resigned himself to his son's death, but he'd never gotten over it. If his son didn't recognize him, he wondered if it would be worse than his death. In a sense, he *wouldn't* have him back.

He'd have a stranger.

Quietly, he cleared his throat.

"I understand," he said softly. "Now, where is he so that I may see him?"

"Papa!"

The scream came from the entry to Lioncross' keep, and they all turned to see Penelope launching herself from the doorway, racing across the bailey as fast as her legs would carry her. William opened up his arms for his youngest child, his baby, and she leapt into his arms, gleeful at the sight of him.

"Sweetheart," William breathed as he held her tightly. "It is so good to see you."

Penelope hugged her father so tightly that she nearly cut off his circulation. "You came!" she gasped, releasing him long enough to look him in the face. "Papa, it's true. What I wrote to you in the missive – it's true!"

William put a hand up, stroking her soft cheek, drinking in the sight of the lovely young woman. "I know," he said softly. "Chris was telling me what has happened. I… I can hardly believe it, any of it. I feel as if this is a dream."

Penelope hugged him again. "Nay, Papa," she said. "It is not a dream. He is inside, in the great hall. He knows that you are here. I told him to wait in the hall and that I would bring you to him. And, Papa… he brought his wife with him. He is married."

William's eyebrows lifted. "He took a wife?"

The brothers were listening. "Rose married years ago," Troy reminded his father what he already knew. "She is pregnant with her second child with her new husband."

William scratched his head in thought. "That complicates things a bit," he said. He looked at Penelope. "Did you tell him that he was already married?"

Penelope shook her head. "He seems so happy with Asmara," she said. "That is her name – Asmara. She is a great-granddaughter of a great Welsh king and I like her very much. They are so happy, Papa. You should see them together – I know that he and Rosie loved one another, but I never saw him with Rosie the way he is with Asmara. It is something magical and I did not want to ruin it."

William wasn't sure what to do about it, in fact. It seemed like quite a complex situation to him, one he didn't particularly want to deal with at the moment. Rose married over three years ago and she was very happy with her new husband. It just didn't seem fair that the unexpected return of James should complicate it, even though, technically, he and Rose were probably still married. He looked around at his sons, and at Chris and the others, as he spoke.

"Until I can speak with a priest, then I suggest no one tell him that he was already married," he said. "We must deal with one issue at a time. At this moment, I do not consider this an important detail. We will address it when we must. Now… may we go inside?"

They understood about the marriage issue, a silent agreement to keep quiet on the matter. As the group turned for the keep, William looked to the entry and suddenly came to a halt. When Penelope saw what he was looking at, she came to a halt, too, as did everyone else.

At the top step of the keep entry stood Blayth and Asmara.

The afternoon sun illuminated them and, for a moment, no one moved. It was as if time itself came to a halt, just for a brief moment, but for William, it was much more than that. His eyesight wasn't very good these days, and he didn't see things at a distance very well, so he was staring for quite a different reason – mostly, he simply couldn't see. But he could see enough to know that what he was looking at was his son.

It really was James.

Maybe he truly hadn't believed it until this very moment, until he actually saw his son in the flesh, and now that he was seeing him, he hardly knew what to do. As William stood there with his sons, unsure what to do next, Penelope let go of her father and scurried over to Blayth and Asmara. As she mounted the steps, Bhrodi emerged from the keep and looked sheepishly at his wife.

"He did not want to remain in the hall," he told her. "Unless I was going to wrestle the man to the ground, I could not make him remain."

Blayth heard him. He, too, had been staring at the men in the bailey as if in a trance, but Bhrodi's voice broke the spell. He tore his gaze off the men in the bailey as he turned to Bhrodi.

"I would not have given you much of a fight, great lord," he said. "But I probably would have pleaded quite a bit. Knowing they are out here… I simply could not wait any longer."

Bhrodi understood. He patted Blayth on the shoulder as Penelope took him by the hand. "Come," she said, her eyes glimmering with joy. "Papa has come to see you. He has brought Scott and Troy and Patrick with him. Come and see them, Blayth. Please."

She wasn't calling him James any longer because, as she'd discovered yesterday, the name meant nothing to him. The only name he remembered was Blayth, so she honored that. But even so, Penelope was coming to swear that there was a spark in him that remembered her because even though he looked differently and acted somewhat differently, the same gentle humor was there. She had tried to teach Asmara a board game last night and Blayth sat on the table, watching them, alternately praising his wife's skill and then accusing Penelope of cheating. It had been good-natured, but it seemed to Penelope that it was very much something James of old would have done to her.

She'd never been so happy to be called a cheater.

Even now, as she coaxed him off the steps and into the bailey, there was something in his gaze that looked just like James to her. She was relishing this moment, when her father would finally meet the son he thought was dead. But when she turned to look at her father and older brothers standing in a group, she could see the shock washing over their faces.

She knew why, for she'd had nearly the same reaction when she saw James for the first time. He didn't look the way they remembered; with his shaved head, more muscular physique, and missing ear, it took some time to become accustomed to the new appearance. It was the new James, who really wasn't James at all.

But quickly, the gap closed between them. William was standing before them and Penelope smiled at her father, still holding Blayth's hand.

The moment had arrived.

"Blayth," she said. "This is our father, William de Wolfe."

Those were words Blayth would remember for the rest of his life.

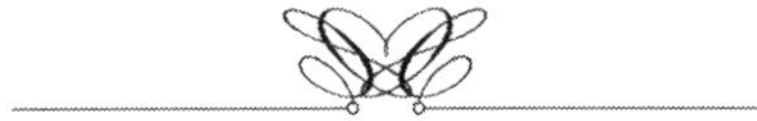

IT WAS STRANGE, really.

He'd been sitting inside Lioncross' cavernous hall, engaged in conversation with Bhrodi de Shera and knowing full well that the man he had ultimately come to seek was out in the bailey, having arrived with his army.

Blayth thought that, perhaps, they'd been trying to keep it from him. They'd spoken of the approach of William de Wolfe in hushed tones and Blayth overheard, so he finally asked Penelope about it, who sheepishly told him the truth. William de Wolfe was coming, and he was coming to see the son he thought was dead. That information alone had prepared Blayth for this moment.

So he thought.

But the truth was it really hadn't prepared him at all. He stood there, looking at a very big man with a patch over his left eye and a face that was careworn and leathery. But it didn't diminish the gleam in the one remaining eye or the expression that bespoke of the joy in his heart. The man was looking at the son he thought was dead, but he wasn't rushing forth with hysteria – he was being very measured, fearful that anything he did or said might turn his lost son away from him, so he wasn't really reacting at all. Blayth thought that was rather strange until he happened to look down at William's hands to see that they were shaking.

His entire body was shaking.

That told Blayth that there was a geyser of emotions ready to spew out at any moment and, in truth, he had quite enough emotion of his own. His gaze moved from William to the very tall man behind him, with dark hair and green eyes, then to the shorter man next to him, also with dark hair but with hazel eyes, and then finally to another tall man next to him with dark blond hair and green eyes. They were all looking at Blayth with such warmth and he had no idea why. He didn't know these men and wondered why they were gazing at him so fondly.

And then, it occurred to him – he'd seen these men before.

In his dreams.

It was as if a great weight had suddenly been lifted from Blayth. He felt lightheaded with the abrupt realization and, along with that sensation, he could feel a rush of happiness as he'd never felt in his life. Tears stung his eyes and he started to blink, rapidly, breathing deeply through his nose as if he couldn't quite catch his breath.

Scott!

Atty!

Those were the names of the men he saw in those dreams, men with swords, men he'd fought with, men he saw in brief glimpses. These were the men that Morys told him had captured him and tortured him, and he knew in his heart that Morys hadn't been right. He'd never felt anything but affection and warmth for these men, and now here they were, looking at him. They appeared slightly different from the way they'd been in his dreams, but the eyes… he knew those eyes.

Blinking back the tears, his focus returned to William.

"I was told you left me behind at Llandeilo," he said. "Tell me that was not true."

It was such a painful question and William immediately started to tear up. "Nay, lad," he breathed. He felt he was answering the very question that had been his worst nightmare. "I never thought I would be able to speak to you again, not in this lifetime, and I was prepared to answer this question when we found each other in heaven. We did all we could to take you with us when we fled Llandeilo, but we were overwhelmed by the Welsh. The worst day of my life was leaving you behind. Had there been another way, I would have taken it. You must believe that."

Blayth sniffled, wiping at his nose, which was beginning to leak. All he could feel was the emotion of the moment, swamping him, and he knew he recognized William's voice. He'd heard that in his dreams, too.

He remembered it very specifically.

"I do not know how much you have been told, but I remember nothing of my life before I awoke in a darkened hut five years ago," he said. "I have had to learn to talk again and think again. I have had to learn to walk and run and fight. But I have heard your voice in my dreams, and I have seen you there, too, but I did not realize those were memories of the *before* time. Before I was injured. I simply thought they were people that I had created."

There were tears on William's face. "What do you remember of your dreams, lad?"

Blayth didn't say anything for a moment. Then, he reached out a hand to William, who took it quickly. The moment their flesh touched, William hung his head and quietly wept. He was touching his son, a man he believed dead, and it was too much for him to take.

Blayth could see that. He took a step towards him, still holding his hand, and put his free hand on William's shoulder.

"I needed to know that you left me because you had no other choice, not because I was unwanted," he said hoarsely. "I believe I recognize your voice, although I am not sure how much I truly know of you. But I do not think I have to remember you to realize that I love you. Something inside me tells me that I do. Something tells me that you are the greatest man I have ever known, the man I most wish to emulate. I do not know why those words come to me, but they do."

William was still weeping softly, his head coming up and a hand going to Blayth's bearded face. "That is because you said those exact words to me, once," he said. "I remember them as clearly as if you said them yesterday. My son, I never thought I would have this moment with you in this life, and because God has been good to us, I have a second chance with you. And I must tell you something – I must tell you how much I love you and how proud I am of you. I thought I'd lost you, but I have not, and even if you return to Wales and we never see one another again, please know how very much to you mean to me and to your mother, and we shall love you as much as we always have no matter where your life takes you."

Other than with Asmara, Blayth had never felt true love or true acceptance until that very moment. He knew William meant every word and he simply nodded his head, unable to speak for the lump in his throat. As William struggled to compose himself, Blayth's attention turned to the three men standing behind him.

His brothers.

The impact of that realization was powerful. Releasing William, he made his way to Scott, the first of the three, and looked him in the eye. He was a little taller than Scott, but not by much. Wiping the tears from his face, he smiled weakly at the man.

"I should know you," he said. "Forgive me that I do not. What is your name?"

Scott was smiling at him, tears stinging his eyes as he gazed into his brother's face. "Scott," he said. "I am Scott, your eldest brother."

Blayth's eyebrows lifted. "Scott," he repeated. "I know that name. I have dreamed of it often."

"Then you have not forgotten me, after all."

Blayth smiled at the realization. As Scott patted him on the cheek, his attention turned to Troy, who wasn't as emotional as Scott was. At least, he was keeping it in check a little better. But out of the two of them, Troy tended to be the more volatile. At the moment, he was managing that particular trait.

"I am Troy," he said quietly. "I am also your elder brother, although by virtue of birth order, Scott is the eldest. And the ugliest, although he will not admit to that."

Blayth grinned, full-on. "Troy," he repeated, feeling the name upon his tongue and realizing that it didn't feel all that strange. "If you call Scott the ugliest, I wonder what you shall call me?"

Troy laughed softly. "I shall call you nothing until you remember me fully," he said. "Then, I will insult you at every turn just as I have always done, little brother."

Because Troy was laughing, Blayth did, too. He only sensed good humor from the man and nothing malicious. "I look forward to it," he said. He meant it. "Am I allowed to retaliate?"

Troy lifted his shoulders. "If you feel you can defend yourself against me, you may try."

Blayth simply chuckled. "I greatly anticipate that day," he said. Then, his focus turned to the tallest de Wolfe brother, the man with the bright green eyes. "You are another brother because you look like the others."

Patrick cocked an eyebrow. "Are you calling me ugly?"

Blayth started to laugh again. "I can see there is a theme with you three," he said. "Was I part of that theme, also?"

"Of course you were," Patrick said. "The four of us were inseparable until… well, until Llandeilo. It was as Papa said, James… we tried to take you with us, but we were overrun. It soon became a matter of saving our own lives and we had to leave. I cannot tell you how much it tore us apart to have to leave you behind. We are so very sorry it happened."

Blayth's smile faded. "I understand why," he said. "I do not curse you because of it. There was no choice."

Patrick nodded. Then, he reached out, extending his hand to Blayth in friendship and in brotherhood, who took it strongly. That first touch of brother against brother almost undid Blayth, but he fought it. He kept looking at Patrick, seeing something familiar about him, knowing that he'd seen this man in his dreams, probably more than the others. He couldn't explain why, only that he had.

And then, it occurred to him.

"Atty," he said. "Your name is Atty."

Patrick grinned, a smile that was brighter than the sun. "Aye," he said. "I am Atty. Welcome home, James. We have missed you."

With that, he threw his arms around him, hugging him tightly as Troy and Scott also crowded around, hugging James when Patrick finally decided to let him go. There wasn't a dry eye among them as they realized Blayth did remember some things about them and perhaps with time, he would remember more.

In fact, there wasn't a dry eye among anyone watching the reunion, the return of a brother believed to be dead, who, by some miracle, had found a second chance at life. Blayth didn't remember his life as James de Wolfe, but his heart, and his soul, knew these men even if his conscious mind did not. He planned to spend the rest of his life getting to know them again and perhaps with that, the rest of his memories would return.

He certainly intended to find out.

Chris and his sons, and Corbett, began to filter back into the keep, with Chris demanding a feast fit for his de Wolfe guests, which sent his wife into a frenzy to realize she had important guests. Bhrodi, who was still on the steps of the keep, watched as Blayth was surrounded by his family, including Penelope, who latched on to his hand and began to drag him towards the keep. It was a family reunion sent from heaven as far as the de Wolfes were concerned, and they were delighted beyond measure to have a second chance with the brother they thought they'd lost.

There was so very much to be thankful for.

As the group neared the steps of the keep, Bhrodi came forward and pulled his wife away, muttering something in her ear. She gasped and quickly looked behind her brothers to see Asmara bringing up the rear, walking alone. Penelope left her brothers, father, and husband to rush to Asmara, appalled that she'd left the woman alone during this most important moment.

"Come, my lady," she said, taking her by the hand. "I am very sorry you were left alone. We did not mean to neglect you. Please come inside and get to know my father and brothers. I am sure they will like you very much."

But Asmara didn't seem put out in the least. In fact, she wasn't at all. She'd stood by and watched Blayth become acquainted with the father he'd been told had abandoned him, and brothers who clearly adored him. She'd watched it all, so very happy for Blayth, thrilled beyond words that he'd found his family again. The quest they'd set out to accomplish had ended rather quickly, but it was the best possible ending imaginable.

Blayth found what he'd been looking for.

"I do not feel neglected," she said, pausing as the men mounted the stairs. She watched Blayth as he laughed with Troy. "In fact, my heart is full as I watch my husband with his brothers and his father. He set out on this journey to find answers to his past, and this is greater than he could have hoped for."

Because Asmara came to a halt, Penelope did, too. She also watched as Blayth entered the keep, surrounded by his brothers, as William and Bhrodi brought up the rear. All of the men filtering into the great hall to become better acquainted, and to begin making new memories for a man who had none at all.

They had a whole lifetime ahead of them to do it.

"I feel as if I am living a dream," Penelope said. "We had reconciled ourselves to James' death, and for him to return makes this feel so very surreal. But if it is a dream, I do not want to wake up from it."

Asmara looked at her. "Nor I," she said. "I have lived all my life in Wales, but I did not start living until Blayth came into my life. Whether he remains Blayth, or becomes James again, does not matter to me. He is the man I love, and I shall go with him wherever he wishes to go, and

I will call him whatever he wishes to be called. The mark of a man is not in his name, but in his character."

"And in his heart," Penelope finished softly. When Asmara smiled at her, she smiled in return. "But you will tell me the story of Blayth the Strong, will you not? All I have heard is what de Lohr and Payton-Forrester have told me. I want to hear of his legend through your eyes. Will you share it with me?"

Asmara thought back to the first time she'd ever seen Blayth the Strong. She'd tripped over him and fell in the mud and he'd thrown her in a trough. Then, she thought of him as they'd assaulted Llandarog Castle, how she'd scaled the walls and how he'd used brute strength to subdue an entire garrison. She remembered their time at Gwendraith and their very first kiss in that musty stable. The man who didn't remember his past but who had an uncanny skill as a warrior was someone she'd loved from the start. In fact, she couldn't remember when she hadn't loved him. And as he wandered into the great hall of Lioncross with his family, her love for him only grew.

Blayth the Strong was unwanted no longer.

"I will be happy to tell you," she said as they began to follow the men into the hall. "The first time I met him, he threw me into a horse trough."

Penelope looked at her with surprise. "Is that true?" she said. "The first time I met my husband, I challenged him to a fight."

Asmara grinned. "Did you win?"

"Of course I did. I am a de Wolfe; I was born with a sword in my hand."

"As was I, practically."

When they reached the top of the stairs, Penelope put her arms around Asmara and hugged her tightly.

"Then you are going to fit into this family perfectly," she said.

Asmara hoped so. As she entered the great hall, she saw Blayth sitting at the massive feasting table with his brothers, being served great cups of ale by the servants. He caught a glimpse of her and when their eyes met, she would never forget the look of joy on the man's face.

It was the joy of a man who was loved fully, and who loved fully. It was the joy of a story with a happy ending, and the joy of a legend whose dreams had actually come true.

James de Wolfe had risen from the dead, and now he was home to stay.

EPILOGUE

Castle Questing
One month later

"YOU LOOK VERY beautiful," Blayth said. "I have the most beautiful wife in all the world."

Asmara cast him a look that could only be described as hateful. It was late on a mild autumn day as they rode with William, Scott, Troy, Patrick, and eight hundred de Wolfe soldiers on their return to Castle Questing. The comment had come from Blayth because his wife was dressed in a lovely frock, courtesy of Penelope, on the occasion of visiting Castle Questing and, consequently, meeting family and relatives for the first time.

But it had been a hard fight.

Penelope and Asmara were roughly the same size, with coloring that was also similar, so before departing Lioncross Abbey, Penelope had given Asmara three lovely gowns she'd brought with her so that Asmara would have something nice to wear. It had been a very sweet gesture, as Penelope and Asmara had become very close over the past month, but Asmara had never worn feminine clothing in her life and was very embarrassed to do so.

She felt like a fool.

But the appreciative expressions of her husband, and his brothers, had changed that attitude somewhat. Not much, but a little. Asmara was receiving attention she normally didn't receive and it was flattering, although she didn't want to admit it. Penelope had even shown Asmara how to fashion her hair so that it was both pretty and practical. No more long, silky strands of dark hair blowing in the wind. Now, it was braided and pinned to the nape of her neck. She kept scratching at her neck, at the iron pins that poked, while Blayth watched her with amusement.

One too many amused looks and she punched him.

But he'd laughed at her, taking it in stride. The de Wolfe brothers knew better than to comment to Asmara; they'd grown up with a sister who was also a warrior, and fine compliments would only bring them pain. Therefore, they let Blayth take the brunt of Asmara's frustration with her new ladylike appearance. But the truth was that she looked quite lovely.

Beneath a crisp blue sky, the returning de Wolfe party mounted the hill that led to Castle Questing, and Blayth and Asmara were once again faced with an enormous English castle that took up nearly the entire top of a hill. William had explained that Scotland wasn't far off, and it was his job to police this portion of the border, but Asmara found it all quite fascinating. The landscape this far north was different from that of Wales, but just as beautiful, she thought. She had thoroughly enjoyed the trip and the opportunity to see parts of England. Although she missed her home, and her family, she could not have been happier, or more content, with Blayth.

She knew her father would have approved.

In truth, the past month for them had been life-changing for them both. Blayth had spent the time with his brothers and father at Lioncross, listening to night after night of tales from his past, as they all tried to stir memories long buried.

William refused to believe that they were gone completely, so he'd spent his days with Blayth, speaking of events from his childhood and from the days when he'd fostered. Asmara listened as well, learning of her husband's past. Sometimes, Blayth thought he might actually remember what he was being told, but other times, there was no recognition at all.

But the fact remained that William, Scott, Troy, and Patrick never gave up. They were so thrilled to have their son and brother returned to them that it was a genuine joy speaking on things he no longer remembered. Even though he'd changed somewhat, and his memory was mostly gone, they all saw characteristics in the man that had never left him. He was still quiet, with a ready humor, and he still became quite emotional about certain things. That was the brother they remembered. And the love he felt for his family, even though he didn't really remember much about them, was ready and prevalent.

Love was something that couldn't be forgotten.

But those conversations about the past also brought up conversations about the future, and it was quickly determined that Blayth really couldn't return to Wales, nor did he want to. What he'd left there was an episode of his life and he genuinely wanted to return to the House of de Wolfe and resume his former life as best he was able, with Asmara by his side.

It was then that William was forced to tell him that he had been married before, and he had two children as a result. Ronan had been six years of age and his daughter, Isabella, had been born when he'd been in Wales. The little girl was five years of age now and the only father she'd ever known was the man her mother had married two years after her father's "passing". Owen le Mon was from a fine family, a knight who had served at a neighboring castle, and he'd accepted Ronan and Isabella as if they were his own.

Blayth had heard that his children and his first wife had resumed their happy life after his disappearance and he had no intention of disturbing that. But the fact remained that he had been married before, putting his marriage to Asmara in jeopardy. William and Blayth consulted with a priest local to Lioncross to discuss the issue, but after much discussion with the priest and a good deal of deliberation, the priest decided that James, for the most part, no longer existed and the man Blayth had taken his place. In the church's view, that meant there was no marriage between Blayth and Rose.

It wasn't only Blayth who had been relieved to hear that, but Asmara.

Suspecting she was pregnant, she didn't particularly want her child to be born a bastard. And as they finally arrived in Questing's enormous bailey, Asmara had the confidence in her marriage and in her husband enough to be secure in their love and in their future.

And that was why they had come to Castle Questing.

"Come down, *cariad*," Blayth said as he dismounted his steed and quickly came around her horse to help her dismount. "Get down and stretch your legs. You must be exhausted."

Asmara slid into his arms, feeling his strength around her. She kissed his fuzzy face. "I am fine," she said, looking around. "I am much more interested in this place. It is enormous."

Blayth held on to her as she stretched out her back. He, too, was looking around, feeling a twinge of recognition. It was another place he'd seen in his dreams, with big towers and sand-colored walls.

"It is," he agreed quietly. "I was born here, so I am told."

Asmara heard the tone in his voice and she turned to look at him. "Do you recognize it?"

He nodded, faintly. "I think so," he said. "I feel as if I do. It is a very strange feeling, as if I have been here before."

As they stood there, Patrick and Troy came to stand with them. On the trip north, they had left Scott at his home in the south of Cumbria, but Troy and Patrick's homes were here in the north, with their father. They had continued onward, all the way to Questing.

"Well?" Patrick said. "Do you recognize the place?"

Blayth nodded. "I was telling Asmara that I feel as if I have been here before."

"You should," Troy said. "You have spent a large portion of your life here. Of our siblings, no one lives here year-round any longer, but they are all nearby with the exception of Penelope and Scott. And

Katheryn, your twin, lives at Berwick. I am sure you will see her shortly."

Blayth smiled faintly. "I should like to," he said. But his attention moved back to the vast castle around them. "I am looking forward to getting reacquainted with everyone."

Patrick started to speak, but something over Blayth's head caught his attention. He cleared his throat softly.

"Mother is coming," he said quietly.

Everyone turned to see William walking towards them, his arm around the shoulders of a petite woman clad in a cloak against the cool autumn breeze. Her honey-blonde hair was pulled back into a bun at the back of her head, and she wore a loose wimple about her head and neck. She was older, but the expression on her face was intense and ageless. Her green eyes were riveted on Blayth as she came closer, and closer still.

Troy and Patrick backed away, affording their mother some private space as she came face to face with the son she thought she'd lost. When Jordan came to within a foot or so of Blayth, William spoke.

"Blayth," he said softly, "this is your mother, Jordan."

Blayth stared at the woman. Unlike his father or brothers, where there had been only a small amount of recognition, the moment he looked into his mother's eyes, he *knew* her. It was a very strong feeling he had, a connection he didn't have with any of the other members of his family. The bond between mother and child was like nothing else and, in this case, it broke the boundaries of amnesia. His eyes grew moist when she reached out, offering him her hand. He took it quickly.

"I have seen ye in my dreams for five long years," she said in her heavy Scots accent. "I've talked tae ye in my dreams and told ye how much I loved ye. Have ye heard me?"

Tears pooled in his eyes. "I think I have."

Jordan smiled. "When ye were a wee lad, I called ye Jamie," she said. "Do ye remember?"

He sniffled. "I do not. I am sorry."

Jordan gazed at him a moment, studying the new man her son had become, before lifting her hand to touch the damaged side of his head. Her fingers were gentle as she acquainted herself with the new side of him, tender yet probing, as only a mother could be.

It was a deeply poignant moment and Blayth closed his eyes, tears streaming down his cheeks as he felt his mother's touch for the first time that he could remember. She touched that terrible side of his head without fear, without revulsion.

Only love.

"When ye were born, ye were a weak little lad," she finally said. "We were a-feared ye would not live. I spent so much time with ye, rocking ye, holding ye, and telling ye what a great man ye would become someday. I'm not sure if I believed it, but I wanted ye tae know that I had faith in ye. I had faith that ye would fulfill yer destiny. I think… I think that even though yer destiny wasna as we'd planned, it is still a fine one. Yer father sent me a missive when he found ye at Lioncross, and he explained what became of ye. I wanted ye tae know that I'm very proud of ye, because ye've been a hero tae people who trusted ye, and that's a grand destiny for any man."

Blayth bent over, kissing her hands as he held them. He was so choked up that he couldn't even speak. Jordan touched the top of his head, the thick blond strands that she remembered so well. Perhaps he went by another name now, and perhaps he didn't remember everything of his life as a de Wolfe, but to Jordan, he was still her little boy.

He was still her Jamie.

As Blayth bent over her, wrought with emotion, Jordan's attention moved to the young woman next to him. Tall, dark-haired, she had a fine-featured face, and Jordan smiled at her.

"Ye must be Asmara," she said. "I am very happy tae meet ye."

Asmara smiled timidly. "Thank you, my lady," she said. "I am happy to know you, too."

Blayth, realizing he'd been rude by not introducing his wife, stood up and wiped the tears from his face. Still holding Jordan's hand, he put his arm around Asmara's shoulders.

"She is a great woman and I am undeserving of her, but she loves me anyway," he said. "I know you two will become great friends."

Jordan squeezed her son's hand before letting it go, moving to Asmara and reaching for the woman. She took Asmara's hands, gazing into the face of the woman her husband's missive had also told her about. It had been a very long missive that explained everything. *Dragon Princess*, William had said about James' new wife. She was a great woman among the Welsh. But all Jordan saw was the woman her son clearly adored.

"Of course we will," she said. "Come inside with me. Ye must be weary."

Asmara was immediately at ease with Jordan's sweet manner. She didn't even hesitate as the woman pulled her along, towards the enormous keep of Castle Questing. She, too, felt instant comfort at Castle Questing and as Jordan pulled her away, Blayth moved to follow. William, however, stopped him.

"Wait," he said quietly. "There is someone else you must see."

Blayth looked at him curiously, but his father indicated a dark-haired woman and two small children who were standing several feet away. In fact, Jordan and Asmara walked right past them, close enough to touch them had they tried. As soon as dark-haired woman saw that William's attention was on her, she moved forward with her children.

"This is Rose," William told Blayth quietly. "The children with her are yours."

Blayth found himself looking at a pretty woman, very pretty, and two very handsome children. The boy was older, having seen eleven summers, but the little girl was small and shy.

Rose walked right up to him, her expression serious as she saw all of the damage to his head. It was her former husband, but he'd transformed into something else. She almost didn't recognize him. She'd had weeks to prepare for this moment, but now that it was here, it wasn't as gut-wrenching or emotional as she thought it would have been. There was a peace about it, in fact. James was here, but only in the literal sense. The man he was had died at Llandeilo; the man she saw before her was what came in his place.

It was a strange realization, but not uncomfortable.

When their eyes met, she forced a smile.

"Greetings," she said. "Do you remember me?"

Blayth almost did, but he wasn't sure. He had that feeling so often that it was frustrating. "I wish I did," he said. "Greetings, Lady le Mon."

He was acknowledging her married name, the name that was no longer his. Rose, too, knew that her marriage to James was no longer valid, thanks to the same missive William had sent to his wife. It was a missive that had contained, and explained, a great many things, so Rose knew the situation for what it was. In truth, she felt relief and she felt joy, if only for William and Jordan's sake. She wasn't quite sure how James would fit into the life of her son now, for he was the only child who remembered him, but she had every faith that everything would happen as it should. She had her father's philosophy on life, and considering she'd spent many an hour with Kieran speaking on this very subject, she'd come to the conclusion that James' return wouldn't disrupt her life.

But it was rather bittersweet to see him again.

"For your family's sake, I am glad that you have returned," she said. "And for Ronan's sake. We have kept your memory alive for him, and he still remembers you."

Blayth looked to the boy with the white-blond hair standing next to Rose. He looked very much as James had when he'd been that age, something that brought William and Jordan much comfort over the years. He smiled at the lad.

"Do you remember me?" he asked.

Ronan had his grandfather's strength, his father's humor, and his mother's wild streak. He looked up at his father, fearlessly. "Aye," he said. "Are… are you really back from the dead?"

Blayth laughed softly. "Some would say so."

"What was it like to be dead?"

Blayth shrugged. "If your mother will allow it, then I should like to spend time with you and tell you," he said. "Of course, only if you will allow it, too."

Ronan looked at his mother, who nodded encouragingly, before lifting his slender shoulders. "I think so," he said. "I have a pony. Would you like to see him?"

Blayth had never heard such a wonderful question. Although he didn't remember his son, the moment he saw the boy, he felt a familiar connection. He wasn't determined to be a father to the boy, because the lad had a father in his mother's new husband, but perhaps he could have some place in his child's life. A friend, a mentor…

He realized that he would like that very much.

"Aye," he said. "I would."

With a wink to his father and brothers, Blayth followed young Ronan as the lad led him off towards the stables of Castle Questing. William watched him go, feeling a sense of contentment that he couldn't begin to describe. His son was home, and even though the world was different now, it was no less wonderful. It could only get better.

He could see the old James in the folds of Blayth's persona, and he knew in his heart that James would make a full return someday.

He could feel it.

"Well," Patrick said, breaking William from his train of thought. "It seems to me that all is well in the world again. Blayth seems happy, doesn't he?"

They had all taken to calling him Blayth because it was the only name he remembered. His family had to accept that James, for the moment, was no longer with them. To Patrick's question, William nodded.

"He does," he said, turning to Troy and Patrick. "As am I. My son was dead, but I got him back. For every parent who has lost a child, that is the dream. Today, I am living my dream."

Patrick and Troy understood. And in particular, Troy did. Having lost two children of his own to a terrible accident years before, what his father said was particularly poignant.

He understood, indeed.

As the two brothers headed off to take care of the horses and help disband the army, William continued to stand there, thinking that he was incredibly blessed to have all of his children returned to him, even if it wasn't exactly as it had been before. In truth, he didn't care that it wasn't. He was very happy with this new world he lived in. As he stood there, pondering what the future would bring for Blayth and Asmara, Rose came to stand next to him.

"Uncle William?"

William turned to her, the lovely young woman who had been his son's first wife. He still loved her like a daughter. Reaching out, he picked up Isabella, kissing the little girl on the cheek.

"You were very brave, Rosie," he said. "I cannot imagine this was easy for you."

Rose shrugged. "To tell the truth, I was not sure how I would feel," she said. "Hearing that James was alive, and then understanding the circumstances of his return, I truly wasn't sure how I would feel. But when I saw him… it wasn't James. I do not know if it makes any sense, but that isn't the man I loved. He is very different."

William nodded. "He is, indeed," he said. "But our James is still there. I catch a glimpse of him now and again. But this Blayth… I like him, too."

Rose simply smiled. She knew how devastated William had been at James' death, but she was glad to see that he wasn't disappointed that the James he knew wasn't the James that returned. There were no unrealistic expectations on William's part, only gratitude.

"I am glad," she said, patting his arm. She, too, turned her attention towards the stables, where she could see her son and Blayth disappearing into the structure, but her mind was elsewhere. Her manner sobered. "You have not asked about my father, Uncle William."

William's entire manner seemed to tense. He'd been so happy, and now Rose had brought about a subject that instantly brought him down. He was afraid to even continue the conversation, but he forced himself.

"I know," he said. "I have not asked anyone about him. I am afraid to."

Rose turned to him. Like everyone else at Questing, she knew how William had been dealing with Kieran's illness. Or not dealing with it, as it were. He couldn't bring himself to. Gently, she put a hand on his shoulder.

"He is waiting for you," she said softly. "He knows you have returned."

William's eye filled with tears and his composure took a hit. "In his chamber?" he asked hoarsely. "Or in his new crypt in the chapel?"

Rose could see his tears coming and it choked her up to see how emotional he was. "In his chamber," she said. "My mother is with him. That is why she is not here to greet James."

William blinked, tears dripping down his face. "Rosie… how is he?"

"Failing."

William inhaled deeply, steadying himself, as he handed Isabella over to Rose. "Then I shall not make him wait."

With that, he crossed the bailey and entered the cool, dark keep of Castle Questing. There were only a few servants around as he took the mural stairs up to the Hage living quarters, and he found that he was almost running as he made his way to Kieran's chamber at the end of the corridor. The more he moved, the more urgent his desire to see his old friend.

One last time.

He didn't even knock. Slowly, he pushed the door open, his gaze immediately going to the big bed where he knew his dearest friend was laying. Stepping into the chamber, he saw Jemma sitting beside her husband, but she stood up quickly when she saw who it was. William approached the bed, his focus on his dying friend.

"Thank God," Jemma said. "Ye've returned. And James?"

William came around the bed to where she was standing. "He is here," he said. "My son has come home."

Jemma closed her eyes briefly, a gesture of thanks and relief. "Then I shall go and see him," she said. But she paused, looking William in the face. "He hasna eaten in a week, William, and he hasna spoken in a few days. I believe he was waiting for ye tae return. He was holding out as long as he could."

William nodded, but he was fighting off a roar of tears. He sat down in the seat vacated by Jemma as she kissed him on the temple and quietly left the chamber. His attention was on Kieran as the man lay there, drawn and pasty and sleeping heavily. His chest lifted slowly, and unsteadily, the only sign that the man was alive. Leaning forward, William took Kieran's big hand in his.

"I have returned," he whispered tightly. "I have brought James with me. I do not know how much you have been told, but he does not remember anything, Kieran. The damage to his head, the blow we thought killed him, erased most of his memory. Scott and Troy and Patrick and I have spent the past month trying to help him remember who he was, but the truth is that he has been living as a hero to the Welsh. Can you imagine? A de Wolfe being a hero to the Welsh?"

Kieran twitched, and William was positive the man heard him. He squeezed his friend's big hand. "He has married, too," he continued. "A lovely lass, a great-granddaughter of a Welsh king. It seems that two of my children have married Welsh royalty, which means I can no longer fight Edward's wars in Wales. I would be fighting my own kin. But, then again, I married a Scots and still do battle in Scotland, so I suppose I am traitor to my family all the way around."

He meant it as a joke, hoping it would stir Kieran, and he was rewarded when the man moved a bit more, as if he were trying to open his eyes He hadn't really expected the man to awaken for him. Hell, he hadn't expected the man to even be alive upon his return, but he was.

And perhaps, it was all William's fault.

William had expressed such distress over Kieran's health, repeatedly telling the man that he couldn't do without him, and as he looked at the dying man on the bed, it occurred to him that Kieran might be hanging on because of William's complaints. It further occurred to William just how selfish he had been.

Oh, he'd fully admitted his selfishness, but seeing Kieran lying pale and sickly on the bed, he realized just how horrible he'd been about the entire situation. William didn't want Kieran to die, and by sheer willpower alone, Kieran was still alive. For William, the man had fought off the jaws of death. But as William looked at his gallant friend, he remembered something Kieran had told him –

I am tired, William. I am tired of being ill, of not being able to function as a normal man. I spend my days in this bed, remembering when I was young and strong and healthy. I do not like my family seeing me this way. It is no way for a knight's life to end. I had always imagined that I would die a glorious death in battle, but it seems as if I am to die an old man in my bed.

But even now, because of William's selfishness, Kieran wouldn't let go.

William knew it was time to *make* him let go.

"Kieran," he said, the tears beginning to fall again. "I know you waited for me to return, and return I have. James has come home, and he is happy and whole. Rosie is also happy. There is no trouble with her having seen James. She understands that he is not the same man. And I am happy because my son has returned. As much as I love you and as much as I am going to miss you, it is okay for you to go now. It is okay for you to leave me because I will be okay in the end. I will do everything I promised; I shall make sure our grandsons remember you, and I shall make sure your memory is honored. We shall all remember your greatness, for generations to come. You no longer need to remain here. Be young and strong again, my friend. Be free."

After that, he couldn't say anything more. He was too overcome by emotion, but he was also overcome by a sense of peace. Peace that this was the right thing for Kieran, and for them all.

It was time.

William remained with Kieran, holding the man's hand, until his breathing grew weaker, and more erratic. When that time came, he sent a servant for Jemma, but he continued to sit there, holding the man's hand and whispering of past adventures, of the battles they'd fought together, and of the humorous events of their youth.

When Kieran finally breathed his last, it was with William's voice in his ear, speaking of a particular battle where the fighting had been so vicious, an enemy blade sliced through the garters holding up the mail on Kieran's left leg. When the mail trousers slid down, so did part of his breeches, leaving his naked leg and bare arse exposed.

The last thing Kieran ever heard was William's soft laughter in his ear.

And that was the way he wanted it.

☙ THE END ❧

Blayth and Asmara's children:

Maddock

Bowen

Caius

Garreth

POST SCRIPT

I don't normally do a post script. But with this book, I thought I should.

It's quite a tale that old Mr. Nolwynn told, isn't it? Helped along by Jestin, of course. I hope you enjoyed the novel and I hope the passing of an old de Wolfe knight touched you like it touched me. It was ugly crying for me as I wrote it, so don't be ashamed if that was your reaction, too. Although I don't normally write about the deaths of any of my heroes (or even significant secondary characters), I felt that I had to address it because according to the novel *Scorpion*, which is Kevin Hage's story, the year Kieran died was, indeed, the year A WOLFE AMONG DRAGONS is set in.

Therefore, I couldn't ignore it. I decided to make his passing something we could all experience, like the passing of a favorite uncle, and that is why I put it at the very end of the book. Blayth and Asmara have had their happily ever after, but it was time for all of us to move Kieran on. I warned you to get the tissues before this book even started. I wasn't kidding.

Also, the biggest question readers will ask is did Cader ever get to see his grandsons, and did Fairynne end up marrying Pryce?

The answer, to both, is yes.

But look for that in a future de Wolfe novel.

And the de Wolfe pack lives on…

~ *KL*

About Kathryn Le Veque

Medieval Just Got Real.

KATHRYN LE VEQUE is a USA TODAY Bestselling author, an Amazon All-Star author, and a #1 bestselling, award-winning, multi-published author in Medieval Historical Romance and Historical Fiction. She has been featured in the NEW YORK TIMES and on USA TODAY's HEA blog. In March 2015, Kathryn was the featured cover story for the March issue of InD'Tale Magazine, the premier Indie author magazine. She was also a quadruple nominee (a record!) for the prestigious RONE awards for 2015.

Kathryn's Medieval Romance novels have been called 'detailed', 'highly romantic', and 'character-rich'. She crafts great adventures of love, battles, passion, and romance in the High Middle Ages. More than that, she writes for both women AND men – an unusual crossover for a romance author – and Kathryn has many male readers who enjoy her stories because of the male perspective, the action, and the adventure.

On October 29, 2015, Amazon launched Kathryn's Kindle Worlds Fan Fiction site WORLD OF DE WOLFE PACK. Please visit Kindle Worlds for Kathryn Le Veque's World of de Wolfe Pack and find many action-packed adventures written by some of the top authors in their genre using Kathryn's characters from the de Wolfe Pack series. As Kindle World's FIRST Historical Romance fan fiction world, Kathryn Le Veque's World of de Wolfe Pack will contain all of the great storytelling you have come to expect.

Kathryn loves to hear from her readers. Please find Kathryn on Facebook at Kathryn Le Veque, Author, or join her on Twitter @kathrynleveque, and don't forget to visit her website and sign up for her blog at www.kathrynleveque.com.

Please follow Kathryn on Bookbub for the latest releases and sales: bookbub.com/authors/kathryn-le-veque.

Made in the USA
San Bernardino,
CA

56589744R00231